The Scold's Bridle

MINETTE WALTERS

The Scold's Bridle

St. Martin's Press
New York

Library of Congress Cataloging-in-Publication Data

Walters, Minette.
The scold's bridle / Minette Walters.
p.   cm.
ISBN 0-312-11377-3
I. Title.
PR6073.A744S28   1994
823'.914—dc20   94-25776   CIP

First published in Great Britain by Macmillan London.

First U.S. Edition: October 1994
10 9 8 7 6 5 4 3 2 1

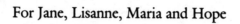
For Jane, Lisanne, Maria and Hope

'**Scold** *skold*, n. a rude clamorous woman or other'
Chambers English Dictionary

'**Branks** *brangks*, (Scot.) n.pl., rarely in sing., a scold's bridle; an instrument of punishment used in the case of scolds, etc., consisting of a kind of iron framework to enclose the head, having a sharp metal gag or bit which entered the mouth and restrained the tongue.'
Oxford English Dictionary

'Create her child of spleen, that it may live
And be a thwart disnatur'd torment to her!
Let it stamp wrinkles in her brow of youth;
With cadent tears fret channels in her cheeks;
Turn all her mother's pains and benefits
To laughter and contempt; that she may feel
How sharper than a serpent's tooth it is
To have a thankless child!'

Shakespeare, *King Lear*

'Forty-two!' yelled Loonquawl. 'Is that all you've got to show for seven and a half million years' work?'

'I checked it very thoroughly,' said the computer, 'and that quite definitely is the answer. I think the problem, to be quite honest with you, is that you've never really known what the question is . . . Once you know what the question is, you'll know what the answer means.'

Douglas Adams, *The Hitch Hiker's Guide to the Galaxy*

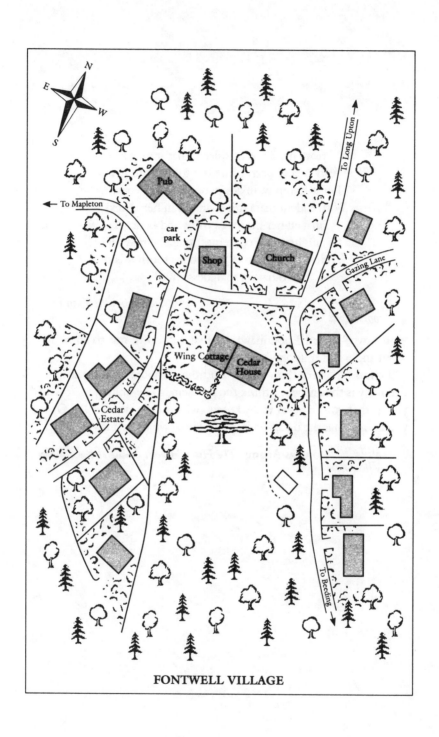

FONTWELL VILLAGE

I wonder if I should keep these diaries under lock and key. Jenny Spede has disturbed them again and it's annoying me. She must have opened a volume inadvertently while dusting, and reads them now out of some sort of prurient curiosity. What does she make, I wonder, of an old woman, deformed by arthritis, stripping naked for a young man? A vicarious lust, I am sure, for it beggars belief that anyone other than her brute of a husband has ever regarded her with anything but revulsion.

But, no, it can't be Jenny. She's too lazy to clean so thoroughly and too stupid to find anything I say or do either interesting or amusing. The later volumes seem to be attracting the most attention but, at the moment, I can't see why. I am only interested in beginnings for there is so much hope at the beginning. The end has no merit except to demonstrate how badly that hope was misplaced.

'In the dead vast and middle of the night . . . How weary, stale, flat, and unprofitable seem to me all the uses of this world.'

Who then? James? Or am I going senile and imagining things? Yesterday I found Howard's offer open on my desk, but I could have sworn I put it back in the file. 'O judgement, thou art fled . . .'

The pills worry me more. Ten is such a round number to be missing. I fear Joanna is up to her wretched tricks again, worse, I wonder if Ruth is going the same way. Blood will always out . . .

One

DR SARAH BLAKENEY stood beside the bath and wondered how death could ever be described as a victory. There was no triumph here, no lingering sense that Mathilda had abandoned her earthly shell for something better, no hint even that she had found peace. The dead, unlike the sleeping, offered no hope of a re-awakening. 'You want my honest opinion?' she said slowly, in answer to the policeman's question. 'Then no, Mathilda Gillespie is the last person I'd have expected to kill herself.'

They stared at the grotesque figure, stiff and cold in the brackish water. Nettles and Michaelmas daisies sprouted from the awful contraption that caged the bloodless face, its rusted metal bit clamping the dead tongue still in the gaping mouth. A scattering of petals, curling and decayed, clung to the scraggy shoulders and the sides of the bath, while a brown sludge below the water's surface suggested more petals, waterlogged and sunk. On the floor lay a bloodied Stanley knife, apparently dropped by the nerveless fingers that dangled above it. It was reminiscent of Marat in *his* bath, but so much uglier and so much sadder. Poor Mathilda, thought Sarah, how she would have hated this.

The police Sergeant gestured at the pitiful grey head. 'What in God's name is *that* thing?' His voice grated with repugnance.

Sarah waited a moment until she felt her own voice was under control. 'It's a scold's bridle,' she told him, 'a primitive instrument of repression. They were used in the Middle Ages to curb the tongues of nagging women. It's been in Mathilda's family for years. I know it looks awful like that, but she kept it downstairs in the hall over a pot of geraniums. As a decoration it was rather effective.' She raised a hand to her mouth in distress and the policeman patted her shoulder awkwardly. 'They were white geraniums and they poked their heads through the iron framework. Her coronet weeds, she always called them.' She cleared her throat. 'She was rather fine, you know. Very proud, very snobbish, very intolerant and not overly friendly, but she had a brilliant mind for someone who had never been trained to do anything more than keep house and she had a wonderful sense of humour. Dry and incisive.'

'Coronet weeds,' echoed the pathologist thoughtfully. 'As in:

> "There with fantastic garlands did she come,
> Of crowflowers, nettles, daisies, and long purples,
> That liberal shepherds give a grosser name,
> But our cold maids do dead men's fingers call them:
> There, on the pendent boughs her coronet weeds – "'

'*Hamlet*,' he explained apologetically to the policeman. 'Ophelia's end. I had to learn it for O level. Amazing what you remember as you get older.' He stared at the bath. 'Did Mrs Gillespie know *Hamlet*?'

Sarah nodded unhappily. 'She told me once that her entire education was based on learning chunks of Shakespeare by heart.'

'Well, we're not going to learn much by standing staring at the poor woman,' said the policeman abruptly. 'Unless Ophelia was murdered.'

Dr Cameron shook his head. 'Death by drowning,' he said thoughtfully, 'while of unsound mind.' He glanced at Sarah. 'Was Mrs Gillespie depressed at all?'

'If she was, she never gave any indication of it.'

The policeman, decidedly more uncomfortable in the presence of death than either of the two doctors, ushered Sarah on to the landing. 'Many thanks for your time, Dr Blakeney. I'm sorry we had to subject you to that but as her GP you probably knew her better than most.' It was his turn to sigh. 'They're always the worst. Old people, living alone. Society's rejects. Sometimes it's weeks before they're found.' His mouth turned down in a curve of distaste. 'Very unpleasant. I suppose we're lucky she was found so quickly. Less than forty hours according to Dr Cameron. Midnight Saturday, he estimates.'

Sarah leant her back against the wall and stared across the landing towards Mathilda's bedroom where the open door showed the old oak bed piled high with pillows. There was a strange sense of ownership still, as if her possessions retained the presence that her flesh had lost. 'She wasn't that old,' she protested mildly. 'Sixty-five, no more. These days that's nothing.'

'She looks older,' he said matter-of-factly, 'but then she would, I suppose, with all the blood drained out of her.' He consulted his notebook. 'A daughter, you say, living in London, and you think a granddaughter at boarding school.'

'Don't Mr and Mrs Spede know?' She had caught a glimpse of them in the library as she came in, grey faces curiously blank from shock, hands clasped tightly together like petrified children. 'They've been coming in twice a week for years. He looks after the garden and she cleans. They must know more about her than anyone.'

He nodded. 'Unfortunately we've had nothing but hysterics out of them since Mrs Spede found the body. We'll be asking round the village, anyway.' He looked towards the bedroom. 'There's an empty bottle of barbiturates on her bedside table beside the remains of a glass of whisky. It looks like a belt and braces job. Whisky for courage, sleeping pills, then the Stanley knife in the bath. Do you still say you wouldn't have expected her to kill herself?'

'Oh, lord, I don't know.' Sarah ran a worried hand through her short dark hair. 'I wouldn't have prescribed barbiturates if I thought there was a chance she'd abuse them, but one can never be certain about these things. And anyway, Mathilda had been taking them for years, they were commonly prescribed once. So yes, I would rule out suicide from what I knew of her, but we had a doctor–patient relationship. She had severe pain with her arthritis and there were nights when she couldn't sleep.' She frowned. 'In any case, there can't have been many of the sleeping pills left. She was due for another prescription this week.'

'Perhaps she was hoarding them,' he said unemotionally. 'Did she ever open her heart to you?'

'I doubt she opened her heart to anyone. She wasn't the type. She was a very private person.' She shrugged. 'And I've only known her – what? – twelve months. I live in Long Upton, not here in Fontwell, so I haven't come across her socially either.' She shook her head. 'There's nothing in her records to suggest a depressive personality. But the trouble is—' She fell silent.

'The trouble is what, Dr Blakeney?'

'The trouble is we talked about freedom the last time I saw her, and she said freedom is an illusion. There's no such thing in modern society. She quoted Rousseau at me, the famous rebel-cry of students in the sixties: "Man was born free, and everywhere he is in chains." There was only one freedom left, according to Mathilda, and that was the freedom to choose how and when to die.' Her face looked bleak. 'But we had conversations like that every time I saw her. There was no reason to assume that one was any different.'

'When was this conversation?'

Sarah sighed heavily. 'Three weeks ago during my last monthly visit. And the awful thing is, I laughed. Even that wasn't a freedom any more, I said, because doctors are so damn scared of prosecution they wouldn't dream of giving a patient the choice.'

The policeman, a large detective nearing retirement, placed a comforting hand on her arm. 'There now, it's nothing to fret about. It was slitting her wrists that killed her, not barbiturates. And the chances are we're looking at murder anyway.' He shook his head. 'I've seen a few suicides one way and another, but I've yet to see an old woman turn herself into a flower arrangement in her bath. It'll be money that's behind it. We all live too long and the young get desperate.' He spoke with feeling, Sarah thought.

An hour later, Dr Cameron was more sceptical. 'If she didn't do it herself,' he said, 'you'll have the devil's own job proving it.' They had removed the body from the bath and lain it, still with the scold's bridle in place, on plastic sheeting on the floor. 'Apart from the incisions in her wrists there's not a mark on her, bar what one would expect, of course.' He pointed to the lividity above and around the wrinkled buttocks. 'Some post mortem hypostasis where the blood has settled but no bruising. Poor old thing. She didn't put up any sort of a fight.'

Sergeant Cooper leaned against the bathroom doorjamb, drawn to look at the poor grey body, but deeply repulsed by it. 'She couldn't if she was drugged,' he murmured.

Cameron peeled off his gloves. 'I'll see what I can find out for you back at the lab, but my advice is, don't hold your breath. I can't see your Chief Super wasting too much time and resources on this one. It's about as neat as anything I've seen. Frankly, unless something pretty unusual shows up in the post mortem, I'll be recommending a suicide verdict.'

'But what does your gut tell you, Doctor? The nettles are telling mine it was murder. Why would she deliberately sting herself before she died?'

'Self-reproach, probably. Good God, man, there's no logic to this kind of thing. Suicides are hardly in their right mind when they top themselves. Still,' he said thoughtfully, 'I am surprised she didn't leave a note. There's so much of the theatre about this headdress that I'd have expected something by way of explanation.' He began to tuck the plastic sheet about the body. 'Read *Hamlet*,' he suggested. 'The answer's in there, I expect.'

Mr and Mrs Spede hovered in the library like two squat spectres, so unprepossessing and shifty in their appearance that Cooper wondered if they were quite normal. Neither seemed able to meet his gaze and every question required unspoken consultation between them before one would offer an answer. 'Dr Blakeney tells me Mrs Gillespie has a daughter living in London and a granddaughter at boarding school,' he said. 'Can you give me their names and tell me where I can contact them?'

'She kept her papers very neat,' said Mrs Spede eventually, after receiving some sort of permission to speak from her husband. 'It'll all be in the papers.' She nodded towards the desk and an oak filing cabinet. 'In there some place. Very neat. Always very neat.'

'Don't you know her daughter's name?'

'Mrs Lascelles,' said the man after a moment. 'Joanna.' He tugged at his lower lip which drooped oddly as if it had been tugged many times before. With a petulant frown his wife smacked him on the wrist and he tucked the offending hand into his pocket. They were very childlike, thought Cooper, and wondered if Mrs Gillespie had employed them out of compassion.

'And the granddaughter's name?'

'Miss Lascelles,' said Mrs Spede.

'Do you know her Christian name?'

'Ruth.' She consulted with her husband behind lowered lids. They're not nice, either of them. The Mrs is rude to Mr Spede about his gardening and the Miss is rude to Jenny about her cleaning.'

'Jenny?' he queried. 'Who's Jenny?'

'Jenny is Mrs Spede.'

'I see,' said Cooper kindly. 'It must have been a terrible shock for you, Jenny, to find Mrs Gillespie in her bath.'

'Oh, it was that,' she howled, grabbing her husband's arm. 'A terrible, terrible shock.' Her voice rose on a wail.

With some reluctance, because he feared an even louder outburst, Cooper took the polythene bag containing the Stanley knife from his pocket and laid it across his broad palm. 'I don't want to upset you any more, but do you recognize this? Is it a knife you've seen before?'

Her lips puckered tragically but she stopped the wailing to nudge her husband into speech. 'The kitchen drawer,' he said. 'It's the one from the kitchen drawer.' He touched the handle through the bag. 'I scratched an h'aitch on it for "house". The one I keep in the shed has a gee on it for "garden".'

Cooper examined the crude 'h' and nodded as he tucked the bag back out of sight into his pocket. 'Thank you. I'll need the one from the garden for comparison. I'll ask an officer to go out with you when we've finished.' He smiled in a friendly way. 'Now, you presumably have keys to the house. May I see them?'

Mrs Spede drew a string from around her neck, revealing a key that had lain within the cleft of her bosom. 'Only me,' she said. 'Jenny had the key. Mr Spede didn't need one for the garden.' She gave it to Cooper and he felt the warmth of her body seeping into his hand. It repelled him because it was damp and oily with sweat, and this made him feel guilty because he found them both deeply unattractive and knew that, unlike Mrs Gillespie, he could not have tolerated them about his house for even half an hour.

Mathilda Gillespie's nearest neighbours lived alongside her in a wing adjoining the house. At some stage Cedar House must have been one residence, but now a discreet sign indicated the door to Wing Cottage at the western end of the building. Before Cooper knocked on it, he walked along a gravel path to the rear corner and surveyed the patio

at the back, neatly bordered by tubs of everlasting pansies, beyc
which a clipped box hedge separated this garden from the expanse
lawn and distant trees that belonged to Cedar House. He fel
sudden envy for the occupants. How drear his own small box was
comparison, but then it was his wife who had chosen to live o
modern estate and not he. He would have been happy with crumbl
plaster and a view; she was happy with all mod. cons and neighbo
so close they rubbed shoulders every day. It was a policeman's lot
give in to a wife he was fond of. His hours were too unpredictable
allow him to impose his own yearning for isolation on a woman w
had tolerated his absences with stoical good humour for thirty yea

He heard the door open behind him and turned, producing
warrant card from his breast pocket, to greet the fat elderly man w
approached. 'DS Cooper, sir, Dorset police.'

'Orloff, Duncan Orloff.' He ran a worried hand across his wi
rather pleasant face. 'We've been expecting you. Dear me, dear me
don't mind admitting Jenny Spede's howling is a little difficult to ta
after a while. Poor woman. She's a good soul as long as nothi
upsets her. I can't tell you what it was like when she found Mathil
She came rushing out of the house screaming like a banshee and
her wretched husband off in sympathy. I realized something dread
must have happened which is why I phoned your people and
ambulance. Thank God they came quickly and had the sense to bri
a woman with them. She was really quite excellent, calmed the Spe
down in record time. Dear me, dear me,' he said again, 'we live su
a quiet life. Not used to this sort of thing at all.'

'No one is,' said Cooper. 'You've been told what's happened
suppose.'

He wrung his hands in distress. 'Only that Mathilda's dead. I k
the Spedes here until the police car arrived – thought it best, real
what with them collapsing in heaps about me – mind you, I was
going to let my wife downstairs till it was safe – one can't be cert
about things – anyway the uniformed chaps told me to wait ur
someone came to ask questions. Look, you'd better come in. Viole
in the drawing-room now, not feeling too well in the circumstanc
and who can blame her? Frankly, not feeling a hundred per ce
myself.' He stood aside to let Cooper enter. 'First door on the righ
he said. He followed the policeman into a cosy, over-furnished roc

9

with a television on low volume in the corner, and bent over the prostrate figure of his wife on the sofa. 'There's a Sergeant to see us,' he said, raising her gently to a sitting position with one hand and using the other to swing her legs to the floor. He lowered his large bulk on to the sofa beside her and gestured Cooper towards an armchair. 'Jenny kept screaming about blood,' he confided unhappily. 'Red water and blood. That's all she said.'

Violet shivered. 'And Jesus,' she whispered. 'I heard her. She said Mathilda was "like Jesus".' She raised a hand to her own bloodless lips. 'Dead like Jesus in blood red water.' Her eyes filled. 'What's happened to her? Is she *really* dead?'

'I'm afraid she is, Mrs Orloff. It's only approximate, but the pathologist estimates the time of death between nine o'clock and midnight on Saturday.' He looked from one to the other. 'Were you here during those three hours?'

'We were here all night,' said Duncan. He was clearly drawn between his own perceived good taste of not asking questions and an overwhelming need to satisfy a very natural curiosity. 'You haven't told us what's happened,' he blurted out. 'It's much, much worse if you don't know what's happened. We've been imagining terrible things.'

'She hasn't been *crucified*, has she?' asked Violet tremulously. 'I said she's probably been crucified, otherwise why would Jenny have said she looked like Jesus?'

'I said someone had tried to clean up afterwards,' said Duncan, 'which is why there's red water everywhere. You hear about it every day, old people being murdered for their money. They do terrible things to them, too, before they kill them.'

'Oh, I do hope she wasn't *raped*,' said Violet. 'I couldn't bear it if they'd raped her.'

Cooper had time to feel regret for this elderly couple who, like so many of their peers, lived the end of their lives in terror because the media persuaded them they were at risk. He knew better than anyone that statistics proved it was young men aged between fifteen and twenty-five who were the group most vulnerable to violent death. He had sorted out too many drunken brawls and picked too many stabbed and bludgeoned bodies from gutters outside pubs to be in any doubt of that. 'She died in her bath,' he said unemotionally.

'Her wrists were slit. At the moment the pathologist is inclining towards suicide and we are only asking questions to satisfy ourselves that she did in fact take her own life.'

'But Jesus didn't die in his bath,' said Violet in bewilderment.

'She was wearing a scold's bridle on her head with flowers in it. I think perhaps Mrs Spede thought it was a crown of thorns.' It made no sense otherwise, he thought.

'I *hated* that thing. Mathilda was always *very* peculiar about it.' Violet had a habit, Cooper noticed, of emphasizing words she thought important. 'It must have been suicide, then. She wore it when her arthritis was bad. It took her mind off the *pain*, you know. She always said she'd kill herself if it got so bad she couldn't stand it.' She turned tear-filled eyes to her husband. 'Why didn't she call out to us? I'm sure there's *something* we could have done to help.'

'Would you have heard her?' asked Cooper.

'Oh, yes, especially if she was in the bathroom. She could have rattled the pipes. We'd certainly have heard *that*.'

Cooper transferred his attention to Mr Orloff. 'Did you hear anything at all that night?'

Duncan gave the question long and thoughtful consideration. 'Our days are very uneventful,' he said apologetically. 'All I can say is that if we had heard something, we'd have acted' – he spread his hands in a gesture of surrender – 'like this morning when Jenny started screaming. There was nothing like that on Saturday.'

'Yet you both assumed she'd been murdered by a gang. You mentioned "they".'

'It's difficult to think straight when people are screaming,' he said, reproaching himself with a shake of the head. 'And to be perfectly honest, I wasn't at all sure the Spedes themselves hadn't done something. They're not the brightest couple as you've probably discovered for yourself. Mind you, it wouldn't have been intentional. They're foolish, not dangerous. I assumed there'd been some sort of accident,' he spread his palms on his fat knees, 'I've been worrying that I should have gone in to do something, saved her perhaps, but if she died on Saturday . . . ?' His voice tailed off on a query.

Cooper shook his head. 'You couldn't have done anything for her. What about during the daytime? Did you hear anything then?'

'On Saturday, you mean?' He shook his head. 'Nothing that leaps

11

to mind. Certainly nothing unsettling.' He looked at Violet as if seeking inspiration. 'We notice if the bell rings in Cedar House, because it's very rare for Mathilda to have visitors, but otherwise' – he shrugged helplessly – 'so little happens here, Sergeant, and we do watch a lot of television.'

'And you didn't wonder where she was on Sunday?'

Violet dabbed at her eyes. 'Oh, dear,' she whispered, 'could we have saved her then? How *awful*, Duncan.'

'No,' said Cooper firmly, 'she was certainly dead by three o'clock on Sunday morning.'

'We were friends, you know,' said Violet. 'Duncan and I have known her for fifty years. She sold us this cottage when Duncan retired five years ago. That's not to say she was the *easiest* person in the world to get on with. She could be very cruel to people she didn't like, but the trick with Mathilda was not to *impose*. We never did, of course, but there were those who did.'

Cooper licked the point of his pencil. 'Who for example?'

Violet lowered her voice. 'Joanna and Ruth, her daughter and granddaughter. They *never* left her alone, always complaining, always demanding money. And the vicar was shocking.' She cast a guilty glance at her husband. 'I know Duncan doesn't approve of tittle-tattle but the vicar was always pricking her conscience about the less well off. She was an *atheist*, you know, and very rude to Mr Matthews every time he came. She called him a Welsh leech. To his face, too.'

'Did he mind?'

Duncan gave a rumble of laughter. 'It was a game,' he said. 'She was quite generous sometimes when he caught her in a good mood. She gave him a hundred pounds once towards a centre for alcoholics, saying there but for the grace of her metabolism went she. She drank to deaden the pain of her arthritis, or so she said.'

'Not to excess, though,' said Violet. 'She was never *drunk*. She was too much of a lady ever to get drunk.' She blew her nose loudly.

'Is there anyone else you can think of who imposed on her?' asked Cooper after a moment.

Duncan shrugged. 'There was the doctor's husband, Jack Blakeney. He was always round there, but it wasn't an imposition. She liked him. I used to hear her laughing with him sometimes in the garden.' He paused to reflect. 'She had very few friends, Sergeant. As

12

Violet said, she wasn't an easy woman. People either liked Mathilda or loathed her. You'll find that out soon enough if you're planning to ask questions of anyone else.'

'And you liked her?'

His eyes grew suddenly wet. 'I did,' he said gruffly. 'She was beautiful once, you know, quite beautiful.' He patted his wife's hand. 'We all were, a long, long time ago. Age has very few compensations, Sergeant, except perhaps the wisdom to recognize contentment.' He pondered for a moment. 'They do say slitting the wrists is a very peaceful way to die, although how anyone knows I can't imagine. Did she suffer, do you think?'

'I'm afraid I can't answer that, Mr Orloff,' said Cooper honestly.

The damp eyes held his for a moment and he saw a deep and haggard sadness in them. They spoke of a love that Cooper somehow suspected Duncan had never shown or felt for his wife. He wanted to say something by way of consolation, but what could he say that wouldn't make matters worse? He doubted that Violet knew, and he wondered, not for the first time, why love was more often cruel than it was kind.

I watched Duncan clipping his hedge this afternoon and could barely remember the handsome man he was. If I had been a charitable woman, I would have married him forty years ago and saved him from himself and Violet. She has turned my Romeo into a sad-eyed Billy Bunter who blinks his passion quietly when no one's looking. Oh, that his too, too solid flesh should melt. At twenty, he had the body of Michelangelo's David, now he resembles an entire family group by Henry Moore.

Jack continues to delight me. What a tragedy I didn't meet him or someone like him when I was 'green in judgement'. I learnt only how to survive, when Jack would, I think, have taught me how to love. I asked him why he and Sarah have no children, and he answered: 'Because I've never had the urge to play God.' I told him there was nothing godlike about procreation – doglike perhaps – and it's a monumental conceit that allows him to dictate Sarah's suitability as a mother. 'The vicar would say you're playing the devil, Jack. The species won't survive unless people like you reproduce themselves.'

But he is not an amenable man. If he were, I would enjoy him less. 'You've played God for years, Mathilda. Has it given you any pleasure or made you more content?'

No, and I can say that honestly. I shall die as naked as I was born . . .

Two

A WEEK LATER the receptionist buzzed through to Dr Blakeney's office. 'There's a Detective Sergeant Cooper on the line. I've told him you have a patient with you but he's very insistent. Can you speak to him?' It was a Monday and Sarah was covering afternoon surgery in Fontwell.

She smiled apologetically at the pregnant mother, laid out like a sacrificial offering on her couch. She put her hand over the receiver. 'Do you mind if I take this call, Mrs Graham? It's rather important. I'll be as quick as I can.'

'Get on with you. I'm enjoying the rest. You don't get many opportunities when it's your third.'

Sarah smiled at her. 'Put him through, Jane. Yes, Sergeant, what can I do for you?'

'We've had the results of Mrs Gillespie's post mortem. I'd be interested in your reactions.'

'Go on.'

He shuffled some papers at the other end of the line. 'Direct cause of death: loss of blood. Traces of barbiturates were discovered in her system, but not enough to prove fatal. Traces also discovered in the whisky glass, implying she dissolved the barbiturates before she drank them. Some alcohol absorbed. No bruising. Lacerations on the tongue where the rusted bit of the scold's bridle caused the surface to bleed. Nothing under her fingernails. Slight nettle rash on her temples and cheeks, and minor chafing of the skin beneath the bridle's framework, both consistent with her donning the contraption herself and then arranging it with the nettles and daisies. No indications at all that she put up any sort of struggle. The scold's bridle was not attached to her

17

head in any way and could have been removed, had she wished to do so. The wounds to the wrists correspond precisely with the Stanley knife blade discovered on the bathroom floor, the one on the left wrist made with a downward right-handed stroke, the one on the right with a downward left-handed stroke. The knife had been submerged in water, probably dropped after one of the incisions, but there was an index fingerprint, belonging to Mrs Gillespie, one-point-three centimetres from the blade on the shaft. Conclusion: suicide.' He paused. 'Are you still there?' he demanded after a moment.

'Yes.'

'So what do you think?'

'That I was wrong last week.'

'But surely the barbiturates in the whisky glass trouble you?'

'Mathilda hated swallowing anything whole,' she said apologetically. 'She crushed or dissolved everything in liquid first. She had a morbid fear of choking.'

'But your immediate reaction when you saw her was that she was the last person you'd expect to kill herself. And now you've changed your mind.' It sounded like an accusation.

'What do you want me to say, Sergeant? My gut feeling remains the same.' Sarah glanced towards her patient who was becoming restless. 'I would not have expected her to take her own life, but gut feelings are a poor substitute for scientific evidence.'

'Not always.'

She waited, but he didn't go on. 'Was there anything else, Sergeant? I do have a patient with me.'

'No,' he said, sounding dispirited, 'nothing else. It was a courtesy call. You may be required to give evidence at the inquest, but it'll be a formality. We've asked for an adjournment while we check one or two small details but, at the moment, we aren't looking for anyone else in connection with Mrs Gillespie's death.'

Sarah smiled encouragingly at Mrs Graham. *Be with you in a minute*, she mouthed. 'But you think you should be.'

'I learnt my trade in a simpler world, Dr Blakeney, where we paid attention to gut feelings. But in those days we called them hunches.' He gave a hollow laugh. 'Now, hunches are frowned on and forensic evidence is God. But forensic evidence is only as reliable as the man who interprets it and what I want to know is why there are no nettle

18

stings on Mrs Gillespie's hands and fingers. Dr Cameron began by saying she must have worn gloves but there are no gloves in that house with sap on them, so now he thinks the water must have nullified the reaction. I don't like that kind of uncertainty. My hunch is Mrs Gillespie was murdered but I'm an Indian and the Chief says, drop it. I hoped you'd give me some ammunition.'

'I'm sorry,' said Sarah helplessly. She murmured a goodbye and replaced the receiver with a thoughtful expression in her dark eyes.

'It'll be old Mrs Gillespie, I suppose,' said Mrs Graham prosaically. She was a farmer's wife, for whom birth and death held little mystery. Both happened, not always conveniently, and the whys and where-fores were largely irrelevant. The trick was coping afterwards. 'There's talk of nothing else in the village. Awful way to do it, don't you think?' She shivered theatrically. 'Slitting your wrists and then watch-ing your blood seep into the water. I couldn't do that.'

'No,' agreed Sarah, rubbing her hands to warm them. 'You say you think the baby's head has engaged already?'

'Mm, won't be long now.' But Mrs Graham wasn't to be side-tracked so easily and she'd heard enough of the doctor's end of the conversation to whet her appetite. 'Is it true she had a cage on her head? Jenny Spede's been hysterical about it ever since. A cage with brambles and roses in it, she said. She keeps calling it Mrs Gillespie's crown of thorns.'

Sarah could see no harm in telling her. Most of the details were out already, and the truth was probably less damaging than the horror stories being put about by Mathilda's cleaner. 'It was a family heirloom, a thing called a scold's bridle.' She placed her hands on the woman's abdomen and felt for the baby's head. 'And there were no brambles or roses, nothing with thorns at all. Just a few wild flowers.' She omitted the nettles deliberately. The nettles, she thought, *were* disturbing. 'It was more pathetic than frightening.' Her probing fingers relaxed. 'You're right. It won't be long now. You must have got your dates wrong.'

'I always do, Doctor,' said the woman comfortably. 'I can tell you to the minute when a cow's due but when it's my turn,' she laughed, 'I haven't time to mark calendars.' Sarah linked arms with her to pull her into a sitting position. 'Scold's bridle,' she went on thoughtfully. 'Scold, as in a woman with a vicious tongue?'

Sarah nodded. 'They were used up until two or three centuries ago to shut women up, and not just women with vicious tongues either. Any women. Women who challenged male authority, inside the home *and* outside.'

'So why do you reckon she did it?'

'I don't know. Tired of living perhaps.' Sarah smiled. 'She didn't have your energy, Mrs Graham.'

'Oh, the dying I can understand. I've never seen much sense in struggling for life if the life isn't worth the struggle.' She buttoned her shirt. 'I meant why did she do it with this scold's bridle on her head?'

But Sarah shook her head. 'I don't know that either.'

'She was a nasty old woman,' said Mrs Graham bluntly. 'She lived here virtually all her life, knew me and my parents from our cradles, but she never acknowledged us once. We were too common. Tenant farmers with muck on our shoes. Oh, she spoke to old Wittingham, the lazy sod who owns Dad's farm, all right. The fact he's never done a hand's turn since the day he was born, but lives on his rents and his investments, made him acceptable. But the workers, rough trade like us – ' she shook her head – 'we were beneath contempt.' She chuckled at Sarah's expression. 'There, I'm shocking you. But I've a big mouth and I use it. You don't want to take Mrs Gillespie's death to heart. She wasn't liked, and not through want of trying, believe me. We're not a bad lot here, but there's only so much that ordinary folk can take, and when a woman brushes her coat after you've bumped into her by accident, well, that's when you say enough's enough.' She swung her legs to the floor and stood up. 'I'm not much of a church-goer, me, but some things I do believe in, and one of them's repentance. Be it God or just old age, I reckon everyone repents in the end. There's few of us die without recognizing our faults which is why death's so peaceful. And it doesn't really matter who you say sorry to – a priest, God, your family – you've said it, and you feel better.' She slipped her feet into her shoes. 'I'd guess Mrs Gillespie was apologizing for her vicious tongue. That's why she wore her scold's bridle to meet her Maker.'

*

Mathilda Gillespie was buried three days later beside her father, Sir William Cavendish MP, in Fontwell village churchyard. The coroner's inquest had still to be held but it was common knowledge by then that a verdict of suicide was a foregone conclusion, if not from Polly Graham, then from a simple putting two and two together when the Dorset police removed their seals from Cedar House and returned to headquarters in the nearby coastal resort of Learmouth.

The congregation was a small one. Polly Graham had told the truth when she said Mathilda Gillespie wasn't liked, and few could be bothered to find time in their busy lives to say goodbye to an old woman who had been known only for her unkindness. The vicar did his best in difficult circumstances but it was with a feeling of relief that the mourners turned from the open grave and picked their way across the grass towards the gate.

Jack Blakeney, a reluctant attendant on a wife who had felt duty-bound to put in an appearance, muttered into Sarah's ear: 'What a bunch of white sepulchres, and I am not referring to the tombstones either, just we hypocrites doing our middle-class duty. Did you see their faces when the Rev referred to her as "our much loved friend and neighbour"? They all hated her.'

She hushed him with a warning hand. 'They'll hear you.'

'Who cares?' They were bringing up the rear and his artist's gaze roamed restlessly across the bowed heads in front of them. 'Presumably the blonde is the daughter, Joanna.'

Sarah heard the deliberate note of careless interest in his voice and smiled cynically. 'Presumably,' she agreed, 'and presumably the younger one is the granddaughter.'

Joanna stood now beside the vicar, her soft grey eyes huge in a finely drawn face, her silver-gold hair a shining cap in the sunlight. A beautiful woman, thought Sarah, but as usual she could admire her with complete detachment. She rarely directed her resentment towards the objects of her husband's thinly disguised lust, for she saw them as just that, objects. Lust, like everything in Jack's life apart from his painting, was ephemeral. A brief enthusiasm to be discarded as rapidly as it was espoused. The days when she had been confident that, for all his appreciation of another woman's looks, he wouldn't jeopardize their marriage were long past and she had few illusions left about her own role. She provided the affluence whereby Jack Blakeney, struggling artist, could live and slake his very mundane cravings, but as Polly Graham had said – *there was only so much that ordinary folk could take*.

They shook hands with the vicar. 'It was kind of you both to come. Have you met Mathilda's daughter?' The Reverend Matthews turned to the woman. 'Joanna Lascelles, Dr Sarah Blakeney and Jack Blakeney. Sarah was your mother's GP, Joanna. She joined the practice last year when Dr Hendry retired. She and Jack live at The Mill in Long Upton, Geoffrey Freeling's old house.'

Joanna shook hands with them and turned to the girl beside her. 'This is my daughter Ruth. We're both very grateful to you, Dr Blakeney, for all you did to help my mother.'

The girl was about seventeen or eighteen, as dark as her mother was fair, and she looked anything but grateful. Sarah had only an impression of intense and bitter grief. 'Do you know why Granny killed herself?' she asked softly. 'Nobody else seems to.' Her face was set in a scowl.

'Ruth, please,' sighed her mother. 'Aren't things difficult enough already?' It was a conversation they had clearly had before.

Joanna must be approaching forty, thought Sarah, if the daughter was anything to go by, but against the black of her coat, she looked only very young and very vulnerable. Beside her, Sarah felt Jack's interest quicken and she had an angry impulse to turn on him and berate him publicly once and for all. How far did he think her patience would stretch? How long did he expect her to tolerate his contemptuous and contemptible indifference to her beleaguered pride? She quelled the impulse, of course. She was too trammelled by her upbringing and the behavioural demands of her profession to do anything else. *But, oh God, one day* . . . she promised herself. Instead she turned to the girl. 'I wish I could give you an answer, Ruth, but I can't. The last time I saw your grandmother she was fine. In some pain from her arthritis, of course, but nothing she wasn't used to or couldn't cope with.'

The girl cast a spiteful glance at her mother. 'Then something must have happened to upset her. People don't kill themselves for no reason.'

'Was she easily upset?' asked Sarah. 'She never gave me that impression.' She smiled slightly. 'She was tough as old boots, your grandmother. I admired her for it.'

'Then why did she kill herself?'

'Because she wasn't afraid of death perhaps. Suicide isn't always a negative, you know. In some cases it's a positive statement of choice. I will die now and in this manner. "To be or not to be." For Mathilda "not to be" would have been a considered decision.'

Ruth's eyes filled. '*Hamlet* was her favourite play.' She was tall like her mother but her face, pinched with cold and distress, lacked the other's startling looks. Ruth's tears made her ugly where her mother's, a mere glistening of the lashes, enhanced a fragile beauty.

Joanna stirred herself, glancing from Sarah to Jack. 'Will you come back to the house for tea? There'll be so few of us.'

Sarah excused herself. 'I'm afraid I can't. I have a surgery in Mapleton at four thirty.'

Jack did not. 'Thank you, that's very kind.'

There was a small silence. 'How will you get home?' asked Sarah, fishing in her pocket for her car keys.

'I'll beg a lift,' he said. 'Someone's bound to be going my way.'

One of Sarah's colleagues dropped in as evening surgery was finishing. There were three partners in a practice serving several square miles of Dorset coast and countryside, including sizeable villages, scattered hamlets and farmhouses. Most of the villages had small self-contained surgeries, either attached to the doctors' houses or leased from patients and, between them, the partners covered the whole area, boxing and coxing in neat rotation. Mapleton was Robin Hewitt's home village but, like Sarah, he spent as much time out of it as he did in. They had so far resisted the logic of pooling their resources in one modern clinic in the most central of the villages, but it was doubtful if they could resist for much longer. The argument, a true one, that most of their patients were elderly or lacked transport, was far outweighed by the commercial pressures now existing inside the health service.

'You look tired,' said Robin, folding himself into the armchair beside her desk.

'I am.'

'Trouble?'

'Only the usual.'

'Domestic, eh? Get rid of him.'

She laughed. 'And supposing I told you, as casually, to get rid of Mary?'

'There's a small difference, my darling. Mary is an angel and Jack is not.' But the idea was not without a certain appeal. After eighteen years, Mary's complacent self-assurance was so much less attractive than Sarah's troubled seeking after truths.

'I can't argue with that.' She finished writing some notes and pushed them wearily to one side.

'What's he done this time?'

'Nothing, as far as I know.'

Which sounded about right, thought Robin. Jack Blakeney made a virtue of doing nothing while his wife made a virtue of supporting him in idleness. Their continuing marriage was a complete mystery to him. There were no children, no ties, nothing binding them, Sarah was an independent woman with independent means, and she paid the mortgage on their house. It only required the services of a locksmith to shut the bastard out for ever.

She studied him with amusement. 'Why are you smiling like that?'

He switched neatly away from his mild fantasy of Sarah alone in her house. 'I saw Bob Hughes today. He was very put out to find me on duty and not you.' He fell into a fair imitation of the old man's Dorset burr. '"Where's the pretty one?" he said. "I want the pretty one to do it."'

'Do what?'

Robin grinned. 'Examine the boil on his bum. Dirty old brute. If it *had* been you, he'd have come up with another one, presumably, lurking under his scrotum and you'd have had the fun of probing for it and he'd have had the thrills while you did it.'

Her eyes danced. 'And it's completely free, don't forget. Relief massage comes expensive.'

'That's revolting. You're not telling me he's tried it on before.'

She chuckled. 'No, of course not. He only comes in for a chat. I expect he felt he had to show you something. Poor old soul. I bet you sent him away with a flea in his ear.'

'I did. You're far too amenable.'

'But they're so lonely some of them. We live in a terrible world, Robin. No one has time to listen any more.' She toyed with her pen. 'I went to Mathilda Gillespie's funeral today and her granddaughter asked me why she killed herself. I said I didn't know, and I've been thinking about that ever since. I *should* know. She was one of my patients. If I'd taken a little more trouble with her, I *would* know.' She flicked him a sideways glance. 'Wouldn't I?'

He shook his head. 'Don't start down that route, Sarah. It's a dead end. Look, you were one person among many whom she knew and talked to, me included. The responsibility for that old woman wasn't yours alone. I'd argue that it wasn't yours at all, except in a strict medical sense, and nothing you prescribed for her contributed to her death. She died of blood loss.'

'But where do you draw the line between profession and friendship? We laughed a lot. I think I was one of the few people who appreciated her sense of humour, probably because it was so like Jack's. Bitchy, often cruel, but witty. She was a latterday Dorothy Parker.'

'You're being ridiculously sentimental. Mathilda Gillespie was a bitch of the first water, and don't imagine she viewed you as an equal. For years, until she sold off Wing Cottage to raise money, doctors, lawyers and accountants were required to enter by the tradesman's entrance. It used to drive Hugh Hendry mad. He said she was the rudest woman he'd ever met. He couldn't stand her.'

Sarah gave a snort of laughter. 'Probably because she called him Doctor Dolittle. To his face, too. I asked her once if it was by way of a job description and she said: "Not entirely. He had a closer affinity with animals than he had with people. He was an ass."'

Robin grinned. 'Hugh was the laziest and the least able doctor I've ever met. I suggested once that we check his medical qualifications because I didn't think he had any, but it's a bit difficult when the bloke in question is the senior partner. We just had to bite the bullet and hang on for his retirement.' He cocked his head on one side. 'So what did she call you, if she called him Dr Dolittle?'

She held the pen to her lips for a moment and stared past him. There was a haunting disquiet in her dark eyes. 'She was obsessed with that wretched scold's bridle. It was rather unhealthy really,

25

thinking about it. She wanted me to try it on once to see what it felt like.'

'And did you?'

'No.' She fell silent for a moment, then seemed to make up her mind to something. 'She called her arthritis her "Resident Scold" because it caused her so much nagging pain' – she tapped the pen against her teeth – 'and in order to take her mind off it, she used to don the bridle as a sort of counter-irritant. That's what I mean about her unhealthy obsession with it. She wore it as a sort of penance, like a hair shirt. Anyway, when I took her off that rubbish Hendry had been prescribing and got the pain under some sort of manageable control, she took to calling me her little scold's bridle by way of a joke.' She saw his incomprehension. 'Because I'd succeeded in harnessing the Resident Scold,' she explained.

'So what are you saying?'

'I think she was trying to tell me something.'

Robin shook his head. 'Why? Because she was wearing it when she died? It was a symbol, that's all.'

'Of what?'

'Life's illusion. We're all prisoners. Perhaps it was her final joke. My tongue is curbed for ever, something like that.' He shrugged. 'Have you told the police?'

'No. I was so shocked when I saw her that I didn't think about it.' She raised her hands in a gesture of helplessness. 'And the pathologist and the policeman latched on to what I said she always called the geraniums inside the beastly thing. Her coronet weeds. It comes from the speech about Ophelia's death and, what with the bath and the nettles, I thought they were probably right. But now I'm not so sure.' Her voice tailed off and she sat staring at her desk.

Robin watched her for several seconds. 'Supposing she *was* trying to say that her tongue was curbed for ever. You realize it has a double meaning?'

'Yes,' said Sarah unhappily, 'that someone else curbed it. But that doesn't make sense. I mean, if Mathilda knew she was going to be murdered she wouldn't have wasted time donning the scold's bridle in the hall when all she had to do was run to the front door and scream her head off. The whole village would have heard her. And the murderer would have taken it off anyway.'

'Perhaps it was the murderer who was saying, "Her tongue is curbed for ever".'

'But that doesn't make sense either. Why would a murderer advertise that it's murder when he's gone to so much trouble to make it look like suicide?' She rubbed her tired eyes. 'Without the scold's bridle, it would have looked straightforward. With it, it looks anything *but*. And why the flowers, for God's sake? What were they supposed to tell us?'

'You'll have to talk to the police,' said Robin with sudden decision, reaching for the telephone. 'Dammit, Sarah, who else knew she called you her scold's bridle? Surely it's occurred to you that the message is directed at you.'

'What message?'

'I don't know. A threat, perhaps. You next, Dr Blakeney.'

She gave a hollow laugh. 'I see it more in terms of a signature.' She traced a line on the desk with her fingertip. 'Like the mark of Zorro on his victims.'

'Oh, Jesus!' said Robin, putting the receiver back. 'Maybe it's wiser not to say anything. Look, it was obviously suicide – you said yourself she was unhealthily obsessed with the damn thing.'

'But I was fond of her.'

'You're fond of everyone, Sarah. It's nothing to be proud of.'

'You sound like Jack.' She retrieved the telephone, dialled Learmouth Police Station and asked for Detective Sergeant Cooper.

Robin watched with gloomy resignation – she had no idea how the tongues would wag if they ever got wind of Mathilda's nickname for her – and wondered disloyally why she had chosen to tell him before anyone else. He had the strangest impression that she had been using him. As a yardstick by which to measure other people's reactions? As a confessor?

DS Cooper had already left for home and the bored voice at the other end of the wire merely agreed to pass on Sarah's request to speak to him when he arrived the next morning. There was no urgency, after all. The case was closed.

How I detest my arthritis and the cruel inactivity it imposes. I saw a ghost today but could do nothing about it. I should have struck it down and sent it back to Hell whence it came, instead I could only lash it with my tongue. Has Joanna brought him back to haunt me? It makes sense. She has been plotting something since she found that wretched letter. 'Ingratitude, thou marble-hearted fiend, more hideous when thou show'st thee in a child than the sea monster.'

But to use James of all people. That I shall never forgive. Or is it he who is using her? Forty years haven't changed him. What loathsome fun he must have had in Hong Kong where I've read the boys dress up as girls and give paederasts the thrill of pretended normality as they parade themselves and their disgusting perversion before a naïve public. He looks ill. Well, well, what a charming solution his death would be.

I made a 'most filthy bargain' there. They talk glibly about cycles of abuse these days but, oh, how much more complex those cycles are than the simple brutality visited by parent on child. Everything comes to him who mates . . .

Three

JACK WAS WORKING in his studio when Sarah's key finally grated in the lock at around eleven o'clock. He looked up as she passed his open door. 'Where have you been?'

She was very tired. 'At the Hewitts'. They gave me supper. Have you eaten?' She didn't come in, but stood in the doorway watching him.

He nodded absent-mindedly. Food was a low priority in Jack's life. He jerked his head at the canvas on the easel. 'What do you think?'

How much simpler it would be, she thought, if she were obtuse, and genuinely misunderstood what he was trying to achieve in his work. How much simpler if she could just accept what one or two critics had said, that it was pretentious rubbish and bad art.

'Joanna Lascelles presumably.'

But not a Joanna Lascelles that anyone would recognize, except perhaps in the black of her funeral weeds and the silver gold of her hair, for Jack used shape and colour to paint emotions, and there was an extraordinary turbulence about this painting, even in its earliest stage. He would go on now for weeks, working layer on layer, attempting through the medium of oils to build and depict the complexity of the human personality. Sarah, who understood his colour-coding almost as well as he did, could interpret much of what he had already blocked in. Grief (for her mother?), disdain (for her daughter?), and, all too predictably, sensuality (for him?).

Jack watched her face. 'She's interesting,' he said.

'Obviously.'

His eyes narrowed angrily. 'Don't start,' he murmured. 'I'm not in the mood.'

She shrugged. 'Neither am I. I'm going to bed.'

'I'll work on the jacket tomorrow,' he promised grudgingly. He made a living of sorts by designing book jackets, but the commissions were few and far between because he rarely met deadlines. The disciplines imposed by the profit motive infuriated him.

'I'm not your mother, Jack,' she said coolly. 'What you do tomorrow is your own affair.'

But he was in the mood for a row, probably, thought Sarah, because Joanna had flattered him. 'You just can't leave it alone, can you? No, you're not my mother, but by God you're beginning to sound like her.'

'How odd,' she said with heavy irony, 'and I always thought you didn't get on with her because she kept telling you what to do. Now I'm tarred with the same brush, yet I've done the exact opposite, left you to work things out for yourself. You're a child, Jack. You need a woman in your life to blame for every little thing that goes wrong for you.'

'Is this babies again?' he snarled. 'Dammit, Sarah, you knew the score before you married me, and it was your choice to go through with it. The career was everything, remember? Nothing's changed. Not for me, anyway. It's not my fault if your bloody hormones are screaming that time's running out. We had a deal. No children.'

She eyed him curiously. After all, she thought, Joanna must have been less accommodating than he had hoped. Well, well! 'The deal, Jack, for what it's worth, was that I would support you until you established yourself. After that, all options were open. What we never considered, and for that I blame myself because I relied on my own artistic judgement, was that you might *never* establish yourself. In which circumstance, I suspect, the deal is null and void. So far, I have kept you for six years, two years before marriage and four afterwards, and the choice to marry was as much yours as mine. As far as I remember we were celebrating your first major sale. Your only major sale,' she added. 'I think that's fair, don't you? I can't recall your selling a canvas since.'

'Spite doesn't suit you, Sarah.'

'No,' she agreed, 'any more than behaving like a spoilt brat suits you. You say nothing's changed, but you're wrong, everything's changed. I used to admire you. Now I despise you. I used to find you amusing. Now you bore me. I used to love you. Now I just feel sorry for you.' She smiled apologetically. 'I also used to think you'd make it. Now I don't. And that's not because I think any less of your painting, but because I think less of you. You have neither the commitment nor the discipline to be great, Jack, because you always forget that genius is only one per cent inspiration and ninety-nine per cent sheer, bloody graft. I'm a good doctor, not because I have an especial talent for diagnosis, but because I work my fingers to the bone. You're a rotten artist, not because you lack talent, but because you're too damn lazy and too damn snobbish to get down on your hands and knees with the rest of us and earn your reputation.'

The dark face split into a sardonic grin. 'Hewitt's doing, I suppose? A cosy little supper with Cock Robin and his wife, and then it's dump on Jack. Jesus, he's a greasy little toad. He'd be in your bed quicker than winking if sweet little Mary and the kiddiwinkles weren't guarding his door.'

'Don't be absurd,' she said coldly. 'It's your doing entirely. I ceased having any feelings for you whatsoever the day I had to refer Sally Bennedict for an abortion. I draw the line at being asked to approve the murder of your bastards, Jack, particularly by a selfish bitch like Sally Bennedict. She enjoyed the irony of it all, believe me.'

He stared at her with something like shock, and she saw that for once she had scored a direct hit. He hadn't known, she thought, which was something in his favour at least. 'You should have told me,' he said inadequately.

She laughed with genuine amusement. 'Why? You weren't my patient, Sally was. And, sure as eggs is eggs, she wasn't going to go to term with your little bundle of joy and lose her chance with the RSC. You can't play Juliet six months pregnant, Jack, which is what she would have been when the run started. Oh, I did my bit, suggested she talk it through with you, suggested she talk it through with a counsellor, but I might have been pissing in the wind for all the good it did. She'd have preferred cancer, I think, to an unwanted pregnancy.' Her smile was twisted. 'And let's face it, we both knew what your reaction would be. It's the only time I've felt confident that the wretched foetus, were it born, would be rejected by both parties. I passed the buck on to the hospital and they had *her* in and *it* out within two weeks.'

He swirled his brush aimlessly around the colours on his palette. 'Was that the reason for the sudden move down here?'

'Partly. I had a nasty feeling Sally would be the first of many.'

'And the other part?'

'I didn't think the wilds of Dorset would appeal to you. I hoped you'd stay in London.'

'You should have told me,' he said again. 'I never was very good at taking hints.'

'No.'

He put the palette and the brush on a stool and started to wipe his hands with a kitchen towel dipped in turpentine. 'So how come the year's grace? Charity? Or malice? Did you think it would be more fun to cast me adrift down here than in London where I'd be assured of a bed?'

'Neither,' she said. 'Hope. Misplaced, as usual.' She glanced at the canvas.

He followed her gaze. 'I had tea with her. Nothing more.'

'I believe you.'

'Why so angry then? I'm not making a scene because you had supper with Robin.'

'I'm not angry, Jack. I'm bored. Bored with being the necessary audience that your ridiculous ego requires. I sometimes think that was the real reason you married me, not for security but because you needed somebody else's emotion to stimulate your creativity.' She gave a hollow laugh. 'In that case you should never have married a doctor. We see too much of it at work to play it all out again at home.'

He studied her closely. 'That's it then, is it? My marching orders? Pack your bags, Jack, and never darken my door again.'

She smiled the Mona Lisa smile that had first bewitched him. He thought he could predict exactly what she was going to say. *It's your life, make your own decisions.* For Sarah's strength and her weakness was her belief that everyone was as confident and single-minded as she was.

'Yes,' she said, 'that's it. I made up my mind that if you ever went near Sally again I'd call it quits. I want a divorce.'

His eyes narrowed. 'If this was about Sally, you'd have given me an ultimatum two weeks ago. I made no secret of where I was going.'

'I know,' she said wearily, staring at the painting again. 'Even your betrayals demand an audience now.'

He was gone when she came downstairs the next morning. There was a note on the kitchen table:

Send the divorce papers c/o Keith Smollett. You can find yourself another solicitor. I'll be going for a fifty-fifty split so don't get too attached to the house. I'll clear the studio as soon as I've found somewhere else. If you don't want to see me, then don't change the locks. I'll leave my key behind when I've retrieved my stuff.

Sarah read it through twice then dropped it in the rubbish bin.

Jane Marriott, the receptionist at the Fontwell surgery, looked up as Sarah pushed open the door of the empty waiting-room. Sarah covered Fontwell on Monday afternoons and Friday mornings and, because she was more sympathetic than her male colleagues, her sessions were usually busy ones. 'There's a couple of messages for you, dear,' said Jane. 'I've left them on your desk.'

'Thanks.' She paused by the desk. 'Who's first?'

'Mr Drew at eight forty-five and then it's hectic until eleven thirty. After that, two home visits, I'm afraid, but I've told them not to expect you before midday.'

'Okay.'

Jane, a retired teacher in her sixties, eyed Sarah with motherly concern. 'No breakfast again, I suppose?'

Sarah smiled. 'I haven't eaten breakfast since I left school.'

'Hm, well, you look washed out. You work too hard, dear. Doctoring's like any other job. You should learn to pace yourself better.'

Sarah put her elbows on the desk and propped her chin on her hands. 'Tell me something, Jane. If heaven exists, where exactly is it?' She looked for all the world like one of the eight-year-olds Jane had once taught, puzzled, a little hesitant, but confident that Mrs Marriott would know the answer.

'Goodness! No one's asked me a question like that since I stopped teaching.' She plugged in the kettle and spooned coffee into two cups. 'I always told the children it was in the hearts you left behind. The more people there were who loved you, the more hearts would hold your memory. It was a devious way of encouraging them to be nice to each other.' She chuckled. 'But I thought you were a non-believer, Sarah. Why the sudden interest in the afterlife?'

'I went to Mrs Gillespie's funeral yesterday. It was depressing. I keep wondering what the point of it all is.'

'Oh dear. Eternal truths at eight thirty in the morning.' She put a cup of steaming black coffee in front of Sarah. 'The point to Mathilda Gillespie's life might not emerge for another five generations. She's part of a line. Who's to say how important that line might be in years to come?'

'That's even more depressing,' said Sarah gloomily. 'That means you have to have children to give meaning to your life.'

'Nonsense. I haven't any children but I don't feel it makes me any less valuable. Our lives are what we make them.' She didn't look at Sarah as she spoke, and Sarah had the feeling that the words were just words, without meaning. 'Sadly,' Jane went on, 'Mathilda made very little of hers. She never got over her husband running out on her and it made her bitter. I think she thought people were laughing at her behind her back. Which, of course, a lot of us were,' she admitted honestly.

'I thought she was a widow.' How little she really knew about the woman.

Jane shook her head. 'Assuming he's still alive, then James is her widower. As far as I know they never bothered with a divorce.'

'What happened to him?'

'He went out to Hong Kong to work in a bank.'

'How do you know?'

'Paul and I took a holiday in the Far East about ten years after he and Mathilda separated, and we bumped into him by accident in a hotel in Hong Kong. We'd known him very well in the early days because he and Paul went through the war together.' She gave a quirky little smile. 'He was happy as Larry, living amongst the other expatriates, and quite unconcerned about his wife and daughter back home.'

'Who was supporting them?'

'Mathilda was. Her father left her very well provided for, which was a shame, I sometimes thought. She'd have been a different woman if she'd had to use that brain of hers to keep the wolf from the door.' She tut-tutted. 'It's bad for the character to have everything handed to you on a platter.'

Well, that was certainly true, thought Sarah, if Jack was anything to go by. Fifty-bloody-fifty, she thought wrathfully. She'd see him in hell first. 'So when did he leave her? Recently?'

'Good heavens, no. It was about eighteen months after they married. Well over thirty years ago, anyway. For a year or two we had letters from him, then we lost touch. To be honest, we found him rather tiresome. When we met in Hong Kong he'd taken to the bottle in a big way and he became very aggressive when he got drunk. We were both rather relieved when the letters dried up. We've never heard from him again.'

'Did Mathilda know he'd written to you?' Sarah asked curiously.

'I really couldn't say. We'd moved to Southampton by then and had very little to do with her. Mutual friends mentioned her from time to time, but other than that we lost touch completely. We only came back here five years ago when my poor old chap's health broke down and I took a decision that fresh Dorset air had to be better for him than the polluted city rubbish in Southampton.'

Paul Marriott suffered from chronic emphysema and his wretched wife agonized over his condition. 'It was the best thing you could have done,' said Sarah firmly. 'He tells me he's been much better since he came home to his roots.' She knew from past experience that Jane wouldn't be able to let the subject drop once she'd embarked upon it and contrived to steer her off it. 'Did you know Mathilda well?'

Jane thought about that. 'We grew up together – my father was the doctor here for many years and Paul was her father's political agent for a time – Sir William was the local MP – but I honestly don't think I knew Mathilda at all. The trouble was I never liked her.' She looked apologetic. 'It's awful to say that about someone who's dead but I refuse to be hypocritical about it. She was quite the nastiest woman I've ever met. I never blamed James for deserting her. The only mystery was why he married her in the first place.'

'Money,' said Sarah with feeling.

'Yes, I think it must have been,' Jane agreed. 'He was very much poor gentry, heir to nothing but a name, and Mathilda was beautiful, of course, just like Joanna. The whole thing was a disaster. James learnt PDQ that there were some things worse than poverty. And being dictated to by a virago who held the purse strings was one of them. He *hated* her.'

One of the messages on Sarah's desk was from Ruth Lascelles, a short note, presumably put through the surgery door the previous evening. She had surprisingly childish writing for a girl of seventeen or eighteen. 'Dear Dr Blakeney, Please can you come and see me at Granny's house tomorrow (Friday). I'm not ill but I'd like to talk to you. I have to be back at school by Sunday night. Thanking you in anticipation. Yours sincerely, Ruth Lascelles.'

The other was a telephoned message from Detective Sergeant Cooper. 'Dr Blakeney's call drawn to DS Cooper's attention this morning. He will contact her later in the day.'

It was nearly three o'clock before Sarah found time to call in at Cedar House. She drove up the short gravel drive and parked in front of the dining-room windows which faced out towards the road on the left-hand side of the house. It was a Georgian building in yellowy-grey stone, with deep windows and high-ceilinged rooms. Far too big for Mathilda, Sarah had always thought, and very inconvenient for a woman who, on bad days, was little better than an invalid. Her one concession to poor health had been the introduction of a stair-lift which had allowed her continued access to the upper floor. Sarah had once suggested that she sell up and move into a bungalow, to which Mathilda had replied that she wouldn't dream of any such thing. 'My dear Sarah, only the lower classes live in bungalows which is why they are always called Mon Repos or Dunroamin. Whatever else you do in life, *never* drop your standards.'

Ruth came out as she was opening her car door. 'Let's talk in the summer-house,' she said jerkily. She didn't wait for an answer but set off round the corner of the house, her thin body, dressed only in tee-shirt and leggings, hunched against the biting north wind that was swirling the autumn leaves across the path.

Sarah, older and more susceptible to the cold, retrieved her Barbour from the back seat and followed. Out of the corner of her eye, she caught a glimpse of Joanna watching her from the dark depths of the dining-room. Had Ruth told her mother she'd asked Sarah to call, Sarah wondered, as she tramped across the lawn in the girl's wake. And why so much secrecy? The summer-house was a good two hundred yards from Joanna's listening ears.

Ruth was lighting a cigarette when Sarah joined her amongst the litter of art deco cane chairs and tables, relics from an earlier – happier? – age. 'I suppose you're going to lecture me,' she said with a scowl, pulling the doors to and flopping on to a chair.

'What about?' Sarah took another chair and folded the Barbour across her chest. It was bitterly cold, even with the doors closed.

'Smoking.'

Sarah shrugged. 'I'm not in the habit of lecturing.'

Ruth stared at her with moody eyes. 'Your husband said Granny called you her scold's bridle. Why would she do that if you didn't tick her off for nagging?'

Sarah looked out of the windows to where the huge cedar of Lebanon, after which the house was named, cast a long shadow on the grass. As she watched, the blustery wind drove a cloud across the sun and wiped the shadow away. 'We didn't have that sort of relationship,' she said, turning back to the girl. 'I enjoyed your grandmother's company. I don't recall any occasion when a ticking-off would have been appropriate.'

'I wouldn't have liked being called a scold's bridle.'

Sarah smiled. 'I found it rather flattering. I believe she meant it as a compliment.'

'I doubt it,' said the girl bluntly. 'I suppose you know she used the bridle on my mother when my mother was a child?' She smoked the cigarette nervously, taking short, rapid drags and expelling the smoke through her nose. She saw Sarah's disbelief. 'It's true. Granny told me about it once. She hated people crying, so whenever Mum cried she used to lock her in a cupboard with that thing strapped to her head. Granny's father did it to her. That's why she thought it was all right.'

Sarah waited but she didn't go on. 'That was cruel,' she murmured.

'Yes. But Granny was tougher than Mum and, anyway, it didn't matter much what you did to children when Granny was young, so being punished by wearing a bridle was probably no different from being thrashed with a belt. But it was awful for my mother.' She crushed the cigarette under her foot. 'There was no one to stand up for her and take her side. Granny could do what she liked whenever she liked.'

Sarah wondered what the girl was trying to tell her. 'It's an increasingly common problem, I'm afraid. Men, under stress, take their problems out on their wives. Women, under stress, take theirs out on their children, and there's nothing more stressful for a woman than to be left holding the baby.'

'Do you condone what Granny did?' There was a wary look in her eyes.

'Not at all. I suppose I'm trying to understand it. Most children in your mother's position suffer constant verbal abuse, and that is often as damaging as the physical abuse, simply because the scars don't show and nobody outside the family knows about it.' She shrugged. 'But the results are the same. The child is just as repressed and just as flawed. Few personalities can survive the constant battering of criticism from a person they depend on. You either crawl or fight. There's no middle way.'

Ruth looked angry. 'My mother had both, verbal and physical. You've no idea how vicious my grandmother was to her.'

'I'm sorry,' said Sarah helplessly. 'But if it's true that Mathilda was also punished brutally as a child, then she was as much a victim as your mother. But I don't suppose that's any consolation to you.'

Ruth lit another cigarette. 'Oh, don't get me wrong,' she said with an ironic twist to her mouth, 'I loved my grandmother. At least she had some character. My mother has none. Sometimes I hate her. Most of the time I just despise her.' She frowned at the floor, stirring the dust with the toe of one shoe. 'I think she killed Granny and I don't know what to do about it. Half of me blames her and the other half doesn't.'

Sarah let the remark hang in the air for a moment while she cast around for something to say. What sort of accusation was this? A genuine accusation of murder? Or a spiteful sideswipe by a spoilt child against a parent she disliked? 'The police are convinced it was suicide, Ruth. They've closed the case. As I understand it, there's no question of anyone else being involved in your grandmother's death.'

'I don't mean Mum actually did it,' she said, 'you know, took the knife and did it. I mean that she drove Granny to killing herself. That's just as bad.' She raised suspiciously bright eyes. 'Don't you think so, Doctor?'

'Perhaps. If such a thing is possible. But from what you've told me of your mother's relationship with Mathilda, it sounds unlikely. It would be more plausible if it had happened the other way round and Mathilda had driven your mother to suicide.' She smiled apologetically. 'Even then, that sort of thing doesn't happen very often, and there would be a history of mental instability behind the person who saw suicide as their only escape from a difficult relationship.'

But Ruth wasn't to be persuaded so easily. 'You don't understand,' she said. 'They could be as unpleasant as they liked to each other and it didn't matter a damn. Mum was just as bad as Granny, but in a different way. Granny said what she thought while Mum just went on chipping away with snide little remarks. I hated being with them when they were together.' Her lips thinned unattractively. 'That was the only good thing about being sent to boarding school. Mum moved out then and went to London, and I could choose whether to come here for my holidays or go to Mum's. I didn't have to be a football any more.'

How little Sarah knew about these three women. Where was Mr Lascelles, for example? Had he, like James Gillespie, run away? Or was Lascelles some kind of courtesy title that Joanna had adopted to give her daughter legitimacy? 'How long did you and your mother live here, then, before you went away to school?'

'From when I was a baby to when I was eleven. My father died and left us without a bean. Mum had to come crawling home or we'd have starved. That's her story at least. But personally I think she was

41

just too snobbish and too lazy to take a menial job. She preferred Granny's insults to getting her hands dirty.' She wrapped her arms about her waist and leaned forward, rocking herself. 'My father was a Jew.' She spoke the word with contempt.

Sarah was taken aback. 'Why do you say it like that?'

'It's how my grandmother always referred to him. *That Jew*. She was an anti-Semite. Didn't you know?'

Sarah shook her head.

'Then you didn't know her very well.' Ruth sighed. 'He was a professional musician, a bass guitarist, attached to one of the studios. He did the backing tracks when the groups weren't good enough to do them themselves, and he had a band of his own which did gigs occasionally. He died of a heroin overdose in 1978. I don't remember him at all, but Granny took great delight in telling me what a worthless person he was. His name was Steven, Steven Lascelles.' She lapsed into silence.

'How did your mother meet him?'

'At a party in London. She was supposed to get off with a deb's delight but got off with the guitarist instead. Granny didn't know anything about it until Mum told her she was pregnant, and then the shit hit the fan. I mean, can you imagine it? Mum up the spout by a Jewish rock guitarist with a heroin habit.' She gave a hollow laugh. 'It was a hell of a revenge.' Her arms were turning blue with cold but she didn't seem to notice it. 'So, anyway, they got married and she moved in with him. They had me and then six months later he was dead after spending all their money on heroin. He hadn't paid the rent for months. Mum was a widow – before she was twenty-three – on the dole with a baby and no roof over her head.'

'Then coming back here was probably her only option.'

Ruth pulled a sour face. 'You wouldn't have done it though, not if you knew you'd never be allowed to forget your mistake.'

Probably not, thought Sarah. She wondered if Joanna had loved Steven Lascelles or if, as Ruth had implied, she had taken up with him simply to spite Mathilda. 'It's easy to be wise after the event,' was all she said.

The girl went on as if she hadn't heard. 'Granny tried to change my name to something more WASP – you know, White Anglo-Saxon

Protestant – to erase the Hebrew in me. She called me Elizabeth for a while but Mum threatened to take me away, so Granny gave in. Other than that and her refusal to let Granny put the bridle on me when I cried, Mum let Granny dictate terms on everything.' Her eyes flashed scornfully. 'She was so wet. But it was easy to stand up to my grandmother. I did it all the time and we got on like a house on fire.'

Sarah had no desire to be drawn into a domestic squabble between a mother and daughter she barely knew. She watched the long shadow creep across the lawn again as the sun emerged from behind a cloud. 'Why did you ask me to come here, Ruth?'

'I don't know what to do. I thought you'd tell me.'

Sarah studied the thin, rather malicious face and wondered if Joanna had any idea how much her daughter disliked her. 'Don't do anything. Frankly, I can't imagine what your mother could have said or done that would have driven Mathilda to kill herself and, even if there were something, it would hardly be a chargeable offence.'

'Then it should be,' said Ruth harshly. 'She found a letter in the house last time she was down here. She told Granny she'd publish it if Granny didn't change her will immediately and move out of the house. So Granny killed herself. She's left everything to me, you see. She *wanted* to leave everything to me.' Now there was definite malice in the immature features.

Oh God, thought Sarah. *What were you trying to tell me, Mathilda?* 'Have you seen this letter?'

'No, but Granny wrote and told me what was in it. She said she didn't want me to find out from my mother. So, you see, Mum did drive her to it. Granny would have done anything to avoid having her dirty linen washed in public.' Her voice grated.

'Do you still have the letter she wrote to you?'

Ruth scowled. 'I tore it up. But that one wasn't important, it's the one Mum found that's important. She'll use it to try and overturn Granny's will.'

'Then I think you should find yourself a solicitor,' said Sarah firmly, drawing her legs together under her chair preparatory to getting up. 'I was your grandmother's doctor, that's all. I can't get involved between you and your mother, Ruth, and I'm quite sure Mathilda wouldn't have wanted me to.'

'But she would,' the girl cried. 'She said in her letter that if anything happened to her I was to talk to you. She said you would know what to do for the best.'

'Surely not? Your grandmother didn't confide in me. All I know about your family is what you've told me today.'

A thin hand reached out and gripped hers. It was icy cold. 'The letter was from Granny's uncle, Gerald Cavendish, to his solicitor. It was a will, saying he wanted everything he had to go to his daughter.'

Sarah could feel the hand on hers trembling, but whether from cold or nerves she didn't know. 'Go on,' she prompted.

'This house and all the money was his. He was the elder brother.'

Sarah frowned again. 'So what are you saying? That Mathilda never had any rights to it? Well, I'm sorry, Ruth, but this is way beyond me. You really must find a solicitor and talk it through with him. I haven't a clue what your legal position is, truly I haven't.' Her subconscious caught up with her. 'Still, it's very odd, isn't it? If his daughter was his heir, shouldn't she have inherited automatically?'

'No one knew she was his daughter,' said Ruth bleakly, 'except Granny, and she told everyone James Gillespie was the father. It's my mother, Dr Blakeney. Granny was being fucked by her uncle. It's really sick, isn't it?'

Joanna came to visit me today. She fixed me with that peculiarly unpleasant stare of hers through most of lunch – I was reminded of a terrier Father once had which turned vicious after a beating and had to be put down; there was the same malicious gleam in his eyes just before he sank his teeth into Father's palm and ripped the flesh from the bone – then spent most of the afternoon searching about in the library. She said she was looking for my mother's book on flower arranging, but she was lying, of course. I remember giving that to her when she moved back to London. I did not interfere.

She looked very tarty, I thought – far too much make-up for a trip to the country and in a ridiculously short skirt for a woman of her age. I suspect some man brought her down and was abandoned to forage for himself at the pub. Sex, to Joanna, is a currency to be used quite shamelessly in return for services rendered.

Oh, Mathilda, Mathilda! Such hypocrisy!

Do these men realize, I wonder, how little she cares for and about them? Not through contempt, I think, but through sheer indifference to anyone's feelings but her own. I should have taken Hugh Hendry's advice and insisted on a psychiatrist. She's quite mad, but then, so, of course, was Gerald. 'The wheel is come full circle.'

She came out of the library with his idiotic will held in front of her like some holy relic and cursed me in the most childish and absurd way for stealing her inheritance. I wonder who told her about it . . .

Four

WHEN SARAH ARRIVED home that evening, she made a bee-line for Jack's studio. To her relief, nothing had been moved. She passed the canvas on the easel without so much as a glance, and started rummaging feverishly through the portraits stacked against the far wall. Those she recognized, she left; those she didn't, she lined up side by side, facing into the room. In all, there were three paintings she had no recollection of ever having seen before. She stood back and gazed at them, trying to decipher who they were. More accurately, she was trying to isolate one that might strike a chord.

She hoped quite earnestly that she wouldn't find it. But she did, of course. It screamed at her, a violent and vivid portrayal of bitterness, savage wit and repression, and the whole personality was encaged in a rusted iron framework that was all too clearly the scold's bridle. Sarah's shock was enormous, driving the breath from her body in a surge of panic. She collapsed on to Jack's painting stool and closed her eyes against the jeering anger of Mathilda's image. *What had he done?*

The doorbell rang, jerking her to her feet like a marionette. She stood for a moment, wide-eyed with shock, then, without consciously rationalizing why she was doing it, she seized the picture, turned it round and thrust it amongst the others against the wall.

It crossed DS Cooper's mind that Dr Blakeney wasn't well. She looked very pale when she opened the door, but she smiled a welcome and stepped back to let him in, and by the time they were settled on chairs in the kitchen some of the colour had returned to her cheeks. 'You telephoned last night,' he reminded her, 'left a message saying you had more information about Mrs Gillespie.'

'Yes.' Her mind raced. *She said you would know what to do for the best*. But I don't! I DON'T! 'I've been worrying about why she wore the bridle,' she said slowly. 'I've come to the conclusion that she was trying to tell me something, although I must emphasize that I don't know what that something could have been.' As clearly as she could, she repeated what she had told Robin Hewitt the night before about Mathilda's nickname for her. 'It's probably just me being fanciful,' she finished lamely.

The Sergeant frowned deeply. 'She must have known you'd make a connection. Could she have been accusing you, perhaps?'

Sarah showed an unexpected relief. 'I hadn't thought of that,' she admitted. 'You mean a slap over the knuckles to bring me down a peg or two. Doctors can't cure unhappiness, Sarah. Something along those lines?'

He found her relief puzzling. 'It's possible,' he agreed. 'Who else knew that she called you her scold's bridle, Dr Blakeney?'

She folded her hands in her lap. 'I don't know. Whoever she mentioned it to, presumably.'

'You didn't tell anyone?'

She shook her head. 'No.'

'No one at all? Not even your partners or your husband?'

'No.' She forced a light chuckle. 'I wasn't altogether sure that she meant it as a compliment. I always took it as such because it would have strained our relationship if I hadn't, but she might have been implying that I was as repressive and tormenting as the instrument itself.'

He nodded thoughtfully. 'If she killed herself, then you and I will be puzzling over the significance of this for the rest of our lives.' His eyes watched Sarah's face. 'If, however, somebody else killed her, and that person knew she called you her scold's bridle, then it does seem to me that the message is very direct. Namely, I have done this *for* you, Dr Blakeney, or *because of* you. Would you agree with that?'

'No,' she said with a spark of anger. 'Of course I wouldn't. You can't possibly make assumptions like that. In any case I was under the impression that the inquest verdict was a foregone conclusion. The only reason I felt I should tell you all this was because it's been worrying me, but at the end of the day I'm probably reading far more into it than Mathilda intended. I suspect the pathologist was right, and that she simply wanted to deck herself out like Ophelia.'

He smiled pleasantly. 'And, of course, you may not have been the only person she used the nickname on.'

'Well, exactly.' She plucked a hair from the front of her jacket. 'May I ask you something?'

'By all means.'

'Does the pathologist's report come down firmly in favour of suicide or is there any room for doubt?'

'Not much,' the policeman admitted. 'He's unhappy about the absence of a letter of explanation, particularly in view of the rather dramatic way she killed herself, and he's unhappy about the flower arrangement.'

'Because the nettles stung her?'

'No. If she was set on killing herself the way she did, a few nettle stings wouldn't have worried her.' He tapped his pencil on the table top. 'I persuaded him to do some experiments. He's been unable to reproduce the arrangement she came up with without assistance.' He drew a quick diagram in his notebook. 'If you remember, the Michaelmas daisies were set upright in the forehead band, which incidentally is so rusted it can't be tightened, and the nettles hung down like a veil over her hair and cheeks. The stems were alternate, a nettle down, a daisy up, completely symmetrical all the way round. Now that is impossible to achieve without help. You can hold half the arrangement in place with one hand but the minute you get beyond the stretch of the fingers, the flowers start to drop out. It's only when three-quarters of the arrangement is in place that the gap between the frame and the head has reduced enough to retain the other quarter without dropping them, assuming the same circumference head as Mrs Gillespie. Do you follow?'

She frowned. 'I think so. But couldn't she have used cotton wool or tissues to pad the gap while she put in the flowers?'

'Yes. But if she had, then something in that house would have had rust marks on it. We searched it from top to bottom. There was nothing. So what happened to the padding?'

Sarah closed her eyes and pictured the bathroom. 'There was a sponge on the bathrack,' she said, remembering. 'Perhaps she used that and then washed it in the bath.'

'It does have particles of rust on it,' he admitted, 'but then the bath was full of them. The sponge could have picked them up when it was soaked by the water.' He pursed his lips in frustration. 'Or, as you say, it could have been used as padding. We don't know, but what worries me is this: if she did it herself, then she must have sat at her dressing-table to do it. It's the only surface where we've discovered any sap.' He made a vague gesture with his hand. 'We picture it something like this. She placed the flowers on the dressing-table, sat down in front of the mirror and then set about arranging them in the framework on her head, but she wouldn't have discovered she needed padding until she was half-way round, at which point the natural thing to do would have been to reach for some Kleenex or some cotton wool, both of which were there in front of her. So why go to the bathroom for the sponge?' He fell silent for a moment or two. 'If, however, someone else killed her and arranged the flowers after she was in the bath, then the sponge would have been the obvious thing to use. It's a far more logical scenario and would explain the absence of nettle rash on Mrs Gillespie's hands and fingers.'

'You said the pathologist's report mentioned nettle rash on her cheeks and temples,' said Sarah apologetically. 'But she'd have to have been alive for her skin to react to the stings.'

'It was only slight,' he amended. 'The way I see it, her killer didn't wait till she was dead – you don't hang about when you're murdering someone – he or she shoved the nettles in while she was dying.'

Sarah nodded. 'It sounds plausible,' she agreed, 'except—' She didn't finish the sentence.

'Except what, Dr Blakeney?'

'Why would anyone want to murder her?'

He shrugged. 'Her daughter and her granddaughter had strong enough motives. According to the will, the estate is to be divided equally between the two of them. Mrs Lascelles gets the money and Miss Lascelles gets Cedar House.'

'Did they know?'

He nodded. 'Mrs Lascelles certainly did because she showed us where to find the will – Mrs Gillespie was very methodical, kept all her papers and correspondence in neat files in a cabinet in the library – but whether *Miss* Lascelles knew the precise terms, I don't know.

She claims her grandmother intended her to have everything and is very put out to discover she is only going to get the house.' His face assumed a somewhat ironic expression. 'She's a greedy young woman. There's not many seventeen-year-olds would turn their noses up at a windfall like that.'

Sarah smiled slightly. 'Presumably you've checked to find out where they were the night she died?'

He nodded again. 'Mrs Lascelles was at a concert in London with a friend; Miss Lascelles was thirty miles away under the watchful eye of a housemistress at school.'

She forced another smile. 'Which puts them out of the picture.'

'Maybe, maybe not. I never set much store by alibis and someone had to get into Cedar House.' He frowned. 'Apart from Mrs Spede and Mrs Gillespie herself, the Lascelles women were the only other ones with keys.'

'You're determined to make it murder,' protested Sarah mildly.

He went on as if she hadn't spoken. 'We've questioned everyone in the village. Mrs Spede was at the pub with her husband and, as far as friends are concerned, we can't find anyone who was on calling terms with Mrs Gillespie, let alone at around nine o'clock on a Saturday night in November.' He shrugged. 'In any case, her neighbours, Mr and Mrs Orloff, say they would have heard the bell ringing if someone had come to her door. When Mrs Gillespie sold them their part of the house, she simply had the bell moved from the kitchen, which is now theirs, to the corridor outside which remained hers. I tested it. They couldn't have missed it if it was rung that night.'

Sarah caught his eye. 'Then it seems fairly obvious that it must have been suicide.'

'Not to me, Dr Blakeney. In the first place, I intend to put those two alibis under a microscope and, in the second place, if Mrs Gillespie's murderer was someone she knew, they could have tapped on the windows or the back door without the Orloffs hearing them.' He closed his notebook and tucked it into his pocket. 'We'll get them eventually. Probably through their fingerprints.'

'You're going on with it then? I thought your boss had decided to drop it.'

'We raised a number of fingerprints in that house which don't belong to Mrs Gillespie or the three women who had keys. We'll be asking everyone in the village and outsiders like you, who knew her, to let us take prints for comparison purposes. I've persuaded the Chief to find out who else went in there before he draws a line under this one.'

'You seem to be taking Mrs Gillespie's death very personally.'

'Policing's no different from any other job, Doctor. The higher up the ladder you are the better the pension at the end.' His amiable face grew suddenly cynical. 'But promotion has more to do with empire-building than ability, and to date my light has always been hidden under some other sod's bushel. I do take Mrs Gillespie's death personally. It's my case.'

Sarah found this bleakly amusing. She wondered how Mathilda would feel about a policeman benefiting from her death, assuming, of course, he could prove it was murder and then convict the murderer. She might have felt happier if she wasn't so convinced that he was going to score on both counts.

'Keith? It's Sarah. Sarah Blakeney. Has Jack been in touch with you, by any chance?' She toyed with the telephone wire while she listened to the sound of Cooper's car fading into the distance. There were too many shadows in this hall, she thought.

'Not recently,' said Keith Smollett's pleasant voice. 'Should he have been?'

There was no point beating about the bush. 'We had a row. I told him I wanted a divorce and he's gone off in a huff. He left a note saying I could contact him through you.'

'Oh, good God, Sarah! Well, I can't act for both of you. Jack will have to find himself another solicitor.'

'He's opted for you. I'm the one who has to find someone else.'

'Bugger that,' said Keith cheerfully. '*You're* my client, sweetheart. The only reason I've ever done anything for that lazy good-for-nothing is because you married him.' He and Sarah had been friends from university days and there had been a time, before Jack entered the frame, when Keith had had designs on Sarah himself. Now, he was happily married with three strapping young sons, and only thought about her on the rare occasions when she telephoned.

'Yes, well, that's a side issue at the moment. The main issue is that

I need to talk to him rather urgently. He's bound to contact you so will you let me know where he is as soon as he does. It's desperately important.' She glanced towards the stairs, her face a pale glimmer in the reflected light from the kitchen. Far too many shadows.

'Will do.'

'There's something else. What's my legal position with regard to a police investigation into a possible murder?' She heard his indrawn breath. 'I don't mean I'm involved or anything but I think I've been given some information that I really ought to pass on. The police don't seem to know about it, but it's incredibly sensitive stuff and very second-hand, and if it doesn't have any bearing then I shall be betraying a confidence that's going to affect quite a few lives really badly.' She drew to a halt. *Why had Ruth told her about the letter and not Cooper? Or had she told Cooper as well?* 'Does any of that make any sense?'

'Not much. My advice, for what it's worth, is don't withhold anything from the police unless it's confidential medical information on a patient. Force them to go through the proper channels for that. They'll do it, of course, but you'll be squeaky-clean.'

'The person who told me isn't even a patient.'

'Then you don't have a problem.'

'But I could ruin lives by speaking out of turn,' she said doubtfully. 'We're talking ethics here, Keith.'

'No, we're not. Ethics don't exist outside church and ivory towers. We're talking big, bad world, where even doctors go to prison if they obstruct the police in their enquiries. You won't have a leg to stand on, my girl, if it turns out you withheld information that could have resulted in a conviction for murder.'

'But I'm not sure it *is* murder. It looks like suicide.'

'Then why is your voice quivering about two pitches higher than normal? You sound like Maria Callas on a bad night. It's only a snap judgement, of course, but I'd say you're one hundred per cent certain that you're looking at murder and ninety-nine per cent certain that you know who did it. Talk to the police.'

She was silent for so long that he began to wonder if the line had been cut. 'You're wrong about the ninety-nine per cent,' she said at last. 'Actually, I haven't a clue who might have done it.' With a muted goodbye, she hung up.

The telephone started to ring before she had removed her hand from the receiver, but her nerves were so shot to pieces that it was several moments before she could find the courage to pick it up.

The following morning, Saturday, a solicitor drove from Poole to Fontwell with Mathilda's will in his briefcase. He had telephoned Cedar House the previous evening to introduce himself and to unleash his bombshell, namely that all Mathilda's previous wills were rendered null and void by the one she had signed in his office two days before she died. He had been instructed by Mrs Gillespie to break the news to her daughter and granddaughter in person as soon as convenient after her funeral, and to do it in the presence of Dr Sarah Blakeney of Mill House, Long Upton. Dr Blakeney was free tomorrow. Would eleven o'clock be convenient for Mrs and Miss Lascelles?

The atmosphere in Mathilda's drawing-room was icy. Joanna stood by the french windows, staring out over the garden, her back to both Sarah and her daughter. Ruth smoked continuously, darting malicious glances between the rigid back of the one woman and the obvious discomfort of the other. No one spoke. To Sarah, who had always loved this room with its mish-mash of beautiful antiques: Georgian corner cabinets, old and faded chintz covers on the Victorian sofa and chairs, nineteenth-century Dutch watercolours and the Louis XVI Lyre clock on the mantelpiece, this unwelcome and unwelcomed return was depressing.

The sound of car tyres on the gravel outside broke the tension. 'I'll go,' said Ruth, jumping up.

'I can't even remember what he said his name was,' declared Joanna, turning back into the room. 'Dougall, Douglas?'

'Duggan,' said Sarah.

Joanna frowned. 'You know him, then.'

'No. I wrote his name down when he phoned last night.' She fished a piece of paper from her pocket. 'Paul Duggan of Duggan, Smith and Drew, Hills Road, Poole.'

Joanna listened to her daughter greeting someone at the door. 'My mother seems to have had considerable faith in you, Dr Blakeney. Why was that, do you suppose? You can only have known her —

what? – a year?' Her face was impassive – schooled that way, thought Sarah, to preserve her youthfulness – but her eyes were deeply suspicious.

Sarah smiled without hostility. She had been placed in a very invidious position, and she wasn't enjoying the experience. She had considerable sympathy for Joanna, one way and another, and she was becoming increasingly troubled by Mathilda's memory. Their relationship, a light-hearted one at best, was turning oppressive in retrospect, and she resented the old woman's assumption that she could manipulate her doctor after her death and without prior permission. It was neither Sarah's business nor her wish to act as mediator in an acrimonious legal battle between Joanna and her daughter. 'I'm as much in the dark as you are, Mrs Lascelles, and probably just as annoyed,' she said frankly. 'I've a week's shopping to do, a house to clean and a garden to take care of. I'm only here because Mr Duggan said if I didn't come then he would have to postpone this meeting until I could. I thought that would be even more upsetting for you and Ruth' – she shrugged – 'so I agreed to it.'

Joanna was on the point of answering when the door swung open and Ruth walked in, followed by a smiling middle-aged man carrying a video recorder with a briefcase balanced on top of it. 'Mr Duggan,' she said curtly, flopping into her chair again. 'He wants to use the television. Would you believe, Granny's made a frigging video-will?'

'Not strictly true, Miss Lascelles,' said the man, bending down to place the recorder on the floor beside the television. He straightened and held out a hand to Joanna, guessing correctly that she was Mathilda's daughter. 'How do you do, Mrs Lascelles.' He moved across to Sarah, who had stood up, and shook her hand also. 'Dr Blakeney.' He gestured to the chairs. 'Please sit down. I'm very aware that all our time is precious, so I don't intend to take up more of it than I need to. I am here as one of the joint executors of the last written will and testament of Mrs Mathilda Beryl Gillespie, copies of which I will give you in a few minutes, and from which you may satisfy yourselves that it does in fact supersede any previous will or wills made by Mrs Gillespie. The other joint executor is Mr John Hapgood, currently manager of Barclays Bank, Hills Road, Poole. In both instances, of course, we hold our responsibilities as executors on behalf of our firms so should either of us cease employment with the said firms, then another executor will be appointed in our place.' He paused briefly. 'Is all that quite clear?' He glanced from one to the other. 'Good. Now, if you'll bear with me for a moment, I'll just connect the video to the television.' He produced a coil of coaxial cable like a magician from his pocket and plugged one end into the television and the other into the video recorder. 'And now a power socket,' he murmured, unrolling a wire and a plug from the back of the video. 'If I remember correctly, it's above the skirting board to the right of the fireplace. Ah, yes, here we are. Splendid. And just in case you're wondering how I knew, then let me explain that Mrs Gillespie invited me here to make an inventory of all her possessions.' He beamed at them. 'Purely to avoid acrimonious arguments between the relative parties after the will has been read.'

Sarah was aware that her mouth had been hanging open since he entered the room. She shut it with a conscious effort and watched him deftly tune the television to receive the signal from the recorder, then open his briefcase and remove a video cassette which he inserted into the recorder before standing back to let Mathilda speak for herself. You could have heard a pin drop, she thought, as Mathilda's face materialized on the screen. Even Ruth sat as if carved in stone, her cigarette temporarily forgotten between her fingers.

The well-remembered voice, with its strident upper-class vowels, spoke confidently from the amplifier.

'Well, my dears,' Mathilda's lips thinned scornfully, 'I'm sure you're wondering why I insisted on bringing you together like this. Joanna, I have no doubt, is cursing me quietly under her breath, Ruth is nursing yet another grievance and Sarah, I suspect, is beginning to wish she had never met me.' The old woman gave a dry laugh. 'I am, by now, impervious to your curses, Joanna, so if there is awareness after death, which I doubt, they won't be troubling me. And, Ruth, your grievances have become so tiresome recently that, frankly, I'm bored with them. They won't be troubling me either.' Her voice softened a little. 'The irritation, however, that I am sure Sarah is feeling at my unilateral decision to involve her in my family's affairs *does* concern me. All I can say is that I have valued your friendship and your strength of character, Sarah, during the time I've known you, and I cannot think of anyone else who could even begin to support the burden that I am about to place on your shoulders.'

There was a brief pause while she consulted some notes on her lap. To Sarah, whose uncritical affection now appeared naïve in the face of the universal dislike which Mathilda had inspired in those who knew her, the old woman's eyes were uncharacteristically cruel. Where, she wondered, had her humour gone?

'I wish to make it absolutely clear that Joanna is not James Gillespie's daughter, but the daughter of my uncle, Gerald Cavendish. He was my father's elder brother and . . .' she sought for the right words to express herself, 'the liaison between us began some four years after he invited me and my father to live with him in Cedar House following the death of my mother. My father had no money of his own because the estate had been settled on the elder son, Gerald. My mother's money reverted to her family when she died, apart from a small inheritance which was left in trust for me. Without Gerald's invitation to live with him in Cedar House, my father and I would have been homeless. To that extent I was grateful. In every other respect I despised and loathed the man.' She smiled coldly. 'I was a child of thirteen when he first raped me.'

Sarah was shocked – not just by what Mathilda was saying, but by the way she was saying it. This was not a Mathilda *she* recognized. Why was she being so brutal, so coldly calculating?

'He was a drunken monster, like my father, and I hated them both. Between them, they destroyed any chance I might ever have had of forming a lasting and successful relationship. I have never known if my father knew what Gerald was doing but, even if he did, I am in no doubt whatsoever that he would have let it continue for fear of Gerald evicting us from Cedar House. My father was an intensely lazy man who scrounged off his wife's family until she died, and then scrounged off his brother. The only time I ever knew him to work was later, when he stood for election to the House of Commons, and then only because he saw membership as an easy route to a knighthood. Once elected, of course, he reverted to what he truly was – a contemptible man.' She paused again, her mouth turned down in bitter remembrance.

'Gerald's abuse of me continued on and off for twelve years when, in desperation, I told my father about it. I cannot adequately explain why it took me so long, except to say that I lived in constant terror of both of them. I was a prisoner, financially and socially, and I was brought up to believe, as many of my generation were, that men held natural authority within a family. I thank God those times are passing because I see now that natural authority belongs only to those who earn the respect to exercise it, be they male or female.' She paused for a moment. 'My father, of course, blamed me for what had happened, calling me a disgusting slut, and was disinclined to do anything. He preferred, as I knew he would, to maintain the status quo at my expense. But he was vulnerable. He was now a Member of Parliament, and in desperation I threatened to write to the Conservative Party and the newspapers in order to expose what sort of family the Cavendishes really were. As a result of this, a compromise was reached. I was allowed to marry James Gillespie who had declared an interest in me, and in return I agreed to say nothing. Under these conditions, we made some attempt to resume our lives although my father, fearing perhaps that I would go back on my word, insisted that my marriage to James take place immediately. He secured James a position at the Treasury, and packed us off to a flat in London.'

There was a longer silence this time while she turned to another page of her notes, adjusting her glasses as she did so. 'Unfortunately, I was already pregnant, and when Joanna was born less than five months after our marriage, even James, by no means the brightest of men, realized the baby couldn't possibly be his. Life became very difficult after that. Not unreasonably, he resented us both, and this led to bouts of violence whenever he had too much to drink. We continued in this unhappy vein for another eighteen months until, mercifully, James announced that he had secured a job abroad and would be sailing the next day without us. I have never regretted his departure or cared one iota what happened to him. He was a very unpleasant piece of work.' The old eyes stared straight out of the screen, arrogant and disdainful, but for Sarah at least there was a sense of something withheld. Mathilda, she thought, was not being quite honest.

'It is tedious now to recall the difficulties of those months after his departure. Suffice it to say that money was short. Joanna experienced similar problems herself when Steven died. The difference was that my father refused to help me – he had by now received his knighthood and enough water had passed under the bridge to mitigate my threats of exposure – while *I* did help *you*, Joanna, although you have never thanked me for it. In the end, when it was clear that eviction was becoming a real possibility, I wrote in desperation to Gerald and asked him to support his daughter. This, I gather, was the first he knew of Joanna's existence,' she smiled cynically, 'and my letter prompted him into the one honourable act of his life. He killed himself with an overdose of barbiturates. The pity is he didn't have the decency to do it sooner.' Her voice was brittle with dislike. 'A verdict of accidental death was recorded, but I cannot believe the two things were unrelated, particularly in view of the letter he sent to his solicitor, making Joanna heir to all his property.'

She turned to what was obviously the last page of her notes. 'I now come to what has prompted me to make this film. Joanna first. You threatened me with exposure if I refused to leave Cedar House immediately and make the property over to you. I have no idea who suggested you look for your father's letter, although,' she smiled grimly, 'I have my suspicions. But you were very misinformed about your rights. Gerald's absurd will could not break the trust whereby his father granted him a life interest in the property after which it passed to the nearest male relative, namely my father. By dying, Gerald merely conferred on his brother and his brother's heirs a permanent interest in the Cavendish wealth. He knew it, too. Please don't imagine that his pathetic codicil was anything more than a weak man's atonement for sins of commission and omission. Perhaps he was naïve enough to believe that my father would honour the obligation, perhaps he just thought that God would be less harsh if he showed willing to make amends. Either way he was a fool. He did, however, have the sense to send me a copy of the codicil and, by threatening to go to court with it in order to challenge the trust, I was able to use it to influence my father. He agreed to finance you and me in London while he remained alive and to make the property over to me on his death which he was entitled to do. As you know, he was dead within two years, and you and I moved back to Cedar House.' Her eyes, staring fixedly into the lens, picked out her daughter. 'You should never have threatened me, Joanna. You had no reason to, whereas I had every reason to threaten my father. I have made some very handsome settlements on you, one way and another, and feel that I have discharged all my obligations towards you. If you haven't already taken me to court when you see this, then I urge you not to waste your money after I'm gone. Believe me, I have given you more than the law ever entitled you to.

'Now, Ruth.' She cleared her throat. 'Your behaviour since your seventeenth birthday has appalled me. I can find no way to account for it or excuse it. I have always told you that the property would be yours when I died. I was referring to Cedar House but you assumed, without any prompting from me, that the contents and the money would be yours, too. That was a false assumption. My intention was always to leave the more valuable contents and the money to Joanna, and the house to you. Joanna, I assumed, would not wish to move from London, and you would have had the choice either to sell up or stay but you would have sold, I'm sure, because the house would have lost its charms once the estate was approved. What little remained to the property would never have satisfied you because you're as greedy as your mother. In conclusion, I can only repeat what I said to Joanna: I have made some very handsome settlements on you and feel that I have more than discharged my obligations to you. It may be the fault of inbreeding, of course, but I have come to realize that neither of you is capable of a decent or a generous thought.' Her eyes narrowed behind her glasses. 'I therefore intend to leave everything I own to Dr Sarah Blakeney of Mill House, Long Upton, Dorset, who will, I am confident, use her windfall wisely. In so far as I have ever been capable of feeling fondness for anyone I have felt it for her.' She gave a sudden chuckle. 'Don't be angry with me, Sarah. I must have died without changing my mind, or you wouldn't be watching this. So remember me for our friendship and not for this burden I have laid on you. Joanna and Ruth will hate you, as they have hated me, and they will accuse you of all manner of beastliness, just as they have accused me. But "what's done cannot be undone", so take it all with my blessing and use it to promote something worthwhile in my memory. Goodbye, my dear.'

'When sorrows come, they come not as single spies but in battalions.' I am afraid that Ruth's behaviour is becoming compulsive but am reluctant to tackle her about it for fear of what she might do to me. She is not above taking a stick to an old woman who annoys or frustrates her. I see it in her eyes, an awareness that I am more valuable to her dead than alive.

It was truly said: 'He that dies pays all debts.'

If I knew where she was going every day, it would help, but she lies about that as she lies about everything. Could it be schizophrenia? She is certainly the right age for it. I trust the school will do something about it next term. I am not strong enough for any more scenes nor will I be blamed for what was never my fault. God knows, there was only one victim in all this, and that was little Mathilda Cavendish. I wish I could remember her, that loving lovely child, but she is as insubstantial to me now as memories of my mother. Forgotten wraiths, both of them, unloved, abused, neglected.

Thank God for Sarah. She convinces me that like Shakespeare's sad old man 'I am more sinned against than sinning . . .'

Five

PAUL DUGGAN switched off the television set and spoke into the silence. 'The video recording, of course, has no legal standing which is why I referred to Mrs Gillespie's last *written* will and testament.' He reached into his briefcase and produced some sheaves of paper. 'These are photocopies only but the original is available for inspection at my office in Hills Street.' He handed a copy to each of the women. 'Mrs Gillespie felt you might try to contest this document, Mrs Lascelles. I can only advise you to consult a solicitor before you do so. As far as Dr Blakeney is concerned' – he turned to Sarah – 'Mr Hapgood and I will need to discuss details with you as soon as possible. We can offer you three mornings next week. Tuesday, Wednesday or Thursday. In my office for preference, although we will come to Long Upton if necessary. You understand, however, that executors are entitled to charge for expenses.' He beamed encouragingly at Sarah, waiting for an answer. He appeared to be completely unaware of the brewing hostility in the room.

Sarah gathered her scattered wits together. 'Do I have any say in this at all?'

'In what, Dr Blakeney?'

'In the will.'

'You mean, are you free to reject Mrs Gillespie's bequest?'

'Yes.'

'There's an alternative provision which you will find on the last page of the document.' Joanna and Ruth rustled through their copies. 'If for any reason you are unable to take up the bequest, Mrs Gillespie instructed us to sell her entire estate and donate the proceeds to the Seton Retirement Home for donkeys. She said, if you couldn't or

wouldn't have her money, then it might as well go to deserving asses.'
He was watching Sarah closely and she thought that, after all, he
wasn't quite so complacent as he seemed. He was expecting that
remark to strike a chord. 'Tuesday, Wednesday or Thursday, Dr
Blakeney? I should point out that an early meeting is essential. There
is the future of Mrs Lascelles and her daughter to be considered, for
example. Mrs Gillespie recognized that they would be in residence at
Cedar House when the will was read and had no wish that we as
executors should demand their immediate vacation of the property. It
was for this reason, and without any offence intended,' he smiled
amiably at the two women, 'that a full inventory of the contents was
made. I'm sure the last thing any of us wants is a battle royal over just
what was in the house at the time of Mrs Gillespie's death.'

'Oh, bloody fabulous,' said Ruth scathingly, 'now you're accusing
us of theft.'

'Not at all, Miss Lascelles. It's standard procedure, I assure you.'

Her lip curled unattractively. 'What's our future got to do with
anything, anyway? I thought we'd ceased to exist.' She dropped her
cigarette butt deliberately on to the Persian carpet and ground it out
under her heel.

'As I understand it, Miss Lascelles, you have another two terms at
boarding school before you take your A levels. To date, your
grandmother paid your fees but there is no provision in the will for
further expenditure on your education so, in the circumstances,
whether you remain at Southcliffe may well depend on Dr Blakeney.'

Joanna raised her head. 'Or on me,' she said coolly. 'I am her
mother, after all.'

There was a short silence before Ruth gave a harsh laugh. 'God,
you're a fool. No wonder Granny didn't want to leave her money to
you. What are you planning to pay with, Mother dear? No one's
going to give you an allowance any more, you know, and you don't
imagine your sweet little flower arrangements are going to produce
four thousand a term, do you?'

Joanna smiled faintly. 'If I contest this will then, presumably,
things will continue as normal in the meantime.' She looked enquiringly at Paul Duggan. 'Do you have the authority to give the money
to Dr Blakeney if I, too, am laying claim to it?'

'No,' he admitted, 'but, by the same token, you will receive nothing either. You are putting me in a difficult position, Mrs Lascelles. I was your mother's lawyer, not yours. All I will say is there are time limits involved and I urge you to seek independent legal advice without delay. Things will not, as you put it, continue as normal.'

'So in the short term Ruth and I lose either way?'

'Not necessarily.'

She frowned. 'I'm afraid I don't understand.'

Ruth flung herself out of the sofa and stormed across to the window. 'God, why do you have to be so obtuse? If you behave nicely, Mother, Dr Blakeney may feel guilty enough about inheriting a fortune to keep subsidizing us. That's it, isn't it?' She glared at Duggan. 'Granny's passed the buck of trying to create something decent out of the Cavendishes to her doctor.' Her mouth twisted. 'What a frigging awful joke! She warned me about it, too. Talk to Dr Blakeney. She'll know what to do for the best. It's so unfair.' She stamped her foot. 'It's so bloody unfair.'

Joanna's face was thoughtful. 'Is that right, Mr Duggan?'

'Not strictly, no. I will admit that Mrs Gillespie's reading of Dr Blakeney's character was that she would honour some of the undertakings Mrs Gillespie made to you and your daughter, but I must stress that Dr Blakeney is not obliged to do so. There is nothing in the will to that effect. She is free to interpret your mother's wishes any way she chooses, and if she believes that she can promote something worthwhile in Mrs Gillespie's memory by ignoring you and building a clinic in this village instead, then she is entitled to do so.'

There was another silence. Sarah looked up from a prolonged study of the carpet to discover all their eyes upon her. She found herself echoing Ruth's words. *What a frigging awful joke*. 'Thursday,' she said with a sigh. 'I'll come to your office on Thursday and I shall probably bring my own solicitor with me. I'm not happy about this, Mr Duggan.'

'Poor Dr Blakeney,' said Joanna with a tight smile. 'I do believe you're finally beginning to realize what a ruthless bitch my mother was. From the moment she seduced Gerald, she had her hands on the Cavendish purse strings and she kept them there, through threats and blackmail, upwards of fifty years.' A look of compassion crossed her curiously impassive face. 'And now she's appointed you to carry on her tyranny. The dictator is dead.' She gave a small, ironic bow. 'Long live the dictator.'

Sarah stood by Paul Duggan's car as he packed the video recorder into the boot. 'Have the police seen that film?' she asked him as he straightened up.

'Not yet. I've an appointment with a Sergeant Cooper in half an hour or so. I'll give him a copy then.'

'Shouldn't you have shown it to them straight away? Mathilda didn't sound to me like a woman who was about to commit suicide. *I must have died without changing my mind* . . . She wouldn't have said that if she was planning to kill herself two days later.'

'I agree.'

His moon face beamed at her and she frowned her irritation. 'You're very relaxed about it,' she said tartly. 'I hope, for your sake, DS Cooper understands why you've delayed producing it. I certainly don't. Mathilda's been dead two weeks and the police have been tying themselves in knots trying to find evidence of murder.'

'Not my fault, Dr Blakeney,' he said amiably. 'It's been with the film company who made it for the last two weeks, waiting to have titles and music added. Mrs Gillespie wanted Verdi playing in the background.' He chuckled. 'She chose *Dies Irae* – The Day of Wrath. Rather appropriate, don't you think?' He paused briefly, waiting for a reaction, but she was in no mood to oblige. 'Anyway, she wanted to vet it afterwards and they told her to come back in a month for a viewing. These things can't be hurried, I gather. They were very put out to hear from me that she was already dead. All of which lends weight to your argument, that she wasn't planning to kill herself.' He shrugged. 'I wasn't there when she made it, so I didn't know what was in it. As far as I was concerned it was a message to her family. I saw it for the first time last night, at which point I rang for an appointment with the boys in blue.' He glanced at his watch. 'And I'm going to be late. I'll see you on Thursday, then.'

Sarah watched him drive away with a horrible feeling of insecurity chewing at the pit of her stomach. She should have guessed, prepared herself a little. *Talk to Dr Blakeney. She will know what to do for the best.* And what about Jack? Had *he* known?

She felt suddenly very lonely.

Sarah was raking up leaves when DS Cooper arrived that afternoon. He picked his way across the grass and stood watching her. 'Hard work,' he murmured sympathetically.

'Yes.' She propped the rake against a tree and thrust her hands into her Barbour pockets. 'We'd better go in. It's warmer inside.'

'Don't worry on my account,' he said. 'I'd just as soon stay out and have a smoke.' He fished a crumpled pack of Silk Cut from inside his coat and lit up with obvious enjoyment. 'Disgusting habit,' he murmured, eyeing her warily. 'I'll give it up one day.'

Sarah lifted an amused eyebrow. 'Why are smokers always so consumed with guilt?'

'Cigarettes reveal the weakness of our character,' he said morosely. 'Other people give up, but we can't. To tell you the truth I've never understood why society treats us like pariahs. I've yet to meet the smoker who's beaten his wife after one too many fags or killed a child while in charge of a car, but I could show you a hundred drunks who've done it. I'd say drink is a far more dangerous drug than nicotine.'

She led him to a bench seat beside the path. 'The moral majority will get round to condemning the drinkers, too, eventually,' she said. 'And then the whole world will be jogging around in its vest and pants, bristling with good health, eating vegetables, drinking carrot juice and never doing anything remotely detrimental to its health.'

He chuckled. 'Shouldn't you applaud that, as a doctor?'

'I'll be out of a job.' She leant her head against the back of the seat. 'Anyway, I have a problem with the moral majority. I don't like it. I'd rather have free-thinking individuals any day than politically correct mobs who behave the way they're told to because somebody else has decided what's socially acceptable.'

'Is that why you liked Mrs Gillespie?'

'Probably.'

'Tell me about her.'

'I can't really add anything to what I've told you already. She was quite the most extraordinary person I've ever met. Completely cynical. She had no respect for anyone or anything. She didn't believe in God or retribution. She loathed mankind in general and the people of Fontwell in particular, and she considered everybody, past and present, beneath her. The only exception to that was Shakespeare. She thought Shakespeare was a towering genius.' She fell silent.

'And you *liked* her?'

Sarah laughed. 'I suppose I enjoyed the anarchy of it all. She put into words what most of us only think. I can't explain it any better than that. I always looked forward to seeing her.'

'It must have been mutual or she wouldn't have left you her money.'

Sarah didn't answer immediately. 'I had no idea what she was planning,' she said after a moment or two. She thrust a hand into her hair, fluffing it skyward. 'It's come as a nasty shock. I feel I'm being manipulated and I don't like that.'

He nodded. 'According to Duggan, Mrs Gillespie instructed the two executors to keep the whole thing secret.' He examined the glowing tip of his cigarette. 'The trouble is, we can't be sure that she herself didn't tell someone.'

'If she had,' said Sarah, 'she would probably still be alive. Assuming she was murdered, of course.'

'Meaning whoever killed her didn't know you were the beneficiary but thought they were?'

She nodded. 'Something like that.'

'Then it must have been the daughter or the granddaughter.'

'It depends what was in the previous will. She may have made other bequests. People have been murdered for far tinier amounts than Joanna or Ruth were expecting to get.'

'But that's assuming she was murdered for her money. It's also assuming that neither you nor anyone dependent on you murdered her.'

'True,' she said unemotionally.

'Did you murder her, Dr Blakeney?'

'I wouldn't have done it that way, Sergeant. I would have taken my time.' She gave a light chuckle. A little forced, he thought. 'There was no hurry, after all. I've no outstanding debts and I certainly wouldn't want to link her death so closely to a will changed in my favour.' She bent forward, clasping her hands between her knees. 'And it would have looked very natural, too. Doctors have a built-in advantage when it comes to committing the perfect murder. A period of illness, followed by a gentle death. Nothing so dramatic or traumatic as slitting the wrists while wearing an instrument of torture.'

'It might be a magnificent bluff,' he said mildly. 'As you say, who would suspect a doctor of doing something so crass within hours of an old lady making over three-quarters of a million pounds?'

Sarah stared at him with undisguised horror. 'Three-quarters of a million?' she echoed slowly. 'Is that what she was worth?'

'More or less. Probably more. It's a conservative estimate. Duggan's valued the house and its contents at around four hundred thousand, but the clocks alone were insured for well over a hundred thousand and that was based on a ten-year-old valuation. I'd hate to guess what they're worth now. Then there's the antique furniture, her jewellery and, of course, Mrs Lascelles's flat in London, plus innumerable stocks and shares. You're a rich woman, Dr Blakeney.'

Sarah put her head in her hands. 'Oh, my God!' she groaned. 'You mean, Joanna doesn't even own her own flat?'

'No. It's part of Mrs Gillespie's estate. If the old woman had had any sense she'd have made it over to her daughter in annual dollops to avoid anyone having to pay inheritance tax on it. As it is, the Treasury's going to have almost as big a windfall as you're getting.' He sounded sympathetic. 'And it'll be your job to decide what has to be sold off to pay the bill. You're not going to be very popular with the Lascelles women, I suspect.'

'That must be the understatement of the year,' said Sarah bleakly. 'What on earth was Mathilda thinking of?'

'Most people would see it as manna from heaven.'

'Including you?'

'Of course, but then I live in a very ordinary house, I've three grown-up children who touch me for money whenever they can, and I dream about retiring early and taking the wife on an extended cruise round the world.' He glanced about the garden. 'In your shoes, I'd probably react as you are reacting. You're not exactly short of a bob or two, and your conscience will stop you spending it on yourself.

She was right when she said she was laying a burden on your shoulders.'

Sarah digested this for a moment or two in silence. 'Does that mean you don't think I murdered her?'

He looked amused. 'Probably.'

'Well, thank God for small mercies,' she said dryly. 'It's been worrying me.'

'Your dependants, however, are a different matter. They stand to benefit just as much as you do from Mrs Gillespie's death.'

She looked surprised. 'I don't have any dependants.'

'You have a husband, Dr Blakeney. I'm told he's dependent on you.'

She stirred some leaves with the toe of her wellington boot. 'Not any more. We're separated. I don't even know where he is at the moment.'

He took out his notebook and consulted it. 'That must be fairly recent then. According to Mrs Lascelles, he attended the funeral two days ago, went on to Cedar House afterwards for tea and then asked her to drive him back here at around six o'clock, which she did.' He paused to look at her. 'So when exactly did the separation begin?'

'He left some time that night. I found a note from him in the morning.'

'Was it his idea or yours?'

'Mine. I told him I wanted a divorce.'

'I see.' He regarded her thoughtfully. 'Was there a reason for choosing that night to do it?'

She sighed. 'I was depressed by Mathilda's funeral. I found myself exploring that old chestnut, the meaning of life, and I wondered what the point of *her* life was. I suddenly realized that my own life was almost as pointless.' She turned her head to look at him. 'You probably think that sounds absurd. I'm a doctor, after all, and you don't enter medicine without some sort of vocation. It's like police work. We're in it because we believe we can make a difference.' She gave a hollow laugh. 'There's an awful arrogance in a statement like that. The presumption is that we know what we're doing when, frankly, I'm not sure that we do. Doctors strive officiously to keep people alive, because the law says we must, and we talk grandly about quality of life. But what *is* quality of life? I kept Mathilda's pain under

70

control with some sophisticated drugs but the quality of her life was appalling, not because of pain, but because she was lonely, bitter, intensely frustrated and very unhappy.' She shrugged. 'I took a long hard look at myself and my husband during the funeral, and I realized that the same adjectives could be applied to the two of us. We were both lonely, both bitter, both frustrated and both unhappy. So I suggested a divorce, and he left.' She smiled cynically. 'It was as simple as that.'

He felt sorry for her. Nothing was ever that simple, and it sounded to him as if she had tried to bluff a hand at poker, and lost. 'Had he met Mrs Lascelles before the funeral?'

'Not as far as I know. *I* hadn't, so I can't imagine how he could have done.'

'But he knew Mrs Gillespie?'

She looked out across the garden, playing for time. 'If he did, then it wasn't through me. He never mentioned meeting her.'

DS Cooper's already lively interest in the absent Jack Blakeney was growing. 'Why did he go to the funeral?'

'Because I asked him to.' She straightened. 'I hate funerals but I always feel I have to go to them. It seems so churlish to turn your back on a patient the minute they're dead. Jack was very good about lending support.' Unexpectedly, she laughed. 'To tell you the truth, I think he rather fancies himself in his black overcoat. He enjoys looking satanic.'

Satanic. The Sergeant pondered over the word. Duncan Orloff had said Mathilda liked Blakeney. Mrs Lascelles had described him as 'a peculiar man who said very little and then demanded to be taken home'. Ruth had found him 'intimidating'. The vicar, on the other hand, had had a great deal to say when Cooper had approached him about the various members of the funeral congregation. 'Jack Blakeney? He's an artist though not a very successful one, poor chap. If it wasn't for Sarah, he'd be starving. Matter of fact, I like his work. I'd buy a canvas if only he'd lower his sights a little, but he knows his worth, or says he does, and refuses to sell himself cheap. Did he know Mathilda? Yes, he must have done. I saw him leaving her house one day with his sketchpad under his arm. She'd have been a wonderful subject for his type of work. He couldn't have resisted her.'

He took the bull by the horns. 'The Reverend Matthews tells me

71

your husband was painting a portrait of Mrs Gillespie. He must have known her quite well to do that.' He lit another cigarette and watched Sarah through the smoke.

She sat for a long time in silence, contemplating a distant cow in a far field. 'I feel inclined to say I won't answer any more questions until my solicitor's present,' she murmured at last, 'except that I have a nasty feeling you'd regard that as suspicious.' He didn't say anything, so she glanced at him. There was no sympathy in the pleasant face, only a patient confidence that she would answer in the affirmative, with or without a solicitor. She sighed. 'I could deny a portrait quite easily. They're all in the studio, and there isn't a chance in a million you'd recognize Mathilda's. Jack doesn't paint faces. He paints personalities. And you have to understand his colour-coding and the way he uses dynamics in shape, depth and perspective to interpret what he's done.'

'But you're not going to deny it?' he suggested.

'Only because Jack won't, and I'm not particularly keen to perjure myself.' She smiled and her eyes lit with enthusiasm. 'Actually, it's brilliant. I think it's probably the best thing he's ever done. I found it yesterday just before you came.' She pulled a wry face. 'I knew it would be there because of something Ruth said. According to her, Jack mentioned that Mathilda called me her scold's bridle.' She sighed again. 'And he couldn't have known that unless Mathilda had told him, because I never did.'

'May I see this painting?'

She ignored the question. 'He wouldn't have murdered her, Sergeant, not for money, anyway. Jack despises materialism. The only use he has for money is as a guide to the value of his genius. Which is why he never sells anything. His own valuation of his art is rather higher than everybody else's.' She smiled at his frown of disbelief. 'Actually, it makes sense in a funny sort of way, but it's irritating because it's so conceited. The argument goes something like this: your average prole is incapable of recognizing genius so he won't be interested in buying your picture whatever price you put on it. While a Renaissance man, on the other hand, will recognize genius and will pay handsomely for it. Ergo, if you're a genius, you put a high price on yourself and wait for the right person to come and discover you.'

'If you'll pardon the language, Dr Blakeney, that is bullshit.' He felt quite angry. 'The man's conceit must be colossal. Has anyone else said he's a genius?'

'No one said Van Gogh was a genius either until after he was dead.' Why, she wondered, did Jack's single-minded view of himself always put people's backs up? Was it because, in an uncertain world, his certainty was threatening? 'It really doesn't matter,' she said calmly, 'what sort of an artist Jack is. Good, bad, indifferent. I happen to think he's good, but that's a personal opinion. The point is he would never have killed Mathilda for her money, assuming he knew she'd made the will in my favour, which I doubt. Why should she have told him when she never told me?'

'Except that he thought you were going to divorce him and push him into the cold.'

'Hardly. That would leave me enjoying the loot all by myself, wouldn't it? How could he get his hands on the inheritance if he and I were divorced?' *I'll be going for a fifty-fifty split* . . . She pushed that thought away. 'And in any case, two weeks ago when Mathilda died, he didn't know I wanted to divorce him. How could he? I didn't know myself.'

Cooper took that with a pinch of salt. 'These things don't happen out of the blue, Dr Blakeney. He must have had an inkling that the marriage was in difficulties.'

'You're underestimating Jack's egotism,' she answered with a somewhat bitter irony. 'He's far too self-centred to notice anyone else's unhappiness unless he's painting them. Believe me, my decision *did* come out of the blue. For him, anyway.'

He puffed thoughtfully on his cigarette. 'Do you expect him to come back at all?'

'Oh, yes. He'll want to collect his paintings if nothing else.'

'Good. Some of the fingerprints we lifted may well be his. It will help if we can eliminate them. Yours, too, of course. There'll be a team taking prints in Fontwell on Wednesday morning. I assume you've no objections to giving yours? They'll be destroyed afterwards.' He took her silence for assent. 'You say you don't know where your husband is, but can you think of anyone who might be in contact with him?'

'Only my solicitor. He's promised to let me know the minute he hears anything.'

The Sergeant dropped his cigarette end on to the damp grass and stood up, drawing his mackintosh about him. 'No friends he might have gone to?'

'I've tried everyone I can think of. He's not been in touch with any of them.'

'Then perhaps you'll be so kind as to write out your solicitor's name and phone number while I take a look at this painting.' He grinned. 'In view of what you've said, I'm fascinated to see if I can make anything of it.'

Sarah found his careful appraisal of the picture rather impressive. He stood for a long time without saying anything, then asked her if Jack had done a portrait of her. She fetched hers from the drawing-room and placed it alongside the one of Mathilda. He resumed his silent study.

'Well,' he said at last, 'you're quite right. I would never have guessed that this was a portrait of Mrs Gillespie, any more than I would have guessed that that was a portrait of you. I can see why no one else considers him a genius.'

Sarah's disappointment surprised her. But what had she expected? He was a country policeman, not a Renaissance man. She forced the polite smile to her lips that was her customary response to other people's often rude comments on Jack's paintings and wondered, not for the first time, why she was the only person who seemed able to appreciate them. It wasn't as if she were blinded by love – rather the reverse in fact – and yet, to her, the portrait of Mathilda was extraordinary and brilliant. Jack had worked layer on layer to bring a deep golden translucence into the heart of the painting – Mathilda's wit, she thought, shining through the complex blues and greys of cruelty and cynicism. And round it all the browns of despair and repression, and the rusted red of iron, shorthand in Jack's work for backbone and character, but moulded here into the shape of the scold's bridle.

She shrugged. After all, perhaps it was a mercy the Sergeant couldn't see it. 'As I said, he paints personalities and not faces.'

'When did he paint the one of you?'

'Six years ago.'

'And has your personality changed in six years?'

'I shouldn't think so. Personalities change very little, Sergeant, which is why Jack likes to paint them. You are what you are. A generous person remains generous. A bully remains a bully. You can smooth the rough edges but you can't transform the core. Once painted, the personality should be recognizable for ever.'

He rubbed his hands together in anticipation of a challenge. 'Then let's see if I can work out his system. There's a lot of green in yours and your most obvious characteristics are sympathy – no – ' he contradicted himself immediately, 'empathy – you enter into other people's feelings, you don't make a judgement on them. So, empathy, honour – you're an honourable woman or you wouldn't feel so racked with guilt about this bequest – truthful – most people would have lied about this painting – nice.' He turned to look at her. 'Does niceness count as a personality trait or is it too flabby?'

She laughed. 'Far too flabby, and you're ignoring the unpleasant aspects. Jack sees two sides to everybody.'

'All right.' He stared at her portrait. 'You're a very opinionated woman who is confident enough to fly in the face of established fact, otherwise you wouldn't have liked Mrs Gillespie. A corollary to that is that you are also naïve or your views wouldn't be so divergent from everyone else's. You're inclined to be rash or you wouldn't be regretting your husband's departure, and that implies a depth of affection for hopeless causes which is probably why you became a doctor and probably, too, why you were so fond of the old bitch in this amazing painting next to you. How am I doing for a prole?'

She gave a surprised chuckle. 'Well, I don't think you are a prole,' she said. 'Jack would adore you. Renaissance man in all his glory. They are good, aren't they?'

'How much does he charge for them?'

'He's only ever sold one. It was a portrait of one of his lovers. He got ten thousand pounds for it. The man who bought it was a Bond Street dealer, who said Jack was the most exciting artist he'd ever come across. We thought our ship had come in, then three months later the poor soul was dead, and no one's expressed an interest since.'

'That's not true. The Reverend Matthews told me he'd buy a canvas like a shot if they were cheaper. Come to that, so would I. Has he ever done a man and wife? I'd go to two thousand for me and the old girl over the mantelpiece.' He studied Mathilda closely. 'I take it the gold is her one redeeming feature of humour. My old lady's a laugh a minute. She'd be gold through and through. I'd love to see it.'

There was a sound behind them. 'And what colour would you be?' asked Jack's amused voice.

Sarah's heart leapt, but Sergeant Cooper only eyed him thoughtfully for a moment or two. 'Assuming I've interpreted these pictures correctly, sir, I'd say a blend of blues and purples, for hard-headed cynicism-cum-realism, common to your wife and Mrs Gillespie, some greens which I think must represent the decency and honour of Dr Blakeney because they are markedly absent from Mrs Gillespie's portrait,' he smiled, 'and a great deal of black.'

'Why black?'

'Because I'm in the dark,' he said with ponderous humour, fishing his warrant card from his inside pocket. 'Detective Sergeant Cooper, sir, Learmouth Police. I'm enquiring into the death of Mrs Mathilda Gillespie of Cedar House, Fontwell. Perhaps you'd like to tell me why she sat for you with the scold's bridle on her head? In view of the way she died, I find that fascinating.'

Arthritis is a brute. It makes one so vulnerable. If I were a less cynical woman, I would say Sarah has the gift of healing, though, frankly, I'm inclined to think anyone would have been an improvement on that old fool, Hendry. He was lazy, of course, and didn't bother to keep up his reading. Sarah tells me there have been huge advances in the field which he obviously knew nothing about. I am rather inclined to sue, if not on my own behalf, then on Joanna's. Clearly, it was he who set her on the path to addiction.

Sarah asked me today how I was, and I answered with a line from King Lear: *'I grow; I prosper. Now, gods, stand up for bastards.' She quite naturally assumed I was referring to myself, laughed good-naturedly and said: 'A bitch, possibly, Mathilda, but never a bastard. There's only one bastard I know, and that's Jack.' I asked her what he had done to deserve such an appellation. 'He takes my love for granted,' she said, 'and offers his to anyone who's foolish enough to flatter him.'*

How very flawed are human relationships. This is not a Jack I recognize. He guards his love as jealously as he guards his art. The truth, I think, is that Sarah perceives both herself and him 'through a glass darkly'. She believes he strays, but only, I suspect, because she insists on using his effect on women as a criterion by which to judge him. His passions frighten her because they exist outside her control, and she is less adept than she thinks she is at seeing where he directs them.

I adore the man. He encourages me to 'dare damnation', for what is life if it is not a rebellion against death . . .

Six

VIOLET ORLOFF stood motionless in the kitchen of Wing Cottage, listening to the row that had broken out in the hall of Cedar House. She had the guilty look of an eavesdropper, torn between going and staying, but, unlike most eavesdroppers, she was free of the fear of discovery, and curiosity won out. She took a glass from the dishwasher, placed the rim against the wall, then pressed her ear to the base. The voices drew closer immediately. Perhaps it was a mercy she couldn't see herself. There was something indecent and furtive about the way she bent to listen, and her face wore the same expression that a Peeping Tom might wear as he peers through a window to see a woman in the nude. Excited. Leering. Expectant.

'. . . think I don't know what you do in London? You're a fucking whore, and Granny knew it, too. It's your bloody fault all this, and now you're planning to whore him, I suppose, to cut me out.'

'Don't you dare speak to me like that. I've a damn good mind to wash my hands of you. Do you think I care tuppence whether you get to university or not?'

'That's you every time. Jealousy, jealousy, fucking JEALOUSY! You can't stand me doing anything you didn't do.'

'I'm warning you, Ruth, I won't listen to this.'

'Why not? Because it's true, and the truth hurts?' The girl's voice was tearful. 'Why can't you behave like a mother sometimes? Granny was more of a mother than you are. All you've ever done is hate me. I didn't ask to be born, did I?'

'That's childish.'

'You hate me because my father loved me.'

'Don't be absurd.'

'It's true. Granny told me. She said Steven used to moon over me, calling me his angel, and you used to fly into a ·temper. She said if you and Steven had got a divorce, then Steven wouldn't be dead.'

Joanna's voice was icy. 'And you believed her, of course, because it's what you wanted to hear. You're your grandmother all over again, Ruth. I thought there'd be an end of it once she was dead but I couldn't have been more wrong, could I? You've inherited every drop of poison that was in her.'

'Oh, that's great! Walk away, just like you always do. When are you going to face up to a problem, Mother, instead of pretending it doesn't exist? Granny always said that was your one true accomplishment, to brush every unpleasantness under the carpet, and then carry on as if nothing had happened. For Christ's SAKE' – her voice rose to a shout – 'YOU HEARD THE DETECTIVE.' She must have caught her mother's attention because her tone dropped again. 'The police think Granny was murdered. So what am I supposed to tell them?'

'The truth.'

Ruth gave a wild laugh. 'Fine. So I tell them what you spend your money on, do I? I tell them Granny and Dr Hendry thought you were so bloody mad they were thinking of having you committed? Jesus' – her voice broke – 'I suppose I might just as well be really honest and tell them how you tried to kill me. Or do I keep quiet because if I don't we won't have a hope in hell's chance of putting in a counter-claim for the money? You're not allowed to benefit from the murder of your mother, you know.'

The silence went on for so long that Violet Orloff began to wonder if they had moved to another part of the house.

'It's entirely up to you, Ruth. I've no compunction at all about saying you were here the day your grandmother died. You shouldn't have stolen her earrings, you stupid little bitch. Or, for that matter, every other damn thing your sticky little fingers couldn't resist. You knew her as well as I did. Did you really think she wouldn't notice?' Joanna's voice grated with sarcasm. 'She made a list and left it in her bedside drawer. If I hadn't destroyed it you'd be under arrest by now. You're making no secret of your panic over this idiotic will, so the police will have no trouble believing that if you were desperate enough to steal from your grandmother, you were probably desperate enough to murder her as well. So I suggest we both keep our mouths shut, don't you?'

A door was slammed so forcefully that Violet felt the vibrations in her kitchen.

Jack perched on his stool and rubbed his unshaven jaw, squinting at the policeman through half-closed lids. Satanic, thought DS Cooper, suited him well. He was very dark with glittering eyes in a hawklike face, but there were too many laughter-lines for a Dracula. If this man was a devil, he was a merry one. He reminded Cooper of an unrepentant Irish recidivist he had arrested on innumerable occasions over a period of twenty years. There was the same 'take-me-as-I-am' expression, a look of such startling challenge that people who had it were impossible to ignore. He wondered with sudden curiosity if the same expression had looked out of Mathilda Gillespie's eyes. He hadn't noticed it on the video, but then the camera invariably lied. If it didn't, no one would tolerate having their picture taken.

'I'll do it,' said Jack abruptly.

The policeman frowned. 'Do what, Mr Blakeney?'

'Paint you and your wife for two thousand pounds, but I'll string you up from a lamp-post if you tell anyone what you're paying.' He stretched his arms towards the ceiling, easing the muscles of his back. 'I'd say two thousand from you is worth ten thousand any day from the likes of Mathilda. Perhaps a sliding scale isn't such a bad idea, after all. It should be the dent in the sitter's pocket that sets the value on the painting, not my arbitrary pricing of my worth.' He raised sardonic eyebrows. 'What right have I to deprive impoverished vicars and policemen of things of beauty? You'd agree with that, wouldn't you, Sarah?'

She shook her head at him. 'Why do you always have to be so offensive?'

'The man likes my work, so I'm offering him a subsidized portrait of himself and the wife in blues, purples, greens and golds. What's offensive about that? I'd call it a compliment.' He eyed Cooper with amusement. 'Purples represent your libido, by the way. The deeper they are, the randier you are, but it's how I see you, remember, not how you see yourself. Your wife might have her illusions shattered if I paint you in deep purple and her in pale lilac.'

Sergeant Cooper chuckled. 'Or vice versa.'

Jack's eyes gleamed. 'Precisely. I don't set out to flatter anyone. As long as you understand that, we can probably do business.'

'And presumably, sir, you need the money at the moment. Would your terms be cash in advance, by any chance?'

Jack bared his teeth in a grin. 'Of course. At that price you could hardly expect anything else.'

'And what guarantee would I have that the portrait would ever be finished?'

'My word. As a man of honour.'

'I'm a policeman, Mr Blakeney. I never take anyone's word for anything.' He turned to Sarah. 'You're a truthful woman, Doctor. Is your husband a man of honour?'

She looked at Jack. 'That's a very unfair question.'

'Sounds fair to me,' said Jack. 'We're talking two thousand pounds here. The Sergeant's entitled to cover himself. Give him an answer.'

Sarah shrugged. 'All right. If you're asking me: will he take your money and run? Then, no, he won't. He'll paint your picture for you, and he'll do it well.'

'But?' prompted Jack.

'You're not a man of honour. You're far too thoughtless and inconsiderate. You respect no one's opinion but your own, you're disloyal, and you're insensitive. In fact,' she gave him a twisted smile, 'you're a shit about everything but your art.'

Jack tipped a finger to the policeman. 'So, do I have a commission, Sergeant, or were you simply working on my wife's susceptibilities to get her to spill the beans about me?'

Cooper pulled forward a chair and offered it to Sarah. She shook her head so he sat in it himself with a faint sigh of relief. He was getting too old to stand when there was a seat available. 'I'll be honest with you, sir, I can't commission anything from you at the moment.'

'I knew it,' said Jack contemptuously. 'You're just like that slime-ball Matthews.' He aped the vicar's sing-song Welsh accent. 'I do love your work, Jack, and no mistake, but I'm a poor man as you know.' He slammed his fist into his palm. 'So I offered him one of my early ones for a couple of thousand, and the bastard tried to negotiate me down to three miserable hundred. Jesus wept!' he growled. 'He gets paid more than that for a few lousy sermons.' He glared at the Sergeant. 'Why do you all expect something for nothing? I don't see you taking a pay cut,' he flicked a glance at Sarah, 'or my wife either for that matter. But then the state pays you while I have to graft for myself.'

It was on the tip of Cooper's tongue to point out that Blakeney had chosen the path he was following, and had not been forced down it. But he refrained. He had had too many bruising arguments with his children on the very same subject to want to repeat them with a stranger. In any case, the man had misunderstood him. Deliberately, he suspected. 'I am not in a position to commission anything from you *at the moment*, sir,' he said with careful emphasis, 'because you were closely connected with a woman who may or may not have been murdered. Were I to give you money, for whatever reason, it would be extremely prejudicial to your chances in court if you were unfortunate enough to appear there. It will be a different matter entirely when our investigations are concluded.'

Jack eyed him with sudden fondness. 'If *I* paid *you* two thousand, you might have a point, but not the other way round. It's your position you're safeguarding, not mine.'

Cooper chuckled again. 'Do you blame me? It's probably empty optimism, but I haven't quite given up on promotion, and back-handers to murder suspects would go down like a lead balloon with my governor. The future looks a lot brighter if you make Inspector.'

Jack studied him intently for several seconds, then crossed his arms over his tatty jumper. He found himself warming to this rotund, rather untypical detective with his jolly smile. 'So what was your question? Why did Mathilda sit for me with the scold's bridle on her head?' He looked at the portrait. 'Because she said it represented the essence of her personality. She was right, too.' His eyes narrowed in recollection. 'I suppose the easy way to describe her is to say she was repressed, but the repression worked both ways.' He smiled faintly. 'Perhaps it always does. She was abused as a child and grew up incapable of feeling or expressing love, so became an abuser herself. And the symbol of her abuse, both active and passive, was the bridle. It was strapped to her and she strapped it to her daughter.' His eyes flickered towards his wife. 'The irony is that it was also a symbol of her love, I think, or those cessations from hostility that passed for love in Mathilda's life. She called Sarah her scold's bridle and she meant it as a compliment. She said Sarah was the only person she had ever met who came to her without prejudice and took her as she was.' He grinned amiably. 'I tried to explain that that was hardly something to applaud – Sarah has many weaknesses, but the worst in my view is her naïve willingness to accept everyone at his or her own valuation – but Mathilda wouldn't have a word spoken against her. And that's all I know,' he finished ingenuously.

DS Cooper decided privately that Jack Blakeney was probably one of the least ingenuous men he had ever met, but he played along with him for disingenuous reasons of his own. 'That's very helpful, sir. I never knew Mrs Gillespie myself, and it's important for me to understand her character. Would you say she was the type to commit suicide?'

'Without a doubt. And she'd do it with a Stanley knife, too. She found as much enjoyment in making an exit as she did in making an entrance. Possibly more. If she's looking at the three of us now, picking over the bones of her demise, she'll be hugging herself with delight. She was talked about in life because she was a bitch, but that's nothing to the way she's being talked about in death. She'd love every cliff-hanging moment of it.'

Cooper frowned at Sarah. 'Do you agree, Dr Blakeney?'

'It has an absurd sort of logic, you know. She *was* like that.' She thought for a moment or two. 'But she didn't believe in an afterlife, or only the maggot variety which means we're all cannibals.' She smiled at Cooper's expression of distaste. 'A man dies and is eaten by maggots, the maggots are eaten by birds, the birds are eaten by cats, the cats defecate on the vegetables and we eat the vegetables. Or any permutation you like.' She smiled again. 'I'm sorry, but that was Mathilda's view of death. Why would she waste her last, great exit? I honestly believe she would have prolonged it for all it was worth and, in the process, made as many people wriggle as she could. Take that video, for example. Why did she want music and credits added if it was only to be shown after she was dead? She was going to watch it herself, and if someone walked in while she was doing it, then so much the better. She meant to use it as a stick to beat Joanna and Ruth with. I'm right, aren't I, Jack?'

'Probably. You usually are.' He spoke without irony. 'Which video are we talking about?'

She had forgotten he hadn't seen it. 'Mathilda's posthumous message to her family,' she said, with a shake of her head. 'You'd have loved it, by the way. She looked rather like Cruella De Vil out of *The Hundred and One Dalmatians*. Dyed black wings on either side of a white streak, nose like a beak, and mouth a thin line. Very paintable.' She frowned. 'Why didn't you tell me you knew her?'

'You'd have interfered.'

'How?'

'You'd have found a way,' he said. 'I can't paint them when you bleat your interpretations of them into my ear.' He spoke in a mocking falsetto. 'But I like her, Jack. She's really very nice. She's not half as bad as everyone says. She's a softy at heart.'

'I never talk like that,' said Sarah dismissively.

'You should listen to yourself once in a while. The dark side of people scares you, so you close your eyes to it.'

'Is that a bad thing?'

He shrugged. 'Not if you want existence without passion.'

She studied him thoughtfully for a moment. 'If passion means confrontation, then yes, I prefer existence without passion. I lived through the disintegration of my parents' marriage, remember. I'd go a long way to avoid repeating that experience.'

His eyes sparkled in his tired face. 'Then perhaps it's your own dark side that scares you. Is there a fire in there waiting to blaze out of control? A scream of frustration that will topple your precarious house of cards? You'd better pray for gentle breezes and no strong winds, my angel, or you'll find you've been living in a fool's paradise.'

She didn't respond and the room fell silent, its three occupants curiously abstracted like the portraits round the walls. It occurred to DS Cooper, fixed in fascinated immobility upon his chair, that Jack Blakeney was a terrible man. Did he devour everyone in the way he was devouring his wife? *A scream of frustration that will topple your precarious house of cards.* Cooper had held his own scream in check for years, the scream of a man caught in the toils of rectitude and responsibility. Why couldn't Jack Blakeney do the same?

He cleared his throat. 'Did Mrs Gillespie ever tell you, sir, what her intentions were with regard to her will?'

Jack had been watching Sarah intently. He glanced now towards the policeman. 'Not in so many words. She asked me once what I would do if I had her money.'

'What did you say?'

'I said I'd spend it.'

'Your wife told me you despise materialism.'

'Quite right, so I'd use it to enhance my spirituality.'

'How?'

'I'd blow the lot on drugs, alcohol and sex.'

'Sounds very materialistic to me, sir. There's nothing spiritual about surrendering to the senses.'

'It depends who you follow. If you're a Stoic like Sarah, your spiritual development comes through duty and responsibility. If you're an Epicurean like me, though I hasten to say poor old Epicurus probably wouldn't recognize me as an adherent, it comes through the gratification of desire.' He arched an amused eyebrow. 'Unfortunately, we modern Epicureans are frowned upon. There's something infinitely despicable about a man who refuses to acknowledge his responsibilities but prefers to fill his cup at the fountain of pleasure.' He was watching Cooper closely. 'But that's only because society is composed of sheep and sheep are easily brainwashed by advertisers' propaganda. They may not believe that the whiteness of a woman's wash is a symbol of her success, but they sure as hell believe that their kitchens should be as germ-free, their smiles as white, their children as well-mannered, their husbands as hard-working, and their moral decency as obvious. With men it's lager. It's supposed to persuade them they have balls, but all it really persuades them to do is wear a clean jumper, shave regularly, have at least three friends, never get drunk and talk amusingly in the pub.' His grim face cracked into a smile. 'My problem is, I'd rather be stoned out of my mind and rogering a sixteen-year-old virgin any day, particularly if I have to take off her gym slip slowly to do it.'

Christ, thought Cooper in alarm, feeling the weight of the other's gaze upon his bent head. Could the bastard read minds as well? He made a pretence of writing something on his notepad. 'Did you explain all that as graphically to Mrs Gillespie or did you just stick with the spending of her money if you had it?'

Jack glanced at Sarah, but she was staring at Mathilda's portrait and didn't look up. 'She had great skin for her age. I expect I said I'd rather be stoned and rogering a granny.'

Cooper, who was far more respectable than he realized, was shocked into looking up. 'What did she say?'

Jack was enjoying himself. 'She asked me if I'd like to paint her in the nude. I said I would, so she took her clothes off. If it's of any interest to you, the only thing Mathilda was wearing when I made my sketches of her was the scold's bridle.' He smiled, his perceptive eyes searching the policeman's. 'Does that excite you, Sergeant?'

'It does as a matter of fact,' said Cooper evenly. 'Would she also have been in the bath by any chance?'

'No. She was very much alive and lying on her bed in all her glory.' He stood up and went to a chest in the corner. 'And she looked bloody fantastic.' He took a sketchpad from the bottom drawer. 'There.' He flung the pad across the room and it fluttered to the floor at the policeman's feet. 'Be my guest. They're all of Mathilda. One of life's great individuals.'

Cooper retrieved the pad and turned the pages. They did indeed show Mrs Gillespie, nude upon her bed, but a very different Mrs Gillespie from the tragic cadaver in the bath or the bitter harridan with the cruel mouth on the television set. He laid the pad on the floor beside him. 'Did you sleep with her, Mr Blakeney?'

'No. She never asked me to.'

'Would you have done if she *had* asked you?' The question was out before Cooper had time to consider its wisdom.

Jack's expression was unreadable. 'Does that have a bearing on your case?'

'I'm interested in your character, Mr Blakeney.'

'I see. And what would my accepting an elderly woman's invitation to sleep with her tell you? That I was a pervert? Or that I was infinitely compassionate?'

Cooper gave a small laugh. 'I'd say it was an indication that you needed your eyes testing. Even in the dark, Mrs Gillespie could hardly have passed for a sixteen-year-old virgin.' He fished his cigarettes from his pocket. 'Do you mind?'

'Be my guest.' He kicked the wastepaper basket across the floor.

Cooper flicked his lighter to the cigarette. 'Mrs Gillespie has left your wife three quarters of a million pounds, Mr Blakeney. Did you know?'

'Yes.'

The Sergeant hadn't expected that. 'So Mrs Gillespie *did* tell you what her intentions were?'

'No,' said Jack, resuming his seat on the stool. 'I've just spent a delightful two hours at Cedar House.' He stared impassively at Sarah. 'Joanna and Ruth are labouring under the misapprehension that I have some influence over my wife so they put themselves out to be charming.'

Cooper scratched his jaw and wondered why Dr Blakeney put up with it. The man was toying with her in the way a sleek cat playfully inserts its claws into a half-mangled mouse. The mystery was not why she had decided to divorce him so suddenly, but why she had tolerated him for so long. Yet there was a sense of a challenge unmet, for a cat only remains interested while the mouse plays the game, and Cooper had the distinct impression that Jack felt Sarah was letting him down. 'Did you know before that?'

'No.'

'Are you surprised?'

'No.'

'Do your wife's patients often leave her money then?'

'Not as far as I know.' He grinned at the Sergeant. 'If they have, she's never told me.'

'Then why aren't you surprised?'

'Give me a good reason why I should be. If you'd told me Mathilda had left her money to the Police Benevolent Fund or New Age Travellers, that wouldn't have surprised me either. It was hers to do with as she liked, and good luck to her. Mind you, I'm glad it's the *wife*,' he put an offensive emphasis on the word, 'who hit the jackpot. It'll make things considerably easier for me. I don't mind admitting I'm a bit short at the moment.'

Sarah raked him from head to toe with angry eyes. 'My God, Jack, if you knew how close I am to sinking my fist into your self-satisfied gut.'

'Ah,' he murmured, 'passion at last.' He stood up and approached her, spreading his hands wide in an invitation to do it. 'Feel free. It's all yours.'

She took him by surprise and kneed him in the groin instead. 'Next time,' she said through gritted teeth, 'I'll break Mathilda's canvas over your head. And that would be a shame because it's probably the best thing you've ever done.'

'GODDAMMIT, WOMAN, THAT HURT!' he roared, clutching his balls and collapsing back on to the stool. 'I asked for passion not fucking castration.'

Sarah's eyes narrowed. 'It was supposed to hurt, you cretin. Don't even think about getting your hands on Mathilda's money. You're certainly not getting any of mine if I can help it. Fifty–fifty? Fat – bloody – chance. I'll sell up and give it to a cats' home before I see you living the life of Riley on the back of my hard work.'

He poked his fingers into his Levi's pocket and removed a folded piece of paper. 'My contract with Mathilda,' he said, holding it out to her with one hand while he fondled himself gingerly with the other. 'The silly old sod snuffed it before she paid me, so I reckon her executors owe me ten thousand and her heir gets the painting. Jesus, Sarah, I feel really sick. I think you've done me some severe damage.'

She ignored him to read what was on the paper. 'This looks kosher,' she said.

'It *is* kosher. Keith drew it up.'

'He never told me.'

'Why should he? It was none of your business. I just hope I've got a claim on the estate. The way my luck's running, the contract's probably invalid because she's dead.'

Sarah passed the paper to DS Cooper. 'What do you think? It would be a shame if Jack's right. It's his second major sale.'

She was genuinely pleased for the bastard, Cooper thought in surprise. What a peculiar couple they were. He shrugged. 'I'm no expert but I've always understood that debts have to be met out of an estate. If you'd supplied her with new carpeting, which she hadn't paid for, the bill would presumably be honoured. I don't see why a painting should be any different, particularly one where the subject is the deceased. It's not as though you can sell it to anyone else, is it?' He glanced at the canvas. 'Bearing in mind, of course, you might have a problem proving it's Mrs Gillespie.'

'Where would I have to prove it? In court?'

'Possibly.'

His eyes gleamed as he clicked his fingers for the contract. 'I'm relying on you, Sarah,' he said, tucking the paper back into his pocket.

'To do what?'

'Tell the executors not to pay, of course. Say you don't think it's Mathilda. I need the publicity of a court battle.'

'Don't be stupid. I *know* it's Mathilda. If the contract's legally binding on her estate, they'll have to pay.'

But he wasn't listening. He tossed his paints, brushes and bottles of turpentine and linseed oil into a hold-all, then released the canvas of Joanna Lascelles from the easel. 'I've got to go. Look, I can't take the rest of this stuff because I haven't found a studio yet, but I'll try and get back for it during the week. Is that okay? I only came for some clothes. I've been sleeping in the car and this lot's a bit rank.' He padded towards the door, slinging the hold-all over his shoulder and carrying the painting in his hand.

'One moment, Mr Blakeney.' Cooper stood up to block his path. 'I haven't finished with you yet. Where were you on the night Mrs Gillespie died?'

Jack glanced at Sarah. 'I was in Stratford,' he said coolly, 'with an actress called Sally Bennedict.'

Cooper didn't look up, merely licked the point of his pencil and jotted the name on his pad. 'And how can I contact her?'

'Through the RSC. She's playing Juliet in one of their productions.'

'Thank you. Now, as someone with material evidence, I must warn you that if you intend to go on sleeping in your car then you will be required to present yourself at a police station every day, because if you don't I shall be forced to apply for a warrant. We also need your fingerprints so that we can isolate yours from the others we lifted in Cedar House. There will be a fingerprinting team in Fontwell Parish Hall on Wednesday morning but if you can't attend, I shall have to make arrangements for you to come to the station.'

'I'll be there.'

'And your whereabouts in the meantime, sir?'

'Care of Mrs Joanna Lascelles, Cedar House, Fontwell.' He booted open the door into the hall and eased through the gap. It was clearly something he had done many times before to judge by the dents and scratches on the paintwork.

'Jack!' Sarah called.

He turned to look at her. His eyebrows lifted enquiringly.

She nodded to the portrait of Mathilda. 'Congratulations.'

He flashed her an oddly intimate smile before letting the door slam behind him.

The two, left behind in the studio, listened to his footsteps on the stairs as he went in search of clothes. 'He's a law unto himself, isn't he?' said Cooper, drawing thoughtfully on his cigarette.

'One of life's great individuals,' Sarah said, consciously echoing Jack's description of Mathilda, 'and very difficult to live with.'

'I can see that.' He bent down to stub the butt against the rim of the wastepaper basket. 'But equally difficult to live *without*, I should imagine. He leaves something of a vacuum in his wake.'

Sarah turned away from him to look out of the window. She couldn't see anything, of course – it was now very dark outside – but the policeman could see her reflection in the glass as clearly as if it were a mirror. He would have done better, he thought, to keep his mouth shut but there was an openness about the Blakeneys that was catching.

'He's not always like that,' said Sarah. 'It's rare for him to be quite so forthcoming, but I'm not sure if that was for your benefit or mine.' She fell silent, aware that she was speaking her thoughts aloud.

'Yours, of course.'

They heard the front door open and close. 'Why "of course"?'

'I haven't hurt him.'

Their reflected eyes met in the window pane.

'Life's a bugger, isn't it, Sergeant?'

Joanna's demands on my purse are becoming insatiable. She says it's my fault that she's incapable of finding a job, my fault that her life's so empty, my fault that she had to marry Steven and my fault, too, that she was saddled with a baby she didn't want. I forbore to point out that she couldn't get into the Jew's bed quick enough or that the pill had been available for years before she allowed herself to get pregnant. I was tempted to catalogue the hells I went through – the rape of my innocence, marriage to a drunken pervert, a second pregnancy when I'd barely got over the first, the courage it took to climb out of an abyss of despair that she couldn't begin to imagine. I didn't, of course. She alarms me enough, as it is, with her frigid dislike of me and Ruth. I dread to think how she would react if she ever found out that Gerald was her father.

She says I'm a miser. Well, perhaps I am. Money has been a good friend to me and I guard it as jealously as others guard their secrets. God knows, I've had to use every ounce of cunning I possess to acquire it. If shrouds had pockets, I'd take it with me and 'to hell, allegiance!' It is not we who owe our children but they who owe us. The only regret I have about dying is that I won't see Sarah's face when she learns what I've left her. That would, I think, be amusing.

Old Howard quoted Hamlet at me today: 'We go to gain a little patch of ground that hath no profit but the name.' I laughed – he is a most entertaining old brute at times – and answered from The Merchant: *'He is well paid who is well satisfied . . .'*

Seven

VIOLET ORLOFF sought out her husband in the sitting-room, where he was watching the early evening news on the television. She turned down the volume and placed her angular body in front of the screen.

'I was watching that,' he said in mild reproof.

She took no notice. 'Those awful women next door have been screaming at each other like a couple of fishwives, and I could hear every word. We should have taken the surveyor's advice and *insisted* on a double skin with soundproofing. What's going to happen if it's sold to hippies or people with young children? We'll be driven *mad* with their row.'

'Wait and see,' Duncan said, folding his plump hands in his ample lap. He could never understand how it was that old age, which had brought him serenity, had brought Violet only an aggressive frustration. He felt guilty about it. He knew he should never have brought her back to live in such close proximity with Mathilda. It was like placing a daisy beside an orchid and inviting comparisons.

She scowled at him. 'You can be so infuriating at times. If we wait and see, it'll be too late to do anything. I think we should demand that something be done *before* it's sold.'

'Have you forgotten,' he reminded her gently, 'that we were only able to afford this house in the first place precisely because there was no soundproofing and Mathilda agreed to a five thousand pound discount when the surveyor pointed out the deficiency? We're hardly in a position to demand anything.'

But Violet hadn't come in to discuss demands. 'Fishwives,' she said again, 'screaming at each other. The police now think Mathilda was *murdered*, apparently. And do you know what Ruth called her mother? A whore. She said she knew her mother was a whore in London. Rather *worse*, in fact. She said Joanna was,' her voice dropped to a whisper while her lips, in exaggerated movement, mouthed the words, 'a *fucking* whore.'

'Good lord,' said Duncan Orloff, startled out of his serenity.

'Quite. And Mathilda thought Joanna was mad, and she tried to murder Ruth, and she's spending her money on something she shouldn't and, worst of all, Ruth was in the house the night Mathilda died and she took Mathilda's earrings. *And,*' she said with particular emphasis, as if she hadn't already said 'and' several times, 'Ruth has stolen other things as well. They obviously haven't told the police any of it. I think we should report it.'

He looked slightly alarmed. 'Is it really any of our business, dear? We do have to go on living here, after all. I should hate any more unpleasantness.' What Duncan called serenity, others called apathy, and the hornets' nest stirred up two weeks ago by Jenny Spede's screams had been extremely unsettling.

She stared at him with shrewd little eyes. 'You've known it was murder all along, haven't you? *And* you know who did it.'

'Don't be absurd,' he said, an edge of anger in his voice.

She stamped her foot angrily on the floor. 'Why do you insist on treating me like a child? Do you think I didn't *know*? I've known for forty years, you silly man. Poor Violet. Only second best. Always second best. What did she tell you, Duncan?' Her eyes narrowed to slits. 'She told you *something*. I know she did.'

'You've been drinking again,' he said coldly.

'You never accused Mathilda of drinking, but then *she* was perfect. Even drunk, Mathilda was perfect.' She tottered very slightly. '*Are* you going to report what I heard? Or will I have to do it? If Joanna or Ruth murdered her they don't deserve to get away with it. You're not going to tell me you don't care, I hope. I *know* you do.'

Of course he cared – it was only Violet for whom he felt a numbing indifference – but had she no sense of self-preservation? 'I don't imagine Mathilda was killed for fun,' he said, holding her gaze for a moment, 'so I do urge you to be very cautious in what you say and how you say it. On the whole I think it would be better if you left it to me.' He reached past her to switch up the volume on the television set. 'It's the weather forecast,' he pointed out, gesturing her gravely to one side, as if tomorrow's atmospheric pressures across the United Kingdom were of any interest to a fat, flabby old man who never stirred out of his armchair if he could possibly avoid it.

Ruth opened the door to Jack with a sullen expression in her dark eyes. 'I hoped you wouldn't come back,' she said bluntly. 'She always gets what she wants.'

He grinned at her. 'So do I.'

'Does your wife know you're here?'

He pushed past her into the hall, propping the canvas of Joanna against a wall and lowering the hold-all to the floor. 'Is that any of your business?'

She shrugged. 'She's the one with the money. We'll all lose out if you and Mum put her nose out of joint. You must be mad.'

He was amused. 'Are you expecting me to lick Sarah's arse so that you can live in clover for the rest of your life? Forget it, sweetheart. The only person I lick arse for is myself.'

'Don't call me sweetheart,' she snapped.

His eyes narrowed. 'Then don't judge me by your own standards. My best advice to you, Ruth, is to learn a little subtlety. There is no bigger turn-off than a blatant woman.'

For all her outward maturity, she was still a child. Her eyes filled. 'I hate you.'

He studied her curiously for a moment, then moved off in search of Joanna.

No one could accuse Joanna of being unsubtle. She was a woman of understatement, in words, dress and action. She sat now in the dimly lit drawing-room, a book open on her lap, face impassive, hair a silver halo in the light from the table lamp. Her eyes flickered in Jack's direction as he entered the room, but she didn't say anything, only gestured towards the sofa for him to sit down. He chose to stand by the mantelpiece and watch her. He thought of her in terms of ice. Glacial. Dazzling. Static.

'What are you thinking?' she asked after several moments of silence.

'That Mathilda was right about you.'

There was no expression in her grey eyes. 'In which particular respect?'

'She said you were a mystery.'

She gave a faint smile but didn't say anything.

'I liked her, you know,' Jack went on after a moment.

'You would. She despised women but looked up to men.'

There was a lot of truth in that, thought Jack. 'She liked Sarah well enough.'

'Do you think so?'

'She left her three-quarters of a million pounds. I'd say that was a pretty good indication she liked her.'

Joanna leant her head against the back of the sofa and stared at him with a disconcertingly penetrating gaze. 'I assumed you knew Mother better than that. She didn't *like* anyone. And why ascribe such a mundane motive to her? She would have viewed a bequest of three-quarters of a million pounds in terms of the power it could buy her, not as a sentimental hand-out to someone who had done her a small kindness. Mother never intended that will to be her last. It was a piece of theatre, made for Ruth and me to find. Money buys power just as effectively if you threaten to withhold it.'

Thoughtfully, Jack rubbed his jaw. Sarah had said something very similar. 'But why Sarah? Why not leave it to a dogs' home? It would have achieved the same purpose.'

'I've wondered about that,' she murmured, her eyes straying towards the window. 'I think perhaps she disliked your wife even more than she disliked me. Do you imagine Ruth and I would have kept quiet if we'd seen that video while Mother was alive?' She stroked her hand rhythmically up and down her arm as she spoke. It was an extraordinarily sensuous action but she seemed unaware that she was doing it. She brought her head round to look at Jack again. Her eyes were strangely glassy. 'Your wife's position would have become untenable.'

'What would you have done?' asked Jack curiously.

Joanna smiled. 'Nothing very much. Your wife would have lost all her patients within six months once it got out that she had persuaded a rich patient to make over her entire estate. She'll lose them anyway.'

'Why?'

'Mother died in suspicious circumstances and your wife is the only person to benefit from her death.'

'Sarah didn't kill Mathilda.'

Joanna smiled to herself. 'Tell that to the people of Fontwell.' She stood up and smoothed her black dress over her flat stomach. 'I'm ready,' she said.

He frowned. 'What for?'

'Sex,' she said matter-of-factly. 'It's what you came for, isn't it? We'll use Mother's room. I want you to make love to me the way you made love to her.' Her strange eyes rested on him. 'You'll enjoy it far more with me, you know. Mother didn't like sex, but then I presume you discovered that for yourself. She never did it for pleasure, only for gain. A man's humping disgusted her. She said it reminded her of dogs.'

Jack found the remark fascinating. 'I thought you said she looked up to men?'

Joanna smiled. 'Only because she knew how to manipulate them.'

The news that Mathilda Gillespie had left Dr Blakeney three-quarters of a million pounds spread through the village like wildfire. The information surfaced after matins on Sunday, but precisely who started the fire remained a mystery. There was no doubt, however, that it was Violet Orloff who let slip the interesting snippet that Jack Blakeney had taken up residence at Cedar House. His car had remained on the gravel drive all Saturday night and looked like remaining there indefinitely. Tongues began to wag.

Jane Marriott was careful to keep her expression neutral when Sarah put in a surprise appearance at lunchtime on Wednesday. 'I wasn't expecting you,' she said. 'Shouldn't you be on your way to Beeding?'

'I had to give my fingerprints in the parish hall.'

'Coffee?'

'I suppose you've heard. Everyone else has.'

Jane switched on the kettle. 'About the money or about Jack?'

Sarah gave a humourless laugh. 'That makes life a lot easier. I've just spent an hour in a queue outside the hall, listening to heavy-handed hints from people who should have been diagnosed brain-dead years ago. Shall I tell you what the current thinking seems to be? Jack has left me to live with Joanna because he is as shocked as everyone else that I used my position as Mathilda's GP to persuade her to forget her duty to her family in favour of me. This being the same Jack Blakeney who, only last week, everyone loved to hate because he was living off his wretched wife.'

'Oh dear,' said Jane.

'They'll be saying next that I killed the old witch before she could change the will back.'

'You'd better believe it,' said Jane dispassionately. 'There's no point burying your head in the sand.'

'You're joking.'

Jane handed her a cup of black coffee. 'I'm serious, dear. There were two of them discussing it here in the waiting-room this morning. It goes something like this: none of the locals had reason to hate Mathilda more than usual in the last twelve months so none of them is likely to have murdered her. Therefore it has to be a newcomer, and you're the only newcomer with a motive who had access to her. Your husband, afraid for himself and Mrs Lascelles, has moved in to protect her. Ruth is safe because she's at school. And last, but by no means least, why did Victor Sturgis die in such peculiar circumstances?'

Sarah stared at her. 'You *are* serious, aren't you?'

''Fraid so.'

'Do I gather I'm supposed to have killed Victor as well?'

Jane nodded.

'How? By suffocating him with his own false teeth?'

'That seems to be the general view.' Jane's eyes brimmed with laughter suddenly. 'Oh dear, I shouldn't laugh, really I shouldn't. Poor old soul, it was bad enough that he swallowed them himself, but the idea of you wrestling with a ninety-three-year-old in order to ram his dentures down his throat' – she broke off to mop her eyes – 'it doesn't bear thinking about. The world is full of very foolish and very envious people, Sarah. They resent your good fortune.'

Sarah mulled this over. 'Do you think I'm fortunate?'

'Good lord, yes. It's like winning the pools.'

'What would you do with the money if Mathilda had left it to you?'

'Go on a cruise. See the world before it sinks under the weight of its own pollution.'

'That seems to be the most popular choice. It must be something to do with the fact that we're an island. Everyone wants to get off it.' She stirred her coffee then licked the spoon absent-mindedly.

Jane was dying of curiosity. 'What are you going to do with it?'

Sarah sighed. 'Use it to pay for a decent barrister, I should think.'

DS Cooper stopped at Mill House on his way home that evening. Sarah offered him a glass of wine which he accepted. 'We've had a letter about you,' he told her while she was pouring it.

She handed him the glass. 'Who from?'

'Unsigned.'

'What does it say?'

'That you murdered an old man called Victor Sturgis for his walnut desk.'

Sarah pulled a wry face. 'Actually, he did leave me a desk and it's rather a nice one, too. The matron at the nursing home gave it to me after he died. She said he wanted me to have it. I was very touched.' She lifted weary eyebrows. 'Did it say how I murdered him?'

'You were seen suffocating him.'

'It makes a weird sort of sense. I was trying to prise his dentures out of his throat. The poor old boy swallowed them when he dozed off in his chair.' She sighed. 'But he was dead before I even started. I had a vague idea of trying mouth-to-mouth if I could unblock his airway. I suppose, from a distance, it might have looked as if I were suffocating him.'

Cooper nodded. He had checked the story already. 'We've had a few letters, one way and another, and they're not all about you.' He took an envelope from his pocket and handed it to her. 'This is the most interesting. See what you make of it.'

'Should I touch the letter?' she asked doubtfully. 'What about fingerprints?'

'Well, that's interesting in itself. Whoever wrote it wore gloves.'

She took the letter from the envelope and spread it on the table. It was printed in block capitals:

RUTH LASCELLES WAS IN CEDAR HOUSE THE DAY MRS GILLESPIE DIED. SHE STOLE SOME EARRINGS. JOANNA KNOWS SHE TOOK THEM. JOANNA LASCELLES IS A PROSTITUTE IN LONDON. ASK HER WHAT SHE SPENDS HER MONEY ON. ASK HER WHY SHE TRIED TO KILL HER DAUGHTER. ASK HER WHY MRS GILLESPIE THOUGHT SHE WAS MAD.

Sarah turned the envelope over to look at the frank mark. It had been posted in Learmouth. 'And you've no idea who wrote it?'

'None at all.'

'It can't be true. You told me yourself that Ruth was under the watchful eye of her housemistress at school.'

He looked amused. 'As I told you, I never set much store by alibis. If that young lady wanted to sneak out I can't see her housemistress stopping her.'

'But Southcliffe's thirty miles away,' Sarah protested. 'She couldn't have got here without a car.'

He changed tack. 'What about this reference to madness? Did Mrs Gillespie ever mention to you that her daughter was mad?'

She considered this for a moment. 'Madness is a relative term, quite meaningless out of context.'

He was unruffled. 'So Mrs Gillespie did mention something of the sort?'

Sarah didn't answer.

'Come on, Dr Blakeney. Joanna's not your patient so you're not giving away any confidences. And let me tell you something else, she's not doing you any favours at the moment. Her view is that you had to kill the old lady PDQ before she had time to change her will back, and she isn't keeping those suspicions to herself.'

Sarah fingered her wine glass. 'The only thing Mathilda ever said on the subject was that her daughter was unstable. She said it wasn't Joanna's fault but was due to incompatibility between Mathilda's genes and Joanna's father's genes. I told her she was talking rubbish but, at the time, I didn't know that Joanna's father was Mathilda's uncle. I imagine she was concerned about the problems of recessive genes but, as we didn't pursue it any further, I can't say for sure.'

'Inbreeding, in other words?'

Sarah gave a small shrug of acquiescence. 'Presumably.'

'Do you like Mrs Lascelles?'

'I hardly know her.'

'Your husband seems to get on with her well enough.'

'That's below the belt, Sergeant.'

'I don't understand why you're bothering to defend her. She's got her knife into you right up to the hilt.'

'Do you blame her?' She leaned her chin on her hand. 'How would you feel if in a few short weeks, you discovered that you were the product of an incestuous relationship, that your father killed himself with an overdose, that your mother died violently either by her own hand or someone else's and that, to cap it all, the security you were used to was about to be snatched away and given to a stranger? She seems remarkably sane to me in the circumstances.'

He took a drink from his glass. 'Do you know anything about her being a prostitute?'

'No.'

'Or what she spends her money on?'

'No.'

'Any ideas?'

'It's nothing to do with me. Why don't you ask her?'

'I have. She told me to mind my own business.'

Sarah chuckled. 'I'd have done the same.'

He stared at her. 'Has anyone ever told you you're too good to be true, Dr Blakeney?' He spoke with a touch of sarcasm.

She held his gaze, but didn't say anything.

'Women in your position drive their husband's car through their rival's front door, or take a chainsaw to the rival's furniture. At the very least, they feel acute bitterness. Why don't you?'

'I'm busy shoring up my house of cards,' she said cryptically. 'Have some more wine.' She filled her own glass, then his. 'It's not bad, this one. Australian Shiraz and fairly inexpensive.'

He was left with the impression that, of the two women, Joanna Lascelles was the less puzzling. 'Would you have described yourself and Mrs Gillespie as friends?' he asked.

'Of course.'

'Why "of course"?'

'I describe everyone I know well as a friend.'

'Including Mrs Lascelles.'

'No. I've only met her twice.'

'You wouldn't think it to listen to you.'

She grinned. 'I have a fellow-feeling with her, Sergeant, just as I have with Ruth and Jack. You don't feel comfortable with any of us. Joanna or Ruth might have done it if they didn't know the will had been changed, Jack or I might have done it if we did. On the face of it, Joanna appears the most likely which is why you keep asking me questions about her. I imagine you've quizzed her pretty thoroughly about when she first learnt who her father was, so you'll know that she threatened her mother with exposure?' She looked at him enquiringly, and he nodded. 'At which point, you're thinking, Mathilda turned round and said, any more threats like this and I'll cut you out altogether. So, in desperation, Joanna dosed her mother with barbiturates and slit the old lady's wrists, unaware that Mathilda had altered the will already.'

'What makes you think I don't feel comfortable with that scenario?'

'You told me Joanna was in London that night.'

He shrugged. 'Her alibi is very shaky. The concert ended at nine thirty which meant she had plenty of time to drive down here and kill her mother. The pathologist puts the time of death somewhere between nine p.m. on the Saturday night and three a.m. the following morning.'

'Which does he favour?'

'Before midnight,' Cooper admitted.

'Then her defence barrister will tear your case to shreds. In any case, Mathilda wouldn't have bothered with pretence. She'd have told Joanna straight out she'd changed the will.'

'Perhaps Mrs Lascelles didn't believe her.'

Sarah dismissed this with a smile. 'Mathilda always told the truth. That's why everyone loathed her.'

'Perhaps Mrs Lascelles just suspected that her mother might change the will.'

'It wouldn't have made any difference as far as Joanna was

concerned. She was preparing to use her father's codicil to fight her mother in court. At that stage, it didn't matter a twopenny damn who Mathilda left the money to, not if Joanna could prove she had no right to it in the first place.'

'Perhaps it wasn't done for money. You keep wondering about the significance of the scold's bridle. Perhaps Mrs Lascelles was revenging herself.'

But Sarah shook her head. 'She hardly ever saw her mother. I think Mathilda mentioned that she came down once in the last twelve months. It would be a remarkable anger that could sustain itself at fever pitch over such a lengthy cooling period.'

'Not if Mrs Lascelles is unstable,' murmured Cooper.

'Mathilda wasn't killed in a mad frenzy,' said Sarah slowly. 'It was all done with such meticulous care, even down to the flowers. You said yourself the arrangement was difficult to reproduce without help.'

The Sergeant drained his glass and stood up. 'Mrs Lascelles works freelance for a London florist. She specializes in bridal bouquets and wreaths. I can't see her finding a few nettles and daisies a problem.' He walked to the door. 'Good night, Dr Blakeney. I'll see myself out.'

Sarah stared into her wine glass as she listened to his footsteps echoing down the hall. She felt like screaming, but was too afraid to do it. Her house of cards had never seemed so fragile.

There was a conscious eroticism to every movement Joanna made and Jack guessed she had posed before, probably for photographs. For money or for self-gratification? The latter, he thought. Her vanity was huge.

She was obsessed with Mathilda's bed and Mathilda's bedroom, aping her mother's posture against the piled pillows. Yet the contrast between the two women could not have been greater. Mathilda's sexuality had been a gentle, understated thing, largely because she had no interest in it; Joanna's was mechanical and obtrusive, as if the same visual stimuli could arouse all men in the same way on every occasion. Jack found it impossible to decide whether she was acting out of contempt for him or out of contempt for men in general.

'Is your wife a prude?' she demanded abruptly after a long period of silent sketching.

'Why do you ask?'

'Because what I'm doing shocks you.'

He was amused. 'Sarah has a very open and healthy libido and far from shocking me, what you're doing offends me. I resent being categorized as the sort of man who can be turned on by cheap pornographic posturing.'

She looked away from him towards the window and sat in strange self-absorption, her pale eyes unfocused. 'Then tell me what Sarah does to excite you,' she said finally.

He studied her for a moment, his expression unreadable. 'She's interested in what I'm trying to achieve in my work. That excites me.'

'I'm not talking about that, I'm talking about sex.'

'Ah,' he said apologetically, 'we're at cross purposes then. *I* was talking about love.'

'How very twee.' She gave a small laugh. 'You ought to hate her, Jack. She must have found someone else or she wouldn't have kicked you out.'

'Hate is too pervasive,' he said mildly. 'It leaves no room for anything else.' With an idle flick of his fingers he tossed a torn page of his sketchpad towards her and watched it flutter to the bed beside her. 'Read that,' he invited. 'If you're interested, it's my assessment of your character after three sittings. I jot down my impressions as I go along.'

With a remarkable lack of curiosity – most women, he thought, would have seized on it with alacrity – she retrieved it and gave a cursory glance to both sides of the paper. 'There's nothing on it.'

'Exactly.'

'That's cheap.'

'Yes,' he agreed, 'but you've given me nothing to paint.' He passed her the sketchpad. 'I don't do glossy nudes and so far that's all you've offered me, bar a dreary and unremitting display of Electra complex, or more accurately demi-Electra complex. There's no attachment to a father, only a compulsive hostility towards a mother. You've talked about nothing else since I've been here.' He shrugged. 'Even your daughter doesn't feature. You haven't mentioned the poor kid once since she went back to school.'

Joanna got off the bed, wrapped herself in her dressing-gown and walked to the window. 'You don't understand,' she said.

'Oh, I understand,' he murmured. 'You can't con a conman, Joanna.'

She frowned. 'What are you talking about?'

'One of the most colossal egos I've ever come across, and God knows I should recognize one when I see it. You may persuade the rest of the world that Mathilda wronged you, but not me. You've been screwing her all your life,' he tipped a finger at her, 'although you probably didn't know until recently just why you were so damn good at it.'

She didn't say anything.

'I'll hazard a guess that your childhood was one endless tantrum, which Mathilda attempted to control with the scold's bridle. Am I right?' He paused. 'And then what? Presumably you were bright enough to work out a way to stop her using it.'

Her tone was frigid. 'I was terrified of the beastly thing. I used to convulse every time she produced it.'

'Easily done,' he said with amusement. 'I did it myself as a child when it suited me. So how old were you when you worked that one out?'

Her peculiarly fixed gaze lingered on him, but he could feel the growing agitation underneath. 'The only time she ever showed me any affection was when she put the scold's bridle over my head. She'd put her arms about me and rub her cheek against the framework. "Poor darling," she'd say, "Mummy's doing this for Joanna."' She turned back to the window. 'I hated that. It made me feel she could only love me when I was at my ugliest.' She was silent for a moment. 'You're right about one thing. It wasn't until I found out that Gerald was my father that I understood why my mother was afraid of me. She thought I was mad. I'd never realized it before.'

'Didn't you ever ask her why she was afraid?'

'You wouldn't even put that question if you'd really known my mother.' Her breath misted the glass. 'There were so many secrets in her life that I learnt very rapidly never to ask her anything. I had to make up a fantasy background for myself when I went to boarding school because I knew so little about my own.' She dashed the mist away with an impatient hand and turned back into the room. 'Have you finished? I've things to do.'

He wondered how long he could stall her this time before the demands of her addiction sent her scurrying for the bathroom. She was always infinitely more interesting under the stress of abstinence than she ever was drugged. 'Southcliffe?' he asked. 'The same school Ruth's at now?'

She gave a hollow laugh. 'Hardly. Mother wasn't so free with her money in those days. I was sent to a cheap finishing school which made no attempt to educate, merely groomed cattle for the cattle market. Mother had ambitions to marry me off to a title. Probably,' she went on cynically, 'because she hoped a chinless wonder would be so inbred himself he wouldn't notice the lunacy in me.' She glanced towards the door. 'Ruth has had far more spent on her than I ever had, and not because Mother was fond of her, believe me.' Her mouth twisted. 'It was all done to stamp out the Jew in her after my little faux pas with Steven.'

'Did you love him?'

'I've never loved anyone.'

'You love yourself,' he said.

But Joanna had already gone. He could hear her scrabbling feverishly through the vanity case in the bathroom. For what? he wondered. Tranquillizers? Cocaine? Whatever it was, she wasn't injecting it. Her skin was flawless and beautiful like her face.

Sarah Blakeney tells me her husband is an artist. A painter of personalities. I guessed he would be something in that line. It's what I would have chosen myself. The arts or literature.

'I have heard of your paintings too, well enough. God hath given you one face and you make yourselves another.' Funnily enough, that might have been written for Sarah. She projects herself as a frank and open person, with strong, decided views and no hidden contradictions, but in many ways she is very insecure. She positively loathes confrontation, preferring agreement to disagreement, and will placate if she can. I asked her what she was afraid of, and she said: 'I was taught to be accommodating. It's the curse of being a woman. Parents don't want to be left with spinsters on their hands so they teach their daughters to say "yes" to everything except sex.'

Times haven't changed then . . .

Eight

SARAH WAS WAITING outside the doorway of Barclays Bank in Hills Street when Keith Smollett arrived. She had her coat collar pulled up around her ears and looked pale and washed out in the grey November light. He gave her a warm hug and kissed her cold cheek. 'You're not much of an advertisement for a woman who's just scooped the jackpot,' he remarked, holding her at arm's length and examining her face. 'What's the problem?'

'There isn't one,' she said shortly. 'I just happen to think there's more to life than money.'

He smiled, his thin face irritatingly sympathetic. 'Would we be talking Jack by any chance?'

'No, we would not,' she snapped. 'Why does everyone assume that my equanimity depends on a shallow, two-faced skunk whose one ambition in life is to impregnate every female he meets?'

'Ah!'

'What's that supposed to mean?' she demanded.

'Just, ah!' He tucked her hand into his arm. 'Things are pretty bad at the moment, then?' He gestured towards the road. 'Which way to Duggan's office?'

'Up the hill. And, no, things are not pretty bad at the moment. At the moment things are pretty good. I haven't felt so calm and so in control for years.' Her bleak expression belied her words. She allowed herself to be drawn out on to the pavement.

'Or so lonely, perhaps?'

'Jack's a bastard.'

Keith chuckled. 'Tell me something I don't know.'

'He's living with Mathilda Gillespie's daughter.'

Keith slowed down and eyed her thoughtfully. 'Mathilda Gillespie as in the old dear who's left you her loot?'

Sarah nodded.

'Why would he want to live with her daughter?'

'It depends who you listen to. Either because he feels guilty that I, his greedy wife, have deprived poor Joanna of her birthright, or he is protecting her and himself from my murderous slashes with a Stanley knife. No one appears to give any credence to the most obvious reason.'

'Which is?'

'Common-or-garden lust. Joanna Lascelles is very beautiful.' She pointed to a door ten yards ahead. 'That's Duggan's office.'

He stopped and drew her to one side. 'Let me get this straight. Are people saying you murdered the old woman for her money?'

'It's one of the theories going the rounds,' she said dryly. 'My patients are abandoning me in droves.' Dampness sparkled along her lashes. 'It's the absolute pits if you want to know. Some of them are even crossing the road to avoid me.' She blew her nose aggressively. 'And my partners aren't happy about it either. Their surgeries are overflowing while mine are empty. If it goes on, I'll be out of a job.'

'That's absurd,' he said angrily.

'No more absurd than an old woman leaving everything she had to a virtual stranger.'

'I talked with Duggan on the phone yesterday. He said Mrs Gillespie was clearly very fond of you.'

'I'm very fond of you, Keith, but I don't intend to leave you all my money.' She shrugged. 'I probably wouldn't have been surprised if she'd left me a hundred quid or even her scold's bridle, but leaving me the whole caboodle just doesn't make sense. I didn't do anything to deserve it, except laugh at her jokes from time to time and prescribe a few pain-killers.'

He shrugged in his turn. 'Perhaps that was enough.'

She shook her head. 'People don't dispossess their families in favour of a slight acquaintance who turns up once a month for half an hour. It's completely crazy. Old men besotted with young girls might be foolish enough to do it, but not tough old boots like Mathilda. And, if she was that way inclined, then why didn't she leave

112

it to Jack? According to him, he knew her so well she was happy to let him paint her in the nude.'

Keith felt unreasonably irritated as he pushed open the door of Duggan, Smith and Drew and ushered Sarah inside. There was, he thought, something deeply offensive about Jack Blakeney persuading a wretched old woman to strip for him. And why would she want to anyway? He couldn't get to grips with that at all. But then Blakeney's attraction, if it existed at all, was entirely lost on Keith. He preferred conventional types who told amusing anecdotes, bought their own drinks and didn't rock the boat by speaking or acting out of turn. He consoled himself with the idea that the story wasn't true. But in his heart of hearts he knew it must be. The real crippler about Jack Blakeney was that women *did* take their clothes off for him.

The meeting dragged on interminably, bogged down in technical details about the 1975 family provision legislation, which, as Duggan had warned Mathilda, might entitle Joanna, as a dependent, to claim reasonable provision for maintenance. 'She ignored my advice,' he said, 'and instructed me to draw up the will leaving all her assets at the time of her death to you. However, it is my considered opinion that in view of the allowance she was paying her daughter and the fact that Mrs Lascelles does not own her own flat, Mrs Lascelles has a good case in law for claiming maintenance. In which case a capital sum now, without prejudice, is worth consideration. I suggest we take counsel's opinion on it.'

Sarah lifted her head. 'You're jumping the gun a little. I haven't yet said that I'm prepared to accept the bequest.'

He could be very direct when he chose. 'Why wouldn't you?'

'Self-preservation.'

'I don't follow.'

'Probably because you haven't had a policeman parked on your doorstep for the last three weeks. Mathilda died in very mysterious circumstances and I'm the only person who stands to gain by her death. I'd say that makes me rather vulnerable, wouldn't you?'

'Not if you didn't know about the bequest.'

'And how do I prove *that*, Mr Duggan?'

He smiled in his amiable way. 'Let me put it to you another way, Dr Blakeney, how will refusing the bequest prove that you didn't murder her? Won't everyone just say you've taken fright because your attempt to make it look like suicide didn't work?' He paused for a moment, but went on when she didn't say anything. 'And no one will applaud you for your magnanimity, you know, because the money won't go to Mrs Lascelles or her daughter but to a handful of donkeys. At least if you accept the bequest, they've a chance of a capital sum.'

Sarah stared past him towards the window. 'Why did she do it?'

'She said she was fond of you.'

'Didn't you question that at all? I mean, do you normally have rich old ladies turning up out of the blue, saying that they want to make new, secret wills which they don't wish their families to know about? Shouldn't you have tried to persuade her out of it? It might have been a spur-of-the-moment whim which we're all saddled with because she died on us. People are saying I used undue influence.'

He turned his pencil in his fingers. 'It wasn't spur-of-the-moment. She first approached me about three months ago and, yes, as a matter of fact I did try to persuade her out of it. I pointed out that, as a general rule, family money is best left with families however much one individual may dislike his or her children. I argued, with no success at all, that she should not regard the Cavendish wealth as hers but as a sort of inherited trust to be passed on to succeeding generations.' He shrugged. 'She wouldn't have it. So I tried to persuade her to discuss it with you first, but I'm afraid she wouldn't have that either. She was quite adamant that you were to inherit but weren't to know about it in advance. For the record, and as I told the police, I was satisfied there was no question of undue influence.'

Sarah was appalled. '*Three months*,' she echoed slowly. 'Have you told the police that?'

He nodded. 'They were also working on the theory that it was a sudden whim.'

She put unsteady fingers to her lips. 'I could just about prove I couldn't have known about it if she made the will two days before she died. There is no way I can prove ignorance if she'd been planning it for three months.'

John Hapgood, the bank manager, cleared his throat. 'It does seem to me, Dr Blakeney, that you are concentrating on entirely the wrong issue. The night Mrs Gillespie died was a Saturday if I remember correctly. Where were you that night, and what were you doing? Let's establish whether you *need* to prove your ignorance of the bequest.'

'I was at home on call. I checked when I learnt about the will.'

'And did you receive any calls?'

'Only one, shortly before eight o'clock. It was nothing serious so I dealt with it over the phone.'

'Was your husband with you?'

'No, he was in Stratford that weekend. No one was with me.' She smiled faintly. 'I'm not a complete moron, Mr Hapgood. If I had an alibi I'd have produced it by now.'

'Then I think you must have more faith in the police, Dr Blakeney. Despite what you read in the papers, they are probably still the best in the world.'

She studied him with amusement. 'You may be right, Mr Hapgood, but, personally, I have no faith at all in my ability to prove I didn't kill Mathilda for her money, and I have a nasty feeling the police know it.' She held up her fingers and ticked off point after point. 'I had motive, I had opportunity and I provided at least half the means.' Her eyes glittered. 'In case you didn't know, she was drugged with the barbiturates I prescribed for her before the incisions were made in her wrists. On top of that, I did twelve months in a pathology department because I was considering a career in forensic medicine before I became a GP, so if anyone would know how to fake a suicide it would be me. Now give me one good argument that I can quote in my defence when the police decide to arrest me.'

He steepled his fingers under his chin. 'It's an interesting problem, isn't it?' He beetled his white eyebrows into a ferocious scowl. 'What were you doing that Saturday?'

'The usual. Gardening, housework. I think I used most of that Saturday to prune the roses.'

'Did anyone see you?'

'What difference does it make whether anyone saw me or not?' She spoke with considerable irritation. 'Mathilda was killed some time during the night, and I certainly wasn't gardening in the dark.'

'What *were* you doing?'

Cursing Jack. Feeling sorry for myself. 'I was painting one of the bedrooms.'

'After doing the garden all day?'

'Someone had to do it,' she said curtly.

There was a short silence.

'You're obviously a workaholic,' said Mr Hapgood lamely. She reminded him of his wife, always on the move, always restless, never pausing long enough to work out where she was going.

Sarah gave a slight smile. 'Most women are. We can't shrug off the responsibility of the home just because we want a career. We got the worst of both worlds when we set out to storm the male bastions.' She pressed her thumb and forefinger to her tired eyes. 'Look, none of this is relevant to why we're here. As far as I can see Mathilda has put me in an impossible position. Whatever I do, I shall be saddled with guilt over her daughter and granddaughter. Is there no way I can simply side-step the issue and leave them to fight it out between themselves?'

'There's nothing to stop you giving it back to them in the form of a gift,' said Duggan, 'once it's yours. But it would be a very inefficient use of the money. The tax liability would be colossal.' He smiled apologetically. 'It would also be flying in the face of Mrs Gillespie's wishes. Whatever the rights and wrongs of it, she did not want Mrs Lascelles or Miss Lascelles to inherit her estate.'

Keith reached for his briefcase. 'Is there any hurry for Dr Blakeney to make her decision,' he asked reasonably, 'or can I suggest we put the whole thing on a back burner for another week or two until the police resolve this one way or another? I can't help feeling Dr Blakeney will find it easier to make her decision once the inquest has been held.'

And so it was agreed, although for Sarah it was simply the postponement of a choice already made.

Keith and Sarah had lunch in a small restaurant at the bottom of the hill. Keith watched her over the rim of his wine glass. 'Was that an act or are you genuinely afraid of being arrested?'

She shrugged. 'Does it matter?' He thought how deeply Jack's departure had affected her. He had never encountered Sarah's bitterness before.

'Of course it matters,' he said bluntly. 'If you're worried, then I suggest I come with you now to sort it out with the police. Where's the sense in tearing yourself apart over something that may never happen?'

She smiled faintly. 'It was an act,' she said. 'I got very tired of them discussing me as if I wasn't there. I might have been as dead as Mathilda. It's the money that excites them.'

Unfair, he thought. Both men had gone out of their way to sympathize with the difficult situation in which Sarah found herself but she was determined to see everyone as an enemy. *Including himself?* Impossible to judge. He turned his glass, letting the sober wall-lights gleam through the red wine. 'Do you want Jack back? Is that why you're so angry? Or are you just jealous because he's found someone else?'

'Can you be *just* jealous?'

'You know what I mean.'

She smiled again, a bitter smile that twisted her mouth. 'But I don't, Keith. I've been jealous for years. Jealous of his art, jealous of his women, jealous of his talent, jealous of him and his ability to bedazzle every damn person he meets. What I feel now is nothing like the jealousy I've felt before. Perhaps it's there but, if it is, it's overlaid with so many other emotions that it's difficult to isolate.'

Keith frowned. 'What do you mean, his ability to bedazzle everyone he meets? I can't stand the man, never have been able to.'

'But you think about him. Mostly with irritation and anger, I expect, but you do think about him. How many other men do you dwell on with the compulsion with which you dwell on Jack? The policeman who's dogging my tracks put it rather well: he said: "He leaves something of a vacuum in his wake."' She held Keith's gaze. 'That's one of the best descriptions I've ever heard of him, because it's true. At the moment I'm living in a vacuum and I'm not enjoying it. For the first time in my life I do not know what to do and it frightens me.'

'Then cut your losses and formalize the separation. Make the decision to start again. Uncertainty is frightening. Certainty never is.'

With a sigh she pushed her plate to one side. 'You sound like my mother. She has a homily for every situation and it drives me mad. Try telling a condemned man that certainty isn't frightening. I doubt he'd agree with you.'

Keith beckoned for the bill. 'At the risk of blotting my copybook again I suggest you go for a long walk by the sea and blow the cobwebs out of your head. You're allowing sentiment to cloud your judgement. There are only two things to remember at a time like this: one, *you* told Jack to leave, not he you; and two, you had good reasons for doing so. It doesn't matter how lonely, how rejected or how jealous you feel now, it cannot affect the central issue, namely that you and Jack do not get on as man and wife. My advice is to get yourself a decent husband who'll stand by you when you need him.'

She laughed suddenly. 'There's not much hope of that. The decent ones are all spoken for.'

'And whose fault's that? You had your chance, but you chose not to take it.' He handed a credit card to the waitress, watched her walk away to the counter, then transferred his gaze to Sarah. 'I don't suppose you'll ever know how much you hurt me, not unless what you're feeling now is something like the hurt that I felt then.'

She didn't answer immediately. 'Now who's being sentimental?' she said at last, but he thought he saw dampness in her eyes again. 'You've forgotten that you only found me truly desirable after you lost me, and by then it was too late.'

And the tragedy was, he knew she was right.

The door of Cedar House opened six inches in answer to Keith's ring. He smiled pleasantly. 'Mrs Lascelles?'

A tiny frown creased her forehead. 'Yes.'

'I'm Jack Blakeney's solicitor. I'm told he's staying here.'

She didn't answer.

'May I come in and talk to him? I've driven all the way from London.'

'He's not here at the moment.'

'Do you know where I can find him? It is important.'

She gave an indifferent shrug. 'What's your name? I'll tell him you called.'

'Keith Smollett.'
She closed the door.

Violet Orloff, sheltering by the corner of the house, beckoned to him as he walked back to his car. 'I do hope you won't think I'm *interfering*,' she said breathily, 'but I couldn't help overhearing what you said. She's in a funny mood at the moment, won't talk to anyone, and if you've come all the way from London . . .' She left the rest of the sentence unsaid.

Keith nodded. 'I have, so if you can tell me where Jack is I'd be very grateful.'

She cast a nervous sideways glance towards Joanna's door, then gestured rapidly to the path running round the far corner of the house. 'In the garden,' she whispered. 'In the summer-house. He's using it as a studio.' She shook her head. 'But don't tell *her* I told you. I thought Mathilda's tongue was wicked, but *Joanna's* – ' she cast her eyes to heaven, 'she calls Mr Blakeney a homosexual.' She shooed at him. 'Quickly now, or she'll see you talking to me and Duncan would be *furious*. He's so afraid, you know.'

Somewhat bewildered by this eccentric behaviour, Keith nodded his thanks and followed the same route that Sarah had taken with Ruth. Despite the cold, the doors to the summer-house stood open and he could hear a woman singing a Cole Porter song as he approached across the lawn. The voice was unmistakable, rich and haunting, backed by a simple piano accompaniment.

> Every time we say goodbye, I die a little,
> Every time we say goodbye, I wonder why a little,
> Why the gods above me, who must be in the know,
> Think so little of me they allow you to go . . .

Keith paused in the entrance. 'Since when were you a Cleo Laine fan, Jack? I thought Sarah was the aficionado.' He pressed the eject button on the recorder and removed the tape to read the handwritten label on the front. 'Well, well. Unless I'm very much mistaken, this is the one I made for her before you married. Does she know you've got it?'

Jack surveyed him through half-closed lids. He was on the point of telling him to put his hackles down, his customary response to Smollett's invariably critical opening remarks, when he thought better of it. For once, he was pleased to see the pompous bastard. In fact, he admitted to himself, he was so damn pleased he could be persuaded to change the habits of the last six years and greet him as a friend instead of a marriage-breaking incubus. He stuck his paintbrush in a jar of turpentine and wiped his hands down the front of his jumper, producing a huge paint-smeared palm as a peace-offering. 'I suppose Sarah's sent you.'

Keith pretended not to see the hand, instead eyed the sleeping-bag, abandoned in a dishevelled heap in a corner, then pulled forward a chair. 'No,' he said, folding himself into it. 'I left her in Poole. She doesn't know I'm here. I've come to try and talk some sense into you.' He studied the portrait. 'Mrs Lascelles presumably.'

Jack crossed his arms. 'What do you think?'

'Of her or the portrait?'

'Either.'

'I only saw six inches of her through the gap in the door.' He cocked his head on one side to examine the painting. 'You've been pretty heavy-handed with the purples. What is she, a nymphomaniac? Or is that just wishful thinking on your part?'

Jack lowered himself gingerly into the chair opposite – the cold and the floorboards were wreaking havoc on the muscles of his back – and wondered if the gentlemanly thing was to bop Keith on the nose now or wait till the man was on guard. 'Not all the time,' he said, answering the question seriously, 'only when she's stoned.'

Keith digested this in silence for a moment or two. 'Have you told the police?'

'What?'

'That she's a user.'

'No.'

'Then I think it's better all round if you never told me and I never heard it.'

'Why?'

'Because I'm on the side of law and order and I don't have your freedom to behave as I like.'

'Don't blame your profession for your lack of freedom, Smollett,' Jack growled, 'blame yourself for selling out to it.' He nodded towards the house. 'She needs help and the best person to give it to her is the one she won't see. Sarah, in other words. What good would a policeman be to her?'

'He could prevent her murdering someone else.'

Thoughtfully, Jack rubbed his unshaven jaw. 'Meaning that because she's degenerate enough to use drugs, she's ipso facto degenerate enough to kill her mother. That's crap, and you know it.'

'It gives her a damn sight better motive than the one Sarah's been saddled with. It's expensive to feed a habit, not to mention the effect it has on the personality. If she didn't kill the old woman for money, then she's probably unpredictable enough to have done it out of sudden fury.'

'You'd have no qualms about briefing a barrister with that codswallop either, would you?' murmured Jack.

'No qualms at all, particularly if it's Sarah's neck that ends up on the line.' Keith turned the cassette in his fingers, then reached out to put it beside the recorder. 'You do know she's worried sick about losing her patients and being arrested for murder, I suppose, while you're here mooning over a drug-addicted nymphomaniac? Where's your loyalty, man?'

Was this Sarah talking? Jack wondered. He hoped not. 'Mooning' was not a word he recognized as part of her vocabulary. She had too much self-respect. He gave a prodigious yawn. 'Does Sarah want me back. Is that why you're here? I don't mind admitting I'm pretty fed up with freezing my balls off in this miserable dump.'

Keith breathed deeply through his nose. 'I don't *know* what she wants,' he said, bunching his fists in his lap. 'I came because I had an absurd idea that you and I could discuss this mess in an adult way without either of us needling the other. I should have known it was impossible.'

Jack squinted at the bunched fists, while doubting that Keith could ever be provoked into using them. 'Did she tell you why she wanted a divorce?'

'Not precisely.'

He linked his hands behind his head and stared at the ceiling. 'She took against me when she had to arrange an abortion for my lover. It's been downhill ever since.'

Keith was genuinely shocked. *That* explained Sarah's bitterness all right. With a shake of his head, he pushed himself out of his chair and stood by the door, gazing out across the garden. 'If I wasn't so sure I'd lose, I'd invite you out there for a thrashing. You're a shit, Jack. JE-SUS!' he said, as the full import of what the man had said slowly dawned. 'You had the bloody nerve to make Sarah murder *your* baby. That is so damn sick I can hardly believe it. She's your wife, for God's sake, not some sleazy back-street abortionist slaughtering wholesale for money. No wonder she wants a divorce. Don't you have any sensibilities at all?'

'Clearly not,' said Jack impassively.

'I warned her not to marry you.' He turned back bludgeoning the air with his finger because he hadn't the courage to bludgeon Jack with a fist. 'I knew it wouldn't last, told her exactly what to expect, what sort of a man you were, how many women you'd used and discarded. But not this. Never this. How could you *do* such a thing?' He was almost in tears. 'Dammit, I wouldn't even turn my back on the baby, but to make your own wife responsible for its murder. You're sick! Do you know that? You're a sick man.'

'Put like that, I rather agree with you.'

'If I have my way you won't get a penny out of this divorce,' he said ferociously. 'You do realize I'm going to report this back to her, and make sure she uses it in court?'

'I'm relying on you.'

Keith's eyes narrowed suspiciously. 'What's that supposed to mean?'

'It means, Smollett, that I expect you to repeat every word of this conversation verbatim.' His expression was unreadable. 'Now do me a favour and take yourself off before I do something I might regret. Sarah's friendships are entirely her concern, of course, but I admit I've never understood why she always attracts domineering little men who think she's vulnerable.' He flipped the tape, pushed it back into the recorder and pressed the 'play' button. This time it was Richard Rodney Bennett's 'I never went away' that drifted in melancholy splendour upon the air.

> No matter where I travelled to,
> I never went away from you . . .
> I never went away . . .

Jack closed his eyes. 'Now bugger off,' he murmured, 'before I rip your arms off. And don't forget to mention the sleeping-bag, there's a good chap.'

Duncan and Violet Orloff are the most absurd couple. They spent the entire afternoon on the lawn with Duncan fast asleep and Violet twittering non-stop drivel at him. She's like a manic little bird, constantly twitching her head from side to side for fear of predators. As a result she never once looked at Duncan and was quite oblivious to the fact that he wasn't listening to a word she said. I can't say I blame him. She was empty-headed as a child and age has not improved her. I still can't decide whether it was a good or a bad idea to offer them Wing Cottage when Violet wrote and said they'd set their hearts on spending their retirement in Fontwell. 'We do so want to come home,' was her appallingly sentimental way of putting it. The money was very useful, of course – Joanna's flat was a shocking expense, as is Ruth's education – but, on balance, neighbours should be eschewed. It's a relationship that can all too easily descend into forced intimacy. Violet forgot herself and called me 'love' last week, then went into paroxysms of hysteria when I pointed it out, beating her chest with her hands and ululating like some peasant woman. A most revolting display, frankly. I'm inclined to think she's going senile.

Duncan, of course, is a very different kettle of fish. The wit is still there, if somewhat slower through lack of practice. Hardly surprising when it has been blunted for forty years on Violet's plank of a brain. I wonder sometimes how much they remember of the past. I worry that Violet will twitter away to Joanna or Ruth one day and let cats out of bags that are better confined. We all share too many secrets.

I read back through my early diaries recently and discovered, somewhat to my chagrin, that I told Violet the week before her wedding that her marriage would never last. If the poor creature had a sense of humour, she could reasonably claim the last laugh . . .

125

Nine

JOANNA SHOWED little surprise at finding Sarah on her doorstep at noon the next day. She gave the faintest of smiles and stepped back into the hall, inviting the other woman inside. 'I was reading the newspaper,' she said, as if Sarah had asked her a specific question. She led the way into the drawing-room. 'Do sit down. If you've come to see Jack, he's outside.'

This was a very different reception from the one Keith described having the previous evening, and Sarah wondered about Joanna's motives. She doubted that it had anything to do with the drug addiction Keith had harped on about, and thought it more likely that curiosity had got the better of her. It made sense. She was Mathilda's daughter and Mathilda had been insatiably curious.

She shook her head. 'No, it's you I've come to see.'

Joanna resumed her own seat but made no comment.

'I always liked this room,' said Sarah slowly. 'I thought how comfortable it was. Your mother used to sit over there,' she pointed to a high-backed chair in front of the french windows, 'and when the sun shone it turned her hair into a silver halo. You're very like her to look at but I expect you know that.'

Joanna fixed her with her curiously inexpressive eyes.

'Would it help, do you think, if you and I talked about her?'

Again Joanna didn't answer and to Sarah, who had rehearsed everything on the assumption that the other woman would be a willing party to their conversation, the silence was as effective as a brick wall. 'I hoped,' she said, 'that we could try to establish some sort of common ground.' She paused briefly but there was no response. 'Because, frankly, I'm not happy about leaving everything

127

in the hands of solicitors. If we do, we might just as well burn the money now and be done with it.' She gave a tentative smile. 'They'll pick the bones clean and leave us with a worthless carcase. Is that what you want?'

Joanna turned her face to the window and contemplated the garden. 'Doesn't it make you angry that your husband's here with me, Dr Blakeney?'

Relieved that the ice was broken, though not in a way she would have chosen herself, Sarah followed her gaze. 'Whether it does or doesn't isn't terribly relevant. If we bring Jack into it, we'll get nowhere. He has a maddening habit of hi-jacking almost every conversation I'm involved in, and I really would prefer, if possible, to keep him out of this one.'

'Do you think he slept with my mother?'

Sarah sighed inwardly. 'Does it matter to you?'

'Yes.'

'Then, no, I don't think he did. For all his sins, he never takes advantage of people.'

'She might have asked him to.'

'I doubt it. Mathilda had far too much dignity.'

Joanna turned back to her with a frown. 'I suppose you know she posed in the nude for him. I found one of his sketches in her desk. It left nothing to the imagination, I can assure you. Do you call that dignified? She was old enough to be his mother.'

'It depends on your point of view. If you regard the female nude as intrinsically demeaning or deliberately provocative, then, yes, I suppose you could say it was undignified of Mathilda.' She shrugged. 'But that's a dangerous philosophy which belongs to the dark ages and the more intolerant religions. If, on the other hand, you see the nude figure, be it male or female, as one of nature's creations, and therefore as beautiful and as extraordinary as anything else on this planet, then I see no shame involved in allowing a painter to paint it.'

'She did it because she knew it would excite him.' She spoke the words with conviction and Sarah wondered about the wisdom of continuing – Joanna's prejudice against her mother was too ingrained for reasoned argument. But the offensiveness of the statement irritated her enough to defend Jack, if only because she had encountered the same sort of blinkered stupidity herself.

'Jack's seen far too many naked women to find nakedness itself a turn-on,' she said dismissively. 'Nudity is only erotic if you want it to be. You might just as well say that I get a thrill every time a male patient undresses for me.'

'That's different. You're a doctor.'

Sarah shook her head. 'It's not, but I'm not going to argue the toss with you. It would be a waste of both our times.' She ran her fingers through her hair. 'In any case your mother was too incapacitated by her arthritis, and in too much pain from it, to want to have intercourse with a virile man thirty years her junior. It's important to keep a sense of proportion, Mrs Lascelles. It might have been different if she had been sexually active all her life or even liked men very much, but neither was true of your mother. She once told me that the reason there were so many divorces these days was because relationships based on sex were doomed to fail. The pleasures of orgasm were too fleeting to make the remaining hours of boredom and disappointment worth while.'

Joanna resumed her study of the garden. 'Then why did she take her clothes off?' It was, it seemed, very important to her. Because she was jealous, Sarah wondered, or because she needed to go on despising Mathilda?

'I imagine it was no big deal, one way or the other, and she was interested enough in art for art's sake to help Jack explore the unconventional side of her nature. I can't see her doing it for any other reason.'

There was a brief silence while Joanna considered this. 'Do you still like her now that she's dead?'

Sarah clasped her hands between her knees and stared at the carpet. 'I don't know,' she said honestly. 'I'm so angry about the will that I can't view her objectively at the moment.'

'Then say you don't want the bequest. Let me and Ruth have it.'

'I wish it was that easy, believe me, but if I turn it down then you'll have to fight the donkeys' charity for it, and I honestly can't see how that will improve your chances unless, presumably, you can show that Mathilda never intended that will to be her last.' She looked up to find Joanna's pale eyes studying her intently.

'You're a very peculiar woman, Dr Blakeney,' she said slowly. 'You must realize that the easiest way for me to do that is to prove that my mother was murdered and that you were the one who did it. It fits so neatly, after all. You knew the will was just a threat to make me and Ruth toe the line, so you killed Mother quickly before she could change it. Once you're convicted, no court on earth will rule in favour of the donkeys.'

Sarah nodded. 'And if you can cajole my husband into testifying that I knew about the will in advance, then you're home and dry.' She raised an eyebrow in enquiry. 'But, as I suspect you're beginning to discover, Jack is neither so amenable nor so dishonest. And it wouldn't make any difference, you know, if you did manage to persuade him into bed with you. I've known him for six years and the one thing I can say about him is that he cannot be bought. He values himself far too highly to tell lies for anyone, no matter how much of an obligation they may put him under.'

Joanna gave a small laugh. 'You're very confident that I haven't slept with him.'

Sarah felt compassion for her. 'My solicitor phoned last night to say that Jack's camped out in your summer-house, but I was sure anyway. You're very vulnerable at the moment, and I do know my husband well enough to know he wouldn't exploit that.'

'You sound as though you admire him.'

'I could never admire him as much as he admires himself,' she said dryly. 'I hope he's extremely cold out there. I've suffered for his art for years.'

'I gave him a paraffin heater,' said Joanna with a frown. The memory obviously annoyed her.

Sarah's eyes brimmed with sudden laughter. 'Was he grateful?'

'No. He told me to leave it outside the door.' She gazed through the window. 'He's an uncomfortable person.'

'I'm afraid he is,' Sarah agreed. 'It never occurs to him that other people have fragile egos which need stroking from time to time. It means you have to take his love on faith if you want a relationship with him.' She gave a throaty chuckle. 'And faith has a nasty habit of deserting you just when you most need it.'

There was a long silence. 'Did you talk to my mother like this?' Joanna asked at last.

'Like what?'

Joanna sought for the right words. 'So – easily.'

'Do you mean did I find her easy to talk to?'

'No.' There was a haunted look in the grey eyes. 'I meant, weren't you afraid of her?'

Sarah stared at her hands. 'I didn't need to be, Mrs Lascelles. She couldn't hurt me, you see, because she wasn't my mother. There were no emotional strings to be arbitrarily plucked when she felt like it; no shared family secrets that would lay me open to her vituperative tongue; no weaknesses from my childhood that she could exploit into adulthood whenever she felt like belittling me. If she'd tried, of course, I'd have walked away, because I've had all that from my own mother for years and there is no way I would put up with it from a stranger.'

'I didn't kill her. Is that what you came to find out?'

'I came to find out if bridges could be built.'

'For your benefit or mine?'

'Both, I hoped.'

Joanna's smile was apologetic. 'But I've got nothing to gain by being friendly with you, Dr Blakeney. It would be tantamount to admitting Mother was right and I can't do that, not if I want to contest the will in court.'

'I hoped to persuade you there were other options.'

'Every one of which is dependent on your charity.'

Sarah sighed. 'Is that so terrible?'

'Of course. I served forty years for my inheritance. You served one. Why should I have to beg from you?'

Why indeed? There was no justice in it that Sarah could see. 'Is there any point in my coming here again?'

'No.' Joanna stood up and smoothed the creases from her skirt. 'It can only make matters worse.'

Sarah smiled wryly. 'Can they *be* any worse?'

'Oh, yes,' she said with a twisted little smile. 'I might start to like you.' She waved dismissively towards the door. 'You know your way out, I think.'

DS Cooper was gazing thoughtfully at Sarah's car when she emerged from the front door. 'Was that wise, Dr Blakeney?' he asked as she approached.

'Was what wise?'

'Bearding the lioness in her den.'

'Do lionesses have beards?' she murmured.

'It was a figure of speech.'

'I gathered that.' She observed him with fond amusement. 'Wise or not, Sergeant, it was instructive. I've had my anxieties laid to rest and, as any doctor will tell you, that's the best panacea there is.'

He looked pleased for her. 'You've sorted things out with your husband?'

She shook her head. 'Jack's a life sentence not an anxiety.' Her dark eyes gleamed with mischief. 'Perhaps I should have paid a little more attention when my mother was making her predictions for our future.'

'Marry in haste, repent at leisure?' he suggested.

'More along the lines of "She who sups with the devil needs a long spoon". Which I, of course, countered with "The devil has all the best tunes".' She made a wry face. 'But try forgetting "Hey, Jude" or "Twenty-four hours from Tulsa". Like Jack they have a nasty habit of lingering in the memory.'

He chuckled. 'I'm more of a "White Christmas" man myself, but I know what you mean.' He glanced towards the house. 'So, if it's not your husband who's set your mind at rest it must be Mrs Lascelles. Does that mean she's decided to accept the terms of the will?'

Again Sarah shook her head. 'No. She's convinced me she didn't kill her mother.'

'And how did she manage to do that?' He looked very sceptical.

'Feminine intuition, Sergeant. You'd probably call it naïvety.'

'I would.' He patted her arm in an avuncular way. 'You really must learn not to be so patronizing, Doctor. You'll see things in a different light if you do.'

'Patronizing?' echoed Sarah in surprise.

'We can always call it something else. Intellectual snobbery or self-righteousness, perhaps. They cloak themselves just as happily under the guise of naïvety but, of course, naïvety sounds so much less threatening. You're a very decided woman, Dr Blakeney, and you rush in where angels fear to tread, not out of foolishness but out of an overweening confidence that you know best. I am investigating a murder here.' He smiled grimly. 'I don't pretend that I would ever have liked Mrs Gillespie because I'm rather inclined to accept the established view that she was an evil-minded old bitch who got her kicks out of hurting people. However, that did not give anyone the right to strike her down prematurely. But the point I want to stress to you is that whoever killed her was clever. Mrs Gillespie made enemies right, left and centre, and knew it; she was a bully; she was cruel; and she trod rough-shod over other people's sensibilities. Yet, someone got so close to her that they were able to deck her out in a diabolical headdress and then take her semi-conscious to the bath where they slit her wrists. Whoever this person was is not going to make you a free gift of their involvement. To the contrary, in fact, they will make you a free gift of their non-involvement, and your absurd assumption that you can tell intuitively who is or who is not guilty from a simple conversation is intellectual arrogance of the worst kind. If it was so damned easy – forgive my French – to tell murderers from the rest of society, do you not think by now that we'd have locked them up and confined unlawful killing to the oddities page of the history textbooks?'

'Oh dear,' she said. 'I seem to have exposed a nerve. I'm sorry.'

He sighed with frustration. 'You're still patronizing me.'

She opened her car door. 'Perhaps it would be better if I left, otherwise I might be tempted to return the insult.'

He looked amused. 'Water off a duck's back,' he said amiably. 'I've been insulted by professionals.'

'I'm not surprised,' she said, slipping in behind the wheel. 'I can't be the only person who gets pissed off when you decide to throw your weight about. You don't even know for sure that Mathilda was murdered, but we're all supposed to wave our arms in the air and panic. What possible difference can it make to anyone if I choose to satisfy myself that Mrs Lascelles hasn't disqualified herself from a cut of the will by topping the old lady who made it?'

'It could make a lot of difference to you,' he said mildly. 'You could end up dead.'

She was intensely scornful. 'Why?'

'Have you made a will, Dr Blakeney?'

'Yes.'

'In favour of your husband?'

She nodded.

133

'So, if you die tomorrow, he gets everything, including, presumably, what Mrs Gillespie has left you.'

She started the car. 'Are you suggesting Jack is planning to murder me?'

'Not necessarily.' He looked thoughtful. 'I'm rather more interested in the fact that he is – potentially – a very eligible husband. Assuming, of course, you die before you can change your will. It's worth considering, don't you think?'

Sarah glared at him through the window. 'And you say Mathilda was evil-minded?' Furiously, she ground into gear. 'Compared with you she was a novice. Juliet to your Iago. And if you don't understand the analogy, then I suggest you bone up on some Shakespeare.' She released the clutch with a jerk and showered his legs with gravel as she drove away.

'Are you busy, Mr Blakeney, or can you spare me a few minutes?' Cooper propped himself against the doorjamb of the summer-house and lit a cigarette.

Jack eyed him for a moment, then went back to his painting. 'If I said I was busy would you go away?'

'No.'

With a shrug, Jack clamped the brush between his teeth and took a coarser one from the jar on the easel, using it to create texture in the soft paint he had just applied. Cooper smoked in silence, watching him. 'Okay,' said Jack at last, flipping the brushes into turpentine and swinging round to face the Sergeant. 'What's up?'

'Who was Iago?'

Jack grinned. 'You didn't come here to ask me that.'

'You're quite right, but I'd still like to know.'

'He's a character from *Othello*. A Machiavelli who manipulated people's emotions in order to destroy them.'

'Was Othello the black bloke?'

Jack nodded. 'Iago drove him into such a frenzy of jealousy that Othello murdered his wife Desdemona and then killed himself when he learnt that everything Iago had said about her was a lie. It's a story of obsessive passion and trusts betrayed. You should read it.'

'Maybe I will. What did Iago do to make Othello jealous?'

'He exploited Othello's emotional insecurity by telling him Desdemona was having an affair with a younger, more attractive man. Othello believed him because it was what he was most afraid of.' He stretched his long legs in front of him. 'Before Othello fell on his sword he described himself as "one that lov'd not wisely but too well". It gets misused these days by people who know the quote but don't know the story. They interpret "lov'd not wisely" as referring to a poor choice of companion, but Othello was actually acknowledging his own foolishness in not trusting the woman he adored. He just couldn't believe the adoration was mutual.'

Cooper ground his cigarette under the heel of his shoe. 'Topical stuff then,' he murmured, glancing towards the sleeping-bag. 'Your wife's not loving too wisely at the moment, but then you're hardly encouraging her to do anything else. You're being a little cruel, aren't you, sir?'

Jack's liking for the man grew. 'Not half as cruel as I ought to be. Why did you want to know about Iago?'

'Your wife mentioned him, said I was Iago to Mrs Gillespie's Juliet.' He smiled his amiable smile. 'Mind, I'd just suggested that if she were to die an untimely death you would make an eligible catch for someone else.' He took out another cigarette, examined it then put it back again. 'But I don't see Mrs Gillespie as Juliet. King Lear, perhaps, assuming I'm right and King Lear was the one whose daughter turned on him.'

'Daughters,' Jack corrected him. 'There were two of them, or two who turned on him, at least. The third tried to save him.' He rubbed his unshaven jaw. 'So you've got your knife into Joanna, have you? Assuming I've followed your reasoning correctly, then Joanna killed her mother to inherit the funds, found to her horror that Mathilda had changed her will in the meantime, so immediately made eyes at me to get me away from Sarah with a view to topping Sarah at the first opportune moment and then hitching herself to me.' He chuckled. 'Or perhaps you think we're in it together. That's one hell of a conspiracy theory.'

'Stranger things have happened, sir.'

He eased his stiff shoulders. 'On the whole I prefer Joanna's interpretation. It's more rational.'

'She's accusing your wife.'

'I know. It's a neat little package, too. The only flaw in it is that Sarah would never have done it, but I can't blame Joanna for getting that wrong. She can't see past her own jealousy.'

Cooper frowned. 'Jealousy over you?'

'God no.' Jack gave a rumble of laughter. 'She doesn't even like me very much. She thinks I'm a homosexual because she can't account for my irreverence in any other way.' His eyes gleamed at Cooper's expression, but he didn't elaborate. 'Jealousy over her mother, of course. She was quite happy loathing and being loathed by Mathilda until she discovered she had a rival. Jealousy has far more to do with ownership than it has with love.'

'Are you saying she knew about your wife's relationship with her mother before her mother died?'

'No. If she had, she would probably have done something about it.' He scraped his stubble again, his eyes narrowing thoughtfully. 'But it's too late now, and that can only make the jealousy worse. She'll start to forget her mother's faults, fantasize about the relationship she imagines Sarah had with Mathilda and torment herself over her own missed opportunities. Let's face it, we all want to believe that our mothers love us. It's supposed to be the one relationship we can depend on.'

Cooper lit another cigarette and stared thoughtfully at the glowing tip. 'You say Mrs Lascelles is jealous of your wife's intimacy with Mrs Gillespie. Why isn't she jealous of her daughter? According to the young lady herself she got on with her grandmother like a house on fire.'

'Do you believe her?'

'There's no evidence to the contrary. The housemistress at her boarding school says Mrs Gillespie wrote regularly and always seemed very affectionate whenever she went there. Far more affectionate and interested, apparently, than Mrs Lascelles who puts in infrequent appearances and shows little or no interest in how her daughter's doing.'

'All that says to me is that Mathilda was a magnificent hypocrite. You can't ignore her snobbery, you know, not without distorting the picture. Southcliffe is an expensive girls' boarding school. Mathilda would never have let the side down in a place like that. She always talked about "people of her sort" and regretted the lack of them in Fontwell.'

The Sergeant shook his head in disbelief. 'That doesn't square with what you told me before. You called her one of life's great individuals. Now you're saying she was pandering to the upper classes in order to make herself socially acceptable.'

'Hardly. She was a Cavendish and inordinately proud of the fact. They were bigwigs round here for years. Her father, Sir William Cavendish, bought his knighthood by doing a stint as the local MP. She was already socially acceptable, as you put it, and didn't need to pander to anyone.' He frowned in recollection. 'No, what made her extraordinary, despite all the trappings of class and respectability which she played up to and tossed about in public to keep the proles in their place, was that privately she seethed with contradictions. Perhaps her uncle's sexual abuse had something to do with it, but I think the truth is she was born into the wrong generation and lived the wrong life. She had the intellectual capacity to do anything she wanted, but her social conditioning was such that she allowed herself to be confined in the one role she wasn't suited for, namely marriage and motherhood. It's tragic really. She spent most of her life at war with herself and crippled her daughter and granddaughter in the process. She couldn't bear to see their rebellions succeed where hers hadn't.'

'Did she tell you all this?'

'Not in so many words. I gleaned it from things she said and then put it into the portrait. But it's all true. She wanted a complete explanation of that painting, down to the last colour nuance and the last brush stroke, so' – he shrugged – 'I gave her one, much along the lines of what I've just told you, and at the end she said there was only one thing wrong, and it was wrong because it was missing. But she wouldn't tell me what it was.' He paused in reflection. 'Presumably it had something to do with her uncle's abuse of her. I didn't know about that. I only knew of her father's abuse with the scold's bridle.'

But Cooper was more interested in something he had said before. 'You can't call Mrs Lascelles's rebellion a success. She lumbered herself with a worthless heroin addict who then died and left her penniless.' His gaze lingered on the portrait.

Jack's dark face split into another grin. 'You've led a very sheltered life if you think rebellion is about achieving happiness. It's about anger and resistance and inflicting maximum damage on a hated authority.' He lifted a sardonic eyebrow. 'On that basis, I'd say Joanna scored a spectacular success. If you're calling her husband worthless now, what on earth do you imagine Mathilda's peers said about him at the time? Don't forget she was a very proud woman.'

Cooper drew heavily on his cigarette and looked up towards the house. 'Your wife's just been to see Mrs Lascelles. Did you know?'

Jack shook his head.

'I met her as she was leaving. She told me she's convinced Mrs Lascelles didn't kill her mother. Would you agree with that?'

'Probably.'

'Yet you just told me that Mrs Lascelles's rebellion was to inflict maximum damage on the object of her hatred. Isn't death the ultimate damage?'

'I was talking about twenty-odd years ago. You're talking about now. Rebellion belongs to the young, Sergeant, not to the middle-aged. It's the middle-aged who're rebelled against because they're the ones who compromise their principles.'

'So how is Ruth rebelling?'

Jack studied him lazily from beneath his hooded eyelids. 'Why don't you ask her?'

'Because she's not here,' said Cooper reasonably, 'and you are.'

'Ask her mother then. You're being paid to meddle,' he cocked his irritating eyebrow again, 'and I'm not.'

Cooper beamed at him. 'I like you, Mr Blakeney, though God alone knows why. I like your wife, too, if it's of any interest. You're straightforward types who look me in the eye when you talk to me and, believe it or not, that warms my heart because I'm trying to do a job that the people have asked me to do but for which, most of the time, I get called a pig. Now, for all I know, one or other, or both of you together, killed that poor old woman up there, and if I have to arrest you I'll do it, and I shan't let my liking get in the way because I'm an old-fashioned sod who believes that society only works if it's bolstered by rules and regulations which give more freedom than they take away. By the same token, I don't like Mrs Lascelles or her daughter, and if I was the sort to arrest people I didn't like, I'd have banged them up a couple of weeks ago. They're equally malicious. The one directs her malice against your wife, the other directs hers against her mother, but neither of them has said anything worth listening to. Their accusations are vague and without substance. Ruth says her mother's a whore without principles, and Mrs Lascelles says your wife's a murderess but when I ask them to prove it, they can't.' He tossed his dog-end on to the grass. 'The odd thing is that you and Dr Blakeney, between you, appear to know more about these two women and their relationship with Mrs Gillespie than they do themselves, but out of some kind of misguided altruism you don't want to talk about it. Perhaps it's not politically correct amongst gilded intellectuals to dabble their fingers in the seamy side of life, but make no mistake, without something more to go on, Mrs Gillespie's death will remain an unsolved mystery and the only person who will suffer will be Dr Blakeney because she is the only person who had a known motive. If she is innocent of the murder of her patient, her innocence can only be proved if someone else is charged. Now, tell me honestly, do you think so little of your wife that you'd let her reputation be trampled in the mud for the sake of not wanting to assist the police?'

'My God!' said Jack with genuine enthusiasm. 'You're going to have to let me do this portrait of you. Two thousand. Is that what we agreed?'

'You haven't answered my question,' said the policeman patiently.

Jack reached for his sketchpad and flicked through to a clean page. 'Just stand there for a moment,' he murmured, taking a piece of charcoal and making swift lines on the paper. 'That was some speech. Is your wife as decent and honourable as you are?'

'You're taking the mickey.'

'Actually, I'm not.' Jack squinted at him briefly before returning to his drawing. 'I happen to think the relationship between the police and society is drifting out of balance. The police have forgotten that they are there only by invitation; while society has forgotten that, because it chooses the laws which regulate it, it has a responsibility to uphold them. The relationship should be a mutually supportive one; instead, it is mutually suspicious and mutually antagonistic.' He threw Cooper a disarmingly sweet smile. 'I am thoroughly enchanted to meet a policeman who seems to share my point of view. And, no, of course I don't think so little of Sarah that I'd allow her reputation to suffer. Is that really likely?'

'You've not been out and about much since you moved in here.'

'I never do when I'm working.'

'Then perhaps it's time you left. There's a kangaroo court operating in Fontwell and your wife is their favourite target. She's the newcomer, after all, and you've done her no favours by shacking up with the opposition. She's lost a goodly number of patients already.'

Jack held the sketchpad at arm's length to look at it. 'Yes,' he said, 'I'm going to enjoy doing you.' He started to pack his hold-all. 'It's too damn cold here anyway, and I've got enough on Joanna to finish her at home. Will Sarah have me back?'

'I suggest you ask her. I'm not paid to meddle in domestic disputes.'

Jack tipped a finger in acknowledgement. 'Okay,' he said, 'the only thing I know about Ruth is what Mathilda told me. I can't vouch for its accuracy, so you'll have to check that for yourself. Mathilda kept a float of fifty pounds locked in a cash-box in her bedside table and opened it up one day because she wanted me to go to the shop and buy some groceries for her. It was empty. I said, perhaps she'd already spent the money and forgotten. She said, no, it's what came of having a thief for a granddaughter.' He shrugged. 'For all I know she may have been excusing her own memory lapse by slandering Ruth, but she didn't elaborate and I didn't ask. More than that I can't tell you.'

'What a disappointing family,' said the Sergeant. 'No wonder she chose to leave her money elsewhere.'

'That's where we part company,' said Jack, standing up and stretching towards the ceiling. 'They are Mathilda's creations. She had no business passing the buck to Sarah.'

I had an appalling shock today. I walked into the surgery, completely unprepared, and found Jane Marriott behind the counter. Why did nobody tell me they were back? Forewarned would have meant forearmed. Jane, of course, knowing our paths must cross, was as cool as ever. 'Good morning, Mathilda,' she said. 'You're looking well.' I couldn't speak. It was left to Doctor Dolittle, asinine man, to bray the good news that Jane and Paul have decided to move back to Rossett House following the death of their tenant. I gather Paul is an invalid – chronic emphysema – and will benefit from the peace and quiet of Fontwell after the rigours of Southampton. But what am I to do about Jane? Will she talk? Worse, will she betray me?

'Is there no pity sitting in the clouds, that sees into the bottom of my grief?'

I would feel less desperate if Ruth had not gone back to school. The house is empty without her. There are too many ghosts here and most of them unlaid. Gerald and my father haunt me mercilessly. There are times, not many, when I regret their deaths. But I have high hopes of Ruth. She is bright for her age. Something good will come of the Cavendishes, I'm sure of it. If not, everything I have done is wasted.

'Hush! Hush! Whisper who dares! Mathilda Gillespie is saying her prayers.' I have such terrible headaches these days. Perhaps it was never Joanna who was mad, but only I . . .

Ten

RUTH, SUMMONED OUT of a chemistry lesson, sidled into the room set aside for Sergeant Cooper by her housemistress and stood with her back to the door. 'Why did you have to come back?' she asked him. 'It's embarrassing. I've told you everything I know.' She was dressed in mufti and, with her hair swept back into a tight bun, she looked more than her seventeen years.

Cooper could appreciate her embarrassment. Any school was a goldfish bowl but a boarding school peculiarly so. 'Police investigations are rarely tidy things,' he said apologetically. 'Too many loose ends for tidiness.' He gestured towards a chair. 'Sit down, Miss Lascelles.'

With a bad grace, she did so, and he caught a brief glimpse of the gawky adolescent beneath the pseudo-sophistication of the outer shell. He lowered his stocky body on to the chair in front of her and studied her gravely but not unkindly.

'Two days ago we received a letter about you,' he said. 'It was anonymous. It claimed you were in Cedar House the day your grandmother died and that you stole some earrings. Are either of those facts true, Miss Lascelles?'

Her eyes widened but she didn't say anything.

'Since which time,' he went on gently, 'I have been told on good authority that your grandmother knew you were a thief. She accused you of stealing money from her. Is that also true?'

The colour drained from her face. 'I want a solicitor.'

'Why?'

'It's my right.'

He stood up with a nod. 'Very well. Do you have a solicitor of

143

your own? If you do, you may give your housemistress the number and ask her to telephone him. If not, I'm sure she will be happy to call the one the school uses. Presumably they will charge it to the fees.' He walked to the door. 'She may even offer to sit in herself to safeguard your interests. I have no objection to either course.'

'No,' she said sharply, 'I want the duty solicitor.'

'Which duty solicitor?' He found her transparency oddly pathetic.

'The one the police provide.'

He considered this during a prolonged and thoughtful silence. 'Would you be referring to duty solicitors at police stations who act on behalf of persons who have no legal representation of their own?'

She nodded.

He sounded genuinely sympathetic. 'With the best will in the world, Miss Lascelles, that is out of the question. These are harsh recessionary times, and you're a privileged young woman, surrounded by people only too willing to watch out for your rights. We'll ask your housemistress to contact a lawyer. She won't hesitate, I'm sure. Apart from anything else, she will want to keep the unpleasantness under wraps so to speak. After all, she does have the school's reputation to think of.'

'Bastard!' she snapped. 'I just won't answer your questions then.'

He manufactured a look of surprise. 'Do I gather you don't want a solicitor after all?'

'No. Yes.' She hugged herself. 'But I'm not saying anything.'

Cooper returned to his seat. 'That's your privilege. But if I don't get any answers from you, then I shall have to ask my questions elsewhere. In my experience, thieves do not confine themselves to stealing from just one person. I wonder what will happen if I call the rest of your house together and ask them en masse if any of their possessions have gone missing in the last year or so. The inference, surely, will be obvious because they know my only connection with the school is you.'

'That's blackmail.'

'Standard police procedure, Miss Lascelles. If a copper can't get his information one way, then he's duty-bound to try another.'

She scowled ferociously. 'I didn't kill her.'

'Have I said you did?'

She couldn't resist answering, it seemed. 'It's what you're think-ing. If I was there I must have killed her.'

'She probably died during the early half of the night, between nine o'clock and midnight, say. Were you there then?'

She looked relieved. 'No. I left at five. I had to be back in time for a physics lecture. It's one of my A level subjects and I gave the vote of thanks at the end.'

He took out his pad. 'What time did the lecture start?'

'Seven thirty.'

'And you were there for the start?'

'Yes.'

'How did you manage to do that? You clearly didn't walk thirty miles in two and a half hours.'

'I borrowed a bicycle.'

He looked deeply sceptical. 'What time did you arrive at your grandmother's, Miss Lascelles?'

'I don't know. About three thirty, I suppose.'

'And what time did you leave the school?'

'After lunch.'

'I see,' he said ponderously, 'so you rode thirty miles in one direction in two hours, rested for an hour and a half with your grandmother and then rode thirty miles back again. You must be a very fit young woman. May I have the name of the person whose bicycle you borrowed?' He licked the point of his pencil and held it poised above the page.

'I don't know whose it was. I borrowed it without asking.'

He made a note. 'Shall we call a spade a spade and be done with the pretence? You mean you stole it. Like the earrings and the fifty pounds.'

'I put it back. That's not stealing.'

'Back where?'

'In the bike shed.'

'Good, then you'll be able to identify it for me.'

'I'm not sure. I just took the best one I could find. What difference does it make which bicycle it was?'

'Because you're going to hop on board again and I'm going to follow closely behind you all the way to Fontwell.' He looked amused.

'You see, I don't believe you're capable of riding thirty miles in two hours, Miss Lascelles, but I'm quite happy for you to prove me wrong. Then you can have an hour and a half's rest before you ride back again.'

'You can't do that. That's just fucking – ' she cast about for a word ' – harassment.'

'Of course I can do it. It's called a reconstruction. You've just put yourself at the scene of a crime on the day the crime was committed, you're a member of the victim's family with easy access to her house and you thought you were going to inherit money from her. All of which puts you high on the list of probable suspects. Either you prove to my satisfaction that you did go by bicycle, or you tell me now how you really got there. Someone drove you, didn't they?'

She sat in a sullen silence, scraping her toe back and forth across the carpet. 'I hitched,' she said suddenly. 'I didn't want to tell you because the school would throw a fit if they knew.'

'Was your grandmother alive when you left Cedar House at five o'clock?'

She looked put out by the sudden switch of direction. 'She must have been, mustn't she, as I didn't kill her.'

'So you spoke to her?'

Ruth eyed him warily. 'Yes,' she muttered. 'I left my key at school and had to ring the doorbell.'

'Then she'll have asked you how you got there. If you had to hitch, she won't have been expecting you.'

'I said I had a lift from a friend.'

'But that wasn't true, was it, and, as you knew you were going to have to hitch back to school again on a dark November evening, why didn't you ask your grandmother to drive you? She had a car and, according to you, she was fond of you. She'd have done it without a murmur, wouldn't she? Why would you do something so dangerous as hitching in the dark?'

'I didn't think about it.'

He sighed. 'Where did you hitch from, Miss Lascelles? Fontwell itself, or did you walk the three miles along Gazing Lane to the main road? If it was Fontwell, then we'll be able to find the person who picked you up.'

'I walked along Gazing Lane,' she said obligingly.

'And what sort of shoes were you wearing?'

'Trainers.'

'Then they'll have mud from the lane squeezed into every seam and crevice. It was raining most of that afternoon. The boys at forensic will have a field day. Your shoes will vindicate you if you're telling the truth. And if you're not . . .' he smiled grimly, 'I will make your life a misery, Miss Lascelles. I will interview every girl in the school, if necessary, to ask them who you consort with, who's had to cover for you when you've gone AWOL, what you steal and why you're stealing it. And if at the end of it you have an ounce of credibility left, then I'll start all over again. Is that clear? Now, who drove you to your grandmother's?'

There were tears in her eyes. 'It's got nothing to do with Granny's death.'

'Then what can you lose by telling me?'

'I'll be expelled.'

'You'll be expelled far quicker if I have to explain why I'm carting your clothing off for forensic examination.'

She buried her face in her hands. 'My boyfriend,' she muttered.

'Name?' he demanded relentlessly.

'Dave – Dave Hughes.'

'Address?'

She shook her head. 'I can't tell you. He'd kill me.'

Cooper frowned at the bent head. 'How did you meet him?'

She raised her tear-stained face. 'He did the tarmac on the school drive.' She read censure in his eyes and leapt to defend herself. 'It's not like that.'

'Like what?'

'I'm not a slut. We love each other.'

Her sexual morality had been the last thing on his mind but it was clearly at the forefront of hers. He felt sorry for her. She was accusing herself, he thought, when she called her mother a whore. 'Does he own the house?'

She shook her head. 'It's a squat.'

'But he must have a telephone or you wouldn't be able to contact him.'

'It's a mobile.'

'May I have the number?'

She looked alarmed. 'He'd be furious.'

You bet your life he would, thought Cooper. He wondered what Hughes was involved in. Drugs? Under-age sex? Pornography? Expulsion was the least of Ruth's problems if any of these were true. He showed no impatience for the address or phone number. 'Tell me about him,' he invited instead. 'How long have you known him? How old is he?'

He had to prise the information from her with patient cajoling and, as she spoke and listened to herself, he saw the dawning confirmation of her worst fears: that this was not a story of Montagues and Capulets thwarting innocent love but, rather, a seedy log of sweaty half-hours in the back of a white Ford transit. Told baldly, of course, it lacked even the saving attraction of eroticism and Cooper, like Ruth, found the telling uncomfortable. He did his best to make it easy for her but her embarrassment was contagious and they looked away from each other more often than their eyes met.

It had been going on for six months since the tarmac crew had relaid the drive, and the details of how it began were commonplace. A school full of girls; Dave with an eye for the most likely; she flattered by his obvious admiration, more so when the other girls noticed he only had eyes for her; a wistful regret when the tarmac was done and the crew departed; followed by an apparently chance meeting when she was walking alone; he, streetwise and twenty-eight; she, a lonely seventeen-year-old with dreams of romance. He respected her, he loved her, he'd wait for ever for her, but (how big a word 'but' was in people's lives, thought Cooper) he had her in the back of his transit within a week. If she could forget the squalor of a blanket on a tarpaulin, then she could remember the fun and the excitement. She had crept out of a downstairs window at two o'clock in the morning to be enveloped in her lover's arms. They had smoked and drunk and talked by candlelight in the privacy of the parked van and, yes, all right, he wasn't particularly well educated or even very articulate, but that didn't matter. And if what happened afterwards had not been part of her gameplan, then that didn't matter either because, when it came to it (her eyes belied the words) she had wanted sex as much as he had.

Cooper longed to ask her, why? Why she valued herself so cheaply? Why she was the only girl in the school who fell for it? Why she would want a relationship with an illiterate labourer? Why, ultimately, she was so gullible as to imagine that he wanted anything more than free sex with a clean virgin? He didn't ask, of course. He wasn't so cruel.

The affair might have ended there had she not met him by sheer mischance (Cooper's interpretation, not hers) one day during the holidays. She had heard nothing from him since the night in the van, and hope had given way to depression. She was spending Easter with her grandmother at Fontwell (she usually went to Fontwell, she told Cooper, because she got on better with her grandmother), and caught the bus to Bournemouth to go shopping. And suddenly there was Dave, and he was so pleased to see her, but angry, too, because she hadn't answered his letter. (Sourly, Cooper imagined the touching scene. What letter? Why, the one that had got lost in the post, of course.) After which they had fallen into each other's arms in the back of the Ford, before Dave had driven her home and realized (Cooper reading between the lines again) that Ruth might be good for a little more than a quick tumble on a blanket when he felt horny.

'He took me everywhere that holidays. It was wonderful. The best time I've ever had.' But she spoke the words flatly, as if even the memory lacked sparkle.

She was too canny to tell her grandmother what she was doing – even in her wildest dreams she didn't think Mathilda would approve of Dave – so, instead, like a two-timing spouse, she invented excuses for her absences.

'And your grandmother believed you?'

'I think her arthritis was really bad about then. I used to say I was going somewhere, but in the evening she'd have forgotten where.'

'Did Dave take you to his home?'

'Once. I didn't like it much.'

'Did he suggest you steal from your grandmother? Or was that your idea?'

'It wasn't like that,' she said unhappily. 'We ran out of money, so I borrowed some from her bag one day.'

'And couldn't pay it back?'

'No.' She fell silent.

'What did you do?'

'There was so much stuff there. Jewellery. Ornaments. Bits of silver. She didn't even like most of it. And she was so mean. She could have given me a better allowance, but she never did.'

'So you stole her things and Dave sold them.'

She didn't answer.

'What happened to Dave's job with the tarmac crew?'

'No work.' She shrugged. 'It's not his fault. He'd work if he could.'

Did she really believe that? 'So you went on stealing from your grandmother through the summer term and the summer holidays?'

'It wasn't stealing. I was going to get it anyway.'

Dave had indoctrinated her well – or was this Ruth herself speaking? 'Except that you didn't.'

'The doctor's no right to it. She's not even related.'

'Dave's address, please, Miss Lascelles.'

'I can't,' she said with genuine fear. 'He'll kill me.'

He was out of patience with her. 'Well, let's face it, it won't be much of a loss whichever way you look at it. Your mother won't grieve for you, and to the rest of society you'll be a statistic. Just another young girl who allowed a man to use and abuse her.' He shook his head contemptuously. 'I think the most depressing aspect of it all is how much money has been wasted on your education.' He looked around the room. 'My kids would have given their eye-teeth to have had your opportunities, but then they're a good deal brighter than you, of course.' He waited for a moment then shut his notebook and stood up with a sigh. 'You're forcing me to do it the hard way, through your headmistress.'

Ruth hugged herself again. 'She doesn't know anything. How could she?'

'She'll know the name of the firm that was employed to do the drive. I'll track him down that way.'

She wiped her damp nose on her sleeve. 'But, you don't understand, I have to get to university.'

'Why?' he demanded. 'So that you and your boyfriend can have a field day with gullible students? What does he deal in? Drugs?'

Tears flowed freely down her cheeks. 'I don't know how else to get away from him. I've told him I'm going to Exeter, but I'm not, I'm trying for universities in the north because they're the farthest away.'

Cooper was strangely moved. It occurred to him that this was very likely true. She did see running away as the only option open to her. He wondered what Dave had done to make her so afraid of him. Grown impatient, perhaps, and killed Mrs Gillespie to hasten Ruth's inheritance? He resumed his seat. 'You never knew your father, of course. I suppose it's natural you should have looked for someone to take his place. But university isn't going to solve anything, Miss Lascelles. You may have a term or two of peace before Dave finds you, but no more. How did you plan to keep it a secret? Were you going to tell the school that they were never to reveal which university you'd gone to? Were you going to tell your mother and your friends the same thing? Sooner or later there'd be a plausible telephone call and someone would oblige with the information.'

She seemed to shrink in front of his eyes. 'Then there's nothing I can do.'

He frowned. 'You can start by telling me where to find him.'

'Are you going to arrest him?'

'For what?'

'Stealing from Granny. You'll have to arrest me, too.'

He shrugged. 'I'll need to talk to your grandmother's executors about that. They may decide to let sleeping dogs lie.'

'Then you're just going to ask him questions about the day Granny died?'

'Yes,' he agreed, assuming it was what she wanted to hear.

She shook her head. 'He does terrible things to me when he's angry.' Her eyes flooded again. 'If you don't put him in prison then I can't tell you where to find him. You just don't understand what he's like. He'll punish me.'

'How?'

But she shook her head again, more violently. 'I can't tell you that.'

'You're protected here.'

'He said he'd come and make a scene in the middle of the school if I ever did anything he didn't like. They'll expel me.'

Cooper was perplexed. 'If you're so worried about expulsion, why did you ever go out and meet him in the first place? You'd have been expelled on the spot if you'd been caught doing that.'

She twisted her fingers in the hem of her jumper. 'I didn't know then how much I wanted to go to university,' she whispered.

151

He nodded. 'There's an old saying about that. You never miss the water till the well runs dry.' He smiled without hostility. 'But all of us take things for granted so you're not alone in that. Try this one: desperate diseases call for desperate remedies. I suggest you make a clean breast of all this to your headmistress, throw yourself on her mercy, so to speak, before she finds out from me or Hughes. She might be sympathetic. You never know.'

'She'll go mad.'

'Do you have a choice?'

'I could kill myself,' she said in a tight little voice.

'It's a very weak spirit,' he said gently, 'that sees cutting off the head as the only solution to a headache.' He slapped his hands against his knees. 'Find a bit of courage, girl. Give me Dave's address and then sort things out with your headmistress.'

Her lip wobbled. 'Will you come with me if I do?'

Oh, good grief, he thought, hadn't he had to hold his own children's hands often enough? 'All right,' he agreed, 'but if she asks me to leave I shall have to. I've no authority here as your guardian, remember.'

'Twenty-three, Palace Road, Bournemouth,' she whispered. 'It was my mother who told you I was a thief, wasn't it?' She sounded desperately forlorn, as if she realized that, for her, there was no one left.

'No,' said Cooper compassionately. 'More's the pity, but your mother hasn't told me anything.'

When Sarah pulled into her driveway later that Friday afternoon, she was greeted by the unexpected sight of Jack's car and Cooper's car nestling side by side against the wall in cosy intimacy. Her first inclination was to turn round and drive away again. She hadn't the stomach for a confrontation with either of them, even less for another baring of her soul in front of Cooper while her husband severed his remaining ties. But second thoughts prevailed. Dammit all – she banged her fist angrily against the steering wheel – it was *her* house. She was buggered if she was going to drive around for hours just to avoid her scumbag of a husband and a pompous policeman.

Quietly, she let herself in through the front door, half-thinking that if she tiptoed past the studio, she could possess herself of the kitchen before they knew she was there. As her mother had once said, slamming the kitchen door on Sarah's father: 'An Englishman's home may be his castle, but an Englishwoman's kitchen is where he eats his humble pie.' The sound of voices drifted down the corridor, however, and she knew they had possessed it before her. With a sigh, she fastened her dignity about her like armour plating, and advanced.

Jack, DS Cooper and Ruth Lascelles looked up from their glasses of wine with differing shades of alarm and embarrassment colouring their faces.

'Hi,' said Sarah into the silence. 'You found the '83 Cheval Blanc with no trouble then.'

'Have some,' said Jack, reaching for a clean glass off the draining board. 'It's good.'

'It should be,' she said. 'It's a St Emilion, Premier Grand Cru Classé, and it cost me a small fortune when I laid it down.'

'Don't be so stuffy, woman. You've got to try them from time to time, otherwise you'll end up with a collector's item that's totally undrinkable.' He filled the glass and pushed it across the table, his eyes bright with mischief. She felt a surge of affection for the randy bastard – love, she thought, was the most stubborn of all the diseases – but hid it under a ferocious glare. 'The consensus view amongst the three of us,' he went on cheerfully, 'is dark ruby colour, brilliant legs, and a very exotic nose – curranty fruit, cigar box and hints of herbs and spices.'

'It's a vintage wine, you moron. It's supposed to be savoured and appreciated, not drunk at five o'clock in the afternoon round the kitchen table. I bet you didn't let it breathe. I bet you just poured it out like Lucozade.'

Cooper cleared his throat. 'I'm sorry, Dr Blakeney. We did say we'd be happier with tea.'

'You pusillanimous rat,' said Jack with imperturbable good humour. 'You drooled when I waved the bottle under your nose. Well, come on, old thing, you might as well try it. We're all dying for second helpings but we thought it would be tactful to wait till you arrived before we opened another one.'

'Your life expectancy would be nil if you had,' she said, dropping her handbag and shrugging her coat to the floor. 'All right. Give it here, but I can tell you now it won't be drinkable. It needs another three years at least.' She sat in the vacant chair and drew the glass towards her, covering it with one hand and swirling it gently to release the bouquet. She sniffed appreciatively. 'Who smelt cigar boxes?'

'I did,' said Cooper nervously.

'That's good. The book says the bouquet should be smoky oak and cedar. Curranty fruit?'

Cooper indicated himself again. 'Me.'

'Have you done this before?' He shook his head. 'You should take it up. You've obviously got a nose for it.'

'Ruth and I sussed the herbs and spices,' said Jack. 'What's the verdict?'

Sarah took a sip and let the flavours play across her tongue. 'Spectacular,' she said finally, 'but you're bloody well not opening another bottle. The book says another three years, and I'm going by the book. You can use the wine box for refills. What are you all doing here anyway?' Her eyes rested on Ruth. 'Shouldn't you be at school?'

There was an uncomfortable silence.

'Ruth's been expelled,' said Jack. 'We're all wondering if she can live here with you and me until something more permanent is sorted out.'

Sarah took another sip of her wine and eyed him thoughtfully. 'You and me?' she queried silkily. 'Does that mean you intend to inflict your company on me again?'

The dark face softened. 'That rather depends, my angel.'

'On whether or not I'm prepared to have you back?'

'No. On whether I come back on my terms or your terms.'

'My terms,' she said bluntly, 'or not at all.'

He gave a ghost of a smile. 'Shame,' he murmured.

Sarah held his gaze for a moment, then transferred her attention to Ruth. 'So why were you expelled?'

Ruth, who had been staring at her hands since Sarah came in, flicked a sideways glance at Cooper. 'The Sergeant knows. He can tell you.'

'I'd rather hear it from you.'

'I broke the school rules.' She resumed her study of her hands.

'All of them or one in particular?'

'Leaving school without permission.'

'Times haven't changed then. A friend of mine was expelled for sneaking down the fire escape and talking to some boys at the bottom of it. She was only caught because the rest of us were hanging out of the windows giggling. We were making such a row the housemistress heard us and expelled her on the spot. She's a barrister now. Rather a good one, too.'

'I've been sleeping with someone,' Ruth whispered, 'and the headmistress said I was a bad influence on the others. She said I was immoral.'

Sarah raised enquiring eyebrows at Cooper, who nodded. 'Ah, well, perhaps times have changed, after all,' she said matter-of-factly. 'I can't imagine any of us having the courage to do anything so daring, not after we'd had it firmly dinned into us that a prospective husband could always tell if a girl wasn't a virgin.' She gave a throaty chuckle. 'We knew a great deal about love bites and the bruising effects of frantic French kissing, and absolutely nothing about anything else. We were convinced we'd turn green or break out in pustules if we let a man loose below the neckline. It came as something of a shock to discover we'd been sold a lie.' She took another sip of her wine. 'Was it worth getting expelled for?'

'No.' A tear ran down the girl's face and on to the table. 'I don't know what to do. I want to go to university.'

'Surely the most sensible thing would be to go back to Cedar House and your mother. She'll have to find you another school.' Why had Cooper brought her here anyway? *Or was it Jack who'd brought her?*

Cooper rumbled into life. 'Her boyfriend's liable to cut up rough, once I've had a word with him, and Cedar House will be the first place he goes looking. It's an imposition, I know, but off-hand I couldn't think of anywhere else, not after the way the school dealt with her.' He looked quite put out. 'She was told to pack a suitcase while they ordered a taxi to take her home, so I said, forget the taxi, I'll take her. I've never seen the like of it. You'd think she'd committed a hanging offence the way they carried on. And the worst of it was, they wouldn't have known anything about it if I hadn't persuaded her to tell them herself. I feel responsible, I really do, but then I thought they'd give her some credit for being honest and let her off with a caution. It's what I would have done.'

'Does your mother know?' Sarah asked Ruth.

'Jack let me phone.'

'Is she happy about you staying here?'

'I don't know. All she said was she'd heard from Miss Harris and then hung up. She sounded furious.' Ruth kept her head down and dabbed at her eyes with a handkerchief.

Sarah made a wry face at Jack. 'You'll have to be the one to tell her then. I'm not exactly flavour of the month at the moment, and I can't see her being very pleased about it.'

'I've already tried. She hung up on me, too.'

It was on the tip of Sarah's tongue to ask why, before she thought better of it. Knowing Jack, the answer would be as teasingly illusive as the answer to life itself. What puzzled her more was the speed with which events, like the ball in a pinball machine, had taken such an unpredictable course. This morning she'd had only another solitary weekend to look forward to – *and now*? 'Well, someone's got to tell her,' she said irritably, isolating the one fact she could get to grips with. She looked at the Sergeant. 'You'll have to do it. I'm quite happy for Ruth to stay but only if her mother knows where she is.'

Cooper looked wretched. 'Perhaps it would be better if we involved social services,' he suggested, 'asked a third party to intercede, as it were.'

Sarah's eyes narrowed. 'I'm an extremely amenable woman on the whole but I do resent my good nature being taken advantage of. There is no such thing as a free lunch, Sergeant, and I'd like to remind you that you have just drunk some very expensive St Emilion of mine which, at a conservative estimate and allowing for inflation, costs well over seven pounds per glass. In other words, you owe me one, so you will not shuffle your responsibility and this child's future on to some overworked and underpaid social worker whose only solution to the problem will be to place her in a hostel full of disturbed adolescents.'

Cooper's wretchedness grew.

'You have also, by underestimating the old-fashioned ethics that still exist within girls' boarding schools, caused a young woman approaching the most important exams of her life to be expelled. Now, in a world where the renting out of a woman's womb is still the only reliable method that men have discovered to replicate themselves, the very least they can do in return is to allow their women enough education to make the life sentence of child-rearing endurable. To sit and stare at an empty wall is one thing; to have the inner resources, the knowledge and the confidence to turn that wall into a source of endless stimulation is another. And that's ignoring the positive influence that educated and intelligent women have on succeeding generations. Ruth wants to go to university. To do so, she must pass her A levels. It is imperative that Joanna finds another school to accept her PDQ. Which means someone' – she cocked her finger at him – 'namely *you*, must explain to her that Ruth is here, that she is here for a good reason, and that Joanna must come and talk it through before Ruth loses her opportunity to take her education as far as it can go.' She turned her gaze on the girl. 'And if you dare tell me now, Ruth, that you've given up on your future, then I'll put you through the first mangle I can find and, I promise you, the experience will not be a pleasant one.'

There was a long silence.

Finally, Jack stirred. 'Now you begin to see what Sarah's terms consist of. There's no allowing for human frailty. I grant you, there are pages of subtext and small print dealing with the awful imperfections that most of us suffer from – namely, inadequacy, lack of confidence, seeing both sides and sitting on fences – but they are grey areas which she treats with insufferable patience. And, take it from me, you allow her to do that at your peril. It undermines what little self-respect you have left.' He beamed fondly at Cooper. 'I sympathize with you, old son, but Sarah's right as usual. Someone's got to talk to Joanna and you're the one who's run up the most debts. After all, you *did* get Ruth expelled and you *did* drink a glass of wine that cost over seven quid.'

Cooper shook his head. 'I hope Miss Lascelles can put up with the pair of you. I know I couldn't. You'd have me climbing the walls before you could say knife.'

The 'pair' wasn't lost on Sarah. 'How come you know so much more about my domestic arrangements than I do, Sergeant?' she asked casually.

He chuckled amiably, pushing himself to his feet. 'Because I never say never, Doctor.' He winked at her. 'As someone once told me, life's a bugger. It creeps up behind you and gets you where you least expect it every time.'

Sarah felt the girl start to tremble as she pushed open the door of the spare room and switched on the light. 'What's the matter?' she asked.

'It's downstairs,' she blurted out. 'If Dave comes, he could get in.'

'Not my choice. Geoffrey Freeling's. He turned the house upside down so that the reception rooms would have the best views. We're slowly turning it back again, but it takes time.' She pushed open a communicating door. 'It has its own bathroom.' She glanced back at the girl, saw the pinched look to her face. 'You're frightened, aren't you? Would you rather sleep upstairs in my room?'

Ruth burst into tears. 'I'm so sorry,' she wept. 'I don't know what to do. Dave will kill me. I was all right at school. He couldn't have got in there.'

Sarah put her arms about the other's thin shoulders and clasped them tightly. 'Come upstairs,' she said gently. 'You'll be safe with me. Jack can sleep in here.'

And serve the bastard right, she thought. *Ho, ho! For once, sod's law was on the side of the angels.* She had been toying with the ethics of medical castration but was prepared to compromise on a cold bed and a grovelling apology. It was a very partial compromise. She was so damn glad to have him back she felt like doing handsprings.

Joanna moved to the flat in London last week and for the first time since her abortive attempt at marriage I am in sole possession of Cedar House. It is a victory of sorts, but I have a sense of anticlimax. The game, I fear, was not worth the candle. I am lonely.

It occurs to me that in some strange way Joanna and I are necessary to each other. There is no denying the understanding that exists between us. We do not get along, of course, but that is largely irrelevant in view of the fact that we don't get along with anyone else either. There was some comfort in treading the mill of clichéed insults that trundled us quite happily through our lives, so worn and over-used that what we said to each other passed largely unnoticed. I miss the little things. The way she pursued Spede about the garden, taking the wretched man to task if he missed a weed. Her waspish remarks about my cooking. And oddly enough, as they always used to irritate me at the time, her long, long silences. After all, perhaps companionship is less to do with conversation than with the comfort of another human presence, however self-centred that presence might be.

I have a terrible fear that, by pushing her out to fend for herself, I have diminished us both. At least, while we were together, we checked each other's worst excesses. And now? The road to hell is paved with good intentions . . .

Eleven

IT WASN'T UNTIL late the following afternoon, a Saturday, that Sergeant Cooper felt he had enough information on Dave Hughes to make an approach viable. He was pessimistic about bringing charges of theft, but in respect of Mathilda's death there was some room for optimism. Ruth's mention of a white Ford transit had rung bells in his memory and a careful sifting of the statements taken in and around Fontwell in the days after the body was found had produced a gem. When asked if he'd seen anything unusual the previous Saturday, the landlord of the Three Pigeons, Mr Henry Peel, had said:

> I can't swear it had anything to do with Mrs Gillespie, but there was a white Ford transit parked on my forecourt that Saturday afternoon and evening. Had a young lad in it, as far as I could judge. Stayed ten minutes the first time then drove off towards the church and picked someone up. I saw it again that evening. I pointed it out to my wife and said some wretch was using our forecourt but not using the pub. I can't give you the registration number.

Underneath in a PC's handwriting was a short note:

> Mrs Peel disagrees. She says her husband is confusing this with another occasion when white vans were there twice in one day, but her recollection is that the vans were different. Three of our regulars drive white vans, she said.

Cooper talked the problem through with his Detective Chief Inspector. 'I need to question Hughes, Charlie, so do I take a team with me, or what? According to the girl, he's living in a squat, so he won't be alone, and I don't fancy trying to winkle him out from

161

under a mob of squatters. Assuming they let me in at all. It's bloody rich, isn't it?' he grumbled. 'Somebody else's property and they can take it over lock, stock and barrel. The only way the poor sod who owns it can get it back is to pay through the nose for an eviction order, by which time he finds they've turned the place into a cess-pit.'

Charlie Jones's squashed face wore a permanently lugubrious expression which always reminded Cooper of a sad-eyed Pekinese. He was more of a terrier, however, who, once he got his teeth into something, rarely let go. 'Can we charge him with theft on what Miss Lascelles has told you?'

'We could, but he'd be out again in a couple of hours. Bourne-mouth have him on file. He's been brought in three times and he's walked on each occasion. All similar offences to this one, i.e. persuading youngsters to steal for him. It's a clever scam.' He sounded frustrated. 'The children only prey off their families and, so far, the parents have refused to co-operate when they discover that Hughes's prosecution will involve their daughters in a prosecution, too.'

'So how come he was brought in in the first place?'

'Because three indignant fathers have independently accused him of forcing their daughters to steal and demanded that charges be brought. But when the girls were questioned, they told a different story, denied the coercion and insisted that the thieving was their own idea. It's a real honey, this one. You can't do him without the daughters, and the fathers won't have the daughters done.' He smiled cynically. 'Too much unpleasant publicity.'

'What sort of backgrounds?'

'Middle class, wealthy. The girls are all over sixteen, so no question of under-age sex. Mind, I'm sure these three and Miss Lascelles are only the tip of a very large iceberg. It sounds to me as if he's got the whole thing down to a very fine art.'

'*Does* he coerce them?'

Cooper shrugged. 'All Miss Lascelles said was, he does terrible things when he's angry. He threatened to make a scene at the school if she did anything he didn't like, but when I asked her about it in the car on the way to Dr Blakeney's, in other words after that particular threat had lost its sting because she'd already been expelled, she clammed up and burst into tears.' He tugged his nose thoughtfully. 'He must be using some form of coercion because she's terrified he's going to find her. I wondered if he makes videos of them but when I asked Bournemouth if they've found any equipment on him, they said no. Your guess is as good as mine, Charlie. He's got some hold on these girls, and it must be fear because they're desperate to get shot of him the minute they're found out. But precisely what's involved, I don't know.'

The Inspector frowned. 'Why aren't they afraid to name him?'

'Presumably because he's given them permission to shop him if they're caught. Look, he must know how easy it would be for us to track him down. If Miss Lascelles hadn't proffered the information, all I had to do was ask the headmistress for the tarmac firm and take it from there. I think his MO goes something like this: target a girl who's young enough and cosseted enough to warrant her parents' protection, win her over, then use some sort of threat to make sure she accuses herself along with him when she's caught. That way he's as sure as he can be that charges won't be brought and, if they are, he'll take her down with him. Perhaps his threat is as simple as that.'

The Inspector was doubtful. 'He can't make much out of it. How long before the parents notice what's going on?'

'You'd be amazed. One of the girls was borrowing her mother's credit card for months before the father queried the amount his wife was spending. It was a jointly held card, the balance was paid off automatically out of the current account, and neither of them noticed that it had increased by upwards of five hundred pounds a month. Or if they did, they assumed the other partner's expenditure was behind it. It's a different world, Charlie. Both parents working and earning a good screw, and enough money sloshing around in the coffers to obscure their daughter's thieving. Once they started looking into it, of course, they discovered she'd sold bits of silver, jewellery that her mother never wore, some valuable first editions of her father's and a five-hundred-pound camera that her father thought he'd left on a train. I'd say Hughes is doing very nicely out of it, particularly if he's running more than one of them at the same time.'

'Good grief! How much has Ruth Lascelles stolen then?'

Cooper took a piece of paper from his pocket. 'She made a list of what she could remember. That's it.' He put it on the desk. 'Same pattern as the other girl. Jewellery that her grandmother had forgotten about. Silver-backed hairbrushes from the spare room that were never used. China ornaments and bowls that were kept in cupboards because Mrs Gillespie didn't like them, and some first editions out of the library. She said Hughes told her the sort of thing to look for. Valuable bits and pieces that wouldn't be missed.'

'What about money?'

'Twenty pounds from her grandmother's handbag, fifty pounds from the bedside table and, a few weeks later, five hundred out of the old lady's account. Went to the bank as cool as cucumber with a forged cheque and a letter purporting to come from Mathilda, instructing them to hand over the loot. According to her, Mrs Gillespie never even noticed. But she did, of course, because she mentioned the fifty-pound theft to Jack Blakeney and, when I tackled her bank this morning, they told me she had queried the five-hundred-pound withdrawal on her statement, and they advised her that Ruth had drawn it out on her instructions.' He scratched his jaw. 'According to them, she agreed that it was her mistake and took no further action.'

'What date was that?'

Cooper consulted his notes again. 'The cheque was cashed during the last week in October, Ruth's half-term in other words, and Mrs Gillespie rang the bank as soon as she got the statement, which was the first week in November.'

'Not long before she died then, and *after* she'd made up her mind to change the will. It's a bugger that one. I can't get the hang of it at all.' He thought for a moment. 'When did Ruth steal the fifty pounds?'

'At the beginning of September before she went back to school. She had some idea apparently of buying Hughes off. She said: "I thought he'd leave me alone if I gave him some money."'

'Dear God!' said Charlie dismally. 'There's one born every minute. Did you ask her if Hughes put pressure on her to cash the five hundred at half-term?'

'I did. Her answer was: "No, no, no. I stole it because I wanted to," and then she turned the waterworks on again.' He looked very rueful. 'I've left the ball in Dr Blakeney's court. I had a word with her on the phone this morning, gave her the gist of what Hughes has been up to and asked her to try and find out why none of the girls will turn QE against him. She may get somewhere but I'm not counting on it.'

'What about the mother? Would Ruth talk to her?'

Cooper shook his head. 'First, you'd have to get *her* to talk to Ruth. It's unnatural, if you ask me. I stopped off last night to tell her the Blakeneys had taken her daughter in and she looked at me as if I'd just climbed out of a sewer. The only thing she was interested in was whether I thought Ruth's expulsion meant she'd killed her grandmother. I said, no, that as far as I knew there were no statistics linking truancy and promiscuous sex to murder, but there were a great number linking them to poor parenting. So she told me to eff off.' He chuckled happily at the memory.

Charlie Jones grunted his amusement. 'I'm more interested in friend Hughes at the moment, so let's break this down into manageable proportions. Have Bournemouth tried getting the three families together so that the girls gain strength from numbers?'

'Twice. No go either time. The parents have taken legal advice and no one's talking.'

Charlie pursed his lips in thought. 'It's been done before, you know. George Joseph Smith did it a hundred years ago. Wrote glowing references for pretty servant girls, then found them placements in wealthy households. Within weeks of starting work they would steal valuables from their employers and take them faithfully to George to convert into ready cash. He was another one with an extraordinary pulling-power over women.'

'George Smith?' said Cooper in surprise. 'I thought he did *away* with women. Wasn't he the brides-in-the-bath murderer?'

'That's him. Started drowning wives when he discovered how easy it was to get them to make wills in his favour upon marriage. Interesting, isn't it, in view of the way Mrs Gillespie died.' He was silent for a moment. 'I read a book about Smith not so long ago. The author described him as a professional and a literal lady-killer. I wonder if the same thing applies to Hughes.' He rapped a tattoo on his desk-top with his knuckles. 'Let's pull him in for questioning.'

'How? Do I take an arrest warrant?'

Charlie reached for his phone. 'No. I'll get Bournemouth to pick him up tomorrow morning and hold him on ice till you and I get there.'

'Tomorrow's Sunday, Charlie.'

'Then with any luck he'll have a hangover. I want to see his expression when I tell him we have reason to believe he murdered Mrs Gillespie.'

Cooper was sceptical. 'Have we? The landlord's statement won't stand close scrutiny, not if his wife's claiming he was confused.'

A wolfish grin spread across the Inspector's features, and the sad Pekinese became a Dobermann. 'But we know he was there that afternoon because Ruth told us he was, and I'm inclined to be a little creative with the rest. He was using Mrs Gillespie's granddaughter to extort money. He has a history of ruthless exploitation of women, and he's probably feeding a habit because his outgoings far exceed his income. If they didn't, he wouldn't have to live in squats. I'd say his psychological profile runs something like this: a dangerously unstable, psychopathic addict, whose hatred of women has undergone a dramatic change recently and taken him from their brutal manipulation to their destruction. He will be the product of a broken home and inadequate education, and boyhood fear of his father will govern most of his actions.'

Cooper looked even more sceptical. 'You've been reading too many books, Charlie.'

Jones allowed himself a laugh. 'But Hughes doesn't know that, does he? So let's try and dent his charisma a little and see if we can't stop him using other people's little girls to do his dirty work.'

'I'm trying to solve a murder,' said Cooper in protest. 'That's what I want answers on.'

'But you've still to convince me it *was* a murder, old son.'

Ruth crept stealthily down the stairs and stood to one side of the studio doorway, watching Jack's reflection in her tiny hand mirror. Not that she could see him very well. He was sitting with his back to the window, working on a portrait but, because the easel was placed directly between him and the door, the canvas obscured all but his legs. From the bedroom window she had watched Sarah leave the house two hours ago, so she knew they were alone. *Would Jack notice when she slipped past the doorway?* She waited for ten minutes in panicky indecision, too afraid to take a step.

'If you want something to eat,' he murmured finally into the silence, 'then I suggest you try the kitchen. If you want someone to talk to, then I suggest you come in here, and if you're looking for something to steal, then I suggest you take Sarah's engagement ring which belonged to my grandmother and was valued at two thousand pounds four years ago. You'll find it in the left-hand drawer of her dressing-table.' He leaned to one side so that she could see his face in her mirror. 'You might as well show yourself. I'm not going to eat you.' He nodded curtly as she came round the doorjamb. 'Sarah gave me strict instructions to be sympathetic, patient and helpful. I'll do my best, but I warn you in advance I can't stand people who sniff into handkerchiefs and creep about on tiptoe.'

Ruth's cheeks lost what little colour they had left. 'Do you think it would be all right if I made myself a cup of coffee?' She looked very unattractive, damp hair clinging to her scalp, face puffy and blotched with crying. 'I don't want to be a nuisance.'

Jack returned to his painting so that she wouldn't see the flash of irritation in his eyes. Self-pity in others invariably brought out the worst in him. 'As long as you make me one, too. Black and no sugar, please. The coffee's by the kettle, sugar's in the tin marked "sugar", milk's in the fridge and lunch is in the oven. It will be ready in half an hour so, unless you're starving, my advice is to skip breakfast and wait for that.'

'Will Dr Blakeney be here for lunch?'

'I doubt it. Polly Graham's gone into labour and as Sarah agreed to a home-birth, she could be there for hours.'

Ruth hovered for a moment, then turned to go to the kitchen, only to change her mind again. 'Has my mother phoned?' she blurted out.

'Did you expect her to?'

'I thought—' She fell silent.

'Well, try thinking about making me a cup of coffee instead. If you hadn't mentioned it, I probably wouldn't have wanted one, but as you have, I do. So get your skates on, woman. This is not a hotel and I'm not in the best of moods after being relegated to the spare room.'

She fled down the corridor to the kitchen and, when she returned five minutes later with a tray and two cups, her hands were shaking so much that the cups chattered against each other like terrified teeth. Jack appeared not to notice but took the tray and placed it on a table in the window. 'Sit,' he instructed, pointing to a hard-backed chair and swinging his stool round to face her. 'Now, is it me you're frightened of, the boyfriend, men in general, Sarah not coming home for lunch, the police, or are you worried about what's going to happen to you?'

She shrank away from him as if he'd struck her.

'Me then.' He moved the stool back a yard to give her more room. 'Why are you afraid of me, Ruth?'

Her hands fluttered in her lap. 'I'm – you—' Her eyes widened in terror. 'I'm not.'

'You feel completely secure and at ease in my presence?'

'Yes,' she whispered.

'You have an odd way of showing it.' He reached for his coffee cup. 'How old were you when your father died?'

'I was a baby.'

'Since which time you've lived with your mother and your grandmother and, latterly, a bevy of women at boarding school.' He took a sip of coffee. 'Am I right that this Hughes character is the first boyfriend you've ever had?'

She nodded.

'So he's your only experience of men?'

She stared at her hands.

'Yes or no?' he demanded, the words whipping out impatiently.

'Yes,' she whispered again.

'Then you obviously require lessons on the male of the species. There are only three things to remember. One: most men need to be told what to do by women. Even sex improves when women take the trouble to point the man in the right direction. Two: compared with women, most men are inadequate. They are less perceptive, have little or no intuition, are poorer judges of character and, therefore, more vulnerable to criticism. They find aggression immensely intimidating because they're not supposed to and, in short, are by far the more sensitive of the two sexes. Three: any man who does not conform to this pattern should be avoided. He will be a swaggering, uneducated brute whose intellect will be so small that the only way he can give himself a modicum of authority is by demeaning anyone who's foolish enough to put up with him, and, finally, he will lack the one thing that all decent men have in abundance, namely a deep and abiding admiration for women.' He picked up her coffee cup and held it under her nose so that she had to take it. 'Now I don't pretend to be a paragon, but I'm certainly not a brute, and between you, me and the gatepost, I am extremely fond of my irascible wife. I accept that what I did was open to interpretation, but you can take it from me that I went to Cedar House for one reason only and that was simply to paint your mother. The temptation to capture two generations of one family was irresistible.' He eyed her speculatively. Almost as irresistible, he was thinking, as the temptation to capture the third generation. 'And if my much-put-upon wife hadn't chosen that precise moment to expel me, well,' he shrugged, 'I wouldn't have had to freeze on your mother's summer-house floor. Does all that set your mind at rest or are you going to go on quaking like a great jelly every time you see me?'

She stared at him with stricken eyes. She was beautiful after all, he thought, but it was a tragic beauty. Like her mother's. Like Mathilda's.

'I'm pregnant,' she said finally, exhausted tears seeping on to her cheeks.

There was a moment of silence.

'I thought – I hoped – my mother—' She dashed at her eyes with a sodden tissue. 'I don't know what – I ought to go – I shouldn't have told you.'

Somewhere in the recesses of his heart, Jack blushed for himself. Was the self-pity of a child under intolerable stress so despicable that he had to savage it? He reached across and took her hand, drawing her off the chair and into his arms, holding her tight and stroking her hair as her father would have done had he lived. He let her weep for a long time before he spoke. 'Your grandmother once said to me that mankind was doomed unless he learnt to communicate. She was a wise old lady. We talk a lot but we rarely communicate.' He eased her off his chest and held her at arm's length so that he could look at her. 'I'm glad you told me. I feel rather privileged that you felt you could. Most people would have waited until Sarah came home.'

'I was going—'

He stopped her with a chuckle and released her back on to her chair. 'Let me hang on to my illusions. Let me believe just once that someone thought I could be as easy to confide in as Sarah. It's not true, of course. There is no one in the world who can listen as well as my wife, or who can impart such sound advice. She'll look after you, I promise.'

Ruth blew her nose. 'She'll be angry with me.'

'Do you think so?'

'You said she's irascible.'

'She is. It's not so frightening. You just keep your head down till the saucepans stop flying.'

She dabbed frantically at her eyes. 'Saucepans? Does she—'

'No,' he said firmly. 'It was a figure of speech. Sarah's a nice person. She brings home wounded pigeons, splints their wings, and watches them die in slow and terrible agony with an expression of enormous sympathy on her face. It's one of the things they teach them at medical school.'

She looked alarmed. 'That's awful.'

'It was a joke,' he said ruefully. 'Sarah is the most sensible doctor I know. She will help you reach a decision about what you want to do and then take it from there. She won't force you to have the baby, and she won't force you not to have it.'

The tears welled again. 'I don't want it.' She clenched her hands in her lap. 'Is that wrong, do you think?'

'No,' he said honestly. 'If I were in your shoes, I wouldn't want it either.'

'But I made it. It was my fault.'

'It takes two to make babies, Ruth, and I can't see your boyfriend showing much enthusiasm when it's fully-fledged and bawling its head off. It's your choice, not his. Sperm comes two-a-penny and most of it gets washed down the sink. Wombs and their foetuses come extremely expensive. Sarah's right when she says it's a life sentence.'

'But isn't it alive? Won't I be murdering it?'

He was a man. How could he begin to understand the agony that women suffered because a biological accident has given them power over life and death? He could only be honest with her. 'I don't know, but I'd say it's only alive at the moment because you're alive. It has no existence as an individual in its own right.'

'But it could have – if I let it.'

'Of course. But on that basis every egg that any woman produces and every sperm that any man produces has the potential for life, and no one accuses young men of being murderers every time they spill their seed on the ground behind the bike sheds. I think for each of us our own life has priority over the potential life that exists inside us. I don't for a moment pretend that it's an easy decision, or even a black and white one, but I do believe that you are more important at this moment than a life that can only come into being if you are prepared to pay for it, emotionally, physically, socially and financially. And you'll bear that cost alone, Ruth, because the likelihood of Hughes paying anything is virtually nil.'

'He'll say it isn't his anyway.'

Jack nodded. 'Some men do, I'm afraid. It's so easy for them. It's not their body that's been caught.'

She hid her face in her hands. 'You don't understand.' She wrapped her arms around her head. *To protect herself? To hide herself?* 'It might be one of the others'. You see I had to – he made me – Oh, God – I wish—' She didn't go on, only curled herself into a tight ball and sobbed.

Jack felt completely helpless. Her anguish was so strong that it washed over him in swamping waves. He could think only in platitudes – *there's nothing so bad that it might not be worse . . . it's always darkest before the dawn* – but what use were platitudes to a girl whose life lay in tatters before her? He put out an awkward hand and placed it on her head. It was an instinctive gesture of comfort, an echo of a priestly benediction. 'Tell me what happened,' he said. 'Perhaps it's not as bad as you think.'

But it was. What she told him in tones of abject terror rocked the foundations of his own humanity. So shocked was he that he felt physically sick.

Sarah found him in the garden when she came home at three thirty after helping to deliver Polly Graham of a healthy baby daughter. He was forking industriously round some roses and scattering handfuls of fertilizer about the roots. 'It's almost December,' she said. 'Everything's dormant. You're wasting your time.'

'I know.' He looked up and she thought she saw traces of tears in his eyes. 'I just needed to do something active.'

'Where's Ruth?'

'Asleep. She had a headache so I gave her some codeine and packed her off to bed.' He brushed the hair from his forehead with the back of a muddy hand. 'Have you finished for the day?'

She nodded. 'What's happened?'

He leant on the fork and stared across the fields. The slowly fading light gave a misty quality to a landscape in which cows grazed and trees, shorn of their leaves, fingered the sky with dark filigree lacework. 'That's the England men and women die for,' he said gruffly.

She followed his gaze with a small frown creasing her forehead.

Tears glistened on his lashes. 'Do you know that poem by Rupert Brooke? "The Soldier". The one that goes:

> 'If I should die, think only this of me:
> That there's some corner of a foreign field
> That is for ever England. There shall be
> In that rich earth a richer dust concealed;
> A dust whom England bore, shaped, made aware . . .'

He fell silent. When he spoke again, his voice shook. 'It's beautiful, isn't it, Sarah? England *is* beautiful.'

She wiped the tears from his face. 'You're crying,' she said, her heart aching for him. 'I've never seen you cry before. What's happened, Jack?'

He didn't seem to hear her. 'Rupert Brooke died in 1915. A sacrifice of war. He was only twenty-eight, younger than you and me, and he gave his life with all the other millions, whatever country they came from, for the sake of other people's children. And do you know what breaks my heart?' His dark gaze slid away from her, looking into a private hell that only he could see. 'That a man who could write one of the most perfect pieces of poetry about his homeland that has ever been written should have sacrificed himself for the filth that England spawns today.'

'No one's all bad, Jack, and no one's all good. We're just human. The poor kid only wanted to be loved.'

He wiped a weary hand around his jaw. 'I'm not talking about

Ruth, Sarah. I'm talking about the men who attacked her. I'm talking about the animal who taught her obedience by shutting her in a van with a group of low-grade scum who raped her one after the other for five hours to break her spirit.' He stared over the fields again. 'Apparently she objected when Hughes told her to start stealing from Mathilda, said she didn't want to do it. So he locked her in the van with his mates who gave her a graphic demonstration of what was going to happen every time she refused. I've had to give my word that I'm not going to repeat this to anyone except you. She is absolutely terrified they're going to find her and do it again, and when I said we should report it to the police I thought she was going to die on me. Hughes told her that if she was ever caught, all she had to do was say the stealing was her idea. As long as she does that and doesn't mention the rape, he'll leave her alone in the future.' His lips thinned. 'But if she talks, he'll send his goons after her to punish her, and he doesn't care how long he has to wait to do it. Police protection won't save her, marriage won't save her. He'll wait for years if he has to, but for every year her punishment is delayed, he'll add another hour to the final ordeal. She'd have to be a quite extraordinary person to talk to the police with a threat like that hanging over her.'

Sarah was too shocked to respond. 'No wonder she was frightened to sleep downstairs,' she said at last.

'She's hardly slept at all for weeks, as far as I can gather. The only way I could get her to take the codeine was to promise again and again that I wouldn't leave the house. She's paranoid about being caught unawares and she's paranoid about the police asking any more questions.'

'But the Sergeant knows there's something,' Sarah warned him. 'He phoned this morning and asked me to try and find out what it was. His word for it was coercion. Hughes must be using coercion, he said, but we can't do much unless we know what sort of coercion it is. Ruth's not the only one it's happened to. They know of at least three others and they think it's only the tip of the iceberg. None of them talk.'

'She's pregnant,' said Jack flatly. 'I said you'd know what to do. JE-SUS!' He threw the fork like a lance into the middle of the lawn, his bellow of rage roaring into the air. 'I-COULD-KILL-THE-FUCKING-BASTARD!'

Sarah put a hand on his arm to calm him. 'How many weeks is she?'

'I don't know,' he said, rubbing his eyes. 'I didn't ask. I wish to God you'd been here. I did my best but I was so damn useless. She needed a woman to talk to, not a clumsy sod who started out by telling her what nice people men are. I gave her a lecture, for Christ's sake, on male decency.'

She hushed him as his voice started to rise again. 'She wouldn't have talked to you if she hadn't felt comfortable with you. How long's she been asleep?'

He looked at his watch. 'A couple of hours.'

'Okay, we'll leave her a little bit longer, then I'll go and see her.' She linked her arm with his. 'I don't suppose you've eaten.'

'No.'

She drew him towards the house. 'Come on then. Things always look worse on an empty stomach.'

'What are we going to do, Sarah?'

'Whatever's best for Ruth.'

'And to hell with all the other wretched girls who get broken in the future?'

'We can only take one step at a time, Jack.' She looked desperately worried.

'O vile, intolerable, not to be endur'd!' Ruth is crying again and it is driving me mad. I simply cannot bear it. I want to take the wretched child and shake her till her teeth rattle, smack her, hit her, anything to stop this petulant whining. My anger never goes away. Even when she's silent, I find myself waiting for her to begin.

It is so unjust when I went through the same thing with Joanna. If she would only show some interest in her daughter, it wouldn't be so bad, but she does everything she can to avoid her. In desperation this morning, I tried to put the scold's bridle on Ruth's head, but Joanna convulsed at the sight of it. I called Hugh Hendry out again and this time he had the sense to prescribe tranquillizers. He said she was overwrought.

Would to God they had had Valium in my day. As always, I had to cope alone . . .

Twelve

DS COOPER'S CAR had barely drawn to a halt in Mill House driveway later that evening when Jack wrenched open the passenger door and folded himself on to the seat. 'Do me a favour, old son, reverse out slowly with as little noise as possible and drive me a mile or two down the road.' He nodded approval as Cooper eased into gear. 'And next time, phone first, there's a good chap.'

Cooper, apparently unconcerned by this somewhat disrespectful behaviour towards an officer of the law, manoeuvred backwards through the gate, pulling the wheel gently to avoid crunching the gravel. 'Doesn't she trust me?' he asked, changing to first gear and driving off in the direction of Fontwell.

'Not you personally. The police. There's a lay-by about half a mile ahead on the right. Pull in there and I'll walk back.'

'Has she said anything?'

Jack didn't answer and Cooper flicked him a sideways glance. His face looked drawn in the reflected light from the headlamps, but it was too dark to read his expression.

'You're obliged by law to assist the police in their enquiries, Mr Blakeney.'

'It's Jack,' he said. 'What's your name, Sergeant?'

'Just what you'd expect,' said Cooper dryly. 'Thomas. Good old Tommy Cooper.'

Jack's teeth gleamed in a smile. 'Rough.'

'Rough is right. People expect me to be a comedian. Where's this lay-by of yours?'

'A hundred yards or so.' He peered through the windscreen. 'Coming up on your right now.'

177

Cooper drew across the road and brought the car to a halt, placing a restraining hand on Jack's arm as he switched off the engine and killed the lights. 'Five minutes,' he said. 'I really do need to ask you some questions.'

Jack let go of the door handle. 'All right, but I warn you there is very little I can tell you except that Ruth is scared out of her wits and extremely reluctant to have anything more to do with the police.'

'She may not be given a choice. We may decide to prosecute.'

'For what? Stealing from a member of her family who didn't even bother to report the few trinkets that were taken? You can't prosecute Ruth for that, Tommy. And anyway, Sarah as legatee would insist on any charges being dropped. Her position's delicate enough without forcing a criminal record on the child she's effectively disinherited.'

Cooper sighed. 'Call me Cooper,' he said. 'Most people do. Tommy's more of an embarrassment than a name.' He took out a cigarette. 'Why do you call Miss Lascelles a child? She's a young woman, Jack. Seventeen years old and legally responsible for her actions. If she's prosecuted she will be dealt with in an adult court. You really shouldn't allow sentiment to cloud your judgement. We're not talking just trinkets here. She took her grandmother for five hundred pounds a month ago and didn't bat an eyelid while she was doing it. And on the day of the murder she stole some earrings worth two thousand pounds.'

'Did Mathilda report the money stolen?'

'No,' Cooper admitted.

'Then Sarah certainly won't.'

Cooper sighed again. 'I guess you've been talking to a lawyer, told you to keep your mouths shut, I suppose, and never mind what Hughes does to anyone else.' He struck a match and held it to the tip of his cigarette, watching Jack in the flaring light. Anger showed itself in every line of the other man's face, in the aggressive jut of his jaw, in the compressed lips and the narrowed eyes. He seemed to be exercising enormous self-control just to hold himself in. With a flick of his thumbnail Cooper extinguished the match and plunged the car into darkness again. Only the glow of burning tobacco remained. 'Hughes is working to a pattern,' he said. 'I explained as much of it as we have been able to find out to your wife this morning. In essence—'

'She told me,' Jack cut in. 'I know what he's doing.'

'Okay,' said Cooper easily, 'then you'll know how important it is to stop him. There'll be other Ruths, make no mistake about that, and whatever he's doing to these girls to force them to work for him will get more extreme as time goes by. That's the nature of the beast.' He drew on his cigarette. 'He does force them, doesn't he?'

'You're the policeman, Cooper. Arrest the sod and ask him.'

'That's exactly what we're planning to do. Tomorrow. But we'll have a much stronger hand if we know what to ask him *about*. We're stumbling around in the dark at the moment.'

Jack didn't say anything.

'I could get a warrant for Miss Lascelles's arrest and take her down to the station. How would she stand up to the psychological thumbscrews, do you think? You might not have realized it but she's different from the other girls Hughes has used. She doesn't have parents she can rely on to protect her.'

'Sarah and I will do it,' Jack said curtly. 'We're in loco parentis at the moment.'

'But you've no legal standing. We could insist that her mother was present during questioning and if it's of any interest to you the only thing Mrs Lascelles was concerned about last night was whether her daughter's expulsion had anything to do with Mrs Gillespie's murder. She'd break Ruth for us if she thought it would help her get her hands on the old lady's money.'

Jack gave a faint laugh. 'You're all piss and wind, Cooper. You're too damn nice to do anything like that, and we both know it. Take it from me, you'd have it on your conscience for life if you added to the damage that's already been done to that poor kid.'

'It's bad then.'

'I'd say that was a fair assumption, yes.'

'You must tell me, Jack. We won't get anywhere with Hughes if you don't tell me.'

'I can't. I've given my word to Ruth.'

'Break it.'

Jack shook his head. 'No. In my book a word, once given, cannot be taken back.' He thought for a moment. 'There's one thing I could do, though. You deliver him to me and I'll deliver him to you. How does that grab you as an idea?'

Cooper sounded genuinely regretful. 'It's known as aiding and abetting. I'd be kissing goodbye to my pension.'

Jack gave a low laugh. 'Think about it,' he said, reaching for the handle and thrusting open the door. 'It's my best offer.' The smoke from Cooper's cigarette eddied after him as he got out. 'All I need is an address, Tommy. When you're ready, phone it through.' He slammed the door and loped off into the darkness.

Violet Orloff tiptoed into her husband's bedroom and frowned anxiously at him. He was swathed in yards of Paisley dressing-gown and reclined like a fat old Buddha against his pillows, a mug of cocoa in one hand, a cheese sandwich in the other, the *Daily Telegraph* crossword on his knees. 'She's crying again.'

Duncan peered at her over his bifocals. 'It's not our business, dear,' he said firmly.

'But I can *hear* her. She's sobbing her heart out.'

'It's not our business.'

'Except I keep thinking, suppose we'd *done* something when we heard Mathilda crying, would she be dead now? I feel very badly about that, Duncan.'

He sighed. 'I refuse to feel guilty because Mathilda's cruelties to her family, imagined or real, provoked one of them into killing her. There was nothing we could have done to prevent it then, and as you keep reminding me, there is nothing we can do now to bring her back. We have alerted the police to possible motive. I think we should leave it there.'

'But, Duncan,' Violet wailed, 'if we *know* it was Joanna or Ruth, then we must tell the police.'

He frowned. 'Don't be silly, Violet. We don't know who did it, nor, frankly, are we interested. Logic says it had to be someone with a key or someone she trusted enough to let into the house, and the police don't need me to tell them that.' The frown deepened. 'Why do you keep pushing me into meddling, anyway? It's almost as if you want Joanna and Ruth to be arrested.'

'Not *both* of them. They didn't do it together, did they?' She grimaced horribly, screwing her face into an absurd caricature. 'But

Joanna *is* crying again, and I think we should do something. Mathilda always said the house was full of ghosts. Perhaps she's come back.'

Duncan stared at her with open alarm. 'You're not ill, are you?'

'Of course I'm not ill,' she said crossly. 'I think I'll pop round, see if she's all right, talk to her. You never know, she might decide to *confide* in me.' With an arch wave she tiptoed off again, and moments later he heard the sound of the front door opening.

Duncan shook his head in perplexity as he returned to his crossword. *Was* this the beginnings of senility? Violet was either very brave or very foolish to interfere with an emotionally disturbed woman who had, quite clearly, loathed her mother enough to murder her. He could only imagine what Joanna's reaction would be to his wife's naïve assertions that she knew more than she'd told the police. The thought worried him enough to force him out of his warm bed and into his slippers, before padding downstairs in her wake.

But whatever had upset Joanna Lascelles was destined to remain a mystery to the Orloffs that night. She refused to open the door to Violet's ringing and it wasn't until the Sunday at church that they heard rumours about Jack Blakeney returning to his wife and Ruth being so afraid to go home to Cedar House and her mother that she had chosen to live with the Blakeneys. Southcliffe, it was said, had asked her to leave because of the scandal that was about to break around the Lascelles family. This time the furiously wagging tongues centred their suspicion on Joanna.

If Cooper was honest with himself, he could see Dave Hughes's attraction for young middle-class girls. He was a personable 'bit of rough', handsome, tall, with the clean, muscular looks of a Chippendale, dark shoulder-length hair, bright blue eyes and an engaging smile. Unthreatening was the word that leapt immediately to mind, and it was only gradually in the confined atmosphere of a Bournemouth police interview room that the teeth began to show behind the smile. What you saw, Cooper realized, was very professional packaging. What lay beneath the surface was anyone's guess.

Detective Chief Inspector Charlie Jones was another where the packaging obscured the real man. It amused Cooper to see how seriously Hughes underestimated the sad Pekinese face that regarded him with such mild-mannered apology. Charlie took the chair on the other side of the table from Hughes and sifted rather helplessly through his briefcase. 'It was good of you to come in,' he said. 'I realize time's precious. We're grateful for your co-operation, Mr Hughes.'

Hughes shrugged amiably. 'If I'd known I had a choice, I probably wouldn't've come. What's this about then?'

Charlie isolated a piece of crumpled paper and spread it out on the table. 'Miss Ruth Lascelles. She says you're her lover.'

Hughes shrugged again. 'Sure. I know Ruth. She's seventeen. Since when was sex with a seventeen-year-old a crime?'

'It's not.'

'What's the hassle then?'

'Theft. She's been stealing.'

Hughes looked suitably surprised but didn't say anything.

'Did you know she was stealing?'

He shook his head. 'She always told me her granny gave her money. I believed her. The old bitch was rolling in it.'

'Was? You know she's dead then.'

'Sure. Ruth told me she killed herself.'

Charlie ran his finger down the page. 'Ruth says you told her to steal silver-backed hair brushes, jewellery and valuable first editions from Mrs Gillespie's library. Similar items, in fact, to what Miss Julia Sefton claims you told her to steal from her parents. Small bits and pieces that wouldn't be missed but could be disposed of very easily for ready cash. Who sold them, Mr Hughes? You or Ruth?'

'Do me a favour, Inspector. Do I look the sort of mug who'd act as a fence for an over-privileged, middle-class tart who'd drop me in it quick as winking the minute she was rumbled? Jesus,' he said with disgust, 'give me some credit for common sense. They only take up with me because they're bored out of their tiny minds with the jerks their parents approve of. And that should tell you something about the sort of girls they are. They call them slags where I come from, and thieving's in their blood along with the whoring. If Ruth says I set her up to it, then she's lying to get herself off the hook. It's so bloody easy, isn't it? I'm just scum from a frigging squat and she's Miss Lascelles from Southcliffe girls' school. Who's going to believe me?'

Charlie smiled his lugubrious smile. 'Ah, well,' he murmured, 'belief isn't really the issue, is it? We both know you're lying and that Ruth is telling the truth, but the question is can we persuade her to stand up in court and tell the *whole* truth? You made a bad choice there, Mr Hughes. She doesn't have a father, you see, only a mother, and you probably know as well as I do that women are far harder on their daughters than men ever could be. Mrs Lascelles won't protect Ruth the way Julia's father protected *her*. Apart from anything else, she positively loathes the girl. It would have been different, I suspect, if Mrs Gillespie were still alive, she would probably have hushed it up for the sake of the family's reputation, but as she isn't I can't see anybody championing Ruth.'

Hughes grinned. 'Well, go ahead then. Prosecute the thieving little bitch. It's no skin off my nose.'

It was Charlie's turn to look surprised. 'You don't like her?'

'She was okay for the odd screw, no great shakes but okay. Look, I told you, they only make out with me because they want to get back at their folks. So what am I supposed to do? Tug my forelock in gratitude for the use of their very ordinary bodies? I can get as good if not better down the nightclub of a Saturday.' He grinned again, a captivatingly wicked grin, guaranteed to melt female hearts but totally lost on Jones and Cooper. 'I do the business for them, give them their thrills, and I only complain when they try and lay their fucking thieving on me. It really gets up my nose, if you want the truth. You're such bloody suckers, you lot. A pretty face, a posh accent, a sob story, and, bingo, get Dave Hughes down here and give him the works. You just won't accept that they're slags, same as the prozzies on the streets in the red light district.'

Charlie looked thoughtful. 'That's the second time you've called Miss Lascelles a slag. What's your definition of a slag, Mr Hughes?'

'The same as yours, I guess.'

'A vulgar, coarse woman who sells her body for money. I wouldn't say that was a description of Miss Lascelles.'

Hughes looked amused. 'A slag's an easy lay. Ruth was so bloody easy, it was pathetic.'

'You said she was no great shakes as a screw,' Charlie carried on imperturbably. 'That's a very revealing admission, don't you think?'

'Why?'

'It says more about you than it does about her. Didn't she fancy you? Did you have to force her? What is it you like doing that she didn't like you enough to go along with? I find that fascinating.'

'I've had better, that's all I meant.'

'Better what, Mr Hughes?'

'Lovers, for Christ's sake. Women who know what they're doing. Women who handle themselves and me with more fucking finesse. Screwing Ruth was like screwing blancmange. It was me had to do all the work while she just lay there telling me how much she loved me. It pisses me off, that, it really does.'

Charlie frowned. 'Why did you bother with her then?'

Hughes smiled cynically at the all-too-patent trap. 'Why not? She was free, she was available, and I get horny like the next man. Are you going to charge me with doing what comes naturally?'

Charlie thought for a moment or two. 'Did you ever go into Cedar House?'

'The old biddy's place?' He shook his head. 'No way. She'd have done her nut if she'd got wind of who Ruth had hitched herself to. I don't go looking for trouble though you'd be amazed at the girls. Half of them think their parents are going to welcome me with open arms.' He mimicked the clipped diction of the upper classes. 'Mummy, Daddy, I'd like you to meet my new boyfriend, Dave.' The boyish grin again. 'They're so bloody thick, you wouldn't believe.'

'There've been a lot of these girls then. We thought there might have been.'

Hughes tilted his chair back, relaxed, complacent, unbelievably confident. 'I appeal to them, Inspector. It's a talent I have. Don't ask me where it comes from, though, because I couldn't tell you. Perhaps it's the Irish in me.'

'On your mother's side, presumably.'

'How did you guess?'

'You're a type, Mr Hughes. Probably the illegitimate son of a whore who screwed anything for money, if your extreme prejudice against prostitutes is anything to go by. You wouldn't have a clue who your father was because he might have been any one of fifty who shafted her during the week you were conceived. Hence your contempt and hatred for women and your inability to conduct an adult relationship. You had no male role model to learn from or emulate. Tell me,' he murmured, 'does getting it free make you feel superior to the sad, anonymous little man who paid to father you? Is that why it's so important?'

The blue eyes narrowed angrily. 'I don't have to listen to this.'

'I'm afraid you do. You see, I'm very interested in your pathological dislike of women. You can't speak about them without being offensive. That isn't normal, Mr Hughes, and as Sergeant Cooper and I are investigating an extraordinarily abnormal crime, your attitude alarms me. Let me give you a definition of psychopathic personality disorder.' He consulted the piece of paper again. 'It manifests itself in poor or non-existent job performance, persistent criminality, sexual promiscuity and aggressive sexual behaviour. People with this disorder are irresponsible and extremely callous; they feel no guilt over their antisocial acts and find it difficult to make lasting relationships.' He looked up. 'Rather a good description of you, don't you think? Have you ever been treated for this type of disorder?'

'No, I fucking well haven't,' he said furiously. 'Jesus, what is this garbage, anyway? Since when was thieving an abnormal crime?'

'We're not talking about thieving.'

Hughes looked suddenly wary. 'What are we talking about then?'

'The things you do to the girls.'

'I don't get you.'

Charlie leaned forward aggressively, his eyes like flints. 'Oh, yes, you do, you filthy little nonce. You're a pervert, Hughes, and when you go down and the rest of the prisoners find out what you've been banged up for, you'll learn what it's like to be on the receiving end of aggressive behaviour. They'll beat the shit out of you, urinate on your food and use a razor on you if they can get you in the shower alone. It's one of the oddities of prison life. Ordinary prisoners hate sex offenders, particularly sex offenders who can only get a hard-on with children. Whatever they've done themselves pales into insignificance beside what you and people like you do to defenceless kids.'

'Jesus! I don't do kids. I hate bloody kids.'

'Julia Sefton had just turned sixteen when you did her. She could almost have been your daughter.'

185

'That's not a crime. I'm not the first man who's slept with someone young enough to be his daughter. Get real, Inspector.'

'But you always pick young girls. What is it about young girls that gets you so excited?'

'I don't pick them. They pick me.'

'Do older women frighten you? That's the usual pattern with nonces. They have to make out with children because mature women terrify them.'

'How many times do I have to tell you? I don't make out with children.'

Abruptly Jones switched tack. 'Ruth stole some diamond earrings from her grandmother on Saturday, November the sixth, the same day that Mrs Gillespie killed herself. Did you take Ruth there that day?'

Hughes looked as if he was about to deny it, then shrugged. 'She asked me to.'

'Why?'

'Why what?'

'Why did she ask you to take her? What did she want to do there?'

Hughes looked vague. 'She never said. But I never went in the frigging place and I didn't know she planned to steal any frigging earrings.'

'So she rang you at your squat, asked you to drive all the way out to Southcliffe to pick her up, take her from there to Fontwell and then back to Southcliffe, without ever explaining why.'

'Yeah.'

'And that's all you did? Acted as her chauffeur to and fro and waited outside Cedar House while she went in?'

'Yeah.'

'But you've admitted you didn't like her. In fact you despised her. Why go to so much trouble for someone you didn't like?'

'It was worth it for a screw.'

'With blancmange?'

Hughes grinned. 'I felt horny that day.'

'She told my Sergeant she was absent from school for upwards of six hours. It's thirty miles from Southcliffe to Fontwell, so let's say it took you forty minutes each way. That leaves some four and a half hours unaccounted for. Are you telling me you sat in your van in Fontwell village for four and a half hours twiddling your thumbs while Ruth was inside with her grandmother?'

'It wasn't that long. We stopped on the way back for the screw.'

'Where exactly did you park in Fontwell?'

'Can't remember now. I was always waiting for her some place or another.'

Charlie placed his finger on the crumpled page of paper. 'According to the publican at the Three Pigeons your van was parked on his forecourt that afternoon. After ten minutes you drove away, but he saw you stop beside the church to pick someone up. We must presume this was Ruth unless you are now going to tell me you took a third party to Fontwell the day Mrs Gillespie killed herself.'

The wary look was back in Hughes's eyes. 'It was Ruth.'

'Okay, then what were you and Ruth doing for four and a half hours, Mr Hughes? You certainly weren't screwing her. It doesn't take four and a half hours to screw blancmange. Or perhaps it does for someone who suffers from a psychopathic personality disorder. Perhaps it takes you that long to get it up.'

Hughes refused to be needled. 'I guess there's no reason for me to protect the silly bitch. Okay, she asked me to drive her to this backstreet jeweller somewhere in Southampton. I didn't ask why, I just did it. But you can't do me for that. All I did was act as a taxi. If she stole some earrings and then sold them, I knew nothing about it. I was just the patsy with the wheels.'

'According to Miss Lascelles she gave the money to you as soon as she sold the earrings. She said it was six hundred and fifty pounds in cash and that you then drove her straight back to school in time for her physics lecture.'

Hughes didn't say anything.

'You profited from a crime, Mr Hughes. That's illegal.'

'Ruth's lying. She never gave me any money and, even if she did, you'd have to prove I knew she'd thieved something in the first place. She'll tell you it was all her idea. Look, I don't deny she funded me from time to time, but she said the money was hers and I believed her. Why shouldn't I? The old granny was rolling in it. Stood to reason Ruth would be as well.' He grinned again. 'So what if she did

187

give me cash from time to time? How was I to know the silly bitch was stealing it? She owed me something for the petrol I wasted acting as her frigging chauffeur in the holidays.'

'But she didn't fund you that day?'

'I already said no, and no's what I mean.'

'Did you have any money on you?'

'A fiver, maybe.'

'What was the name of the backstreet jeweller in Southampton?' Charlie asked abruptly.

'No idea. I never went in the place. You'll have to ask Ruth. She just told me to go to a road and stop at the end of it.'

'What was the name of the road?'

'Don't know. She had a map, told me right, left, straight on, stop. I just did what I was told. You'll have to ask Ruth.'

'She doesn't know. She says you drove her there, told her which shop to go into, who to ask for and what to say.'

'She's lying.'

'I don't think so, Mr Hughes.'

'Prove it.'

Charlie thought rapidly. He had no doubt that Hughes was telling the truth when he said he hadn't entered Cedar House or the jewellers', not in Ruth's company anyway. The beauty of his scam was that he didn't handle the stolen goods himself, merely transported the girls and the goods to someone who would. That way, the only person who could ever implicate him was the girl, and she wasn't going to because, for whatever reason, she was too frightened of him. 'I intend to prove it, Mr Hughes. Let's start with an account of your movements after you dropped Ruth back at school. Did you go to this nightclub you mentioned? It'll be expensive, they usually are, and coke and ecstasy don't come cheap, both of which I suspect you're on. People will remember you, especially if you were throwing money about.'

Hughes saw another trap and giggled. 'I already said I hadn't got any money, Inspector. I drove around a bit and then went back to the squat.'

'What time was that?'

He shrugged. 'No idea.'

'So if I find someone who says a white transit van was parked in the vicinity of a Bournemouth nightclub that night, you'll say it couldn't have been yours because you were just driving around.'

'That's about the size of it.'

Charlie bared his teeth in a predatory smile. 'I have to inform you, Mr Hughes, that you will be transferred shortly to Learmouth Police Station where you will be questioned at length about the murder of Mrs Mathilda Gillespie.' He gathered his notes together and thrust them back into his pocket.

'Shit!' said Hughes angrily. 'What crap are you trying to lay on me now? You said she killed herself.'

'I was lying. She was murdered and I have reason to believe you were involved in that murder.'

Hughes surged aggressively to his feet. 'I told you I never went in the fucking place. Anyway, the publican's my alibi. He saw me in his car park and watched me pick up Ruth. How could I murder the old lady if I was in my van the whole time?'

'She wasn't murdered at two thirty. She was murdered later that evening.'

'I wasn't there later that evening.'

'Your van was. The publican says you returned that evening and, as you yourself have just told us, you and your van have no alibi for the night of November the sixth. You were driving around, remember?'

'I was here in Bournemouth and so was the van.'

'Prove it.' Charlie stood up. 'Until you do, I'm holding you on suspicion of murder.'

'You're really out of order on this one. I'll get my brief on you.'

'Do that. You'll be allowed your phone call at Learmouth.'

'Why would I want to kill the old cow anyway?'

Charlie lifted a shaggy eyebrow. 'Because you have a history of terrorizing women. This time you went too far.'

'I don't bloody murder them.'

'What do you do to them?'

'Shag 'em that's all. And I don't short change 'em neither. I've never had a complaint yet.'

'Which is probably what the Yorkshire Ripper said every time he came home with his hammer and his chisel in the boot of his car.'

'You're way out of order,' said Hughes again, stamping his foot.

'I didn't even know the old bitch. I didn't *want* to know her. Jesus, you bastard, how could I kill someone I didn't even know?'

'You got born, didn't you?'

'What the hell's that supposed to mean?'

'Birth and death, Hughes. They happen at random. Your mother didn't know your father but you still got born. The not-knowing is irrelevant. You were there that day, you were using her granddaughter to steal from her and Mrs Gillespie knew it. You had to shut her up before she talked to us.'

'I don't work it that way.'

'How do you work it then?'

But Hughes refused to say another word.

I have brought Joanna and her baby home to live with me. I could not believe the squalor I found them in when I arrived in London. Joanna has given up all attempts at caring for the child or even practising elementary hygiene. She is clearly not fit to live alone and, while I abhorred that wretched Jew she married, at least while he was alive she had some pretensions to normality.

I am very afraid that the shock of Steven's death has sent her over the edge. She was in the baby's room this morning, holding a pillow over the cot. I asked her what she was doing, and she said: 'Nothing,' but I have no doubt at all that, had I entered the room a few minutes later, the pillow would have been across the baby's face. The awful part is that I saw myself standing there, like some ghastly reflection in a distorted mirror. The shock was tremendous. Does Joanna suspect? Does anyone, other than Jane, suspect?

There is no cure for inbred insanity. 'Unnatural deeds do breed unnatural troubles . . .'

Thirteen

JANE MARRIOTT MARCHED into Sarah's office in the Fontwell surgery the following morning after the last patient had left and deposited herself firmly in a chair. Sarah glanced at her. 'You're looking very cross,' she remarked as she signed off some paperwork.

'I feel cross.'

'What about?'

'You.'

Sarah folded her arms. 'What have I done?'

'You've lost your compassion.' Jane tapped a stern finger against her watch. 'I know I used to wig you about the length of time you spent on your patients, but I admired you for the trouble you took. Now, suddenly, they're in and out like express trains. Poor old Mrs Henderson was almost in tears. "What have I done to upset Doctor?" she asked me. "She hardly had a kind word for me." You really mustn't let this business over Mathilda get to you, Sarah. It's not fair on other people.' She drew an admonishing breath. 'And don't tell me I'm only the receptionist and you're the doctor. Doctors are fallible, just like the rest of us.'

Sarah pushed some papers about her desk with the point of her pencil. 'Do you know what Mrs Henderson's first words to me were when she came in? "I reckon it's safe to come back to you, Doctor, seeing as how it was that bitch of a daughter what done it." And she lied to you. I didn't have a *single* kind word for her. I told her the truth for once, that the only thing wrong with her is an acidulated spleen which could be cured immediately if she looked for the good in people instead of the bad.' She wagged the pencil under Jane's nose. 'I am rapidly coming to the conclusion that Mathilda was right.

193

This village is one of the nastiest places on earth, peopled entirely by ignorant, evil-minded bigots with nothing better to do in their lives than sit and pass judgement on anyone who doesn't conform to their commonplace, petty-minded stereotypes. It's not compassion I've lost, it's my blinkers.'

Jane removed the pencil from Sarah's grasp before it could lodge itself in her nostril. 'She's a lonely old widow, with little or no education, and she was trying in her very ham-fisted way to say sorry for ever having doubted you. If you haven't the generosity of spirit to make allowances for her clumsy diplomacy then you are not the woman I thought you were. And for your information, she now thinks she is suffering from a very severe condition, namely acidulated spleen, which you are refusing to treat. And she's put that down to the cuts in the Health Service and the fact that, as an old woman, she is now considered expendable.'

Sarah sighed. 'She wasn't the only one. They're all cock-a-hoop because they think Joanna did it and I resent them using me and my surgery to score points off her.' She pulled her fingers through her hair. 'Because that's what today was all about, Jane, a sort of childish yah-boo-sucks at their latest victim, and if Jack hadn't decided to play silly buggers, then there wouldn't have been so much for them to gossip about.'

'Don't you believe it,' said Jane tartly. 'What they can't get any other way they make up.'

'Hah! And you have the nerve to haul me over the coals for cynicism!'

'Oh, don't assume I'm not just as irritated as you are by their silliness. Of course I am, but then I don't expect anything else. They haven't changed just because Mathilda's died, you know, and I must say it's a bit rich accusing Mrs Henderson of only seeing the bad in people when the greatest exponent of that has just left you a small fortune. Mrs Henderson's view of people is positively saintly compared with Mathilda's. *She* really did have an acidulated spleen.'

'All right. Point taken. I'll drop in on Mrs H. on my way home.'

'Well, I hope you'll be gracious enough to apologize to her. Perhaps I'm being over-sensitive but she did seem so upset, and it's not like you to be cruel, Sarah.'

'I feel cruel,' she growled. 'As a matter of interest, do you talk to the male doctors like this?'

'No.'

'I see.'

Jane bridled. 'You don't see anything. I'm fond of you. If your mother were here she would be saying the same things. You should never allow events to sour your nature, Sarah. You leave that particular weakness to the Mathildas of this world.'

Sarah felt a surge of affection for the elderly woman, whose apple cheeks had grown rosy with indignation. Her mother, of course, would say no such thing, merely purse her lips and declare that she had always known Sarah was sour at heart. It took someone with Jane's generosity to see that other people were diplomatically inept, or weak, or disillusioned. 'You're asking me to betray my principles,' she said mildly.

'No, my dear, I'm asking you to stand by them.'

'Why should I condone Mrs Henderson calling Joanna a murderess? There's no more evidence against her than there was against me, and if I apologize it's a tacit acceptance.'

'Nonsense,' said Jane stoutly. 'It's courtesy towards an old lady. How you deal with Joanna is a different matter altogether. If you don't approve of the way the village is treating her then you must demonstrate it in a very public way so that no one is in any doubt of where your sympathies lie. But,' her old eyes softened as they rested on the younger woman, 'don't take your annoyance out on poor Dolly Henderson, my dear. She can't be expected to see things as you and I do. She never enjoyed our liberal education.'

'I will apologize.'

'Thank you.'

Sarah suddenly leaned forward and planted a kiss on the other's cheek.

Jane looked surprised. 'What was that for?'

'Oh, I don't know.' Sarah smiled. 'Standing in for my mother, perhaps. I wonder sometimes if the stand-ins aren't rather better at the job than the real thing. Mathilda did it, too, you know. She wasn't *all* acidulated spleen. She could be just as sweet as you when she wanted to be.'

'Is that why you're looking after Ruth? As a sort of quid pro quo?'

'Don't you approve?'

Jane sighed. 'I don't approve or disapprove. I just feel it's a little provocative in the circumstances. Whatever your reasons for doing it, the village has put the worst interpretation on those reasons. You do know they're saying that Joanna's about to be arrested for the murder of her mother, and that's why Ruth has gone to live with you?'

'I hadn't realized it was quite that bad.' Sarah frowned. 'God, they're absurd. Where do they get this rubbish from?'

'They put two and two together and make twenty.'

'The trouble is' – she paused – 'there's nothing much I can do about it.'

'But, my dear, all that's required is an explanation of why Ruth is with you,' Jane suggested, 'and then you can knock these rumours on the head. There must be one, after all.'

Sarah sighed. 'It's up to Ruth to explain, and at the moment she's not in a position to do that.'

'Then invent one,' said Jane bluntly. 'Give it to Mrs Henderson when you see her this afternoon and it'll be all round the village by tomorrow evening. Fight fire with fire, Sarah. It's the only way.'

Mrs Henderson was touched by Dr Blakeney's apology for her bad temper in the surgery, thought it very handsome of her to take the trouble to come out to her cottage, and quite agreed that if you'd been up all night looking after a seventeen-year-old showing all the symptoms of glandular fever, you were bound to be shirty the next day. Mind, she didn't quite understand why Ruth had to stay with Dr Blakeney and her husband in the circumstances. Wouldn't it be more fitting for her to remain with her mother? Much more fitting, agreed Sarah firmly, and Ruth would prefer it too, of course, but, as Mrs Henderson knew, glandular fever was an extremely painful and debilitating viral infection, and because of the likelihood of its recurring if the patient wasn't cared for properly and bearing in mind this was Ruth's A level year, Joanna had asked Sarah to take her in and get her back on her feet again as quickly as possible. In the circumstances, what with Mrs Gillespie's will and all (Sarah looked suitably embarrassed), she could hardly refuse, could she?

'Not when you're the one what's got all the money,' was Mrs Henderson's considered retort, but her rheumy eyes clouded in puzzlement. 'Ruth going back to Southcliffe then, when she's better, like?'

'Where else would she go?' murmured Sarah unblushingly. 'As I said, it's her A level year.'

'Well, I never! There's some lies being told and no mistake. Who killed Mrs Gillespie, then, if it weren't you and it weren't the daughter?'

'God knows, Mrs Henderson.'

'Happen he does, too, so it's a shame He doesn't pass it on. He's causing a lot of bother by keeping the information to Hisself.'

'Perhaps she killed herself.'

'No,' said the old woman decidedly. 'That I'll never believe. I don't say as I liked her very much but Mrs Gillespie was no coward.'

Sarah knew Joanna was in Cedar House, despite the stubborn silence that greeted her ringing of the doorbell. She'd seen the set white face in the shadows at the back of the dining-room and the brief flicker of recognition before Joanna slipped into the hall and out of sight. Rather more than her refusal to answer the door, it was her flicker of recognition that fuelled Sarah's anger. Ruth was the issue here, not Mathilda's will or Jack's shenanigans, and while she might have sympathized with Joanna's reluctance to open the door to the police, she could not forgive the barricading of it against the person Joanna knew was sheltering her daughter. Sarah set off grimly down the path that skirted the house. What kind of woman, she wondered, put personal enmity before concern for her daughter's welfare?

In her mind's eye, she pictured the portrait Jack was working on. He had trapped Joanna inside a triangular prism of mirrors, with her personality split like refracted light. It was an extraordinary depiction of confused identity, the more so because for each image there was a single image reflected back from the huge encompassing mirror that bordered the canvas. Sarah had asked him what the single image represented. 'Joanna as she wants to be seen. Admired, adored, beautiful.'

She pointed to the prism images. 'And what are they?'

'That's the Joanna she's suppressing with drugs,' he said. 'The ugly, unloved woman who was rejected by mother, husband and daughter. Everything in her life is illusion, hence the mirror theme.'

'That's sad.'

'Don't go sentimental on me, Sarah, or on her either for that matter. Joanna is the most self-centred woman I have ever met. I guess most addicts are. She says Ruth rejected her. That's baloney. It was Joanna who rejected her because Ruth cried whenever Joanna picked her up. It was a vicious circle. The more her baby cried the less inclined she was to love it. She claimed Steven rejected her because he was revolted by the pregnancy, but in the next sentence she admitted she couldn't stand the way he fussed over Ruth. It was she, I think, who rejected him.'

'But why? There must be a reason for it.'

'I suspect it's very simple. The only person she loves or is capable of loving is herself and because her swollen belly made her less attractive in her own eyes, she resented the two people responsible for it, namely her husband and her baby. I'll put money on the fact that she's the one who found the pregnancy repulsive.'

'Nothing's ever that simple, Jack. It could be something quite serious. Untreated post-natal depression. Narcissistic personality disorder. Schizophrenia even. Perhaps Mathilda was right, and she *is* unstable.'

'Maybe, but if she is, then Mathilda was entirely to blame. From what I can gather, she kowtowed to Joanna and Joanna's histrionics from day one.' He gestured towards the painting. 'When I said that everything in her life is illusion, what I meant was: everything is false. This is the fantasy she wants you to believe, but I'm ninety-nine per cent certain she doesn't believe it herself.' He laid his forefinger on the central triangle of the prism, which as yet contained nothing. 'That's where the real Joanna will be, in the only mirror that can't reflect her stylized image of herself.'

Clever stuff, thought Sarah, but was it true? 'And what is the real Joanna?'

He stared at the painting. 'Utterly ruthless, I think,' he said slowly, 'utterly and completely ruthless about getting her own way.'

*

The kitchen door was locked but the key that Mathilda had hidden under the third flowerpot to the right was still there and, with an exclamation of triumph, Sarah pounced on it and inserted it into the Yale lock. It was only after she'd opened the door and was removing the key to lay it on the kitchen table that she wondered if anyone had told the police that entry into Cedar House was that easy if you knew what was under the flowerpot. *She* certainly hadn't, but then she had forgotten all about it until the need to get in had jogged her memory. She had used it once, months ago, when Mathilda's arthritis was so bad that she hadn't been able to get out of her chair to open the front door.

Gingerly, she laid the key on the table and stared at it. Intuition told her that whoever had used the key last had killed Mathilda Gillespie, and she didn't need to be Einstein to work out that if their fingerprints had been on it she had just destroyed them with her own. 'Oh, Jesus!' she said with feeling.

'How dare you come into my house without asking,' announced Joanna in a tight little voice from the hall doorway.

Sarah's glare was so ferocious that the other took a step backwards. 'Will you get off your ridiculous high horse and stop being so pompous,' she snapped. 'We're all in deep shit here and the only thing you ever do is stand on your wretched dignity.'

'Stop swearing. I detest people who swear. You're worse than Ruth and she has a mouth like a sewer. You're not a lady. I can't understand how my mother put up with you.'

Sarah drew a deep angry breath. 'You're unreal, Joanna. Which century do you think you're living in? And what is a lady? Someone like you who's never done a hand's turn in her life but passes muster because she doesn't utter profanities?' She shook her head. 'Not in my book it isn't. The greatest lady I know is a seventy-eight-year-old Cockney who works with the down-and-outs in London and swears like a trooper. Open your eyes, woman. It's the contribution you make to society that earns you respect, not a tight-arsed allegiance to some outmoded principle of feminine purity that died the day women discovered they weren't condemned to a life of endless pregnancy and child-rearing.'

Joanna's lips thinned. 'How did you get in?'

Sarah nodded towards the table. 'I used the key under the flowerpot.'

Joanna frowned angrily. 'Which key?'

'That one, and don't touch it, whatever you do. I'm sure whoever killed your mother must have used it. Can I borrow the phone? I'm going to call the police.' She brushed past Joanna into the hall. 'I'll have to ring Jack as well, tell him I'm going to be late. Do you mind? Presumably the cost will come out of your mother's estate.'

Joanna pursued her. 'Yes, I do mind. You've no business to force your way in. This is my house and I don't want you here.'

'No,' said Sarah curtly, picking up the phone on the hall table, 'according to your mother's will, Cedar House belongs to me.' She flicked through her diary for Cooper's telephone number. 'And you're only in it because I've balked at evicting you.' She held the receiver to her ear and dialled Learmouth Police Station, watching Joanna as she did so. 'But I'm rapidly changing my mind. Frankly, I see no reason why I should show you more consideration than you're prepared to show your own daughter. Detective Sergeant Cooper, please. Tell him it's Dr Blakeney and it's urgent. I'm at Cedar House in Fontwell. Yes, I'll hold.' She put her hand over the mouthpiece. 'I want you to come home with me and talk to Ruth. Jack and I are doing our best but we're no substitute for you. She needs her mother.'

A small tic flickered at the side of Joanna's mouth. 'I resent your interference in matters that don't concern you. Ruth is quite capable of looking after herself.'

'My God, you really are unreal,' said Sarah in amazement. 'You couldn't give a shit, could you?'

'You are doing this deliberately, Dr Blakeney.'

'If you're referring to my swearing, then, yes, you're dead right I am,' said Sarah. 'I want you to be as shocked by me as I am by you. Where's your sense of responsibility, you *sodding* bitch? Ruth didn't materialize out of thin air. You and your husband had a *fucking* good time when you made her, and don't forget it.' Abruptly she transferred her attention to the telephone. 'Hello, Sergeant, yes, I'm at Cedar House. Yes, she's here, too. No, there's no trouble, it's just that I think I know how Mathilda's murderer got in. Has anyone told you she kept a key to the kitchen door under a flowerpot by the coal bunker at the back? I know, but I forgot about it.' She pulled a face. 'No, it's not still there. It's on the kitchen table. I used it to get in.' She held the receiver away from her ear. 'I did not do it on purpose,' she said coldly after a moment. 'You should have searched a bit more thoroughly at the beginning then it wouldn't have happened.' She replaced the receiver with unnecessary force. 'We've both got to stay here until the police come.'

But Joanna's composure had abandoned her. 'GET OUT OF MY HOUSE!' she screamed 'I WILL NOT BE SPOKEN TO LIKE THIS IN MY HOUSE!' She ran up the stairs. 'YOU WON'T GET AWAY WITH IT! I'LL REPORT YOU TO THE MEDICAL COUNCIL! MUD STICKS. I'LL TELL THEM YOU MURDERED MR STURGIS AND THEN MY MOTHER.'

Sarah followed in her wake, watched her run into the bathroom and slam the door, then lowered herself to the floor and sat cross-legged outside it. 'Tantrums and convulsions may have worked a treat with Mathilda but they sure as hell aren't going to work with me. GODDAMMIT!' she roared suddenly, putting her mouth to the oak-panelled door. 'You're a forty-year-old middle-aged woman, you stupid cow, so act your age.'

'DON'T YOU DARE SPEAK TO ME LIKE THAT!'

'But you get up my nose, Joanna. I have only contempt for someone who can't function unless they're doped stupid.' Tranquillizers was Jack's guess.

No answer.

'You need help,' she went on matter-of-factly, 'and the best person to give it to you is based in London. He's a psychiatrist who specializes in all forms of drug addiction but he won't take you on unless you're willing to give up. If you're interested I'll refer you, if you're not then I suggest you prepare yourself for the long term consequences of habitual substance abuse on the human body, beginning with the one thing you don't want. You will get old very much quicker than I will, Joanna, because your physical chemistry is under constant attack and mine isn't.'

'Get out of my house, Dr Blakeney.' She was beginning to calm down.

'I can't, not till Sergeant Cooper gets here. And it's not your house, remember, it's mine. What are you on?'

There was a long, long silence. 'Valium,' said Joanna finally. 'Dr Hendry prescribed it for me when I came back here after Steven died. I tried to smother Ruth in her cot, so Mother called him in and begged him to give me something.'

'Why did you try to smother Ruth?'

'It seemed the most sensible thing to do. I wasn't coping terribly well.'

'And did tranquillizers help?'

'I don't remember. I was always tired, I remember that.'

Sarah believed her, because she could believe it of Hugh Hendry. Classic symptoms of severe post-natal depression, and instead of giving the poor woman anti-depressants to lift her mood, the idiot had effectively shoved her into a state of lethargy by giving her sedatives. No wonder she found it so difficult to get on with Ruth, when one of the tragic consequences of post-natal depression, if it wasn't treated properly, was that mothers found it difficult to develop natural loving relationships with their babies whom they saw as the reason for their sudden inability to cope. God, but it explained a lot about this family if the women had a tendency to post-natal depression. 'I can help you,' she said. 'Will you let me help you?'

'Lots of people take Valium. It's perfectly legal.'

'And very effective in the right circumstances and under proper supervision. But you're not getting yours from a doctor, Joanna. The problems of diazepam addiction are so well documented that no responsible practitioner would go on prescribing them for you. Which means you've got a private supplier somewhere and the tablets won't be cheap. Black market drugs never are. Let me help you,' she said again.

'You've never been afraid. What would you know about anything if you've never been afraid?'

'What were you afraid of?'

'I was afraid to go to sleep. For years and years I was afraid to go to sleep.' She laughed suddenly. 'Not any more, though. She's dead.'

The doorbell rang.

Sergeant Cooper was in very tetchy mood. The last twenty-four hours had been frustrating ones for him and not just because he had had to work over the weekend and miss Sunday lunch with his children and grandchildren. His wife, tired and irritable herself, had delivered the inevitable ticking-off about his lack of commitment to his family.

'You should put your foot down,' she told him. 'The police force doesn't own you, Tommy.'

They had held Hughes overnight at Learmouth Police Station but had released him without charge at lunchtime. After a persistent refusal the previous afternoon to say anything at all, he had reverted that morning to his previous statement, namely that he had been driving around aimlessly before returning to his squat. He gave the time for his return as nine o'clock. Cooper, dispatched by Charlie Jones to interview the youths who shared the squat with him, had come back deeply irritated.

'It's a set-up,' he told the DCI. 'They've got his alibi off pat. I spoke to each one in turn, asked them to give me an account of their movements on the evening of Saturday, the sixth of November, and each one told me the same story. They were watching the portable telly and drinking beer in Hughes's room when Hughes walked in at nine o'clock. He stayed there all night, as did his van which was parked in the road outside. I did not mention Hughes once, nor imply that I was at all interested in him or his blasted van. They offered the information gratuitously and without prompting.'

'How could they know he'd told us nine o'clock?'

'The solicitor?'

Charlie shook his head. 'Very unlikely. I get the impression he doesn't like his client any more than we do.'

'Then it's a prearranged thing. If questioned, Hughes will always give nine o'clock as the time he returns to the squat.'

'Or they're telling the truth.'

Cooper gave a snort of derision. 'No chance. They were scum. If any of them were tamely watching telly that night, I'm a monkey's uncle. Far more likely, they were out beating up old ladies or knifing rival football supporters.'

The Inspector mulled this over. 'There's no such thing as an alibi applicable in all situations,' he said thoughtfully. 'Not unless Hughes always makes a habit of committing crimes after nine o'clock at night, and we know he doesn't do that, because Ruth stole her grandmother's earrings at two thirty in the afternoon.' He fell silent.

'So what are you saying?' asked Cooper when he didn't go on. 'That they're telling the truth?' He shook his head aggressively. 'I don't believe that.'

'I'm wondering why Hughes didn't produce this alibi yesterday. Why did he keep mum for so long if he knew his mates were going to back him up?' He answered his own question slowly. 'Because his solicitor forced my hand this morning and demanded to know the earliest time that Mrs Gillespie might have died. Which means Hughes had already told him he was in the clear from nine o'clock, and hey presto, out comes his alibi.'

'How does that help us?'

'It doesn't,' said Jones cheerfully. 'But if it was the set-up you say it is, then he must have done something else that night that required an alibi from nine o'clock. All we have to do is find out what it was.' He reached for his telephone. 'I'll talk to my oppo in Bournemouth. Let's see what he can come up with on the crime sheet for the night of Saturday, November the sixth.'

The answer was nothing.

Nothing, at least, that remotely fitted the modus operandi of David Mark Hughes.

Hence Cooper's tetchiness.

He tut-tutted crossly at Sarah as he examined the key on the table. 'I thought you had more sense, Dr Blakeney.'

Sarah held on to her patience with an effort, remembering Jane's admonishment not to let events sour her nature. 'I know. I'm sorry.'

'You'd better hope we do raise someone else's fingerprints, otherwise I might be inclined to think this was a stunt.'

'What sort of stunt?'

'A way of leaving your fingerprints on it legitimately.'

She was way ahead of him. 'Assuming I was the one who used it to get in and kill Mathilda and had forgotten to wipe my fingerprints off it at the time, I suppose?' she said tartly.

'Not quite,' he said mildly, 'I was thinking more in terms of a Good Samaritan act on behalf of someone else. Who have you unilaterally decided is innocent this time, Dr Blakeney?'

'You're not very grateful, Cooper,' she said. 'I needn't have told you about it at all. I could have put it back quietly and kept my mouth shut.'

'Hardly. It has your fingerprints all over it and someone would have found it eventually.' He glanced at Joanna. 'Did you really not know it was there, Mrs Lascelles?'

'I've already told you once, Sergeant. No. I had a key to the front door.'

There was something very odd going on between her and Dr Blakeney, he thought. The body language was all wrong. They were standing close together, arms almost touching, but they seemed unwilling to look at each other. Had they been a man and a woman, he'd have said he'd caught them in flagrante delicto; as it was, intuition told him they were sharing a secret although what that secret was and whether it had any bearing on Mrs Gillespie's death was anyone's guess.

'What about Ruth?'

Joanna shrugged indifferently. 'I've no idea but I wouldn't think so. She's never mentioned it to me, and I've only ever known her use her front door key. There's no sense in coming all the way round the back if you can get in through the front. There's no access on this side.' She looked honestly puzzled. 'It must be something Mother started recently. She certainly didn't do it when I was living here.'

He looked at Sarah who spread her hands in a gesture of helplessness. 'All I know is that the second or third time I came to visit her, she didn't answer the door, so I walked round to the french windows and looked into the drawing-room. She was completely stuck, poor old thing, quite unable to push herself out of her chair because her wrists had packed up on her that day. She mouthed instructions through the glass. "Key. Third flowerpot. Coal bunker." I imagine she kept it there for just that kind of emergency. She worried all the time about losing her mobility.'

'Who else knew about it?'

'I don't know.'

'Did you tell anyone?'

Sarah shook her head. 'I can't remember. I may have mentioned it in the surgery. It was ages ago, anyway. She started responding very well to the new medication I gave her and the situation didn't recur. I only remembered it when I came round the back this afternoon and saw the flowerpots.'

Cooper took a couple of polythene bags out of his pocket and used one to inch the key off the table into the other. 'And why did you come round the back, Dr Blakeney? Did Mrs Lascelles refuse to let you in at the front?'

For the first time Sarah glanced at Joanna. 'I don't know about refusing. She may not have heard the bell.'

'But it was obviously something very urgent you needed to discuss with her or you wouldn't have been so determined to get in. Would you care to let me in on what that was? Presumably it concerns Ruth.' He was too old and experienced a hand to miss the look of relief on Joanna's face.

'Sure,' said Sarah lightly. 'You know my views on education. We were discussing Ruth's future schooling.'

She was lying, Cooper thought, and he was startled by the fluency with which she did it. With an inward sigh, he made a mental note to review everything she had told him. He had believed her to be an honest, if naïve, woman, but the naïvety, he realized now, was all on his side. There was no fool like an old fool, he thought bitterly.

But then silly old Tommy had fallen a little in love.

There is no truer saying than 'Revenge is a dish best eaten cold.' It is so much sweeter for the waiting, and my only regret is that I cannot broadcast my triumph to the world. Sadly, not even to James, who is duped but does not know it.

This morning I heard from my bank that he has cashed my cheque for £12,000 and has therefore by default agreed to the insurance settlement. I knew he would. Where money is concerned James has the intemperate greed of a child. He spends it like water because cash in hand is the only thing he understands. Oh, to be a fly on the wall and see how he's living, but I can guess, anyway. Drink and sodomy. There was never anything else in James's life.

I am £36,500 richer today than I was yesterday, and I glory in it. The cheque from the insurance company for the various items stolen from the safe over Christmas while Joanna and I were in Cheshire came to an astonishing £23,500, the bulk of which was for the set of diamond jewellery belonging to my grandmother. The tiara alone was insured for £5,500, although I imagine it was worth more than that as I have not had it valued since Father's death. Extraordinary to have such a windfall for items I, personally, would not be seen dead in. There is nothing so ugly or heavy as ornate Victorian jewellery.

By contrast, James's clocks are anything but vulgar, probably because it was his father who bought them and not James. I took them to Sotheby's to be valued and discovered they are worth more than double the £12,000 they were insured for. Thus, after paying James £12,000, I retain £11,500 from the insurance cheque and have effectively purchased from my contemptible husband a fine investment, valued at £25,000.

As I said, revenge is a dish best eaten cold . . .

Fourteen

EARLIER THAT afternoon, a tall, distinguished-looking man was shown into Paul Duggan's office in Poole. He gave his name as James Gillespie and calmly produced his passport and his marriage certificate to Mathilda Beryl Gillespie to prove it. Aware that he had dropped something of a bombshell, he lowered himself on to a vacant chair and clasped his hands around the handle of his walking-stick, studying Duggan with amusement from beneath a pair of exuberant white eyebrows. 'Bit of a shock, eh?' he said. Even from the other side of the desk, the smell of whisky on his breath was powerful.

The younger man examined the passport carefully, then placed it on the blotting-pad in front of him. 'Unexpected, certainly,' he said dryly. 'I had assumed Mrs Gillespie was a widow. She never mentioned a husband or,' he laid a careful stress upon the next syllable, '*ex*-husband still living.'

'Husband,' grunted the other forcefully. 'She wouldn't. It suited her better to be thought a widow.'

'Why did you never divorce?'

'Never saw the need.'

'This passport was issued in Hong Kong.'

'Naturally. Out there forty years. Worked in various banks. Came back when I realized it was no place to end my days. Too much fear now. Peking's unpredictable. Uncomfortable for a man of my age.' He spoke in clipped staccato sentences like someone in a hurry or someone impatient with social niceties.

'So why have you come to see me?' Duggan watched him curiously. He was striking to look at, certainly, with a mane of white hair and an olive complexion, etched with deep lines around his eyes and mouth, but closer examination revealed an underlying poverty beneath the superficial air of prosperity. His clothes had once been good, but time and usage had taken their toll and both the suit and the camel-hair coat were wearing thin.

'Should have thought it was obvious. Now she's dead – reclaiming what's mine.'

'How did you know she was dead?'

'Ways and means,' said the other.

'How did you know I was her executor?'

'Ways and means,' said the other again.

Duggan's curiosity was intense. 'And what is it that you wish to reclaim?'

The old man took a wallet from his inside pocket, removed some folded sheets of very thin paper and spread them on the desk. 'This is an inventory of my father's estate. It was divided equally amongst his three children on his death forty-seven years ago. My share was those items marked with the initials JG. You will find, I think, that at least seven of them appear on your inventory of Mathilda's estate. They are not hers. They never were hers. I now wish to recover them.'

Thoughtfully, Duggan read through the documents. 'Precisely which seven items are you referring to, Mr Gillespie?'

The huge white eyebrows came together in a ferocious scowl. 'Don't trifle with me, Mr Duggan. I refer, of course, to the clocks. The two Thomas Tompions, the Knibbs, the seventeenth-century mahogany long case, the Louis XVI Lyre clock, the eighteenth-century "pendule d'officier" and the crucifix clock. My father and grandfather were collectors.'

Duggan steepled his hands over the inventory. 'May I ask why you think any of these things appear on the inventory of Mrs Gillespie's estate?'

'Are you telling me they don't?'

The solicitor avoided a direct answer. 'If I understood you correctly you've been absent from this country for forty years. How could you possibly know what might or might not have been in your wife's possession the day she died?'

The old man snorted. 'Those clocks were the only things of value I had, and Mathilda went to a great deal of trouble to steal them from me. She certainly wouldn't have sold them.'

'How could your wife steal them if you were still married?'

'Tricked me out of them, then, but it was still theft.'

'I'm afraid I don't understand.'

Gillespie removed an airmail letter from his wallet and handed it across the desk. 'Self-explanatory, I think.'

Duggan unfolded the letter and read the terse lines. The address was Cedar House and the date was April 1961.

> Dear James,
>
> I am sorry to have to tell you that during a burglary here over Christmas much of value was stolen, including your collection of clocks. I have today received a cheque in settlement from the insurance company and I enclose their invoice, showing that they sent me a total of £23,500. I also enclose a cheque for £12,000 which was the insured value of your seven clocks. You bought my silence by leaving the clocks with me, and I am reimbursing you only because I fear you might return one day to claim them. You would be very angry, I think, to discover I'd cheated you a second time. I trust this means we will not need to communicate again.
> Yours, Mathilda.

Duggan's amiable face looked up in bewilderment. 'I still don't understand.'

'They weren't stolen, were they?'

'But she gave you twelve thousand pounds for them. That was a small fortune in 1961.'

'It was fraud. She told me the clocks were stolen when they weren't. I accepted the money in good faith. Never occurred to me she was lying.' He tapped his walking-stick angrily on the floor. 'Two ways of looking at it. One, she stole the clocks herself and defrauded the insurance company. A crime, in my book. Two, other things were stolen to the value of twenty-three and a half thousand and she saw an opportunity to take the clocks off me. Also a crime. They were my property.' His ancient mouth turned down at the corners. 'She knew their value, knew they'd be the best asset she had. Been to Sotheby's myself. Rough estimate, of course, with only descriptions in the inventory to go by, but we're talking over a hundred thousand at auction, probably a great deal more. I want them back, sir.'

Duggan considered for a moment. 'I don't think the situation is quite as clear-cut as you seem to think, Mr Gillespie. There's a burden of proof here. First, you have to show that Mrs Gillespie deliberately defrauded you; second, you have to show that the clocks in Mrs Gillespie's estate are the precise clocks that were left to you by your father.'

'You've read both inventories. What else could they be?'

For the moment, Duggan avoided the question of how James Gillespie knew there was an inventory of Mathilda's estate or what was on it. Once broached, it was going to be a very unpleasant can of worms. 'Similar clocks,' he said bluntly. 'Maybe even the same clocks, but you will have to prove she didn't buy them back at a later stage. Let's say the collection was stolen, and she passed on the compensation to you as she was supposed to. Let's say, then, that she set out to replace the collection because she had developed an interest in horology. She could quite legitimately have used her own money to buy similar clocks at auction. In those circumstances, you would have no claim on them at all. There is also the undeniable fact that you had a duty, encumbent on you as the owner, to establish to your satisfaction that the money you were paid in 1961 represented a full and fair settlement by the insurance company for the theft of your goods. In accepting twelve thousand pounds, Mr Gillespie, you effectively did that. You abandoned the clocks to sail to Hong Kong, accepted handsome compensation for them without a murmur, and only wish to reclaim them now because after forty years you believe they might have been worth hanging on to. I will admit that this is a grey area, which will require Counsel's opinion, but off the top of my head, I'd say you haven't a leg to stand on. It's an old saying, but a true one. Possession is nine tenths of the law.'

Gillespie was not so easily intimidated. 'Read her diaries,' he growled. 'They'll prove she stole them off me. Couldn't resist boasting to herself, that was Mathilda's trouble. Put every damn thing on those miserable pages, then read them over and over again to remind herself how clever she was. Wouldn't have left out a triumph like this. Read the diaries.'

The younger man kept his face deliberately impassive. 'I will. As a matter of interest, do you know where she kept them? It'll save me the trouble of looking for them.'

'Top shelf of the library. Disguised as the works of Willy

Shakespeare.' He took a card from his wallet. 'You're a solicitor, Mr Duggan, so I'm trusting you to be honest. That's where I'm staying. Expect to hear from you on this in a couple of days or so. Grateful if you'd treat it as a matter of urgency.' He levered himself to his feet with his walking-stick.

'I'd much prefer to deal through your solicitor, Mr Gillespie.'

'I don't have one, sir.' He spoke with a touching dignity. 'My pension won't allow it. I am relying on you being a gentleman. Presumably they still exist in this wretched country. Precious little else does.' He made his way to the door. 'Perhaps you think I treated Mathilda badly by deserting her and the child. Perhaps you think I deserved to be stolen from. Read the diaries. She'll tell you herself what really happened.'

Duggan waited until the door had closed, then reached for the telephone and dialled Learmouth Police Station.

The information about Mathilda's diaries was telephoned through to Cooper as he was about to leave Cedar House. He replaced the receiver with a frown. He'd been over that house from top to bottom, and he was as sure as he could be that there were no handwritten diaries in the library or anywhere else. 'Sorry, ladies, I shall have to trespass on your time a little longer. Will you come with me, please?'

Puzzled, Joanna and Sarah followed him across the hall and into the library.

'What are you looking for?' asked Joanna as he stood staring at the top shelf.

He reached up and tapped the thick mahogany ledge that ran, like its fellows, across the width of the wall. 'Do either of you see the collected works of William Shakespeare up here?'

'They're all over the place,' said Joanna dismissively. 'Which particular edition are you looking for?'

'The one that's supposed to be on this shelf.' He glanced at her. 'Your mother's diaries. I'm told she kept them on the top shelf, disguised as the works of William Shakespeare.'

Joanna looked genuinely surprised. 'What diaries?'

'Our information is that she kept a record of everything that happened to her.'

'I didn't know.'

'The informant was very positive.'

Joanna gestured helplessly. 'I didn't know,' she said again.

'Who's your informant?' asked Sarah curiously.

Cooper was watching Joanna as he spoke. 'James Gillespie,' he said. 'Mrs Lascelles's step-father.'

This time the look of surprise lacked conviction. It was left to Sarah to make the obvious response. 'I thought he abandoned Mathilda years ago,' she said thoughtfully. 'How would he know whether she kept diaries or not? Anyway, he's in Hong Kong, or that's what my receptionist told me.'

'Not any more, Dr Blakeney. According to Mrs Gillespie's solicitor, he's living in Bournemouth.' He addressed Joanna. 'We'll have to search the house again, and I'd prefer it if you were here while we did so.'

'Of course, Sergeant. I'm not planning to go anywhere. This is my house, after all.'

Sarah caught her gaze. 'What about Ruth? You can't just abandon her.'

'Ruth must learn to fend for herself, Dr Blakeney.' She gave an eloquent little shrug. 'Perhaps you should have considered the consequences a little more carefully before you persuaded Mother to change her will. You must see that it's quite impossible for me to support her as things stand at the moment.'

'It's emotional support she needs, and that won't cost you a bean.'

'There's nothing I could say to her that wouldn't make matters worse.' Joanna's pale eyes stared unwinkingly at Sarah. 'She's had more opportunities than I ever had and she's chosen to throw them away. You do realize she was stealing from Mother for months before this sordid little episode at school.' Her mouth thinned unpleasantly. 'You can't imagine the resentment I've felt since Miss Harris telephoned to explain why Ruth was being expelled. Have you any idea of the money that's been wasted on that child's education?'

'Miss Harris has given you a very one-sided view of what happened,' said Sarah carefully, aware that Cooper was all ears beside her. 'You must see that it's only fair to hear Ruth's side as well, at least give her the chance to demonstrate that what happened wasn't entirely her fault.'

'I've lived with my daughter on and off for nearly eighteen years, and I know exactly who's to blame. Ruth is quite incapable of telling the truth. You would be very foolish to assume otherwise.' She smiled very slightly. 'You may tell her that she knows where I am if she wants me, although please make it very clear that, unless this business of the will is settled satisfactorily, then she can expect no help from me either in terms of her continuing education or of her living expenses.'

This woman was using Ruth as a bargaining chip, thought Sarah in disgust, but she reminded herself that in her own way Joanna was as desperate as Ruth. She tried again. 'Money isn't the issue here, Joanna, the only issue is that your daughter would like to see you. She's too frightened to come to Cedar House because the man who persuaded her to steal knows this address and has made threats against her. Please, please, will you come with me to Mill House and talk to her there? She isn't lying, but she's deeply disturbed about everything that's happened and needs reassurance that you haven't rejected her. She has spent most of her time sitting by the telephone, hoping and praying that you would call. I don't think you have any idea how deeply she cares for you.'

There was the briefest of hesitations – *or was that wishful thinking on Sarah's part?* 'You took her in, Dr Blakeney, so I suggest you deal with her. I can't begin to condone anything she's done. Worse, I'm inclined to think it was she who murdered my mother. She's quite capable of it. Please don't be in any doubt about that.'

Sarah shook her head in disbelief. 'Ah, well, perhaps it's better this way. The one thing Ruth doesn't need at the moment is you downloading your hypocritical crap on her. You're tarred with exactly the same brush, or have you forgotten the mess you were in when Mathilda rescued you?' She shrugged. 'I'd made up my mind to turn the bequest down and let you and Ruth have a fair crack at convincing a court you had more rights than the donkeys. Not any more. You'll have to fight me for it now, and you'll be fighting your corner alone because I intend to put money in trust for Ruth so that she doesn't lose out whatever happens.' She walked to the door, flashing Cooper one of the sweet smiles that made his elderly heart race around like a young spring lamb. 'If it's of any interest to you, Sergeant, I am still of the opinion that Joanna did not kill Mathilda. Arthritis or no arthritis, Mathilda would have legged it for the hills the minute this bitch came near her.'

Well, well, Cooper thought, gazing after her as she stormed across the hall, there was passion in Dr Blakeney after all. But he wished he knew what had happened to Ruth that was making her and Jack so angry.

Cadogan Mansions, implying as it did something grand and impressive, was a misnomer for the shabby neglect of the purpose-built block that greeted Cooper the following morning. Sixties architecture, drab, square and unstylish, squeezed into a gap between two suburban villas and constructed solely to provide extra accommodation at minimum cost for maximum profit. How very different towns might look, Cooper always thought, if planners had been prosecuted instead of praised for their urban vandalism.

He climbed the utilitarian stairs and rang the bell of number seventeen. 'Mr James Gillespie?' he asked of the rugged old man who poked his nose round the door and gusted stale whisky in his face. Cooper flipped open his warrant card. 'DS Cooper, Learmouth Police.'

Gillespie's eyebrows beetled aggressively. 'Well?'

'May I come in?'

'Why?'

'I'd like to ask you some questions about your late wife.'

'Why?'

Cooper could see this conversation dragging on interminably. He opted for the direct approach. 'Your wife was murdered, sir, and we have reason to believe you may have spoken to her before she died. I understand that you have been living abroad for some years, so perhaps I should remind you that you are obliged by British law to assist us in any way you can with our enquiries. Now, may I come in?'

'If you must.' He seemed quite unruffled by the policeman's bald statement but led the way past a room with a bed in it to another room containing a threadbare sofa and two plastic chairs. There was no other furniture and no carpets, but a piece of net curtaining was draped in the windows to give a modicum of privacy. 'Expecting bits and pieces from Hong Kong,' he barked. 'Should arrive any day. Camping out meanwhile. Sit down.' He lowered himself on to the sofa, trying somewhat clumsily to hide the empty bottle that lay on the floor at his feet. The room was frowsty with whisky, urine and unwashed old man. The front of his trousers was saturated, Cooper saw. Tactfully, he took out his notebook and concentrated his attention on that.

'You didn't seem very surprised when I told you your wife was murdered, Mr Gillespie. Did you know already?'

'Heard rumours.'

'Who from?'

'My brother. We used to live in Long Upton once. He still knows people there. Hears things.'

'Where does he live now?'

'London.'

'Could you give me his name and address?'

The old man thought about it. 'No harm, I suppose. Frederick Gillespie, Carisbroke Court, Denby Street, Kensington. Won't help you, though. Doesn't know any more than I do.'

Cooper flicked back through the pages of his notebook till he came to Joanna Lascelles's address. 'Your step-daughter lives in Kensington. Does your brother know her?'

'Believe so.'

Well, well, well, thought Cooper. A panorama of intriguing possibilities opened up in front of him. 'How long have you been back in England, Mr Gillespie?'

'Six months.'

The bits and pieces from Hong Kong were eyewash, then. Nothing took that long these days to be freighted round the world. The old boy was destitute. 'And where did you go first? To your brother? Or to your wife?'

'Spent three months in London. Then decided to come back to my roots.'

Frederick couldn't put up with an incontinent drunk. It was guesswork, of course, but Cooper would put money on it. 'And you saw Joanna during that time and she told you that Mathilda was still living in Cedar House.' He spoke as if it were something he had established already.

'Nice girl,' said the old man ponderously. 'Pretty, like her mother.'

'So you went to see Mathilda.'

Gillespie nodded. 'Hadn't changed. Rude woman still.'

'And you saw the clocks. The ones she told you had been stolen.'

'Solicitor's talked, I suppose.'

'I've just come from Mr Duggan. He informed us of your visit yesterday.' He saw the old man's scowl. 'He had no option, Mr Gillespie. Withholding information is a serious offence, particularly where a murder has occurred.'

'Thought it was suicide.'

Cooper ignored this. 'What did you do when you realized your wife had lied to you?'

Gillespie gave a harsh laugh. 'Demanded my property back, of course. She found that very amusing. Claimed I'd accepted money in lieu thirty years ago and no longer had an entitlement.' He searched back through his memory. 'Used to hit her when I lived with her. Not hard. But I had to make her frightened of me. It was the only way I could stop that malicious tongue.' He fingered his mouth with a trembling hand. It was mottled and blistered with psoriasis. 'I wasn't proud of it and I never hit a woman again, not until—' He broke off.

Cooper kept his voice level. 'Are you saying you hit her when she told you you couldn't have your property back?'

'Smacked her across her beastly face.' He closed his eyes for a moment as if the recollection pained him.

'Did you hurt her?'

The old man smiled unpleasantly. 'I made her cry,' he said.

'What happened then?'

'Told her I'd be putting the law on to her and left.'

'When was this? Can you remember?'

He seemed to become suddenly aware of the urine stains on his trousers and crossed his legs self-consciously. 'The time I hit her? Two, three months ago.'

'You went there at other times then?'

Gillespie nodded. 'Twice.'

'Before or after you hit her?'

'After. Didn't want the law on her, did she?'

'I don't follow.'

'Why would you? Doubt you saw her till she was dead. Devious,

218

that's the only way to describe Mathilda. Devious and ruthless. Guessed I'd fallen on hard times and came here the next day to sort something out. Talked about a settlement.' He picked at the scabs on his hand. 'Thought I wouldn't know what the clocks were worth. Offered me five thousand to leave her alone.' He fell silent.

'And?' Cooper prompted when the silence lengthened.

The old eyes wandered about the empty room. 'Realized she'd pay more to avoid the scandal. Went back a couple of times to demonstrate how vulnerable she was. She was talking fifty thousand the day before she died. I was holding out for a hundred. We'd have got there eventually. She knew it was only a matter of time before someone saw me and recognized me.'

'You were blackmailing her.'

Gillespie gave his harsh laugh again. 'Mathilda was a thief. D'you call it blackmail to negotiate back what's been stolen from you? We understood each other perfectly. We'd have reached an agreement if she hadn't died.'

Cooper allowed his revulsion to get the better of him. 'It seems to me, sir, you wanted to have your cake and eat it too. You deserted her forty years ago, left her to fend for herself with a baby, snatched up what the clocks were worth in nineteen sixty-one, spent the whole lot' – he looked pointedly at the empty bottle – 'probably on booze, repeated the exercise with everything else you've ever earned and then came home to leech off the woman you'd abandoned. I'd say it's arguable who was the greater thief. If the clocks were so important to you, why didn't you take them with you?'

'Couldn't afford to,' said Gillespie dispassionately. 'Put together enough for my passage. Nothing left over to freight the clocks.'

'Why didn't you sell one to pay for the freight of the others?'

'She blocked it.' He saw the scepticism in Cooper's expression. 'You didn't know her, man, so don't make judgements.'

'Yet by your own admission you used to beat her to make her frightened of you. How could she stop you selling your own property? You'd have thrashed her.'

'Maybe I did,' he growled. 'Maybe she found another way to stop me. You think I was the first one to try blackmail? She was a past master at it.' He touched his lips again and this time the tremor in his hands was more marked. 'We reached an accommodation, the essence of which was no scandal. She'd let me leave for Hong Kong on the condition that there was no divorce and she kept the clocks. Mutual insurance, she called them. While she housed them, she could be sure of my silence. While I owned them I could be sure of hers. They were worth a bob or two, even in those days.'

Cooper frowned. 'What silence were you buying?'

'This and that. It was an unhappy marriage, and you washed your dirty linen in public when you divorced in those days. Her father was an MP, don't forget.'

She let me leave for Hong Kong . . . Strange use of words, thought Cooper. How could she have stopped him? 'Were you involved in something criminal, Mr Gillespie? Were the clocks a quid pro quo for her not going to the police?'

He shrugged. 'Water under the bridge now.'

'What did you do?'

'Water under the bridge,' the old man repeated stubbornly. 'Ask me *why* Mathilda had to buy my silence. That's a damn sight more interesting.'

'Why then?'

'Because of the baby. Knew who the father was, didn't I?'

Water under the bridge, thought Cooper sarcastically. 'You told Mr Duggan that your wife kept diaries,' he said, 'that they were on the top shelf of her library disguised as the collected works of William Shakespeare. Is that correct?'

'It is.'

'Did you see them when you went to Cedar House or did Mrs Gillespie tell you about them?'

Gillespie's eyes narrowed. 'You saying they're not there now?'

'Will you answer my question, please. Did you see them or are you relying on something Mrs Gillespie told you?'

'Saw them. Knew what to look for, see. I had the first two volumes bound for her as a wedding present. Gave her another eight with blank pages.'

'Could you describe them, Mr Gillespie?'

'Brown calfskin binding. Gold lettering on the spines. Titles courtesy Willy Shakespeare. Ten volumes in all.'

'What sort of size?'

'Eight inches by six inches. An inch thick or thereabouts.' He wrung his hands in his lap. 'They're not there, I suppose. Don't mind telling you, rather relying on those diaries. They'll prove she set out to defraud me.'

'So you read them?'

'Couldn't,' the old man grumbled. 'She never left me alone long enough. Fussed around me like a blasted hen. But the proof'll be there. She'd've written it down, just like she wrote everything else.'

'Then you can't say for sure they were diaries, only that there were ten volumes of Shakespeare on the top shelf which bore a resemblance to some diaries you'd bought for her forty-odd years ago.'

He pursed his lips obstinately. 'Spotted them the first time I was there. They were Mathilda's diaries all right.'

Cooper thought for a moment. 'Did Mrs Lascelles know about them?'

Gillespie shrugged. 'Couldn't say. I didn't tell her. Don't believe in emptying the armoury before I have to.'

'But you told her you weren't her father?'

He shrugged again. 'Someone had to.'

'Why?'

'She was all over me. Wouldn't leave me alone. Pathetic really. Seemed wrong to let her go on believing such a fundamental lie.'

'Poor woman,' murmured Cooper with a new compassion. He wondered if there was anyone who *hadn't* rejected her. 'I suppose you also told her about the letter from her natural father.'

'Why not? Seemed to me she has as much right to the Cavendish wealth as Mathilda had.'

'How did you know about it? It was written after you left for Hong Kong.'

The old man looked sly. 'Ways and means,' he muttered. But he saw something in Cooper's eyes that caused him to reflect. 'There was talk in the village when Gerald topped himself,' he said. 'Word got about he'd written a letter which his brother managed to suppress. Suicide' – he shook his head – 'wasn't the done thing in those days. William hushed it up for the sake of the family. I heard the stories at the time and suggested Joanna look for the letter. Stood to reason what would be in it. Gerald was a sentimental half-wit bound to've mentioned his bastard. Couldn't've resisted it.'

'And perhaps you reached an accommodation with Mrs Lascelles as well. You'd testify in court to her real paternity if she kept you in clover for the rest of your life. Something like that?'

Gillespie gave a dry chuckle. 'She was a great deal more amenable than her mother.'

'Then why did you bother to go on negotiating with Mrs Gillespie?'

'Didn't rate Joanna's chances much, not against Mathilda.'

Cooper nodded. 'So you killed your wife to improve the odds.'

The dry chuckle rasped out again. 'Wondered when you'd pull that one out of the hat. Didn't need to. If she didn't kill herself, then rather think my step-daughter did it for me. She was mighty put out to discover that her mother played the tart with her great-uncle.' Abruptly, like some guilty secret he'd decided to unburden, he fished a full bottle of whisky from where it was tucked down behind the sofa cushions, unscrewed the cap and held it to his mouth. 'Want some?' he asked vaguely after a moment, waving the bottle in Cooper's direction before placing it between his lips again and half-draining it in huge mouthfuls.

The Sergeant, whose experience of drunks was considerable after years of plucking them out of the gutter in sodden heaps, watched in amazement. Gillespie's tolerance levels were extraordinary. In two minutes he had consumed enough neat spirit to put most men on their backs, and the only effect it seemed to have on him was to reduce the tremors in his hands.

'We're having difficulty establishing a motive for your wife's murder,' Cooper said slowly. 'But it seems to me yours is rather stronger than most.'

'Bah!' Gillespie snorted, his eyes bright now with alcoholic affability. 'She was worth more to me alive. I told you, she was talking fifty thousand the day before she died.'

'But you didn't keep your side of the bargain, Mr Gillespie. That meant your wife was free to reveal why you had to abscond to Hong Kong.'

'Water under the bridge,' came his monotonous refrain. 'Water under the bloody bridge. No one'd be interested in my little peccadillo now, but there's a hell of a lot'd be interested in hers. The daughter, for a start.' He raised the bottle to his mouth again, and the shutters went down.

Cooper couldn't remember when anyone or anything had disgusted him quite so much. He stood up, buttoning depression about himself with his coat. If he could wash his hands of this terrible family, he would, for he could find no saving graces in any of them. What's bred in the bone comes out in the flesh, and their corruption was as rank as the stench in that room. If he regretted anything in his life it was being on shift the day Mathilda's body was found. But for that, he might have remained what he had always believed he was – a truly tolerant man.

Unnoticed by Gillespie, he retrieved the empty bottle from the floor with his fingertips and took it with him.

Jack studied the address that Sarah had patiently cajoled out of Ruth. 'You say it's a squat, so how do I get him outside alone?'

She was rinsing some cups under the cold water tap. 'I'm having second thoughts. What happens if you end up in traction for the next six months?'

'It couldn't possibly be worse than what I'm suffering already,' he murmured, pulling out a chair and sitting on it. 'There's something wrong with the spareroom bed. It's giving me a stiff neck. When are you going to boot Ruth out and let me back where I belong?'

'When you've apologized.'

'Ah, well,' he said regretfully, 'a stiff neck it is then.'

Her eyes narrowed. 'It's only an apology, you bastard. It won't kill you. Stiff-necked says it all, if you ask me.'

He gave an evil grin. 'It's not the only thing that's stiff. You don't know what you're missing, my girl.'

She glared at him. 'That's easily cured.' With a swift movement she upended a cupful of freezing water into his lap. 'It's a pity Sally Bennedict didn't do the same.'

He surged to his feet, knocking the chair backwards. 'Jesus, woman,' he roared, 'will you stop trying to turn me into a eunuch!' He gripped her round the waist and lifted her bodily into the air. 'You're lucky we've got Ruth in the house,' he growled, twisting her sideways and holding her head under the running tap, 'otherwise I might be tempted to show you how ineffectual cold water is on a deprived libido.'

'You're drowning me,' she spluttered.

'Serves you right.' He set her on her feet again and turned off the tap.

'You asked for passion,' she said, dripping water over the quarry tiles. 'Don't you like it now that you've got it?'

He tossed her a towel. 'Hell, yes,' he said with a grin. 'The last thing I wanted was a wife who understood. I will not be patronized, woman.'

She shook her head in fury, splattering the kitchen with droplets. 'If one more person calls me patronizing,' she said, 'I will do them some damage. I am *trying* to be charitable towards some of the most useless and self-indulgent egotists it has ever been my misfortune to meet. And it's bloody difficult.' She rubbed her hair vigorously with the towel. 'If the world was made up of people like me, Jack, it would be paradise.'

'Well, you know what they say about paradise, old thing. It's heaven until the horned viper pops his head out from under the fig leaf and spots the moist warm burrow under the bushes. After that all hell breaks loose.'

She watched him pull on his old donkey jacket and take a torch from the kitchen drawer. 'What are you planning to do exactly?'

'Never you mind. What you don't know can't incriminate you.'

'Do you want me to come with you?'

His dark face split into a grin. 'What for? So you can stitch him back together again when I've finished with him? You'd be a liability, woman. Anyway, you'd be struck off if we were caught, and someone's got to stay with Ruth.'

'You will be careful, won't you?' she said, her eyes dark with concern. 'In spite of everything, Jack, I am really very fond of you.'

He touched a finger to her lips. 'I'll be careful,' he promised.

He drove slowly up Palace Road, located number twenty-three and the white Ford transit outside it, made a circuit of the block and drew into a space which gave him an unobstructed view of the house but

224

was far enough away from it not to attract attention to himself. Yellow lamplight gleamed along the street, throwing pools of shadow amongst the houses, but few people were abroad at eight o'clock on a cold Thursday evening in late November, and only once or twice did his heart jump at the unexpected appearance of a dark-clad figure on the pavement. An hour had passed when a dog emerged into a swathe of light ten yards from the car and began to rootle amongst some garbage by a dustbin. It was only after several minutes of watching that Jack realized it wasn't a dog at all but an urban fox, scavenging for food. So prepared was he for a long wait, and so entranced by the delicate scratchings of the fox, that he missed the door of number twenty-three opening. Only the noise of laughter alerted him to the fact that something was going down. With narrowed eyes, he watched a group of young men piling into the back of the van, saw the doors slam and a figure disappear round the side.

Impossible to tell if it was Hughes. Ruth had described him as tall, dark and handsome, but, as all cats are black in the night, so all young men look the same from thirty yards distant on a winter's evening. Jack, gambling on something else she had said, that the van was his and he always drove it, pulled out behind it as it drove away.

The doctor has written 'heart failure' as the cause of Father's death. I had difficulty keeping a straight face when I read it. Of course he died of heart failure. We all die of heart failure. Mrs Spencer, the housekeeper, was suitably distraught until I told her I'd keep her on while she looked about for another niche for herself. After that she rallied with surprising speed. That class has little loyalty to anything except money.

Father looked very peaceful in his chair, his whisky glass still clasped in his hand. 'Taken in his sleep' according to the doctor. How very, very true, in every respect. 'He drank far more than was good for him, my dear. I did warn him about it.' He went on to assure me that I need have no fears about him suffering. I made an appropriate response, but thought: What a pity he hadn't. He deserved to suffer. Father's worst fault was his ingratitude. James was really very lucky. Had I realized how easy it was to get rid of drunks, well, well . . . enough said.

Unfortunately, Joanna saw me. The wretched child woke up and came downstairs just as I was removing the pillow. I explained that Grandpa was ill and that the pillow was to make him more comfortable, but I have the strangest feeling she knows. She refused to go to sleep last night, just lay looking at me with that very unnerving stare of hers.

But what possible significance could a pillow have for a two-year-old . . .

Fifteen

HALF AN HOUR later and well into the better side of town, the van drew to a halt in the shadows of an expensive-looking house to pick up the wide-eyed adolescent girl waiting there. The hairs began to crawl on the back of Jack's neck. He watched her climb with gawky eagerness into the passenger seat, and he knew that she was as unprepared as Ruth had been for the surprise that Hughes had waiting for her in the back.

The van took the coast road east towards Southbourne and Hengistbury Head and, as the traffic thinned, Jack allowed the distance between it and him to lengthen. He toyed with one possibility after another – should he stop to call the police and risk losing the van altogether? – should he ram the van and risk injuring himself and the girl? – should he try to deter them by drawing in beside them when they parked, at the risk of their driving off and giving him the slip? He discarded each idea in turn, seeing only their weaknesses, and suddenly felt a deep regret that he hadn't brought Sarah with him. He had never wanted the comfort of her friendship quite so desperately.

The van turned into a deserted car park on the sea front, and more by instinct than design Jack killed his lights, thrust the gears into neutral and freewheeled to a stop beside the kerb some fifty yards behind it. Every detail of what happened next was lit by a cold, clear moon, but he knew what to expect because Ruth had described Hughes's MO in all too graphic detail. The driver, Hughes for a certainty, flung open his door and jumped out on to the tarmac, dragging the girl after him. There was the briefest of scuffles before he pinioned her in his arms and carried her, kicking and struggling,

229

to the back of the van. He was laughing as he wrenched the rear door open and flung her like a sack of potatoes into the lit interior. The square of light shone out briefly before he closed the doors and strolled away towards the sea shore, lighting a cigarette as he went.

Jack could never explain afterwards why he did what he did. In retrospect he could only really remember his fear. His actions were governed entirely by instinct. It was as if, faced with a crisis, normal reason deserted him and something primeval took over. He focused entirely on the child. The need to help her was paramount, and the only method that presented itself was to open the van doors and physically remove her from danger. He eased into first gear and motored gently towards the transit, watching Hughes as he did so to see if he picked up the throb of the engine above the wash of the waves against the shore. Apparently not. The man stooped lazily to gather stones from the beach and send them spinning out across the black water.

Jack coasted to a halt behind the van and left the engine purring while he unbuckled his belt, drawing it from around his waist and wrapping the end about his fist. He took the heavy rubber torch in his other hand, clicked open the door and slipped out on to the tarmac, sucking in great draughts of air to still the thudding of his heart.

In the distance, Hughes turned round, took in the situation at a glance, and started to pound up the beach.

Adrenaline plays tricks. It floods the body to galvanize it into colossal and spontaneous effort, but the mind observes what happens in slow motion. Thus time, that most relative of phenomena, ceases to exist in any meaningful way, and what Jack would for ever insist took several minutes, in reality took seconds. He burst the van doors open and brought the torch down on the head of the man nearest him, bellowing like a bull. The startled white face of another youth turned towards him and Jack flicked the belt across it in a vicious backhand swipe, crooking his elbow round the first man's neck as he did so and pulling him backwards on to the tarmac. He released his hold and brought the torch round in a scything arc to smash under the chin of the face he'd whipped, toppling the youth off balance into thin air behind him.

The three men left in the van, two holding the girl down, the other bare-arsed on top of her, were frozen into shocked immobility. The violence of the onslaught was so extreme, the noise of Jack's continuous roaring so disorientating, that he was on top of them before they could register what was happening. He used the hand holding the belt to grip the hair of the bastard raping the girl, wrenched his head up and swung the torch in a mighty forehand smash into the wide-eyed, frightened face. Blood erupted from the broken nose in a stream, and the youth slithered sideways with a whimper of pain.

'GET OUT!' Jack shouted at the girl who was scrambling to her knees in terror. 'GET IN THE CAR!' He whipped the belt back and sliced it through the air into the eyes of a boy who was struggling to his feet in the corner. 'YOU BLOODY LITTLE SHITS!' he roared. 'I'M GOING TO KILL YOU.' He brought his boot down on the unprotected groin of the rapist and turned like a madman on the only youth he hadn't touched. With a cry of terror, the boy cowered away, his arms held protectively above his head.

Perhaps, after all, reason hadn't entirely deserted Blakeney. He abandoned the torch and the belt, flung himself precipitately out of the van, bundled into the car after the girl, and roared it into motion, tugging the door closed as he did so. He saw Hughes too late to avoid him as he careered across the tarmac, and caught him a glancing blow with the offside wing, bouncing him into the air like a rag-doll. Jack's anger was out of control, a red frenzy that pounded in his head like cannon-fire. Spinning the wheel, he turned the vehicle in a tight circle and headed back towards the crouching figure, switching on the headlights with a lazy flick of his fingers to catch Hughes's terrified face in the glare as he prepared to mow him down.

He had no idea what stopped him doing it. Perhaps it was the girl's screams. Perhaps his anger abated as rapidly as it had surged into life. Perhaps, quite simply, his humanity triumphed. Instead, he slewed the car to a screaming halt, slammed the door into the man's body and leapt out to wind his fist around the long hair and drag Hughes to his feet. 'Into the back, sweetheart,' he said to the girl, 'as fast as you can.' She was too terrified not to obey and slid in hysterics between the seats. 'Now, you, in,' he said, yanking down on the hair and shoving his knee into the small of Hughes's back, 'or, so help me, I'll break your filthy neck now.'

Hughes believed him. As the lesser of two evils, he allowed himself to be thrust face-down across the seat and sighed as Jack's heavy weight descended across his legs. The car raced into life again, screaming across the tarmac as Jack forced it into gear, the door slamming shut when it impacted against another flying figure. 'PUT YOUR SEAT BELT ON!' he yelled at the screaming girl. 'IF THIS BASTARD MOVES A MUSCLE I'M GOING TO PILE THE SIDE WHERE HIS HEAD IS INTO THE BIGGEST BRICK WALL I CAN FIND.' He changed up, swung out on to the road and set off at a blistering pace through South-bourne with his hand clamped over the horn. If there was any justice in this cess-pit of a world, someone would get the police out before the Ford transit caught up with him.

There was some justice left in the England Rupert Brooke died for. The local police received seventeen 999 calls in three minutes, twelve from elderly widows living alone, four from outraged men, and one from a child. They all reported the same thing. Joy-riders were turning the quiet tree-lined streets of their suburb into a death-trap.

Jack's car and the pursuing white transit were ambushed as they tore on to the main road leading into Bournemouth city centre.

The phone rang in Mill House at eleven thirty that night. 'Sarah?' Jack barked down the wire.

'Hi,' she countered with relief. 'You're not dead then.'

'No. I'm under sodding arrest,' he shouted. 'This is the one telephone call I'm allowed to make. I need help PDQ.'

'I'll come straight away. Where are you?'

'The bastards are going to charge me with joy-riding and rape,' he said furiously, as if she hadn't spoken. 'They're fucking *cretins* here, won't listen to a word I say. Goddammit, they've banged me up along with Hughes and his animals. The poor kid they were having a go at in the back of the van's completely hysterical and thinks I'm one of them. I keep telling them to contact Cooper but they're such bloody morons they won't listen to me.'

'Okay,' she said calmly, trying to make what she could of this alarming speech, 'I'll get Cooper. Now tell me where you are.'

'Some shit-hole in the middle of Bournemouth,' he roared. 'They're about to take swabs off my fucking penis.'

'The address, Jack. I need the address.'

'WHERE THE HELL AM I?' he bellowed at someone in the room with him. 'Freemont Road Police Station,' he told Sarah. 'You'll have to bring Ruth, too,' he said with regret. 'God knows, I never meant to involve her but she's the only one who knows what happened. And get Keith as well. I need a solicitor I can trust. They're all bloody fascists in this place. They're talking about frigging paedophile rings and conspiracies and Christ knows what else.'

'Calm down,' she said sternly. 'Keep your mouth shut till I get there and, for God's sake, Jack, don't lose your temper and hit a policeman.'

'I already have, dammit. The bastard called me a pervert.'

It was well after two o'clock when Sarah, Cooper and Ruth finally arrived bleary-eyed at Freemont Road. The night Sergeant at Learmouth had been adamant in his refusal either to contact Cooper or to give Sarah his home phone number when she put through an urgent call requesting to speak to him. 'DS Cooper is not on duty, madam,' was his measured response. 'If you have a problem, you deal with me or wait until tomorrow morning when he will be on duty.' It was only when he was faced with her angry presence in front of his desk, threatening him with questions in Parliament and court action for negligence, that he was moved to contact the Detective Sergeant. The counter-blast from Cooper's end, not in the best of moods, anyway, after being woken up from a deep sleep, left him shaken. He grumbled away to himself for the rest of his shift. Sod's law said that it didn't matter how considerate a chap tried to be, he was always in the wrong.

Keith, even more irritable than Cooper to be dragged from the arms of Morpheus far away in London, perked up a little to hear that Jack was under arrest for joy-riding and rape. 'Good God,' he said with cynical amusement, 'I had no idea he was so active. I thought he preferred spectator sports.'

'It's not funny, Keith,' said Sarah curtly. 'He needs a solicitor. Can you come down to Bournemouth?'

'When?'

'Now, you oaf. They're taking swabs off him at this very minute.'

'Did he do it?'

'What?'

'The rape,' said Keith patiently.

'No, of course he didn't,' she spluttered angrily. 'Jack's not a rapist.'

'Then there's nothing to worry about. The swabs will prove he hasn't been in contact with the victim.'

'He says they think he's part of a paedophile ring. They may charge him with conspiracy to rape even if they can't charge him with the actual offence.' She sighed. 'At least I think that's what he said. He's very angry and it was all a bit garbled.'

'What on earth's he been up to?'

'I don't know yet,' she said through gritted teeth. 'Just get your arse down here, will you, and earn some of the fortune we've paid you over the years.'

'I'm not much of a criminal lawyer, you know. You might do better to get hold of a specialist from down there. I could give you some names out of the book.'

'He asked for you, Keith. He said he wants a solicitor he can trust, so – ' her voice rose ' – for God's sake will you stop arguing and get in your car. We're wasting time. He's at Freemont Road Police Station in Bournemouth.'

'I'll be there as soon as I can,' he promised. 'In the meantime, tell him to keep quiet and refuse to answer any questions.'

Easier said than done, thought Sarah ruefully, as she and Ruth were given chairs to sit on while Cooper was taken into an interview room. When the door opened, they heard Jack in full spate. '*Look*, how many times do you have to be *told*? I was rescuing her from being raped, not bloody raping her myself. Jesus wept!' His fist pounded on the table. 'I will not talk to morons. Doesn't anyone in this piss-pot have a measurable IQ?' He gave a whoop of relief. 'Hallelujah! Cooper! Where the hell have you been, you bastard?' The door closed again.

Sarah leant her head against the wall with a sigh. 'The trouble with Jack,' she said to Ruth, 'is he never does anything by halves.'

'He wouldn't be here at all if it wasn't for me,' the girl said wretchedly, washing her hands over and over in her lap. She was so nervous she could barely keep her breathing under control.

Sarah glanced at her. 'I think you should be rather proud of yourself. Because of you he obviously stopped someone else getting the treatment you were given. That's good.'

'Not if they think Jack was involved.'

'Cooper will set them straight.'

'Does that mean I won't have to say anything? I don't want to say anything.' The words came out in a rush. 'I'm so frightened,' she said simply, tears welling tragically in the huge dark eyes. 'I don't want anyone to know' – her voice shook – 'I'm so ashamed.'

Sarah, who had had to use a very heavy hand in the shape of emotional blackmail to get her this far, balked at using any more. The girl was in a highly emotional state already, desperately seeking to justify her mother's indifference because then she could justify her own indifference to the growing foetus inside her. But she couldn't justify it, of course, and that made her guilt about wanting an abortion all the stronger. There was no logic to human psychology, thought Sarah sadly. She had said nothing about her visit to Cedar House, merely offered to drive Ruth over to Fontwell. 'In fairness,' she had said, 'all your mother knows is that you've been expelled for going out to meet your boyfriend. I'm sure she'll be sympathetic if you tell her the truth.' Ruth shook her head. 'She wouldn't,' she whispered, 'she'd say I got what I deserved. She used to say it to Granny about her arthritis.' Her face had pinched in pain. 'I wish Granny hadn't died. I did love her, you know, but she died thinking I didn't.' And what could Sarah say to that? She had never come across three people so intent on destroying each other, and themselves.

She put her arm now around the girl's thin shoulders and hugged her tight. 'Sergeant Cooper will sort it out,' she said firmly, 'and he won't force you to say anything you don't want to.' She gave her throaty chuckle. 'He's far too nice and far too soft which is why he's never made Inspector.'

But the law, like the mills of God, grinds slow but exceeding small, and Sarah knew that if any of them emerged unscathed at the end of their brush with it, it would be a miracle.

*

'You realize, Dr Blakeney, we could charge you with being an accessory before the fact,' said an irate Inspector. 'You knew when you helped your husband get hold of Hughes's address that he planned to do something illegal, didn't you?'

'I wouldn't answer that,' said Keith.

'No, I did not,' said Sarah stoutly. 'And what's illegal about preventing a brutal rape? Since when was rescuing somebody a chargeable offence?'

'You're in the wrong ballpark, Doctor. We're talking attempted murder, GBH, abduction, driving without due care and attention, assault on a police officer. You name it, it's down here. Your husband's an extremely dangerous man and you sent him off after Hughes, knowing full well that he was liable to lose control of his temper if confronted. That's a fair summary, isn't it?'

'I wouldn't answer that,' said Keith automatically.

'Of course it isn't,' she snapped. '*Hughes* is the extremely danger-ous man, not Jack. What would you have done if you knew a young girl was about to be brutally attacked by five zombies who are so degenerate and uneducated they'll do anything their sadistic leader tells them to do?' Her eyes flashed. 'Don't bother to answer. I know exactly what you'd have done. You'd have crept off with your tail between your legs to the nearest telephone to dial nine-nine-nine, and never mind the damage that was done to the child in the meantime.'

'It's an offence to withhold information from the police. Why did you not inform us about Miss Lascelles's rape?'

'I really do advise you not to answer that question,' said Keith wearily.

'Because we gave her our word we wouldn't. Why on earth do you think Jack went out tonight if we could have told the police everything?'

Keith held up his hand to forestall the Inspector. 'Any objections to switching off the tape while I confer with my client?'

The other man eyed him for a moment then consulted his watch. 'Interview with Dr Blakeney suspended at 3.42 a.m.' He spoke abruptly, then pressed the 'stop' button.

'Thanks. Now, will you explain something to me, Sarah?' Keith murmured plaintively. 'Why did you drag me all the way down here if neither you nor Jack will listen to a word I say?'

'Because I'm so bloody angry, that's why. They should be grateful to Jack; instead they're condemning him.'

'The Inspector's paid to make you angry. That's how he gets his results, and you're making this very easy for him.'

'I object to that remark, Mr Smollett. I am paid, among other things, to try and get at the truth when a criminal offence has occurred.'

'Then why don't you stop bull-shitting,' suggested Keith amiably, 'and deal in straightforward fact? I can't be the only one here who's bored stiff with all these idiotic threats of criminal prosecution. Of course you can charge Mr Blakeney if you want to, but you'll be a laughing-stock. How many people these days would have bothered to go in and do what he did with only a belt and a torch as protection?' He smiled faintly. 'We're a non-involvement society these days, where heroism is confined to the television screens. There was a case the other day where a woman was sexually assaulted by two men in full view of several taxi-drivers at a taxi rank, and not a single one of them lifted a finger to help her. Worse, they wheeled up their windows to block out her screams for help. Should I infer from your attitude towards Mr Blakeney that that is the sort of behaviour you approve of in our so-called civilized society?'

'Vigilante behaviour is just as dangerous, Mr Smollett. For every case of non-involvement you cite, I can cite another where rough justice has been meted out on innocent people because a lynch mob decides arbitrarily who is or is not guilty. Should I infer from your attitude that you approve of the kangaroo-court approach to justice?'

Keith acknowledged the point with a nod. 'Of course not,' he said honestly, 'and had Mr Blakeney taken a private army with him I'd be on your side. But you're on very thin ice describing him as a lynch mob. He was one man, faced with an impossible decision – to act immediately to stop the rape or to abandon the girl to her fate while he drove off to summon assistance.'

'He would never have been there at all had he and his wife not conspired together to withhold the information about Miss Lascelles. Nor for that matter would Hughes and his gang have been able to subject the young lady Mr Blakeney rescued to the terror she was put through, for the simple reason that they would all have been under lock and key charged with the rape of Miss Lascelles.'

237

'But Miss Lascelles has told you categorically that she would have been too frightened to say anything to the police, assuming the Blakeneys had reported what she told them. She lives in terror of Hughes carrying out his threat to rape her again the minute he's set free, and there's no guarantee, even now, that she – or tonight's victim – will find the courage to give the evidence in court that will convict him. Your best bet, quite frankly, is Jack Blakeney's testimony. If he remains strong, which he will, Ruth will gain courage from his example, and if the other girl and her parents are made aware of just what they owe him, then she, too, may find the courage to speak out. By the same token, if you insist on pursuing these charges against Blakeney, then you can kiss goodbye to any co-operation from two terrified young women. Quite reasonably they will conclude that justice is on Hughes's side and not on theirs.'

The Inspector shook his head. 'What none of you seems able to grasp,' he said irritably, 'is that if we fail to charge Mr Blakeney we make the prosecution case against Hughes so much harder. His defence will have a field day in court pointing up the contrast between police leniency towards the *admitted* violence of a middle-class intellectual and police harshness towards the *alleged* violence of an unemployed navvy. Hughes was outside the van, remember, when the rape was taking place, and he's sitting there now claiming he had no idea what was going on. The lad who was raping the girl when your client burst into that van is only fifteen, a juvenile, in other words, who can be sentenced to detention but not to custody in an adult prison. The oldest boy there, if we exclude Hughes, is eighteen and his age will be taken into account at his trial. At the moment, they're all shell-shocked and fingering Hughes as the instigator and prime mover, but by the time they come to trial it will have become a bit of harmless fun that was the girl's idea and which Hughes knew nothing about because he had wandered off for a walk along the beach. The worst of it is, Mr Blakeney will have to testify to that in court because he saw him doing it.' He rubbed his tired eyes. 'It's a mess, frankly. God knows if we will ever succeed in bringing a conviction. Without clear evidence of intent I can see Hughes getting off scot-free. His MO is to manipulate youngsters into doing his dirty work while he stands aloof and collects the money, and once these boys realize how short their sentences are going to be because the law is relatively powerless against juveniles, they'll stop grassing him up. I'm so confident of that, I'd lay my last cent on it.'

There was a long silence.

Sarah cleared her throat. 'You're forgetting the girls,' she said. 'Won't their evidence carry weight?'

The Inspector's smile was twisted. 'If they're not too frightened to testify, if they don't collapse under cross-examination, if their stealing isn't used by the defence to blacken their characters, if the speed with which they were prepared to spread their legs for Hughes doesn't lose them the sympathy of the jury.' He shrugged. 'Justice is as fickle as fate, Dr Blakeney.'

'Then release him now and be done with it,' she said coldly. 'I mean, let's face it, it's going to be a damn sight easier to fill your productivity quota by prosecuting Jack than by having to put the counselling effort into bringing thieving little tarts up to scratch. Perhaps you should ask yourself why none of these girls felt confident enough to come to the police in the first place?' Her eyes narrowed angrily as she answered her own question. 'Because they believed everything Hughes told them, namely that *he* would always be acquitted, and *they* would always be left to fend for themselves. He was right, too, though I'd never have guessed it if I hadn't heard it from you.'

'He'll be charged and hopefully he'll be held on remand, Dr Blakeney, but what happens at trial is out of my hands. We can do our best to prepare the ground. We cannot, unfortunately, predict the outcome.' He sighed. 'For the moment, I have decided to release your husband without charge. I shall be taking advice, however, which means we may decide to proceed against him at a later date. In the meantime, he will be required to remain at Mill House in Long Upton and, should he wish to travel anywhere, he must advise Detective Sergeant Cooper of his intentions. Is that clear?'

She nodded.

'In addition, please note that if he ever involves himself again in similar activities to those he engaged in tonight, he will be charged immediately. Is that also clear?'

She nodded.

The Inspector's tired face cracked into a smile. 'Off the record, I rather agree with Mr Smollett here. Your husband's a brave man, Doctor, but I'm sure you knew that already.'

'Oh, yes,' said Sarah loyally, hoping that her expression was less sheepish than it felt. For as long as she'd known him Jack had always maintained the same thing. All men were cowards but it was only a few, like himself, who had the courage to admit it. She was beginning to wonder if there were other aspects of his character that she had misjudged so completely.

Father rang today to give me the inquest verdict on Gerald's death. 'They've opted for misadventure, thank God, but I had to pull every string in the book to get it. That damned Coroner was going to bring in suicide if he could.' Poor Father! He could never have shown his face in the House again if his brother had killed himself. Heaven forbid! What stigma is still attached to suicide, particularly amongst the upper classes. Nothing is so bad as the ultimate weakness of taking one's own life.

I am naturally delighted with the verdict, if somewhat piqued to have my brilliance overlooked. There is an extraordinary urge to confess, I find, if only to draw attention to what one has achieved . . . I won't, of course.

Gerald was putty in my hands when it came to writing the codicil because I told him he'd go to prison for raping his niece if he didn't. 'Lord, what fools these mortals be!' The only purpose of the codicil was to convince the idiot solicitor that Gerald had committed suicide when he discovered whose child Joanna really was. Once persuaded, he alerted Father to the fact that a document detailing Gerald's incest existed, and they both performed to perfection. They made such a song-and-dance about pulling their various strings in order to suppress any hint that Gerald might have done away with himself that everyone, including the Coroner, was in no doubt that he had. It is all so very amusing. My only regret is that I had to involve Jane, but I am not unduly concerned about that. Even if she does have any suspicions, she won't voice them. She can't afford to, but in any case no one has questioned where Gerald acquired his barbiturates, or if they have I suspect Father has claimed them as his. He's so drunk most of the time, he probably believes they were.

Father's relief was short-lived. I told him I had a signed carbon copy of the codicil in my possession and he became apoplectic at the other end of the wire. He calls it blackmail. I call it self-preservation . . .

Sixteen

TWO FAXES were waiting on Cooper's desk when he arrived at the station later that morning. The first was brief and to the point:

Fingerprints on Yale key, ref: TC/H/MG/320, identified as belonging to Sarah Penelope Blakeney. 22 point agreement. No other prints. Fingerprints on bottle, ref: TC/H/MG/321 agree in 10, 16 and 12 points respectively with prints located in Cedar House on desk (room 1), chair (room 1), and decanter (room 1). Full report to follow.

The second fax was longer and rather more interesting. After he had read it, Cooper went off in search of PC Jenkins. It was Jenkins, he recalled, who had done most of the tedious legwork around Fontwell in the days following Mrs Gillespie's death.

'I hear you've been busy,' said Charlie Jones, dunking a ginger biscuit into a cup of thick white coffee.

Cooper sank into an armchair. 'Hughes, you mean.'

'I'm going down there in half an hour to have another bash at him. Do you want to come?'

'No thanks. I've had more than enough of Dave Hughes and his fellow-lowlife to last me a lifetime. You wait till you see them, Charlie. Kids, for Christ's sake. Fifteen-year-olds who look twenty-five and have a mental age of eight. It scares me, it really does. If society doesn't do something to educate them and match a man's brain to a man's body, we haven't a hope of survival. And the worst of it is, it's not just us. I saw a ten-year-old boy on the telly the other day,

243

wielding a machine gun in Somalia as part of some rebel army. I've seen children in Ireland throwing bricks at whichever side their bigoted families tell them to, adolescent Palestinian boys strutting their stuff in balaclavas, negro lads in South Africa necklacing each other because white policemen think it's a great way to get rid of them, and Serbian boys encouraged to rape Muslim girls the way their fathers do. It's complete and utter madness. We corrupt our children at our peril, but by God we're doing a fine job of it.'

Charlie eyed him sympathetically. 'Not just a busy night, obviously, but an exhausting one, too.'

'Forget *in vino veritas*,' said Cooper acidly. '*In insomnio veritas* is more like it. I wake up in the early hours of the morning sometimes and see the world as it really is. A bear garden, with religious leaders twisting souls on one side, power-corrupt politicians twisting minds on the other side, and the illiterate, intolerant masses in the middle baying for blood because they're too uneducated to do anything else.'

'Stop the world I want to get off, eh?'

'That's about the size of it.'

'Are there no redeeming features, Tommy?'

Cooper chuckled. 'Sure, as long as no one reminds me of Hughes.' He passed the first fax across the desk-top. 'Gillespie never left the sitting-room, apparently, and the key's a dead-end.'

Jones looked disappointed. 'We need something concrete, old son, and quickly. I'm being pushed to drop this one and concentrate on something that will get a result. The consensus view is that, even if we do manage to prove it was murder, we're going to have the devil's own job bringing a prosecution.'

'I wonder where I've heard that before,' said Cooper sourly. 'If things go on like this, we might as well pack it in and let the anarchists have a go.'

'What about the diaries? Any progress there?'

'Not really. The search was a wash-out, but then I knew it would be. I went through every book in the library the first time we searched Cedar House.' He frowned. 'I had a word with Jack and Ruth last night, but they're claiming ignorance as well, although Jack does remember Mrs Gillespie being in a paddy one day because she said her books were being disturbed.' He fingered his lip. 'I know it's hypothetical but, let's say the diaries did exist and that someone was looking for them, then that might at least explain why the books were disturbed.'

Charlie snorted. 'Hellishly hypothetical,' he agreed, 'and quite unprovable.'

'Yes, but if whoever was looking for them found them, then it might explain why they've been removed.' He took pity on Charlie's baffled expression. 'Because,' he said patiently, 'they could tell us who murdered her and why.'

Charlie frowned. 'You're clutching at straws. First, convince me they existed.'

'Why would James Gillespie lie?'

'Because he's a drunk,' said Charlie. 'You don't need any better reason than that.'

'Then why was Mathilda in a paddy because her books were being disturbed? Explain that, or are you suggesting Jack's lying, too?'

Charlie registered this second use of 'Jack' with an inward sigh. When would the silly fellow learn that it was his inability to keep his distance that scuppered his chances every time? *Unprofessional. Cannot remain objective*, was what Jones's predecessor had written on Cooper's last assessment. 'She must have guessed who it was,' he said. 'It's a narrow field in all conscience. Why didn't she tackle them about it?'

'Perhaps she did. Perhaps that's why she was murdered.' Cooper tapped the fax with his forefinger. 'The key complicates it, though. If whoever it was knew about that, then they could have let themselves in without her knowing. The field becomes much wider then.'

'I suppose you've considered that Gillespie's our man, and only mentioned the diaries to you because he thought everyone else would have known about them.'

'Yes. But why would he take them away and deny all knowledge if he's expecting them to prove she diddled him over the clocks?'

'Double bluff. He read them, discovered they proved the exact opposite, so destroyed them in order to keep his claim alive, then topped her to give himself a free run with Mrs Lascelles who he thought was going to inherit.'

Cooper shook his head. 'It's a possibility, I suppose, but it doesn't feel right. If he stole them himself because he knew they'd destroy his chances of any money, how could he be sure no one else had read them first? It's too iffy, Charlie.'

'It's *all* too iffy, frankly,' said the Inspector dryly. 'If the diaries existed – if the searcher *knew* they existed – if there was something incriminating in them – if he or she knew about the key . . .' He fell silent, dunking his biscuit again. 'There are two things I don't understand. Why did Mrs Gillespie leave all her money to Dr Blakeney and why did her murderer put the scold's bridle on her head and deck it out with nettles and daisies? If I knew the answers to those two questions, I could probably tell you who killed her. Otherwise I'm inclined to make do with a verdict of suicide.'

'I think I know why she left the money to Dr Blakeney.'

'Why?'

'I reckon it was a Pontius Pilate exercise. She'd done a lousy job herself bringing up her daughter and granddaughter, knew they'd destroy themselves with jealous infighting if she left the money to them, so passed the buck to the only person she'd ever got on with and respected. Namely Dr Blakeney. I think she hoped the doctor would succeed where she hadn't.'

'Sentimental twaddle,' said the Inspector amiably. 'And all because you're reasoning backwards, from the effect you see to the cause you imagine a normal person would wish to achieve. Try reasoning forwards. She was a bloody-minded, mean and vicious old woman, who not only acquired a fortune through blackmail and creative insurance scams but also loathed and despised everyone around her for most of her life. Why, having sown nothing but discord for sixty years, did she suddenly endow an easy-going, pleasant stranger with a fortune? Not for the sake of harmony, that's for sure.' The Inspector's eyes narrowed thoughtfully. 'I can go along with the scold's bridle as a sort of symbolic drawing attention to the final curbing of a peculiarly unpleasant tongue, but I cannot go along with the idea that the leopard suddenly changed its spots when it came to making the will.'

'You can't ignore the Blakeneys' view of her character, Charlie. According to them, she was a much pleasanter person than anyone else credited her with being. My guess is they gave her room to breathe, didn't demand anything and the real Mathilda blossomed.' He paused for a moment and took stock. 'Think about this. We've been dwelling on the symbolism of the scold's bridle, largely because of Ophelia's "nettles, daisies and long purples", but look at it in practical terms instead. They were used to keep women quiet, and perhaps the reason she was wearing it was as simple as that. Her murderer didn't want her alerting the next-door neighbours by screaming her head off, so shoved that contraption on her head and then adorned it with flowers to give it a mystical – but misleading – significance.'

Jones steepled his fingers under his chin. 'But she must have taken the barbiturates first or she'd have struggled when the bridle was put on and there'd have been scratches on her face. If she was so doped up that she didn't bother to fight it, then why put it on at all?'

'Do what you told me to do and reason forwards. You want to kill a woman by making it look like suicide, but the neighbours are too close for comfort so you need a method of keeping her quiet in case the barbiturates aren't as effective as you hope. A belt and braces job in other words. You can't use tape or Elastoplast because it'll leave a mark on the skin, and you're canny enough not to use a gag in case bits of fabric are found in the mouth during the post mortem, so you pitch on something you can leave in place which has its own significance to the victim, and you trust to luck that the police will put it down as a macabre example of self-condemnation. Then you carry her to the bath, clasp your hands over hers while you slit each wrist, drop the knife to the floor and leave her to die, knowing that even if she does struggle back to consciousness, the bridle will prevent her calling for help.'

Jones nodded. 'It sounds feasible, but why bother with the bath and the Stanley knife at all? Why not simply overdose her on sleeping pills and kill her that way?'

'Because there weren't enough, presumably, and even if there were, they're very unreliable. Supposing Ruth had come back the next morning and found the old lady still alive. It might have been possible to pump her out and revive her. Plus, of course, Ophelia drowned herself which may have inspired the idea.' He smiled self-consciously. 'I've read the play to see if there are any clues in it and a blood-thirsty piece it is, too. There's no one left standing by the end.'

'Did you find any clues?'

'No.'

'I'm not surprised. It was written four hundred years ago.' Jones tapped his pencil against his teeth. 'I can't see that any of this makes much difference, frankly. You're still describing someone who knew her intimately, which is what we've believed from the start. The only new pieces of information are the discovery of the key and the absence of the diaries. I admit the key may mean that her murderer came in uninvited, but it still had to be someone very close to her or she'd have screamed her head off. And there's so much intimate detail involved – the Stanley knife, the sleeping pills, her yen for Shake-speare, the scold's bridle. Whoever it was probably even knew there were nettles and daisies in her garden *and* where to find them in the dark. And someone *that* close means the Blakeneys, the Lascelles women or Mr and Mrs Spede.'

Cooper took the second fax from his notebook and spread it on the desk. 'According to the fingerprint tests we made, bearing in mind I told the lab to get a move on so these results will have to be double-checked for accuracy, they've made tentative identifications on four of the prints in that house, excluding Mrs Gillespie herself, Mrs Spede, the Blakeneys, Mrs and Miss Lascelles and now James Gillespie. The four are . . .' he ran his finger slowly down the page, 'the Reverend Matthews, matched in ten points with print located on hall mirror; Mrs Orloff, matched in sixteen points with print located on kitchen worktop and in fourteen points with print found on kitchen door; Mrs Spencer, matched in twelve points with print on hall door; and, lastly, Mrs Jane Marriott, matched in eighteen points with two prints on desk in library and one on stair newel post.' He looked up. 'Mrs Orloff is her neighbour. Mrs Spencer runs the local shop and Mrs Marriott is the receptionist at the Fontwell surgery. What's interesting is that the Reverend Matthews, Mrs Orloff and Mrs Spencer all admitted quite happily that they had been inside the house in the week before Mrs Gillespie died. Mrs Marriott didn't. According to Jenkins who interviewed her when he was going door to door, she said she hadn't been near Cedar House for years.'

With careless disregard for the restrictions placed on his movements by the Bournemouth police, Jack waited until Sarah had left for work then set off for Fontwell on the old bicycle that Geoffrey Freeling's next-of-kin had abandoned in the garage. His car was in the pound at Freemont Road and looked like remaining there indefinitely until a decision was reached on whether or not to prosecute him, but he was deeply suspicious about their motives for holding it. They had claimed it was material evidence, but he saw Keith's devious hand at work behind the Inspector. It's unreasonable to expect Dr Blakeney to guard her husband for you, so deprive Jack of his wheels, and he may stay put. For once he was grateful to Smollett's lingering partiality for his wife.

Ruth was dead to the world upstairs, worn out by the mental and physical stress that had taken its toll of her all too meagre reserves the previous night, but he left a note on the kitchen table in case she woke up and panicked to find him gone: 'You're quite safe with Hughes in the nick,' it read, 'but don't answer the door to anyone, just in case. Back soon, love Jack.'

'Mrs Marriott?' Cooper leant on the receptionist's counter in the empty surgery and held up his warrant card. 'DS Cooper, Learmouth Police.'

Jane smiled automatically. 'How can I help you, Sergeant?'

'I'd like a word or two in private, if that's possible.'

'It's private enough here for the moment,' she said. 'The only thing likely to disturb us is the telephone. Would you care for a cup of coffee?'

'Thank you. White, two sugars, please.'

She busied herself with the kettle.

'We've had some interesting results from our fingerprint tests,' said Cooper to her back. 'One way and another the evidence points to quite a few people visiting Mrs Gillespie before she died. You, for example.'

Jane became very still suddenly. 'I hoped you wouldn't find out,' she admitted after a moment, plucking invisible fluff from her jumper. 'And then, of course, you invited us all to give examples of our fingerprints. It was very difficult to know what to do then. Should I confess that I'd told a lie the first time or sit it out in the hopes I hadn't touched anything?'

'Why didn't you want us to know you'd been to Cedar House?'

'Because you'd have asked me my reason for going.'

He nodded. 'Which was?'

She turned back to the coffee cups and poured out the water. 'It had nothing to do with Mathilda's death, Sergeant. It was a very private matter.'

'I'm afraid that really won't do, Mrs Marriott.'

She pushed a cup across the counter and placed the sugar bowl and a spoon beside it. 'Will you arrest me if I refuse to tell you?'

He chuckled good-humouredly. 'Not immediately.'

'When?'

He sidestepped the question. 'If I say to you that, as long as what you tell me really does have no bearing on Mrs Gillespie's death, it will go no further than these four walls, will you trust me enough to keep my word?' He held her gaze with his. 'You've no idea of the sort of publicity you'll face if I have to take you in for questioning. Once the press have their teeth into you, they don't let go easily.'

Jane's plump homely face took on a very bleak expression. 'How Mathilda would adore this if she were still alive,' she said. 'She loved making trouble.'

'You knew her well then.'

'Too well.'

'And you didn't like her?'

'I couldn't bear her. I tried to avoid her as far as I could but that wasn't very easy once I started working here, what with phone calls demanding a doctor's visit and requests for repeat prescriptions.'

'Yet you went to see her?'

'I had to. I saw James coming out of her house the day before she died.' She held a hand to her bosom. 'It was such a shock. I thought he was in Hong Kong.' She fell silent.

'Tell me about it,' Cooper prompted gently.

'You wouldn't understand,' said Jane with conviction. 'You didn't know Mathilda.'

Jack was in a very bad mood by the time he reached Cedar House. He hadn't ridden a bicycle in years, and four miles along rutted country lanes on something that should have been condemned to the scrap heap years ago had given him sore balls and the sort of trembling thighs that would have disgraced a nonagenarian. He abandoned the bicycle against a tree in the Cedar Housing Estate, vaulted the fence

and ran lightly across the grass to the kitchen window. For reasons of
his own, he had no intention of announcing his presence by approaching across the gravel or using the front doorbell.

He tapped lightly but persistently on the window pane, and after
a minute or two, Joanna appeared in the doorway that led from the
kitchen into the hall. 'What do you want?'

He read her lips, rather than heard the words, and gestured
towards the back door. 'Let me in,' he mouthed, his voice barely
above a whisper.

Jane's eyes narrowed as she looked back down the corridors of time.
'You see, you can't assess Mathilda on what people tell you now.
They've forgotten how beautiful she was as a young woman, how
witty she was and how many men desired her. She was the most
eligible girl around – her father was the MP, her uncle was a wealthy
bachelor – ' she shrugged ' – she could have married anybody.'

'Then why didn't she?'

'At the time everyone assumed she was hanging on for something
better, a title perhaps, or a stately home with acres, but I always
thought there was more to it than that. I used to watch her at parties
and it was very clear to me that, while she enjoyed flirting and being
the centre of attention, she couldn't bear men touching her.' She fell
silent.

'Go on,' Cooper prompted after a moment or two.

'It wasn't until ten years later when my husband and I met James
in Hong Kong and he told us the truth about Joanna's parentage that
it made sense.' She sighed. 'Not that I've ever really understood
exactly what happened because, of course, child abuse and incest were
kept under wraps in those days. James believed she encouraged
Gerald, but I never did. It's the one area where I always felt sorry for
her. She was emotionally crippled by it, I think.'

'So you've known for a long time that Mrs Lascelles wasn't James
Gillespie's daughter?'

'Yes.'

'Did Mrs Gillespie know you knew?'

'Oh, yes.'

'Didn't that worry her?'

'She knew I wouldn't tell anyone.'

'How could she know?'

'She just did,' said Jane flatly.

What was it James Gillespie had called it? Mutual insurance.

Without warning, as the back door closed behind him, Jack's huge hand circled Joanna's throat and drove her through the kitchen and into the hall. 'Didn't what happened to Mathilda teach you anything, you silly bitch?' he said in a savage undertone.

Cooper took out a cigarette, remembered where he was and put it back again. 'Was it you who was friendly with Mr Gillespie, or your husband?' he asked Jane.

'Paul and he went through the war together, but I'd known him a long time as well.'

'Why did it shock you so much to see him coming out of Cedar House that day?'

'I'd always hoped he was dead.' She sighed. 'I know you've seen him. Sarah told me. Did he tell you anything?'

'About what, Mrs Marriott?'

She gave a tired smile. 'You'd know if he'd told you, Sergeant.'

'Then I don't think he can have done,' he said honestly. 'But you're obviously afraid he will, so wouldn't it be better coming from you? I presume it's something that only you, he and Mathilda were privy to. You were confident she wouldn't say anything because you could reveal the truth about Joanna's father, but he's a different matter. You have no hold over him, which is why you were so shocked to see him back in England and why you went to see Mathilda, to find out if he was going to spill the beans. Am I right?'

Joanna showed only the slightest flicker of alarm before she relaxed against the wall and stared into his eyes with a look of triumph. 'I knew you'd come back.'

He didn't say anything, just searched her beautiful face and marvelled again at its absolute perfection. It was the face of the Madonna in Michelangelo's Pietà, the face of a mother gazing down in quiet contemplation on the body of her adored son, a study of such simple purity that it had brought tears to his eyes when he first saw it. For years, he had wondered about the woman behind the Madonna. Was she real? Or was she something fabulous that Michelangelo had conjured from his own imagination? Until Joanna, he had believed she must have existed in the eye of her creator because only an artist could have made a thing of such immeasurable beauty. Now he held it beneath his hand and knew that its conception had been as random and as accidental as his own. He closed his eyes to stem the tears that threatened to well again.

Jane nodded unhappily. 'James blackmailed me for five years after we returned home from Hong Kong. In the end, I paid him over ten thousand pounds, which was all the money my mother left me.' Her voice shook. 'He stopped when I sent him copies of my bank statement which showed I had nothing more to give him, but he warned me he'd come back.' She was silent for a moment, striving for control. 'I never saw or heard from him again until that awful day when he came out of Cedar House.'

Cooper studied her bent head with compassion. He could only assume she'd had an affair that James and Mathilda Gillespie had found out about, but why was it so hard to confess to all these years on? 'Everyone has skeletons somewhere in their closet, Mrs Marriott. Mine still bring a blush to my cheeks when I think about them. But do you really think your husband would hold yours against you after thirty-odd years?'

'Oh, yes,' she said honestly. 'Paul always wanted children, you see, and I could never give him any.'

Cooper waited for her to go on but, when she didn't, he prompted her gently: 'What do children have to do with it?'

'Paul had an affair with Mathilda and Mathilda got pregnant. That's why James went to Hong Kong. He said it was the last straw, that he might have coped with Gerald's incestuous bastard but not with Paul's love child as well.'

Cooper was very taken aback. 'And that's what James was

blackmailing you over?' But no, he thought, that didn't make sense. It was the adulterous husband who paid the blackmailer not the deceived wife.

'Not about the affair,' said Jane. 'I knew all about that. Paul told me himself after he resigned. He was Sir William's agent and used to stay with James and Mathilda in their flat in London whenever he had business in town. I don't think the affair was anything more than a brief infatuation on both their parts. She was bored with the tedious domestic routine of washing nappies and keeping house and he . . .' she sighed, 'he was flattered by the attention. You really must try to understand how captivating Mathilda could be, and it wasn't just beauty, you know. There was something about her that drew men like magnets. I think it was the remoteness, the dislike of being touched. They saw it as a challenge, so when she let her guard down for Paul, he fell for it.' She gave a sad little smile. 'And I understood that, believe me. It may sound odd to you but there was a time – when we were young – when I was almost as in love with her as he was. She was everything I always wanted to be and never was.' Her eyes filled. 'Well, you know how attractive she could be. Sarah fell in love with her, just the way I did.'

'Show me how much you love me, Jack.' Joanna's voice, soft and husky, was a lover's caress.

Gently his fingers smoothed the white column of her throat. How could someone so ugly be *so* beautiful? She made a mockery of the wonder of creation. He raised his other hand to the silver-gold hair and, with a violent twist, wrapped the strands around his palm and jerked her head backwards with his fingers still clamped about her throat. 'I love you this much,' he said quietly.

'You're hurting me.' This time her voice rose in alarm.

He tightened his grip on her hair. 'But I enjoy hurting you, Joanna.' His voice echoed through the emptiness of the hall.

'I don't understand,' she cried out, her voice rasping against his fingers on her larynx. 'What do you want?' She saw something in his eyes that brought the fear leaping into hers. 'Oh, my God. It was you who killed my mother.' She opened her mouth to scream but only a thread of sound came out as the pressure on her throat tightened.

'I'm sorry if I'm being particularly slow on the uptake,' said Cooper apologetically, 'but I don't quite see what hold James Gillespie could have had over you that would prompt you to pay him ten thousand pounds. If you already knew about the affair from your husband—' he broke off. 'It was something to do with the pregnancy, presumably. Did you not know about that?'

She compressed her lips in an effort to hold back tears. 'Yes, I did. It was Paul who never knew.' She drew another deep sigh. 'It's so awful. I've kept it secret for so long. I wanted to tell him but there was never a good time. Rather like the lie I told your constable. At what point do you come clean, as it were?' She touched her fingers to her lips in a gesture of despair. 'Being a father. It was all he ever wanted. I prayed and prayed that we would have children of our own, but of course we never did . . .' She tailed off into silence.

Cooper put a large, comforting hand over hers. He was completely at sea here, but was reluctant to press too hard in case she clammed up on him. 'How did you know about the pregnancy if your husband didn't?'

'Mathilda told me. She rang me and asked me to go to London, said if I didn't she'd make sure the whole of Fontwell knew about her and Paul. He'd written her some letters and she said she'd make them public if I didn't do what she wanted.'

'What did she want?'

It was some moments before she could speak. 'She wanted me to help her murder the baby when it came.'

'Good God!' said Cooper with feeling. And she must have done it, he thought, or James Gillespie would never have been able to blackmail her.

There was the sound of footsteps on the gravel outside and a ring on the doorbell. 'Joanna!' called Violet's high-pitched, nervous voice. 'Joanna! Are you all right, dear? I thought I *heard* something.' When

255

she received no answer, she called again: 'Is someone with you? Do answer, please.' Her voice rose even higher. 'Duncan! Duncan!' she called. 'There *is* something wrong. I know there is. You must call the police. I'm going to get help.' Her footsteps skittered away as she ran towards the gate.

Jack stared down into Joanna's drawn and haunted face, then lowered her with surprising gentleness on to the nearest chair. 'You don't deserve it, but you were luckier than your mother,' was all he said, before walking off towards the kitchen and the back door.

Joanna Lascelles was still screaming when Duncan Orloff, in a state of complete panic, used a sledgehammer to break open the front door and confront whatever awaited him in the hall of Cedar House.

'And did you help her?' Cooper asked with a calm that belied his true feelings.

She looked wretched. 'I don't know – I don't know what she did – I can only guess.' She wrung her hands in distress. 'She didn't say anything in so many words. She just asked me to steal some sleeping pills – barbiturates – from my father's dispensary. She said they were for her because she couldn't sleep. I hoped – I thought – she was going to kill herself – and I was glad. I hated her by that time.'

'So you got her the pills?'

'Yes.'

'But she didn't kill herself.'

'No.'

'But you said she wanted you to help her kill the baby.'

'That's what I thought for ten years.' The long-held-back tears oozed slowly from between her lids. 'There was only Joanna, you see. The other baby might never have existed. I didn't think it had ever existed.' She held a shaking hand to her face. 'I thought I'd helped her kill it – and then in Hong Kong, James kept asking me how Gerald could have killed himself with barbiturates, because no doctor would have prescribed them for him, and I realized it was Gerald she'd wanted to kill all along, and I'd given her the means to do it.' She took out a handkerchief and blew her nose. 'I was so *shocked* that James guessed what I'd done. I think he'd always known, though. In many ways, he and Mathilda were very alike.'

Cooper sought desperately to break this down into manageable proportions. There were so many unanswered questions. 'Why would no doctor prescribe barbiturates for Gerald Cavendish? I've checked the coroner's report. There was no question of murder, only a choice between misadventure and suicide.'

'Gerald was . . .' Jane sought for the right word, 'feeble-minded, I suppose, like the Spedes, but today they call it educationally subnormal. It's why the property was kept intact for William. Mathilda's grandfather was afraid Gerald would give it away to anyone who asked for it. But I've never really understood how Mathilda came to sleep with him. He was a very pathetic person. I've always assumed her father forced her into it to protect his legacy somehow, but James said it was all Mathilda's idea. I don't believe that. James hated her so much he'd have said anything to blacken her.'

Cooper shook his head in bewilderment. How uneventful his own life had been, compared with the agonies of this grey-haired motherly soul who looked as if butter wouldn't melt in her mouth. 'Why did you visit James Gillespie in Hong Kong if your husband had had an affair with his wife? There can't have been much love lost between the three of you in all conscience.'

'We didn't or at least not like that. We had no idea James had gone to Hong Kong. Mathilda never told us – why would she? – and we moved away from here after the affair and went to live in Southampton. I became a teacher and Paul worked for a shipping company. We put it all behind us, and then Paul had to go to Hong Kong on business and took me with him for a holiday.' She shook her head. 'And almost the first person we met when we arrived was James. The expatriate community was so small' – she raised her hands in a gesture of helplessness – 'we were bound to meet him. If we'd only known he was there, we'd never have gone. Fate is very cruel, Sergeant.'

He couldn't argue with that. 'Then why did you come back here to live, Mrs Marriott, knowing that Mrs Gillespie was in Cedar House? Weren't you tempting fate a second time?'

'Yes,' she said simply, 'but what could I do about it? Paul knows nothing of any of this, Sergeant, and he's dying – slowly – of emphysema. We kept our house here – it was his parents' house and he was too fond of it to sell it, so we let it out to tenants – and then five years ago, he was retired on health grounds and he begged me to let us come home.' Her eyes flooded again. 'He said I needn't worry about Mathilda, that the only thing he had ever felt for her was compassion, while the only woman he had ever loved was me. How could I tell him then what had really happened? I still thought his baby was dead.' She held her handkerchief to her streaming eyes. 'It wasn't until I went to Cedar House and asked Mathilda about James that she told me she'd put the baby up for adoption.' She buried her face in her hands. 'It was a boy and he's still alive somewhere.'

Cooper pondered the sad ironies of life. Was it providence, God or random selection that made some women fertile and some barren? With a deep reluctance he took her back to the day Mathilda died, knowing there was little chance that what she told him could ever remain a secret.

I am pregnant again, sickeningly and disgustingly pregnant. Barely six months after giving birth to one bastard, I am carrying another. Perhaps James's drunken rages will achieve some good purpose by bringing on a miscarriage. He weeps and rants in turn, screaming insults at me like a fishwife, intent, it seems, on trumpeting my 'whorishness' to the entire building. And all for what? A brief, unlovely affair with Paul Marriott whose clumsy, apologetic gropings were almost past endurance. Then, why, Mathilda?

Because there are days when I could 'drink hot blood, and do such bitter business as the day would quake to look on'. Paul's priggishness annoyed me. He talked about 'dear Jane' as if she mattered to him. Mostly I think about death – the baby's death, James's death, Gerald's death, Father's death. It is, after all, such a final solution. Father connives to keep me in London. He tells me Gerald has sworn to marry Grace if I return. The worst of it is, I believe him. Gerald is so very, very frightened of me now.

I paid a private detective to take photographs of James. And, my, my, what photographs they are! 'The fitchew nor the soiled horse goes to't with such a riotous appetite.' And in a public lavatory too. If the truth be told, I am rather looking forward to showing them to him. What I did was merely sinful. What James does is criminal. There'll be no more talk of divorce, that's for sure, and he'll go to Hong Kong without a murmur. He has no more desire than I to have his sexual activities made public.

Really, Mathilda, you must learn to use blackmail to better effect on Gerald and Father . . .

259

Seventeen

HUGHES, WHO WAS suffering from sleep deprivation and niggling doubts about the continued obedience of the youngsters he had so successfully controlled, was subdued when he faced Chief Inspector Charlie Jones across the table in the interview room at Freemont Road Police Station. Like Cooper, he was in pessimistic mood. 'I suppose you've come to stitch me up for the old cow's murder,' he said morosely. 'You're all the same.'

'Ah, well,' said Charlie in his lugubrious fashion, 'it makes the percentages look better when the league tables get published. We're into business culture in the police force these days, lad, and productivity's important.'

'That stinks.'

'Not to our customers it doesn't.'

'What customers?'

'The law-abiding British public who pay handsomely for our services through their taxes. Business culture demands that we first identify our client base, next, assess its needs, then, finally, respond in a satisfactory and adequate manner. You already represent a handsome profit on the balance sheet. Rape, conspiracy to rape, abduction, holding without consent, conspiracy to hold without consent, assault, sexual assault, theft, conspiracy to commit theft, handling stolen goods, corruption, conspiracy to pervert the course of justice – ' he broke off with a broad smile, 'which brings me to Mrs Gillespie's murder.'

'I knew it,' said Hughes in disgust. 'You're gonna fucking frame me for it. Jesus! I'm not saying another word till my brief gets here.'

'Who said anything about framing you?' demanded Charlie plaintively. 'It's a little co-operation I'm after, that's all.'

Hughes eyed him suspiciously. 'What do I get in return?'

'Nothing.'

'Then it's no.'

Charlie's eyes narrowed to thin slits. 'The question you should have asked me, lad, is what do you get if you don't co-operate? I'll tell you. You get my personal assurance that not a stone will be left unturned until I see you convicted and sent down for the abduction and rape of a child.'

'I don't do children,' Hughes sneered. 'Never have done. Never will. And you won't get me for rape neither. I've never raped a girl in my life. I've never needed to. What those other punks did is their affair. I had no idea what was going on.'

'For an adult male to sleep with a thirteen-year-old girl is rape. She's under age and therefore too young to give consent for what's done to her.'

'I've never slept with a thirteen-year-old.'

'Sure you have, and I'll prove it. I'll work every man under me until he drops in order to turn up just one little girl, *virgo intacta* before you raped her, who lied to you about her age.' He gave a savage grin as a flicker of doubt crossed Hughes's face. 'Because there'll be one, lad, there always is. It's an idiosyncrasy of female psychology. At thirteen, they want to pass for sixteen, and they do. At forty, they want to pass for thirty, and by God they can do that, too, because the one damn thing you can be sure about the female of the species is that she never looks her age.'

Hughes fingered his unshaven jaw. 'What sort of co-operation are you talking about?'

'I want a complete run-down on everything you know about Cedar House and the people in it.'

'That's easy enough. Fuck all's the answer. Never went in. Never met the old biddy.'

'Come on, Dave, you're a pro. You sat outside in your van over the months, waiting while Ruth did her stuff inside. You were her chauffeur, remember, turned up day after day during the holidays to give her a good time. How did she know you were there if you couldn't signal to her? Don't kid me you weren't close enough to watch all the comings and goings in that place.'

Hughes shrugged. 'Okay, so I saw people from time to time, but if I don't know who they were, how's it gonna help you?'

'Did you ever watch the back of the house?'

The man debated with himself. 'Maybe,' he said guardedly.

'Where from?'

'If you're aiming to use this against me, I want my brief.'

'You're in no position to argue,' said Charlie impatiently. 'Where were you watching it from? Outside or inside the garden?'

'I sometimes used to park the van in the housing estate at the side. Ruth reckoned it was safer, what with all the yuppies living there. Wives commuting to work along with their husbands so no one in during the day,' he explained obligingly. 'There's some rough ground next to the fence round Cedar House garden, easy enough to hop over and watch from the trees.'

The Inspector took an ordnance survey map out of his briefcase. 'The Cedar Estate?' he asked, tapping the map with his forefinger.

Hughes sniffed. 'Probably. Ruth said the land once belonged to the house before the old lady sold it off for cash, though Christ knows why she didn't flog the rest while she was about it. What she want with a massive garden, when there's people living on the streets? Jesus, but she was a tight-fisted old bitch,' he said unwarily. 'All that frigging money and no one else got a bloody look-in. Is it true she left the lot to her doctor or was Ruth just spinning me a yarn?'

Charlie stared him down. 'None of your business, lad, but I'll tell you this for free. Ruth didn't get a penny because of what you forced her to do. Her grandmother took agin her when she started stealing. But for you, she'd have had the house.'

Hughes was unmoved. 'Shouldn't have been so quick to open her legs then, should she?'

Charlie looked at the map again, fighting an urge to hit him. 'Did you ever see anyone go in through the back door?'

'The cleaner used to sweep the step now and again. Saw the woman from next door pottering about in her bit and the old boy sunning himself on his patio.'

'I mean strangers. Someone you wouldn't have expected.'

'I never *saw* anyone.' He put unnatural emphasis on the verb.

'Heard then?'

'Maybe.'

'Where were you? What did you hear?'

'I watched Mrs Gillespie go out in her car one day. Thought I'd take a look through the windows, see what was there.'

'Was Ruth with you?'

He shook his head. 'Back at school.'

'Refusing to co-operate, presumably, so you had to find out for yourself what was worth stealing. You were casing the place.'

Hughes didn't answer.

'Okay, what happened?'

'I heard the old lady coming round the path so I dived behind the coal bunker by the kitchen door.'

'Go on.'

'It wasn't her. It was some other bastard who was nosing around like me.'

'Male? Female?'

'An old man. He knocked on the back door and waited for a bit, then let himself in with a key.' Hughes pulled a face. 'So I legged it.' He saw the triumph on Jones's face. 'That what you wanted?'

'Could be. Did he have the key in his hand?'

'I wasn't looking.'

'Did you hear anything?'

'The knocking.'

'Anything else?'

'I heard a stone being moved after the knocking.'

The flowerpot. 'How do you know it was a man if you weren't looking?'

'He called out. "Jenny, Ruth, Mathilda, are you there?" It was a man all right.'

'Describe his voice.'

'Posh.'

'Old? Young? Forceful? Weak? Drunk? Sober? Pull your finger out, lad. What sort of impression did you get of him?'

'I already told you. I reckoned it was an old man. That's why I thought it was *her* coming back. He was really slow and his voice was all breathy, like he had trouble with his lungs. Or was very unfit.' He thought for a moment. 'He might have been drunk, though,' he added. 'He had real trouble getting the words out.'

'Did you go round the front afterwards?'

Dave shook his head. 'Hopped over the fence and went back to the van.'

'So you don't know if he came by car?'

'No.' A flash of something – *indecision?* – crossed his face.

'Go on,' prompted Jones.

'I'd never swear to it, so it's not evidence.'

'What isn't?'

'I was listening, if you get my meaning. He gave me a hell of a shock when I heard him coming so I reckon I'd've heard a car if there'd been one. That gravel at the front makes a hell of a row.'

'When was this?'

'Middle of September. Thereabouts.'

'Okay. Anything else?'

'Yeah.' He fingered his shoulder gingerly where Jack's car door had slammed into it. 'If you want to know who killed the old biddy then you should talk to the bastard who dislocated my fucking arm last night. I sussed him the minute I saw his face in the light. He was forever sniffing round her, in and out that place like he owned it, but he made damn sure Ruth wasn't there at the time. I spotted him two or three times up by the church, waiting till the coast was clear. Reckon he's the one you should be interested in if it's right what Ruth told me, that the old woman's wrists were slit with a Stanley knife.'

Charlie eyed him curiously. 'Why do you say that?'

'He cleaned one of the gravestones while he was waiting, scraped the dirt out of the words written on it. And not just the once neither. He was really fascinated by that stone.' He looked smug. 'Used a Stanley knife to do it, too, didn't he? I went and read it afterwards . . . "Did I deserve to be despised, By my creator, good and wise? Since you it was who made me be, Then part of you must die with me." Some bloke called Fitzgibbon who snuffed it in 1833. Thought I'd use it myself when the time came. Kind of hits the nail on the head, wouldn't you say?'

'You won't be given the chance. They censor epitaphs these days. Religion takes itself seriously now the congregations have started to vanish.' He stood up. 'A pity, really. Humour never harmed anyone.'

'You interested in him now then?'

'I've always been interested in him, lad.' Charlie smiled mournfully. 'Mrs Gillespie's death was very artistic.'

Cooper found the Inspector enjoying a late pint over cheese and onion sandwiches at the Dog and Bottle in Learmouth. He lowered himself with a sigh on to the seat beside him. 'Feet playing you up again?' asked Charlie sympathetically through a mouthful of bread.

'I wouldn't mind so much,' Cooper grumbled, 'if my inside had aged at the same rate as my outside. If I felt fifty-six, it probably wouldn't bug me.' He rubbed his calves to restore the circulation. 'I promised the wife we'd take up dancing again when I retired, but at this rate we'll be doing it with Zimmer frames.'

Charlie grinned. 'So there's no truth in the saying: you're as old as you feel?'

'None whatsoever. You're as old as your body tells you you are. I'll still feel eighteen when I'm a bedridden ninety-year-old and I still won't be able to play football for England. I only ever wanted to be Stanley Matthews,' he said wistfully. 'My dad took me to watch him and Blackpool win the FA cup in 1953 as a sixteenth birthday present. It was pure magic. I've never forgotten it.'

'I wanted to be Tom Kelley,' said Charlie.

'Who's he?'

The Inspector chuckled as he wiped his fingers on a napkin. 'The photographer who persuaded Marilyn Monroe to pose nude for him. Imagine it. Marilyn Monroe entirely naked and you on the other side of the lens. Now, that really would have been magic.'

'We're in the wrong business, Charlie. There's no charm in what we do.'

'Mrs Marriott hasn't raised your spirits then?'

'No.' He sighed again. 'I made a promise to her, said we wouldn't use what she told me unless we had to, but I can't see at the moment how we can avoid it. If it doesn't have a bearing on the case, then I'm a monkey's uncle. First, Joanna Lascelles was not Mrs Gillespie's only child. She had another one thirteen, fourteen months later by Mrs Marriott's husband.' He ran through the background for Charlie's benefit. 'Mrs Marriott believed Mrs Gillespie killed the baby when it was born, but on the morning of the sixth, Mrs Gillespie told her it had been a boy and that she'd put it up for adoption when it was born.'

Charlie leaned forward, his eyes bright with curiosity. 'Does she know what happened to him?'

Cooper shook his head. 'They were screaming at each other, apparently, and that little tit-bit was tossed out by Mrs Gillespie as she closed the door. Mrs Marriott says Mathilda wanted to hurt her, so it might not even be true.'

'Okay. Go on.'

'Second, and this is the real shocker, Mrs Marriott stole some barbiturates from her father's dispensary which she says Mathilda used to murder Gerald Cavendish.' He detailed what Jane had told him, shaking his head from time to time whenever he touched on James Gillespie's part in the tragedy. 'He's evil, that one, blackmails everyone as far as I can judge. The wretched woman's terrified he's going to broadcast what he knows.'

'Serves her right,' said Charlie unsympathetically. 'What a corrupt lot they all were, and they say it's only recently the country started going to pot. You say she went to see Mrs Gillespie on the morning of the murder. What else did Mrs Gillespie tell her?'

'Murder?' queried Cooper with a touch of irony. 'Don't tell me you agree with me at last?'

'Get on with it, you old rogue,' said Jones impatiently. 'I'm on the edge of my seat here.'

'Mrs Gillespie began by being very cool and composed, told Mrs Marriott that the whole matter was out of her hands and that she wasn't prepared to pay the sort of money James was demanding from her. As far as she was concerned she didn't care any more what people said or thought about her. There had never been any doubt that Gerald committed suicide and if Jane wanted to own up to stealing drugs from her father, that was her affair. Mathilda would deny knowing anything about them.' He opened his notebook. '"I'm more sinned against than sinning," she said and advised Mrs Marriott that, in the matter of the baby, things would get worse before they got better. She went on to say that Mrs Marriott was a fool for keeping her husband in the dark all these years. They had a terrible row during which Mrs Marriott accused Mrs Gillespie of ruining the lives of everyone she had ever had contact with, at which point Mrs Gillespie ordered her out of the house with the words: "James has been reading my private papers and knows where the child is. It's quite pointless to keep quiet any longer." She then told Mrs Marriott it was a boy and that she'd put it up for adoption.' He closed the notebook. 'My bet is the "private papers" were the diaries and things were going to get worse because Mrs Gillespie had made up her mind to acknowledge her illegitimate child and spike James's guns.' He rubbed his jaw wearily. 'Not that that scenario really makes a great deal more sense than it did before. We'd more or less decided that whoever was reading the diaries was the same person who stole them and murdered the old lady, and I still say James Gillespie wouldn't have drawn our attention to the diaries if he was the guilty party. The psychology's all wrong. And what motive did he have for killing her? She was far more valuable alive as a blackmail victim. Let's face it, it wasn't just the business of the baby he could hold over her, it was her uncle's murder as well.'

'But he probably couldn't prove that, not so long afterwards, and you're making too many assumptions,' said Charlie slowly. ' "I'm more sinned against than sinning",' he echoed. 'That's a line from *King Lear*.'

'So?'

'King Lear went mad and took to wandering in the fields near Dover with a crown of weeds on his head because his daughters had deprived him of his kingdom and his authority.'

Cooper groaned. 'I thought it was Ophelia who had the crown of weeds.'

'Hers were coronet weeds,' corrected Jones with idle pedantry. 'It was Lear who wore the crown.' He thought of the epitaph on the Fontwell tombstone. 'By God, Tommy, there's a lovely symmetry about this case. Jack Blakeney's been using a Stanley knife to clean inscriptions in Fontwell.'

Cooper scowled at him. 'How many pints have you had?'

Charlie leaned forward again, his keen eyes scouring Cooper's face. 'I studied *King Lear* at school. It's a hell of a play. All about the

268

nature of love, the abuse of power, and the ultimate frailties of the human spirit.'

'Just like *Hamlet* then,' said Cooper sourly. '*Othello*, too, if it comes to that.'

'Of course. They were all tragedies with death the inevitable consequence. King Lear's mistake was to misinterpret the nature of love. He gave more weight to words than to deeds and partitioned his kingdom between two of his daughters, Goneril and Regan, whom he believed loved him but who, in reality, despised him. He was a tired old man who wanted to relinquish the burdens of state and live the rest of his life in peace and tranquillity. But he was also extremely arrogant and contemptuous of anyone's opinions but his own. His rash assumption that he knew what love was sowed the seeds of his family's destruction.' He grinned. 'Not bad, eh? Damn nearly verbatim from an essay I wrote in the sixth form. And I loathed the flaming play at the time. It's taken me thirty years to see its merits.'

'I came up with *King Lear* a few days ago,' remarked Cooper, 'but I still don't see a connection. If she'd divided her estate between Mrs Lascelles and Miss Lascelles there'd have been a parallel then.'

'You're missing the point, Tommy. *King Lear* was the most tragic of all Shakespeare's plays and Mrs Gillespie knew her Shakespeare. Dammit, man, she thought everything he wrote was gospel. There was a third child, don't forget, who was turned off without a penny.' He surged to his feet. 'I want Jack Blakeney in the nick in half an hour. Be a good fellow and bring him in. Tell him your boss wants to talk to him about Mrs Gillespie's adopted son.'

What neither of them knew was that Jack Blakeney had been arrested at Mill House, half an hour previously, following the Orloffs' 999 call and Joanna Lascelles's hysterical assertions that he had not only tried to kill her but had admitted killing her mother.

The Inspector learnt of it as soon as he arrived back from lunch. Cooper was informed by radio and ordered to return post haste. He took time out, however, to sit for five minutes in depressed disillusion in a deserted country lane. His hands were shaking too much to drive with any competence, and he knew, with the awful certainty of defeat, that his time was over. He had lost whatever it was that had made him a good policeman. Oh, he had always known what his superiors said about him, but he had also known they were wrong. His forte had been his ability to make accurate judgements about the people he dealt with, and whatever anyone said to the contrary, he was usually right. But he had never allowed his sympathies for an offender and an offender's family to stand in the way of an arrest. Nor had he seen any validity in allowing police work to dehumanize him or destroy the tolerance that he, privately, believed was the one thing that set man above the animals.

With a heavy heart, he fired the engine and set off back to Learmouth. He had misjudged both the Blakeneys. Worse, he simply couldn't begin to follow Charlie Jones's flights of fancy over *King Lear* or comprehend the awful symmetry behind inscriptions and Stanley knives. Hadn't Mr Spede told him that the Stanley knife on the bathroom floor was the one from the kitchen drawer? The crown he thought he understood. Whoever had decked out Mrs Gillespie in nettles had seen the symbolic connection between her and *King Lear*. How then had Ophelia come to lead them up the garden path? *Coronet weeds,* he recalled, and Dr Blakeney's reference to them in the bathroom.

An intense sadness squeezed about his heart. Poor Tommy Cooper. He was, after all, just an absurd and rather dirty old man, entertaining fantasies about a woman who was young enough to be his daughter.

An hour later, Inspector Jones pulled out the chair opposite Jack and sat down, switching on the tape recorder and registering date, time and who was present. He rubbed his hands in anticipation of a challenge. 'Well, well, Mr Blakeney, I've been looking forward to this.' He beamed across at Cooper who was sitting with his back to the wall, staring at the floor. 'The Sergeant's whetted my appetite with what he's told me about you, not to mention the reports of your contretemps with the police in Bournemouth and this latest little fracas at Cedar House.'

Jack linked his hands behind his head and smiled wolfishly. 'Then I hope you won't be disappointed, Inspector.'

'I'm sure I won't.' He steepled his fingers on the table in front of him. 'We'll leave Mrs Lascelles and the Bournemouth incident to one side for the moment because I'm more interested in your relationship with Mrs Gillespie.' He looked very pleased with himself. 'I've deciphered the floral crown that she was wearing in her bath. Not Ophelia at all, but King Lear. I've just been looking it up. Act IV, Scene IV where Cordelia describes him as "Crown'd with rank fumiter and furrow weeds, With burdocks, hemlock, nettles, cuckoo-flow'rs". And then Scene VI, a stage direction. "Enter Lear, fantastically dressed with weeds." Am I right, Mr Blakeney?'

'It did occur to me that Ophelia was a very unlikely interpretation. I guessed Lear when Sarah described the scene to me.'

'And Lear certainly makes more sense.'

Jack cocked his irritating eyebrow. 'Does it?'

'Oh, yes.' He rubbed his hands in gleeful anticipation. 'It goes something like this, I think. Lear had two vile daughters, Goneril and Regan, and one loving daughter, Cordelia. Cordelia he banished because she refused to flatter him with hollow words; Goneril and Regan he rewarded because they were deceitful enough to tell lies in order to get their share of his wealth. For Goneril and Regan, read Joanna and Ruth Lascelles. For Cordelia, read the son Mrs Gillespie put up for adoption, i.e. the one she banished who never received a penny from her.' He held Jack's gaze. 'Now, in the play, Cordelia comes back to rescue her father from the brutality her sisters are inflicting upon him, and I think it happened in real life, too, though purely figuratively speaking of course. Neither Joanna nor Ruth were *brutal* to Mrs Gillespie, merely desperately disappointing.' He tapped his forefingers together. 'Cordelia, the adopted son whom Mathilda had long since given up on, reappears miraculously to remind her that love does still exist for her, that she is not as embittered as she thought she was and that, ultimately, she has produced at least one person who has qualities she could be proud of. How am I doing, Mr Blakeney?'

'Imaginatively.'

Charlie gave a low laugh. 'The only question is, who is Cordelia?'

Jack didn't answer.

'And did he come looking for his mother or was it pure chance that brought him here? Who recognized whom, I wonder?'

271

Again Jack didn't answer, and Charlie's brows snapped together ferociously. 'You are not obliged to answer my questions, Mr Blakeney, but you would be very unwise to forget that I am investigating murder and attempted murder here. Silence won't help you, you know.'

Jack shrugged, apparently unmoved by threats. 'Even if any of this were true, what does it have to do with Mathilda's death?'

'Dave Hughes told me an interesting story today. He says he watched you clean a gravestone in the cemetery at Fontwell, claims you were obviously so fascinated by it that he went and read it after you'd gone. Do you remember what it says?'

'"George Fitzgibbon 1789–1833. Did I deserve to be despised, By my creator, good and wise? Since you it was who made me be, Then part of you must die with me." I looked him up in the parish records. He succumbed to syphilis as a result of loose living. Maria, his wretched wife, died of the same thing four years later and was popped into the ground alongside George, but she didn't get a tombstone because her children refused to pay for one. There's a written epitaph in the record instead and hers is even better. "George was lusty, coarse and evil, He gave me pox, he's with the devil." Short, and to the point. George's was ridiculously hypocritical by contrast.'

'It all depends who George thought his creator was,' said Charlie. 'Perhaps it was his mother he wanted to take to hell with him.'

Idly Jack traced a triangle on the surface of the table. 'Who told you Mathilda had an adopted son? Someone reliable, I hope, because you're building a hell of a castle on their information.'

Jones caught Cooper's eye, but ignored the warning frown. As Cooper said, their chances of respecting Jane Marriott's confidences were thin. 'Mrs Jane Marriott, whose husband was the boy's father.'

'Ah, well, a *very* reliable source then.' He saw the gleam of excitement in the Inspector's eyes and smiled with genuine amusement. 'Mathilda was not my mother, Inspector. If she had been I'd have been thrilled. I loved the woman.'

Charlie shrugged. 'Then Mrs Gillespie lied about having a son, and it's your wife who's Cordelia. It has to be one or other of you or she wouldn't have made that will. She wasn't going to make Lear's mistake and bequeath her estate to the undeserving daughters.'

Jack looked as if he were about to deny it, then shrugged. 'I imagine Mathilda told Jane Marriott it was a boy out of spite. She never referred to her by name, always called her that "prissy creature at the surgery". It was cruel of her, but then Mathilda was usually cruel. She was a deeply unhappy woman.' He paused to collect his thoughts. 'She told me about her affair with Paul after I'd finished her portrait. She said there was something missing from the painting, and that that something was guilt. She was absolutely racked with it. Guilt for having given up the baby, guilt for not being able to cope, guilt for blaming the second baby's adoption on Joanna's crying, ultimately, I suppose, guilt for her inability to feel affection.' Briefly he fell silent again. 'Then Sarah turned up out of the blue and Mathilda recognized her.' He saw the look of incredulity on Charlie Jones's face. 'Not immediately and not as the baby she'd given away, but gradually as the months went by. There were so many things that matched. Sarah was the right age, her birthday was the same day as the baby's birthday, her parents had lived in the same borough in London where Mathilda's flat was. Most importantly she thought she detected a likeness in Sarah's and Joanna's mannerisms. She said they had the same smile, the same way of inclining their heads, the same trick of looking at you intently while you speak. And from the start Sarah took Mathilda as she found her, of course, the way she takes everyone, and for the first time in years Mathilda felt valued. It was a very potent cocktail. Mathilda was so convinced she'd found her lost daughter that she approached me and commissioned me to paint the portrait.' He smiled ruefully. 'I thought my luck had changed but all she wanted, of course, was an excuse to find out more about Sarah from the only person available who knew anything of value.'

'But you didn't know that while you were painting her?'

'No. I did wonder why she was so interested in us both, what our parents were like, where they came from, if we had brothers and sisters, whether or not I got on with my in-laws. She didn't confine herself to Sarah, you see. If she had, I might have been suspicious. As it was, when she finally told me that Sarah was her lost child, I was appalled.' He shrugged helplessly. 'I knew she couldn't be because Sarah wasn't adopted.'

'Surely that was the first thing Mrs Gillespie asked you?'

'Not in so many words, no. She never put anything as directly as that.' He shrugged again in the face of the Inspector's scepticism.

'You're forgetting that no one in Fontwell knew about this child, except Jane Marriott, and Mathilda was far too proud to give the rest of the village a glimpse of her clay feet. She was looking for a private atonement, not a public one. The closest we ever came to it was when she asked me if Sarah had a good relationship with her mother and I said, no, because they had nothing in common. I can even remember the words I used. I said: "I've often wondered if Sarah was adopted because the only explanation for the disparity between the two of them in looks, words and deeds is that they aren't related." I was being flippant, but Mathilda used it to build castles in the air. Rather as you're doing at the moment, Inspector.'

'But she'd made up her mind before you started painting that portrait, Mr Blakeney. If I remember correctly she began consulting Mr Duggan about the will in August.'

'It was like a faith,' said Jack simply. 'I can't explain it any other way. She needed to make amends to the child who'd had nothing, and Sarah had to be that child. The fact that the ages, birthdays and mannerisms were pure coincidence was neither here nor there. Mathilda had made up her mind and all she wanted from me was the gaps filled in.' He ran his fingers through his hair. 'If I'd known sooner, then I'd have disabused her, but I didn't know, and all I achieved, quite unwittingly, was to fuel the belief.'

'Does Dr Blakeney know any of this?'

'No. Mathilda was adamant she never should. She made me promise to keep it to myself – she was terrified Sarah would treat her differently, stop liking her, even reject her completely – and I thought, thank God, because this way no one gets hurt.' He rubbed a hand across his face. 'I didn't know what to do, you see, and I needed time to work out how to let Mathilda down gently. If I'd told her the truth, there and then, it would have been like taking the baby away from her all over again.'

'When was this, Mr Blakeney?' asked Charlie.

'About two weeks before she died.'

'Why did she tell you, if she didn't want anyone to know?'

Jack didn't answer immediately. 'It was the portrait,' he said after a moment. 'I took it round to show it to her. I still had some work to do on it but I wanted to see what her reaction was so that I could paint that into the picture. I've had some amazing responses in the past: anger, shock, vanity, irritation, disappointment. I record them all beneath my signature so that anyone who understands the code will know what the subject thought about my treatment of his or her personality. It's a sort of visual joke. Mathilda's reaction was intense grief. I've never seen anyone so upset.'

'She didn't like it?' suggested Charlie.

'The exact opposite. She was weeping for the woman she might have been.' His eyes clouded in reflection. 'She said I was the first person who had ever shown her compassion.'

'I don't understand.'

Jack glanced across at the Sergeant who was still sitting staring at the floor. 'Tommy does,' he said. 'Don't you, my old friend?'

There was a brief pause before Cooper raised his head. 'The gold at the heart of the picture,' he murmured. 'That was Mathilda as she was in the beginning before events took over and destroyed her.'

Jack's dark eyes rested on him with affection. 'Goddammit, Tommy,' he said, 'how come I'm the only one to appreciate your qualities? Does anything escape you?'

When I told Father I was pregnant, he fainted. It was an extraordinary example of craven cowardice. Gerald, by contrast, was rather pleased. 'Is it mine, Matty?' he asked. Perhaps I should have been offended, but I wasn't. I found his delight in what he'd achieved rather touching.

Father is all for an abortion, of course, and not just because of the potential scandal. He says the baby will be even more of an imbecile than Gerald. I have refused. Nothing will induce me to go near a backstreet abortionist which is all Father is offering me. He says he knows of somebody in London who will do it for a small fee, but I don't trust him an inch and will not entrust my life to some incompetent woman with knitting needles and gin. In any case, if the child's as defective as Father's suggesting, then it will not survive long. Gerald is only with us in all conscience because his silly mother nursed him devotedly for years.

Every cloud has its silver lining. Gerald has never been easier to manage than he is at the moment. The knowledge that I am carrying his baby has wiped all memories of Grace from his mind. It means I shall have to marry to give the baby legitimacy, but James Gillespie is tiresome in his approaches, and will marry me tomorrow if I agree. Father says James is homosexual and needs a wife to give himself respectability, but as I need a husband for the same reason, I can no doubt tolerate him for the few months till the baby's born.

I have told Father to put a brave face on it, something the silly man is incapable of doing, and to let me and James have the use of his flat in London. Once the baby is born I shall return home. Father will stay at his club on the rare – now, very rare – occasions when he is sober enough to attend a debate at the House. He wept his drunken tears this evening and said I was unnatural, claiming all he had ever wanted me to do was be sweet to Gerald and keep him happy.

But it was Grace who introduced Gerald to sex, not I, and Father knows it. And how was I supposed to keep a sexually active imbecile happy? By playing bridge? By discussing Plato? Dear God, but I have such contempt for men. Perhaps I am unnatural . . .

Eighteen

JONES DRUMMED his fingers impatiently on the table. 'You told the Sergeant you were with an actress in Stratford the night Mrs Gillespie was murdered. You weren't. We've checked. Miss Bennedict said' – he consulted a piece of paper – 'she'd see you in hell before she allowed you near her again.'

'True.' He gave an amiable grin. 'She didn't like the portrait I did of her. She's had it in for me ever since.'

'Then why give her as your alibi?'

'Because I'd already told Sarah that's where I was, and she was listening when the Sergeant asked me.'

Charlie frowned but let this pass. 'Where were you then, if you weren't in Stratford?'

'Cheltenham.' He linked his hands behind his neck and stared at the ceiling.

'Can you prove it?'

'Yes.' He reeled off a phone number. 'Sarah's father's house. He will confirm that I was there from six o'clock on the Friday evening until midday on the Sunday.' He flicked a lazy glance at the Inspector. 'He's a JP, so you can be fairly sure he won't be lying.'

'What were you doing there?'

'I went on the off-chance that he had something I could show Mathilda that would prove Sarah wasn't her daughter. I knew I could talk fairly freely without him blabbing about it. If I'd approached her mother, she'd have been on the phone to Sarah like a shot and then the cat would have been out of the bag with Sarah demanding to know why I wanted proof she wasn't adopted. By the same token, she'd have asked me why I was going to see her father, so I told her I was staying with Sally to put her off the scent.' He looked suddenly pensive. 'Not the most intelligent thing I've ever done.'

Charlie ignored this. 'Did her father give you proof?'

'No. He said he hadn't got anything and that I'd have to talk to her mother. I was planning to bite the bullet and go the next weekend, but, by the Monday, Mathilda was dead and it didn't matter any more.'

'And you still haven't told your wife?'

'No.'

'Why not?'

'I promised Mathilda I wouldn't,' he said evenly. 'If she'd wanted Sarah to know what she believed, she'd have told her herself on the video.'

'Any idea why she didn't?'

Jack shrugged. 'Because she wasn't going to tell her in life either, I suppose. She had too many secrets which she thought would be exposed if she claimed Sarah as her own – and let's face it, she was right. Look what Tommy's unearthed already.'

'It would have been unearthed anyway. People were bound to ask questions the minute they heard she'd left her money to her doctor.'

'But she wouldn't have expected the police to be asking them because she didn't know she was going to be murdered. And, as far as I can make out, from what Sarah has told me of the video, she did the best she could to warn Joanna and Ruth off putting in a counter-claim by dropping enough heavy hints about their lifestyles to give Sarah's barrister a field day if the thing ever went to court.' He shrugged again. 'The only reason either of them feels confident about challenging it now is because Mathilda was murdered. Whatever they've done pales into insignificance beside that.'

Cooper rumbled into life behind him. 'But the video is full of lies, particularly in relation to her uncle and her husband. Mrs Gillespie implies she was the victim of them both, but Mrs Marriott tells a very different story. She describes a woman who was ruthless enough to use blackmail and murder when it suited her. So which is true?'

Jack swung round to look at him. 'I don't know. Both probably. She wouldn't be the first victim to strike back.'

'What about this business of her uncle's feeble-mindedness? She described him on the video as a drunken brute who raped her when she was thirteen, yet Mrs Marriott says he was rather pathetic. Explain that.'

'I can't. Mathilda never talked to me about it. All I know is that she was deeply scarred by her inability to love and when I showed her the portrait with the scarring represented by the scold's bridle, she burst into tears and said I was the first person to show her any compassion. I chose to interpret that as meaning that I was the first person to see her as a victim, but I could have been wrong. You'll have to make up your own mind.'

'We wouldn't have to if we could find her diaries,' said Cooper.

Jack didn't say anything and the room fell silent with only the whirr of the tape to disturb the complete bafflement that at least two of those present were experiencing. Jones, who had approached this interview in the confident expectation that Jack Blakeney would spend tonight in a police cell, was falling prey to the same crippling ambivalence that Cooper had always felt towards this man.

'Why did you tell Mrs Lascelles this morning that you murdered her mother if you already had an alibi for the night Mrs Gillespie died?' he asked at last, rustling the papers in front of him.

'I didn't.'

'She says in this report that you did.'

'I didn't.'

'She says you did.'

'She said what she believed. That's a different thing entirely.'

Jones pondered for a moment. He had a nasty feeling that he would receive almost as dusty an answer to his next question, but he put it anyway. 'Why did you try to murder Mrs Lascelles?'

'I didn't.'

'She says, and I'm quoting, "Jack Blakeney forced me against the wall and started to strangle me. If Violet hadn't interrupted him, he'd have killed me." Is she lying?'

'No. She's telling you what she believes.'

'But it's not true.'

'No.'

'You weren't trying to strangle her?'

'No.'

'I have to tell you, Mr Blakeney, that according to this report she had the marks of a stranglehold on her neck when the car that answered the nine–nine–nine call arrived at Cedar House. Therefore someone did try to strangle her, and she says that someone was you.' He paused, inviting Jack to answer. When he didn't, he tried a different approach. 'Were you in Cedar House at approximately ten thirty this morning?'

'Yes.'

'Did you put your hand about Mrs Joanna Lascelles's throat?'

'Yes.'

'Is she justified in believing that you were trying to strangle her?'

'Yes.'

'Were you trying to strangle her?'

'No.'

'Then explain it to me. What the hell were you doing?'

'Showing you lot where you've been going wrong again. Mind you, it's not the most sensible thing I've done, and I wouldn't have done it at all if I hadn't been so pissed off by that jerk of an Inspector last night.' His eyes narrowed angrily at the memory. 'I don't give a toss about myself, matter of fact I rather hope he decides to prosecute and give me my day in court, but I do care about Sarah and I care very much indeed at the moment about Ruth. He treated them both like shit and I made up my mind then that enough was enough. Joanna's past saving, I suspect, but her daughter isn't, and I want the poor kid free to put this bloody awful mess behind her.' He took a deep angry breath. 'So I sat up last night and did what you should have done, worked out who killed Mathilda and why. And believe me it wasn't difficult.'

Charlie did believe him. Like Cooper, he was beginning to find Jack irresistible. 'Mrs Lascelles,' he said with conviction. 'She's always been top of the list.'

'No, and I satisfied myself of that this morning. I agree she's quite capable of it. She has an almost identical personality to her mother, and if Mathilda could murder to get what she wanted, then Joanna could, too. You don't grow up in an atmosphere of extreme dysfunction and emerge normal at the end of it. But Joanna's relationship with Mathilda was very ambivalent. Despite everything, I suspect they were actually rather fond of each other. Perhaps, quite simply, their fondness was based on mutual understanding, the devil you know being more acceptable than the devil you don't.'

'All right,' said Charlie patiently. 'Then who did kill Mrs Gillespie?'

'I can't prove it, that's your job. All I can do is take you through what I worked out last night.' He took a moment to organize his thoughts. 'You've concentrated entirely on Sarah, me, Joanna and Ruth,' he said, 'and all because of the will. Not unreasonable in the circumstances – but if you take us out of the equation then the balance of probability shifts. So let's assume she wasn't killed for money and take it from there. Okay, I don't believe she was killed in anger either. Anger is a violent, hot-blooded emotion and her death was too well planned and too meticulous. Too symbolic. Whoever murdered her may well have been angry with her, but it wasn't done because someone's patience had finally run out.' He glanced at Jones who nodded. 'Which leaves what? Hatred? She was certainly disliked by a lot of people but as none of them had killed her before, why decide to do it then? Jealousy?' He shrugged eloquently. 'What was there to be jealous of? She was a virtual recluse, and I can't believe Jane Marriott stored her jealousy for years to have it erupt suddenly in November. So, at the risk of stating the obvious, Mathilda must have been murdered because someone wanted her out of the way.'

Jones had difficulty keeping the sarcasm out of his voice. 'I think we can agree on that,' he said.

Jack stared at him for a moment. 'Yes, but *why*? Why did someone want her out of the way? What had she done or what was she going to do that meant she had to be killed? That's the question you've never asked, not outside the context of the will at least.'

'Because I don't find it quite so easy, as you apparently do, to ignore it.'

'But it *is* just a will. Thousands of people make them every week and thousands of people die every week. The fact that Mathilda's was unusually radical becomes completely irrelevant if you absolve Joanna, Ruth, Sarah and me of her death. No one else is directly affected by the way she chose to leave her money.'

Cooper cleared his throat. 'It's a good point, Charlie.'

'All right,' he conceded. 'Why *was* she killed then?'

'I don't know.'

Charlie raised his eyes to heaven. 'God give me strength!' he growled savagely.

Cooper chuckled quietly to himself. 'Get on with it, Jack, before you give the poor man apoplexy,' he suggested. 'We're all running out of patience on this one. Let's take it as read that the will wasn't the motive and that neither the Lascelles women nor you and your wife were involved. Where does that leave us?'

'With Mathilda wearing the scold's bridle. Why? And why did it have half a hedgerow carefully entwined through it? Isn't that what persuaded you it wasn't suicide?'

Cooper nodded.

'Then the logical conclusion has to be that the murderer never intended you to think it *was* suicide. I mean we're not talking about a moron here, we're talking finesse and careful planning. My guess is that someone knew Mathilda thought Sarah was her daughter, knew that both Mathilda and Joanna had been conditioned by the scold's bridle in their childhoods, knew that Joanna was a florist and knew, too, that "scold's bridle" was Mathilda's nickname for Sarah. Hence the contraption on her head and the *King Lear* imagery. If you put all that together with the fact that Ruth was in the house that day, then the aim must surely have been to focus your attention on Sarah, Joanna and Ruth – Lear's three daughters in other words. And that's exactly what happened, even if it was the will that set you thinking along those lines because you mistook the symbolism for Ophelia's coronet weeds. You mustn't forget how close Mathilda played the will to her chest. As far as anyone knew, Joanna and Ruth were going to share the estate between them. Sarah's possible claim as the long-lost daughter was nothing but a wild card when the murder took place so, for the murderer, it came as a sort of bonus.'

Charlie frowned. 'I still don't understand. Were we supposed to arrest one of them? And which one? I mean, was your wife indicated because of the scold's bridle, was Joanna indicated because of the flowers, or was Ruth indicated because she was there?'

Jack shrugged. 'I'd say that's the whole point. It doesn't matter a damn, just so long as you focus your attention on them.'

'But why?' snarled Charlie through gritted teeth.

Jack looked helplessly from him to Cooper. 'There's only one reason that I can see, but maybe I've got it all wrong. Hell dammit!' he exploded angrily. 'I'm not an expert.'

'Confusion,' said Cooper stoutly, a man ever to be relied upon.

'The murderer wanted Mrs Gillespie dead and confusion to follow. And why would they want confusion to follow? Because it would be much harder to proceed with any kind of normality if the mess surrounding Mrs Gillespie's death wasn't sorted out.'

Jack nodded. 'Sounds logical to me.'

It was Charlie's turn to be lost in Cooper's flights of fancy. 'What normality?'

'The normality that follows death,' he said ponderously. 'Wills in other words. Someone wanted the settling of Mrs Gillespie's estate delayed.' He thought for a moment. 'Let's say she was about to embark on something that someone else didn't like, so they stopped her before she could do it. But let's say, too, that whatever it was could be pursued by her beneficiary the minute that beneficiary came into the estate. With a little ingenuity, you throw a spanner in the works by pointing a finger at the more obvious legatees and grind the process to a halt. How does that sound?'

'Complicated,' said Charlie tartly.

'But the pressure was to stop Mathilda,' said Jack. 'The rest was imaginative flair which might or might not work. Think of it as a speculative venture that could, with a little bit of luck, produce the goods.'

'But that brings us right back to square one,' said Cooper slowly. 'Whoever killed her knew her very well and, if we jettison the four who knew her best, then we're left with – ' he pressed his fingers to his eyes in deep concentration, 'Mr and Mrs Spede, Mr and Mrs Marriott, and James Gillespie.'

'You can do better than that, Cooper,' said Jack impatiently. 'The Spedes are simple souls who could never have dreamt up the *Lear* symbolism in a million years; Paul and Jane Marriott have avoided Mathilda like the plague for years so probably couldn't have found their way around her house, let alone known where she kept the Stanley knife; and, as far as I understand it, if what Duggan told Sarah is true, rather than trying to delay the processing of the will, James Gillespie is doing the exact opposite and pressing for the controversy to be settled so that he can lay claim to the clocks.'

'But there isn't anyone else.'

'There is, and I proved it this morning.' He hammered his fist on the table. 'It's Ruth's involvement that should have alerted you.

285

Someone knew she was in the house that day and could therefore figure as a suspect. You've been chasing around in circles since you found out about it, but Sarah says you only learnt she was there because you received an anonymous letter. So who sent it?' He slammed his palm on the table at Cooper's blank expression. 'Who tried to rescue Joanna this morning?'

Violet Orloff opened her front door and stared at the piece of polythene-encased paper that Detective Sergeant Cooper was holding in front of him. He turned it round to read it aloud. '"Ruth Lascelles was in Cedar House the day Mrs Gillespie died. She stole some earrings. Joanna knows she took them. Joanna Lascelles is a prostitute in London. Ask her what she spends her money on. Ask her why she tried to kill her daughter. Ask her why Mrs Gillespie thought she was mad." Would we be right in assuming you wrote this, Mrs Orloff?' he enquired in his friendly way.

'Duncan did, but we were only trying to *help*,' she said breathily, looking from him to the tall figure of Charlie Jones behind him, the collar of whose thick sheepskin jacket was pulled up about his comfortably sad face. She took heart from their mutual lack of hostility. 'I know we probably ought to have come in person, but it's so *difficult*.' She gestured vaguely in the direction of the other part of the house. 'We are neighbours, after all, and Duncan does so hate unpleasantness.' She smiled tentatively. 'But when a murder's been committed – I mean, one can't expect the police to solve it if people who know things stay quiet. It seemed more *tactful*, somehow, not to get involved personally. You do understand, don't you?'

'Perfectly,' said Charlie with an encouraging smile, 'and we're very grateful to you for the trouble you took.'

'That's all right then. I *told* Duncan it was important.'

'Didn't he agree with you?'

She glanced cautiously over her shoulder, then pulled the door to behind her. 'I wouldn't put it quite like *that*,' she said. 'He's grown so lazy since we came here, won't stir himself, won't have his routines upset, can't bear what he calls aggravations. He says he's earned a peaceful retirement and doesn't want it *upset* by lots of bother. He's very unfit, of course, which doesn't help, but I can't help feeling that

286

it isn't good to be so' – she struggled for the right word – '*unenterprising.*'

'Mrs Gillespie's death must have been a shock then, what with the police tramping about the house, and Mrs Lascelles and her daughter coming back.'

'He hasn't *enjoyed* it,' she admitted, 'but he did see there was nothing we could do about it. Don't get so het up, he told me. A little patience and it will all blow over.'

'Still, it must be very unsettling,' said Cooper, 'worrying about what's going to happen to Cedar House now that Mrs Gillespie's dead. Presumably it will be sold, but you won't have any control over who it's sold to.'

'That's just what *I* said. Duncan would go mad with noisy children next door.' She lowered her voice. 'I know one shouldn't take pleasure in other people's misfortune, but I can't deny it's a relief to have Joanna and Dr Blakeney at loggerheads over the will. They're going to court about it, you know, and as Duncan said, that sort of thing takes years.'

'And in the meantime the house will stand empty?'

'Well, *exactly.*'

'So it's definite that Mrs Lascelles intends to contest the will?'

'Oh, yes.'

'She told you that?'

She looked guilty again. 'I heard her and the doctor talking in the drawing-room. I don't make a habit of listening, not as a general rule, but . . .' She left the rest of the sentence unsaid.

'You've been worried and you needed to know what's going on,' suggested Charlie helpfully.

'Well, *exactly*,' she said again. 'Someone has to take an interest. If it's left to Duncan, we'll only know what sort of neighbours we've got when they're living next to us.'

'Like Mrs Gillespie, you mean. I suppose you knew a lot about her one way and another.'

Violet's mouth pinched disapprovingly. 'Not through choice. I don't think she ever realized just how piercing her voice was. Very *strident*, you know, and she was so convinced that her opinions *mattered*. I never really listened, to tell you the truth, but Duncan found her amusing from time to time, particularly when she was being rude on the telephone, which she was, often. She took people to task about the most *trivial* things and she thought they couldn't hear her, you know, unless she shouted. She was a very silly woman.'

Charlie nodded, as if in agreement. 'Then I'm surprised you didn't hear anything the night she died. She must have spoken to her murderer, surely?'

Violet's face flushed a dull red. 'She didn't, you know. Duncan never heard a sound.'

He pretended not to notice her embarrassment. 'And what about you, Mrs Orloff? Did you hear anything?'

'Oh, dear,' she wailed, 'it's not as though it's a *crime* though you'd think it was the way Duncan carries on. I have a tot or two of whisky of an evening, really nothing very much. Duncan's a teetotaller and doesn't approve, but as I always say, where's the harm in it? Mathilda's done it for years – it's unnatural not to, she always said – and she drank far more than I do.' She dropped her voice again. 'It's not as though I'm an *alcoholic.*'

'Good *lord* no,' said Charlie effusively, picking up the loaded speech patterns. 'If I didn't drink enough to send myself to sleep every night, I'd be a nervous wreck come the morning.'

'Well, exactly,' came the repetitive refrain. 'But I do nod off in front of the television, and, of course, I *did* the night Mathilda died. Hardly surprising really since I spent the day in Poole with my sister, and I find that very tiring now. You see, I'm not as young as I used to be, and I won't deny I've been worrying ever since, did Mathilda call for help? Duncan *swears* she didn't but, you know, he's so anti getting involved in anything that he'd have persuaded himself it was just Mathilda being irritating.'

'Any idea what time you nodded off?' asked Cooper, showing more interest in the state of his shoes than in her answer.

'*Very* early,' she said in a whisper. 'We'd just finished supper and sat down to watch *Blind Date*, and the next thing I knew Duncan was shaking me and telling me I was snoring and it was annoying him because it was spoiling *Match of the Day*. Goodness, but I was tired. I went to bed and slept like a *log* till the morning, and I can't help feeling that if I'd only stayed awake, I might have been able to do something for poor Mathilda.'

And that of course was true.

Charlie gestured towards the door. 'May we talk to your husband now, Mrs Orloff?'

'Is that necessary? He won't be able to tell you anything and it'll just make him *grumpy* for the rest of the day.'

'I'm afraid it is.' He produced a paper from his pocket with an air of apology. 'We also have a warrant to search your house, but I assure you, we'll be as careful as we can.' He raised his voice. 'Bailey! Jenkins! Watts! Show yourselves, lads. We're ready to go.'

Quite bewildered by this sudden turn of events, Violet stood meekly to one side while Jones, Cooper and three DCs filed into her hallway. Behind their backs, she crept away with the stealth of a guilty person into the kitchen.

Duncan's small eyes watched the two senior policemen closely as they eased into the cramped living-room, but otherwise he showed remarkably little concern at this sudden invasion of his privacy. 'Forgive me if I don't get up,' he said courteously, 'but I find I'm not as mobile as I used to be.' He waved towards a delicate two-seater sofa, inviting them to sit down. They declined with equal courtesy, afraid of breaking it under their combined weight. 'I've met Detective Sergeant Cooper but I don't know you, sir,' he said, examining Charlie with interest.

'Detective Chief Inspector Jones.'

'How do you do.'

Charlie inclined his head in a brief salute. He was assailed with doubt as he looked at the fat old man in the oversized armchair, his huge stomach overhanging his thighs like the meat from a split sausage skin. Could such ungainly bulk have performed the delicate artistry of Mrs Gillespie's murder? Could he even have abstracted himself from this room without waking his wife? He listened to the shallow wheezing breaths, each one a battle against the smothering pressure of flesh, and recalled Hughes's description of the man who had used the key to open the back door. *His voice was all breathy like he had trouble with his lungs.* 'Was Mrs Gillespie aware that you knew about the key under the flowerpot?' he asked without any attempt at preamble.

Duncan looked surprised. 'I don't understand you, Inspector.'

'No matter. We have a witness who can identify you. He was there when you let yourself in one morning in September.'

But Duncan only smiled and shook his fat cheeks in denial. 'Let myself in where?' There was a sound above them as one of the DCs moved a piece of furniture across the floor, and Duncan's gaze shifted to the ceiling. 'What exactly is all this in aid of?'

Charlie produced the warrant and handed it to him. 'We are searching these premises for Mrs Gillespie's diaries or, more likely, the remains of Mrs Gillespie's diaries. We have reason to believe you stole them from the library of Cedar House.'

'How very peculiar of you.'

'Are you denying it?'

He gave a low chuckle. 'My dear chap, of course I'm denying it. I didn't even know she kept diaries.'

Charlie changed tack. 'Why didn't you tell my Sergeant on the Monday after the murder that Miss Ruth Lascelles had been in Cedar House during the afternoon? Or indeed that Mrs Jane Marriott had had a row with her in the morning?'

'How could I tell him something I didn't know myself?'

'If you were here, Mr Orloff, you could not have avoided knowing. Jane Marriott describes her confrontation with Mrs Gillespie as a screaming match and Ruth says she rang the doorbell because she left her key at school.'

'But I wasn't here, Inspector,' he said affably. 'I took the opportunity of my wife's absence in Poole to go for a long walk.'

There was a gasp from the doorway. 'Duncan!' declared Violet. 'How can you tell such lies? You *never* go for walks.' She advanced into the room like a small ship under sail. 'And don't think I don't know *why* you're lying. You can't be bothered to assist the police in their enquiries, just like you haven't been bothered all along. Of *course* he was here, and of *course* he will have heard Jane and Ruth. We *always* heard Ruth when she came back. She and her grandmother couldn't be in a room together without arguing, any more than she can be in a room with her mother without arguing. Not that I altogether blame her. She wants love, poor child, and neither Mathilda nor Joanna were capable of such an emotion. The only people Mathilda had any fondness for were the Blakeneys, you know, the artist and his wife. She used to laugh with *them*, and I think she even took her clothes off for *him*. I heard her in her bedroom, being very coy and silly, saying things like "Not bad for an old woman" and "I was beautiful once, you know. Men competed for me." And that was true, they *did*. Even Duncan loved her when we were all much younger. He denies it now, of course, but I knew. All us girls knew we were only second best. Mathilda played so hard to get, you see, and that was a challenge.' She paused for breath and Cooper, who was beside her, smelt the whisky on her lips. He had time to feel sadness for this little woman whose life had never blossomed because she had lived it always in the shade of Mathilda Gillespie.

'Not that it *matters*,' she went on. 'Nothing matters that much. And it's years since he lost interest. You can't go on loving someone who's rude all the time, and Mathilda was always rude. She thought it was funny. She'd say the most appalling things, and *laugh*. I won't pretend we had a close relationship, but I did feel sorry for her. She should have done something with her life, something interesting, but she never did and it made her bitter.' She turned a severe gaze on her husband. 'I know she used to *tease* you, Duncan, and call you Mr Toad, but that's no reason not to help find her murderer. Murder is inexcusable. And I can't help feeling, you know, that it was *particularly* inexcusable to put that beastly scold's bridle on her head. You were very upset when she put it on you.' She turned back to Charlie. 'It was one of her horrible jokes. She said the only way Duncan would ever lose weight was if he had his *tongue* clamped, so she crept up behind him one day when he was asleep in the garden with his mouth open and popped that horrid rusty thing over his head. He nearly *died* of shock.' She paused for another breath but this time she had run out of steam and didn't go on.

There was a long silence.

'I suppose that's how you put it on her,' murmured Charlie finally, 'when she was already asleep, but I'd be interested to know how you gave her the barbiturates. The pathologist estimates four or five and she would never have taken that many herself.'

Duncan's gaze rested briefly on his wife's shocked face, before shifting to Cooper's. 'Old women have two things in common,' he said with a small smile. 'They drink too much and they talk too much. You'd have liked Mathilda, Sergeant, she was a very amusing woman, although the memory of her was a great deal more attractive than the real thing. It was a disappointment coming back. Age has few compensations, as I think I told you.' His pleasant face beamed. 'On the whole I prefer male company. Men are so much more predictable.'

'Which is convenient,' remarked Cooper to the Blakeneys in Mill kitchen that evening, 'since he'll probably spend the rest of his life in prison.'

'Assuming you can prove he did it,' said Jack. 'What happens if he doesn't confess? You'll be left with circumstantial evidence, and if his defence has any sense they'll go all out to convince the jury Mathilda committed suicide. You don't even know why he did it, do you?'

'Not yet.'

'Doesn't Violet know?' asked Sarah.

Cooper shook his head, thinking of the wretched woman they'd abandoned at Wing Cottage, wringing her hands and protesting there must be some mistake. 'Claims she doesn't.'

'And you didn't find the diaries?'

'We never really expected to. He'd have destroyed them long ago.'

'But there's so much unexplained,' said Sarah in frustration. 'How did he get her to take the sleeping pills? Why did he do it? Why didn't Violet wake up? Why didn't he tell you Ruth had been there if he wanted her implicated? And then the bit I really don't understand – why on earth did Jane have a row with Mathilda that day?'

Cooper glanced at Jack, then took out his cigarettes. 'I can make a guess at some answers,' he said, planting a cigarette in the side of his mouth and flicking his lighter to the tip. 'Both Mathilda and Violet liked a tipple in the evening and they both drank whisky. I think the chances are it was Mathilda who first introduced Violet to it, made it respectable as it were in the face of Duncan's disapproval, but in any case Violet was certainly in the habit of dozing off in her armchair. The night Mathilda died, Violet went out for the count during *Blind Date* which comes on at six thirty or thereabouts, woke up briefly some time after ten o'clock, when Duncan shook her and told her she was snoring through *Match of the Day,* went up to bed and slept like the dead for the rest of the night.' He tapped ash into his cupped palm. 'That was definitely no doze. That was a barbiturate-induced stupor which is why Duncan leaving the room wouldn't have wakened her. I think he greeted Violet when she got home after a tiring day in Poole with a stiff whisky, laced with sleeping tablets, waited till she fell asleep, then trotted next door and used the same concoction on Mathilda. She kept the drink in the kitchen. How simple just to say: Don't stir yourself. Let me do the honours and get you a top-up.'

'But where did he get the sleeping pills from? He's on my list and I've never prescribed any for him or Violet.'

'Presumably he used the ones you prescribed for Mrs Gillespie.'

Sarah looked doubtful. 'When could he have taken them, though? Surely she'd have noticed if any were missing.'

'If she did,' he said dryly, 'then she probably assumed it was her own daughter who was responsible. With Mrs Lascelles's sort of dependence she must have been raiding her mother's drug cupboard for years.'

Jack looked thoughtful. 'Who told you?'

'As a matter of fact, you did, Jack. But I wasn't too sure what she was on until we searched the house yesterday for the diaries. She's not very good at hiding things, but then she's damn lucky she hasn't fallen foul of the police before. She will, though, now that the money's dried up.'

'I didn't tell you anything.'

Cooper tut-tutted. 'You've told me everything you know about Mrs Lascelles, right down to the fact that you, personally, despise her. I stood and looked at her portrait while we were discussing Othello and Iago, and all I could see was a desperately weak and fragmented character whose existence – ' he used his hands to depict a border ' – depends on external stimulation. I compared the pallid colours and the distorted shapes of Joanna's portrait with the vigour of Mathilda's and Sarah's and I thought, you've painted a woman without substance. The only reality you perceive is a reflected reality, in other words, a personality that can only express itself artificially. I guessed it had to be drink or drugs.'

'You're lying through your teeth,' said Jack bluntly. 'That bastard Smollett told you. Dammit, Cooper, even I didn't see all that and I painted the bloody picture.'

Cooper gave a deep chuckle. 'It's all there, my friend, believe me.

Mr Smollett told me nothing.' His face sobered. 'But you had no business withholding that information, either of you, not in a murder enquiry.' He looked at Sarah. 'And you should never have confronted her with it the other afternoon, if you don't mind me saying so, Doctor. People like that are shockingly unpredictable and you were alone in the house with her.'

'She's not on LSD, Cooper, she's on Valium. Anyway, how do you know I confronted her with it?'

'Because I'm a policeman, Dr Blakeney, and you were looking guilty. What makes you think she's on Valium?'

'She told me she was.'

Cooper raised his eyes to heaven. 'One day, Dr Blakeney, you will learn not to be so gullible.'

'Well, what is she on then?' demanded Jack. 'I guessed tranquillizers, too. She's not injecting. I sketched her in the nude and there wasn't a mark on her.'

'It depends what you were looking for. She's rich enough to do the thing cleanly. It's dirty needles and dirty lavatories that cause most of the problems. Where did you look anyway? Arms and legs?' Jack nodded. 'The veins around her groin?'

'No,' he admitted. 'I was having enough trouble as it was, I didn't want to encourage her by staring at the damn thing.'

Cooper nodded. 'I found half a pharmacy under her floorboards, including tranquillizers, barbiturates, amphetamines and sizeable quantities of heroin and syringes. She's chronically addicted, I'd say, presumably has been for years. And, I'll tell you this for free, her mother's allowance alone couldn't possibly have funded what she'd got stashed away, and nor could fancy flower arranging. I think Duncan and Violet's anonymous letter said it all, Joanna is a high-class prostitute turning tricks to fund a very expensive habit, begun, I would guess, when she married Steven Lascelles.'

'But she looks so . . .' Sarah sought for the right word, 'unsullied.'

'Not for much longer,' said Cooper cynically. 'She's about to discover what it's like to live in the real world where there's no Mathilda to keep the coffers topped up. It's when you get desperate that you start getting careless.' He patted Sarah's hand. 'Don't waste your sympathy on her. She's been a taker all her life and, rather belatedly, her mother has forced her to face up to it.'

Of all absurd things, Gerald has developed a conscience. 'No more, Matty, please,' he said, bursting into tears. 'We'll go to hell for what we've done.' The ingratitude of the man beggars belief. Does he think I get any pleasure from being pawed by a drooling half-wit? It's Father's doing, of course. He lost his temper yesterday and started calling Gerald names. Now Gerald says he's going back to the slut down the road who first seduced him, and this time he says he'll marry her. 'Grace will give Gerry a baby, Matty,' he blubbered, 'and Gerry wants a baby.' Why, oh why, was my grandfather so stupid? How much more sensible it would have been to weather the embarrassment of certifying Gerald than to pretend to the world he was normal.

I sought out Father in the library, drunk as usual, and told him bluntly that Gerald wasn't playing any more. 'You're such a fool,' I stormed at him. 'Grace won't be bought off a second time. Don't imagine she hasn't guessed by now that she'll get more by marrying Gerald than by taking your bribes.' Father cringed away from me as he always does. 'It's not my fault,' he whined, 'it's your grandfather's fault. He should have mentioned me by name in his will instead of referring to Gerald's nearest male relative.' I could have murdered him then. The same old story, never his fault, always someone else's. But in one way he's right. Why did my grandfather create a trust to prevent his idiot first-born disposing of his wealth without clarifying that my father must inherit afterwards? And why did it not occur to him that Gerald might repeat the terms of the will parrot-fashion to any scheming little bitch who cared to listen? Grace must have worked out by now that Gerald is worth marrying just to produce a son who will inherit everything. I suppose my grandfather had no idea that imbeciles were so interested in sex nor, indeed, that they were capable of fathering children.

295

I made Father wear the scold's bridle all evening and he's promised to hold his tongue in future. Gerald, of course, whimpered in the corner, afraid that I would make him wear it, too, but I promised that if we heard no more talk of going to live with Grace, I would be nice to him. Now he is pliable once more.

How strange it is that these two, without a brain between them, can see the scold's bridle for the humiliation it is, while Duncan, who has some pretensions to intelligence, is disgustingly excited by it. For Gerald and Father it is a necessary penance for the sins they wish to commit. For Duncan, it is a fetish that unlocks his potency. He is invariably aroused by wearing it. But what a gutless worm he is. He begs me on his knees to marry him while he allows Violet and her parents to continue with the marriage arrangements. He is not prepared to risk losing her miserable dowry, unless he is first assured of mine.

I could never marry a man who takes pleasure in his own humiliation, for then there would be no pleasure left to me. I can only love them when they cringe. Still, it is odd how many men find cruelty attractive. Like dogs, they lick the hand that whips them. Poor Violet. I have planted fantasies in Duncan's mind that she can never satisfy. Well, well, what a very amusing thought that is. I really couldn't bear to see them happy. But then I can't bear to see anybody happy . . .

Nineteen

SARAH TOPPED UP their wine glasses and viewed the empty bottle with a wry look. 'Thank God my poison is legal,' she murmured. 'I know damn well I need an external stimulant to make the miseries bearable. Did you take her heroin off her, Cooper? She'll be in a desperate state if you did.'

'No,' he admitted, 'but you can keep that information to yourselves.'

'You're a very kind man,' she told him.

'I'm a realist,' he corrected her. 'If Joanna had murdered her mother then I was in a stronger position keeping what I knew up my sleeve than showing my hand before I had to. She would have been very vulnerable to police questioning if we could have charged her with possession and murder both at the same time.'

'You're such a bad liar,' said Sarah fondly. 'You're not going to charge her at all. Will you even tell her you know?'

But Cooper sidestepped that question. 'We were talking about how Duncan murdered Mathilda,' he said. 'So where were we?'

'With Mathilda being immensely suspicious when he came through the back door uninvited and offered to top up her whisky,' said Sarah dryly.

'Oh, yes, well he wouldn't have gone that way. He'd have rung the front door bell. It was quite safe. Violet wasn't going to hear anything, not if she was snoring her head off in front of the television, and I'm sure he had a very convincing reason for knocking on Mathilda's door at seven o'clock on a Saturday evening. He did know a great deal about her life, after all, any bit of which he could tap into as an excuse. She would have to have been deeply paranoid to lock her door against a neighbour she saw almost every day.' Absent-mindedly, he tapped more ash into his palm then turned it upside down to scatter it on the floor. 'Once he'd given her the whisky, and watched her drink it, he made his excuses and left. He's a cautious man and he didn't know how effective the sedative would be, plus he needed to be sure Violet really was dead to the world and hadn't heard the bell ringing. Presumably if he'd found her semi-conscious, he'd have abandoned the project as being too dangerous and, by the same token, he wanted Mathilda well and truly under before he put the scold's bridle over her head.

'From then on, it would all have been very straightforward. He checked on Violet, donned a pair of gloves, collected the appropriate weeds from the garden – he wouldn't have done that during daylight hours in case someone saw him and put two and two together when they heard about Mathilda's flower arrangement. Then he let himself in again, this time through Mathilda's back door, took the Stanley knife from the kitchen drawer, checked Mathilda was asleep, took the weeds, the knife and the scold's bridle upstairs where he left them on the dressing-table, filled the bath, then went back down to collect Mathilda. All he had to do was scoop her up in his arms, put her on the lift, take her upstairs and undress her.

'The time would have been approximately nine thirty, we think, which has made the pathologist very happy. He always favoured earlier rather than later, particularly as Mathilda wouldn't have died immediately.' He cast about in his mind again for the thread of where he had been. 'Right, so once he'd undressed her, he placed her in the warm bath, put the scold's bridle on her head, slit her wrists and then arranged the nettles and daisies in the head-band, probably using the sponge to wedge the gap. Then all he had to do was leave the whisky glass beside the empty sleeping-pill bottle, remove the diaries, wipe the key clean for safety's sake and replace it, before going home to Violet and the television. He undoubtedly took the poor woman to task the next morning over her drinking being so bad that she'd passed out the night before, or she might have told us earlier that she'd been asleep instead of going along with Duncan's story that there had been no sound from next door.' He massaged his chin. 'She's a very pliable woman and, in fairness to her, it obviously never occurred to her that he could have murdered Mathilda. I think she prompted him to write us the anonymous letter because she felt so guilty about letting Mathilda down.' He flicked a glance at Jack. 'She overheard her crying that time you went round to show her the painting, and she's convinced herself that if she'd only spoken to her then she might have prevented the murder.'

He saw the look of puzzled enquiry on Sarah's face, and ploughed on relentlessly. 'As far as Ruth and Jane are concerned, Duncan didn't want to tell us about them being in Cedar House that day because he couldn't afford to draw attention to how much could be heard through the walls. But Violet gave him the perfect opportunity to involve Ruth when she overheard a row between Joanna and Ruth in their hall. She consulted Duncan about the wisdom of reporting it and, while he flatly refused to let her come in person, to avoid any unpleasantness, as he put it, he didn't object to an anonymous letter, although he insisted on wearing gloves to avoid us tracing it through the fingerprints. Violet thought that was *very* exciting,' he concluded with heavy irony.

'It's odd that Mathilda never mentioned hearing them,' said Jack. 'It's the sort of thing that would have driven her mad.'

'Mrs Orloff says she spoke very clearly and decisively, so perhaps she was a little deaf, and if she never heard them, it wouldn't occur to her that they could hear her. In any case, as soon as they realized just how much could be overheard, I suspect they tempered their own volume. It's interesting to watch them. He speaks just above a whisper and whenever she gets excited, he frowns at her and she drops her voice.'

'I suppose that's how he found out about the key,' said Sarah slowly. 'When Mathilda told me where it was that day. He must have heard her.'

Cooper nodded.

'How did he know about the diaries?'

'According to Violet, she often used to talk to herself when no one was there, so I'm guessing she read them aloud. Otherwise, he stumbled on them by accident when he was looking for something else.' He frowned. '*He's* not going to tell us, that's for sure. He's just sitting there at the moment denying everything and challenging us to give one good reason why he would suddenly want to murder a woman he had known for fifty years, when scarcely one cross word had been exchanged between them in all that time. And Violet supports him on that. She says Duncan is far too lazy either to take offence or give it, so Mathilda very quickly got bored with trying to provoke any sort of reaction out of him.'

'He's got you by the short and curlies,' remarked Jack with reluctant admiration. 'You won't get very far with "trying to delay the passage of the will" as a convincing motive for murder. Even if the Prosecution's prepared to run with it, I can't see a jury accepting it. Have you really no idea at all why he wanted her dead? Surely Violet must know something.'

'She's very distressed at the moment. The DCI hopes a little tender care from a sympathetic policewoman will help jog her memory, but, if you want my opinion, she's being genuinely honest when she says she doesn't know. She's a funny little person, seems to live in a world of her own most of the time, talks nineteen-to-the-dozen but doesn't listen. I suspect most of what went on inside Cedar House was just background noise to her.' He glanced from one to the other of them. 'All of which is why I'm here. I need to talk to Ruth. She mentioned that her grandmother wrote her a letter shortly before she died, and it occurred to me that there might have been something in there which might help us.'

'If it's the same one she told me about, then she tore it up,' said Sarah.

'Still, she'll remember what was in it. I really do need to talk to her.'

Sarah shook her head firmly. 'Not now, Cooper. She's paranoid about the police at the moment, what with last night, and Jack being carted off in handcuffs at lunchtime. Okay, I know none of it's your fault, but you've got to show her a little compassion.'

'Don't make me insist,' he begged. 'I really don't have a choice on this one. We can't hold Duncan indefinitely without some very concrete evidence and, once he walks, he'll be free to tidy up anything we've missed.'

She sighed and took one of his large hands in hers. 'Look, I'm going to tell you something that, strictly speaking, I shouldn't because it's Ruth's secret and not mine, but I'd trust you with my life, Cooper, so I think I can trust you with Ruth's.' She gave the hand a quick squeeze before releasing it to reach across for Jack's, her eyes creasing with affection. 'Why do you think this silly sod has been charging about like a bull in a china shop? He says what he's done is rational and sensible. You and I know it isn't. Rather belatedly, he's discovered that he has some very powerful paternal feelings which, because he's the generous soul he is, he does not intend to limit to his own offspring. He is acting in lieu of Ruth's dead father because he wants her to know that there is someone in this shitty world who loves her.'

Jack raised her fingers to his lips. 'Two people,' he corrected her.

She held his gaze for a moment. 'Two people,' she agreed. She took her hand away and transferred her attention back to Cooper. 'Ruth is so vulnerable at the moment that if she's put under any more pressure, then I can guarantee she'll withdraw from reality in the way that Joanna clearly has done and Mathilda probably did as well. It's almost as if there's a self-destructive gene in the family that triggers the withdrawal.' She shook her head. 'Whatever it is, Ruth is not going the same way, not if Jack and I can prevent it. She's pregnant, Cooper. I know she doesn't look it, but she's almost at the legal cut-off point, and if she doesn't make up her mind very quickly about having the pregnancy terminated, then she'll have to go through with it. Jack was trying to buy her the peace and quiet she needs to reach a decision, because as yet she hasn't had the chance to do it.'

Cooper absorbed all this in grave silence. 'Are you helping her reach her decision?' he asked at last.

'I've given her all the information I can, but I don't like to say, do this or do that. It's her mother's role to give advice but Joanna doesn't even know about the rape, let alone about the pregnancy.'

'Hmm,' grunted Cooper, pursing his lips in deep thought. 'Well, I certainly don't intend to add to the poor girl's problems,' he said at last. 'I'm sure her grandmother wouldn't demand justice for herself before consideration for her granddaughter. If she was that way inclined she'd have reported Ruth for thieving when she was still alive.' He stood up and buttoned his coat about him, preparatory to leaving. 'But, if you'll forgive the impertinence, Dr Blakeney, you must take your responsibilities as her adopted mother, temporary or otherwise, a great deal more seriously. It's no good giving her information and leaving it up to her to decide, without making it very clear that you believe it's in her best interests to have an abortion. The chances are she'll scream and yell, say you don't love her and don't care tuppence for her feelings, but parenting is not about patting oneself on the back for being understanding and liberal, it's about guidance, education and training to help the child you love become a man or woman you can respect.' He nodded a friendly goodbye and made for the door, only to pause as he saw Ruth in the shadows of the hall.

'I've been listening,' she said, her wretched eyes full of tears. 'I'm sorry. I didn't mean to.'

'There, there,' said Cooper, gruff with embarrassment, pulling a large white handkerchief from his pocket and offering it to her. 'I'm the one who should apologize. I'd no business to interfere.'

Her eyes brimmed again. 'I don't mind about what you said. I was thinking – if only – you said you wished your children had had my opportunities – do you remember?'

He nodded. He had indeed said that, he thought with chagrin.

'Well, I was just thinking – I wish' – she gave him a watery smile – 'I wish I'd had theirs. I hope they appreciate you, Sergeant Cooper.' She took a letter from her pocket and gave it to him. 'It's Granny's,' she said. 'I didn't throw it away, but I couldn't show it to you because she talks about my stealing.' A tear splashed on to her hand. 'I really did love her, you know, but she died thinking I didn't, and that's almost worse than everything else.'

'Yes,' he said gently, 'I'm sure it is, because there's nothing you can do to mend it.'

'Not ever.'

'Well, as to ever – that I couldn't say. In this life, the best any of us can do is learn from our mistakes and try not to make them again. We're none of us infallible, Ruth, but we owe it to ourselves and to those around us to act with whatever wisdom we possess. Otherwise, how will mankind ever improve?'

She pressed her lips together to hold back the tears. 'And you think it would be wise for me to have an abortion?'

'Yes,' he said with absolute honesty, 'I do.' He placed his broad palm against her stomach. 'At the moment you're not quite old enough or tough enough to be mother and father to another human being, and you're too riddled by guilt over your grandmother, and what you see as your betrayal of her, to give this baby away to someone else.' He smiled rather shyly. 'That's not to say I expect you

302

to agree with me or that I'll turn my back on you if you decide to have your baby. Dr Blakeney's quite right when she says it's your choice. But I'd rather see you pregnant when you've lived a little and found a man you can love who loves you, too. Then your babies will be wanted and you'll be free to be the kind of mother you want to be.'

She tried to thank him, but the words wouldn't come, so Cooper took her in his arms instead and held her tight. Behind them, Sarah turned a tear-streaked face to Jack. 'Remind me of this,' she whispered, 'whenever I get complacent. I've just learnt how little I really know.'

My dear Ruth [Mathilda had written], Your mother and I have fallen out over a letter written by my uncle Gerald Cavendish shortly before he died, making Joanna his heir. She is threatening to take me to court over it because she believes she can use it to overturn my father's will. She won't succeed, but I have been unable to convince her of that. She feels understandably aggrieved and wants to punish me. I realize now there has been too much secrecy within this family and so I am writing to you now to acquaint you with the knowledge she already has, because I do not want you to learn about it from her. She will not, I think, tell you kindly. James Gillespie was not your mother's father. Gerald Cavendish was. I realize how shocked you will be by this information but I urge you to do what I have done all these years and see it as something that happened which should not be regretted. You may find this hard to believe but, despite everything, I have always been fond of your mother, as indeed I have been fond of you.

I am faced now with a difficult choice. I am aware, my dear, that you have been stealing from me for some months. I am aware, too, that your mother has given up on life and prefers the twilight world of drug dependency and the casual relationships that give her the illusion of being loved without the ties of responsibility. You are both allowing yourselves to be abused by men and, in view of my own history, I find that deeply disheartening. I realize I have failed you, and have decided, therefore, to set you both free to make your own decisions about your futures.

My intention is to make over a lump sum to you and your mother on your eighteenth birthday, the amount to be apportioned in the ratio 2:1, with your mother receiving double your share. Perhaps it is something I should have done a long time ago, but I was reluctant to give up what I have worked so hard for in the Cavendish name. As things are now, I see that a name is nothing unless the individuals who bear it stand above their peers, for it is not the accident of our births that makes us great but our individual characters. By setting you and your mother free to lead your lives as you choose, I hope to give you the chance to prove yourselves, just as others – those less fortunate – have already done.

In conclusion, should anything happen to me and you find yourself in need of a friend, then I urge you to talk to Dr Sarah Blakeney, my GP, who will give you nothing but good advice whatever the situation you find yourself in.

With love, Granny.

Cooper placed the letter in front of Detective Chief Inspector Jones. 'I've been asking myself where she was going to get the money from to give lump sums to Mrs and Miss Lascelles if she'd already made a will giving everything to Dr Blakeney.'

Charlie scanned the page rapidly. 'Did you come up with an answer?'

'I reckon it's on the video, if we'd only known what to look for. Do you remember when she was talking to Ruth towards the end and she mentioned her promise to leave the girl Cedar House before Ruth's behaviour of the last six months had persuaded her to change her mind? Okay, well immediately after that she went on to say something like: "You'd have had the choice either to sell up or stay but you'd have sold because the house would have lost its charms for you once the estate was approved." Or words to that effect.'

Charlie nodded.

'I assumed the phrase "once the estate was approved" referred to the goods and chattels being handed over to Joanna as part of her share.'

'Go on.'

'I think now she was talking about an estate of houses. She was planning to sell off the garden for development. How else could she raise a lump sum for the Lascelles women and still be able to leave Cedar House and its contents to Dr Blakeney? Just imagine the impact that would have had on Duncan Orloff. A man who can't bear the thought of noisy children next door sure as hell isn't going to sit tamely by and watch his garden turned into a building site.'

'Prove it,' said Duncan placidly. 'Name the developer. Explain why there's no correspondence with this mythical company. Good grief, man, she wouldn't even have got planning permission for such an enterprise. The days of unravelling the green belt are long gone. They're knitting it back together now just as fast as they can. There's electoral mileage in the environmental vote and none at all in speculative vandalism.'

All of which, thought Charlie gloomily, was true. It was left to Cooper to bring a dose of common sense to the situation.

The following morning, after lengthy consultations with the local borough planning officer, he presented himself at Howard & Sons, building contractors of Learmouth since 1972. A middle-aged secretary, agog with curiosity at this unexpected appearance of a plain-clothes policeman in their midst, ushered him with some ceremony into the office of Mr Howard Snr.

Mr Howard, a thickset elderly man with a scattering of grizzled grey hairs, looked up from a set of plans with a frown. 'Well, Sergeant? What can I do for you?'

'I understand your company was responsible for the Cedar Estate development in Fontwell. It was built ten years ago. Do you recall it?'

'I do,' barked the other. 'What of it? Who's complaining?'

'No one, as far as I know,' said Cooper placidly.

He waved to a chair. 'Sit down, man. You can't be too sure about anything these days. It's a dog-eat-dog world where litigation's the name of the game and the only people who get fat are the solicitors. I had a letter this morning from a tight-fisted bastard who's refusing to pay what he owes because he says we're in breach of contract by putting in one less electric socket than the plans called for. It makes you sick.' He beetled ferocious eyebrows. 'So what's your interest in Cedar Estate?'

'You bought the land for it from a Mrs Mathilda Gillespie of Cedar House, Fontwell.'

'I did. Blood-sucking old bitch she is, too. Paid far more for it than I should have done.'

'*Was*,' Cooper corrected him. 'She's dead.'

Howard eyed him with sudden interest. 'Is that so? Ah, well,' he murmured without regret, 'it comes to us all in the end.'

'In her case rather prematurely. She was murdered.'

There was a short silence. 'And what does that have to do with the Cedar Estate?'

'We're having difficulty establishing a motive. One idea that suggests itself,' he declared ponderously, 'is that she was planning to continue her successful venture with you by selling off the rest of her garden for development. From consultations I've had with the planning department, I understand some sort of second phase has always been on the cards, but this would have made her very unpopular in certain quarters and might have inspired the murder.' He hadn't missed the gleam of interest in the sharp old eyes opposite. 'Have you had any recent correspondence with her on the subject, Mr Howard?'

'Only negative.'

Cooper frowned. 'Could you explain that?'

'She approached us with a view to going forward. We made an offer. She rejected it.' He grunted with annoyance. 'Like I told you, she was a blood-sucking old bitch. Wanted far more for the land than it's worth. The building trade's been through the worst recession in its history and prices have plummeted. I wouldn't mind so much if it wasn't down to us in the first place that she was even in a position to develop the damn thing.' He glared at Cooper as if Cooper were responsible for Mathilda's rejection. 'It was us who established the sodding outline permission on her garden ten years ago which is why we left access space on the south-east boundary. First refusal on the second phase if she decided to go ahead was part of the original contract and she had the gall to turn us down.'

'When was this? Can you remember?'

'The day she turned us down? Bonfire night, November the fifth.' He chuckled suddenly. 'I told her to stick a rocket up her arse and she hung up on me. Mind, I'd said many worse things first time round – I don't mind my Ps and Qs for anyone – and she always came back.'

'You saw her in person?'

'Telephone. She meant it, though, wrote a couple of days later confirming. Claimed she was in no hurry and was prepared to wait for the prices to go back up again. It's in the file, along with a copy of our offer.' The gleam of interest was back in his eyes. 'Still, if she's dead, her heirs might be interested, eh? It's a fair offer. They won't get better from anyone else.'

'Her will's being contested,' said Cooper apologetically. 'I imagine it will be some time before ownership of the property is proved. May I see her letter?'

'Don't see why not.' He pressed the intercom and demanded the Gillespie file. 'So who killed her then?'

'No one's been charged as yet.'

'Well, they do say planning disputes bring out the worst in people. Bit extreme to murder someone over it though. Eh?'

'Any murder's extreme,' said Cooper.

'A few houses more or less. It's hardly a motive.'

'People fear the unexpected,' said Cooper phlegmatically. 'I some-times think that's the root cause of all murders.' He looked towards the door as the secretary popped in with an orange folder. 'The boat rocks and the only solution is to kill the person who's rocking it.'

Howard opened the file and selected a sheet from the top. 'There you are.' He handed it across.

Cooper examined it carefully. It was dated Saturday, November 6th, and typed. As Howard had said, it confirmed her refusal to proceed until prices improved. 'When did you say you got this?'

'Couple of days after the phone call.'

'That would have been a Sunday.'

'The Monday then, or maybe the Tuesday. We don't work weekends, not in the office at least.'

'Did she always type her letters?'

'Don't remember her ever doing it before.' He looked back through the file. 'Copper-plate script every time.'

Cooper thought of her letter to Ruth. That had been written in a beautiful hand. 'Have you any other letters from her? I'd like to compare the signatures.'

Howard licked a finger and flicked over the pages, removing several more sheets. 'You think someone else wrote it?'

'It's a possibility. There's no typewriter in her house and she was dead by the Saturday night. When could she have had it done?' He placed the pages side by side on the desk and squinted at the subscriptions. 'Well, well,' he said with satisfaction, 'the best laid schemes – you've been very helpful, Mr Howard. May I take these with me?'

'I'll want photocopies for my records.' He was consumed with curiosity. 'Never occurred to me it wasn't kosher. What's wrong with it then?'

Cooper placed a finger on the typed letter's signature. 'For a start, he's dotted his "i"s' – he pointed to the others – 'and she hasn't. His "M" is too upright and the "G" runs on to the following "i".' He chuckled. 'The experts are going to have a field day on this. All in all it's a very cack-handed effort.'

'Bit of a fool, is he?'

'Arrogant, I'd say. Forgery is an art like any other. It takes years of practice to be any good.'

'I've a forensic team sifting through a dustbin full of Violet's old cinders,' Charlie told Cooper when he returned to the nick, 'and they tell me they've found the diaries. Or what's left of them at least. There's the odd scrap of paper but several quite substantial pieces of what they say is the calf-skin binding. They're still looking. They're confident of finding at least one scrap with her writing on it.' He rubbed his hands together.

'They might look for scraps of typed paper while they're about it, preferably with a Howard & Sons imprint,' said Cooper, producing his sheaf of letters. 'They made her a formal offer for her land on the first of November, and we certainly didn't find it when we went through her papers. The chances are Orloff swiped an entire file. Howard Snr has a stack of correspondence relating to Cedar Estate, and there wasn't a damn thing on the subject anywhere in the house. If there had been we might have twigged a bit sooner.'

'No one's fault but her own. I suppose she learnt never to trust anyone which is why she played everything so close to her chest. She said it all in her letter to Ruth, "there's been too much secrecy within this family". If she'd mentioned her plans to the solicitor even, she'd probably be alive now.'

'Still, we didn't ask the right questions, Charlie.'

The Inspector gave a dry laugh. 'If the answer's forty-two, then what's the Ultimate Question? Read *The Hitch Hiker's Guide to the Galaxy*, old son. It's harder to ask the right question than it is to come up with the answer, so don't lose any sleep over it.'

Cooper, who somewhat belatedly was trying to improve his reading, took out his notebook and jotted down the title. At the very least, it had to be more palatable than *Othello* which he was struggling through at the moment. He tucked his pencil back into his pocket and took Charlie through his conversation with the developer. 'It was six weeks of hard negotiating the first time before he and she could agree on a price. She used to horse-trade over the phone, apparently, rejecting every offer until he came up with one she could accept. Poor old soul,' he said with genuine feeling. 'Orloff must have thought his ship had come in when he heard her doing it the second time round. She made it so easy for him.' He tapped the typed letter. 'All he had to do was get rid of her and post that off the next day. Howard claims he and his sons lost interest immediately because he'd made it clear to her on more than one occasion that the bottom had dropped out of the market and he wasn't in a position to offer her any more.'

Charlie picked up the letter and examined it. 'There was a portable typewriter on the desk in his sitting-room,' he recalled. 'Let's get the lads out there to make a quick comparison for us. He's put all his effort into forging her signature and forgotten that typewriters have signatures, too.'

'He'd never make it that easy for us.'

But he had.

'Duncan Jeremiah Orloff . . . formally charged with the murder of Mathilda Beryl Gillespie . . . Saturday, November sixth . . .' The voice of the Duty Officer droned on relentlessly, making little impact on Cooper who knew the formula off by heart. Instead, his mind drifted towards an elderly woman, drained of her lifeblood, and the rusted iron framework that had encased her head. He felt an intense regret that he had never known her. Whatever sins she had committed, it would, he felt, have been a privilege.

'. . . request that you be refused bail because of the serious nature of the charges against you. The magistrates will order an immediate remand into custody . . .'

He looked at Duncan Orloff only when the man beat his fat little hands against his breast and burst into tears. It wasn't his fault, he pleaded, it was Mathilda's fault. Mathilda was to blame for everything. He was a sick man. What would Violet do without him?

'Collapse of stout party,' muttered the Duty Officer under his breath to Cooper, listening to the rasping, anguished breaths.

A deep frown creased Cooper's pleasant face. 'By heaven, she deserved better than you, she really did,' he said to Orloff. 'It should have been a brave man who killed her, not a coward. What gave you the right to play God with her life?'

'A brave man wouldn't have had to, Sergeant Cooper.' He turned haunted eyes towards the policeman. 'It wasn't courage that was needed to kill Mathilda, it was fear.'

'Fear of a few houses in your garden, Mr Orloff?'

Duncan shook his head. 'I am what I am' – he held trembling hands to his face – 'and it was she who made me. I have spent my adult life shunning the woman I married in favour of fantasies about the one I didn't, and you cannot live in hell for forty years without being damaged by it.'

'Is that why you came back to Fontwell, to relive your fantasies?'

'You can't control them, Sergeant. They control you.' He fell silent.

'But you returned five years ago, Mr Orloff.'

'I asked nothing from her, you know. A few shared memories perhaps. Peace even. After forty years I expected very little.'

Cooper eyed him curiously. 'You said you killed her out of fear. Was that what you fantasized about? Being so afraid of her that you could bring yourself to kill her?'

'I fantasized about making love,' he whispered.

'To Mathilda?'

'Of course.' He gathered his tears in the palms of his hands. 'I've never made love to Violet. I couldn't.'

Good God, thought Cooper with disgust, did the man have no pity at all for his poor little wife? 'Couldn't or wouldn't, Mr Orloff? There is a difference.'

'Couldn't.' The word was barely audible. 'Mathilda did certain things' – he shivered like a man possessed – 'which Violet was offended by' – his voice broke – 'it was less unpleasant for both of us if I paid for what I wanted.'

Cooper caught the Duty Officer's gaze above Duncan's head, and gave a cynical laugh. 'So this is going to be your defence, is it? That you murdered Mathilda Gillespie because she gave you a taste for something only prostitutes could supply?'

A thready sigh puttered from the moist lips. 'You never had cause to be afraid of her, Sergeant. She didn't own you because she didn't know your secrets.' The sad eyes turned towards him. 'Surely it's occurred to you that when we bought Wing Cottage our solicitor discovered the outline planning permission on the remaining Cedar House land? We went ahead with the purchase because Mathilda agreed to a clause in the contract, giving us a power of veto over any future decision.' He gave a hollow laugh. 'I blame myself because I knew her so much better than Violet ever did. The clause was worth less than the paper it was written on.' Briefly, he pressed his lips together in an effort to control himself. 'She was obliged to tell me about her approach to Howard because she was going to need my signature on the final document, but when I told her that Violet and I would object to the proposed plan, which put the nearest house ten yards from our back wall, she laughed. "Don't be absurd, Duncan. Have you forgotten how much I know about you?"'

When he didn't go on, Cooper prompted him. 'She was going to blackmail you into signing?'

'Of course.' He placed his damp palms to his breasts. 'We were in the drawing-room. She left me for a couple of minutes to fetch a book from the library, and when she came back she read extracts to me.' Distress wheezed from him in quickened breaths. 'It was one of her diaries – full of such terrible lies and obscenity – and not just about me – Violet, too – intimate details that Violet had told her

311

when she was tipsy. "Do you want me to photocopy this, Duncan, and spread it round the village?" she asked. "Do you want the whole of Fontwell to know that Violet is still a virgin because the demands you made of her on your wedding night were so disgusting that she had to lock herself in the bathroom?"' – his voice faltered – 'she was very entertained by it all – couldn't put the book down once she'd started – read me pieces about the Marriotts, the vicar, the poor Spedes – everyone.' He fell silent again.

'So you went back later to read the others?' suggested Cooper.

Duncan shrugged helplessly. 'I was desperate. I hoped I'd find something I could use against *her*. I doubted there'd be anything of value in the early ones, simply because I'd have to find independent proof to challenge her, and, bar references to Joanna's drug addiction, Ruth's stealing and her belief that Sarah Blakeney was the daughter she'd had by Paul Marriott, the later ones were simply a catalogue of her dislikes. They were the product of a diseased mind, and she used them, I think, as a channel for expunging her poison. If she hadn't been able to express herself on paper' – he shook his head – 'she was quite mad, you know.'

'Still,' said Cooper ponderously, 'murder was an extreme solution, Mr Orloff. You could have used her daughter's and her granddaughter's problems against her. She was a proud woman. She wouldn't have wanted those made public, surely?'

The sad eyes fixed on him again. 'I never planned to murder her, or not till that Saturday morning when Jane Marriott went to see her. I intended to threaten her with divulging what I knew to Dr Blakeney. But as I told you, it was fear that killed her. A brave man would have said: "publish and be damned".'

He had lost Cooper. 'I don't understand.'

'She told Jane Marriott that things would get worse before they got better because she knew James had been reading her private papers – it never occurred to her it was me – then she went on to say that she had no intention of keeping quiet any longer.' He wrung his hands. 'So, of course, I went round the minute Jane left and asked her what she meant by "she had no intention of keeping quiet any longer"?' His face was grey with fatigue. 'She picked up the scold's bridle and taunted me with it. "Mathilda Cavendish and Mathilda Gillespie did not write their diaries for fun, Duncan. They wrote them so that one day they could have their revenge. They will not be gagged. I shall see to that."' He paused. 'She really was mad,' he insisted, 'and she knew it. I said I'd call a doctor for her so she laughed and quoted *Macbeth* at me. "More needs she the divine than the physician."' He raised his hands in a gesture of surrender. 'And I thought how all of us, who would be destroyed by her diaries, needed the divine more than the physician, and I made up my mind during that terrible afternoon to play . . . God.'

Cooper was deeply sceptical. 'But you must have planned it all in advance because you stole the sleeping pills beforehand.'

He sighed. 'They were for me – or Violet – or both of us.'

'So what made you change your mind?'

'Sergeant, I am, as you rightly say, a coward and I realized that I could not destroy the diaries without destroying her as well. *She* was the poison, the diaries were only the outward manifestation. At least I have allowed all the others to keep their dignity.'

Cooper thought of the ones he cared about, Jack and Sarah, Jane and Paul Marriott; Ruth above all.

'Only if you plead guilty, Mr Orloff, otherwise this will all come out in court.'

'Yes. I owe Violet that much,' he said.

After all, it is easy to manipulate a man if all he wants is something as worthless as love. Love is easily given when it is the body that's invaded and not the mind. My mind can withstand anything. I am Mathilda Cavendish and what does Mathilda care when the only thing she feels is contempt?

> *Man, proud man,*
> *Drest in a little brief authority,*
> *Most ignorant of what he's most assur'd,*
> *His glassy essence, like an angry ape,*
> *Plays such fantastic tricks before high heaven,*
> *As make the angels weep.*

If angels weep Mathilda sees no sign of it. They do not weep for me . . .

Twenty

JANE MARRIOTT replaced the telephone receiver and held a shaking hand to her lips. She walked through to the living room where her invalid husband was dozing quietly in the bright winter sunshine which poured through the window. She sat beside him and took her hand in his. 'That was Sergeant Cooper on the phone,' she said. 'James Gillespie was found dead in his flat this morning. A heart attack, they think.'

Paul didn't say anything, only stared out across the garden.

'He says there's nothing to worry about any more, that no one need ever know. He also said' – she paused briefly – 'he also said that the child was a girl. Mathilda lied about your having a son.' She had told him everything after her return home from the surgery the day Sergeant Cooper had questioned her.

A tear squeezed from between his lids. 'I'm so sorry.'

'For James?'

For – everything. If I'd known—' He fell silent.

'Would it have made a difference, Paul?'

'We could have shared the burden, instead of you bearing it alone.'

'It would have destroyed me,' she said honestly. 'I couldn't have coped with you knowing that Mathilda had had your child.' She studied his face closely. 'As time went by, you would have thought more of her and less of me.'

'No.' His marbled hand clutched at hers. 'She was in every sense of the word a brief madness so, even if I'd known about the child, it wouldn't have changed anything. I have only ever loved you.' His eyes grew damp. 'In any case, my dear, I think your first instincts

317

were right, and that Mathilda would have killed the baby. We can none of us put any faith in what she said. She lied more often than she told the truth.'

'Except that she left her money to Sarah,' said Jane in a rush, 'and Sergeant Cooper said the baby was a girl. Suppose Sarah—?' She broke off and squeezed his hand encouragingly. 'Nothing's ever too late, Paul. Would it do any harm, do you think, to ask a few tactful questions?'

He looked away from her eager face and, in Cooper's earlier footsteps, traced the fickleness of fate. He had lived his life believing he was childless, and now, at the age of seventy, Jane had told him he was a father. But of whom? Of a son? Of a daughter? Or had Mathilda lied about this as she had lied about so much else? For himself, it hardly mattered – he had long since come to terms with being childless – but for Jane, Mathilda would always cast a long and spiteful shadow. There were no guarantees that Sarah Blakeney was his daughter, no guarantees even that the child, if it existed at all, would welcome the intrusion of parents into its life, and he couldn't bear to see Jane's hopes dashed in this as surely as her hope in his fidelity had been dashed. In the end, wasn't it better to live with the illusion of happiness than the awful certainty of trust betrayed?

'You must promise me you will never say anything.' He laid his head against the back of the chair and struggled for breath. 'If I am her father, then Mathilda never told her, or I'm sure she would have come here of her own accord.' His eyes filled with tears. 'She has a loving father already who has done a fine job – a very fine job – in bringing her up. Don't force her to choose between us, my dearest one. Rejections are such painful things.'

Jane smoothed the thinning hair from his forehead. 'Perhaps, after all, some secrets are best kept secret. Shall we share this one together and dream a little from time to time?' She was a wise and generous woman who, just occasionally, acknowledged that it was Mathilda's treachery that had given her insights into herself and Paul that she hadn't had before. After all, she thought, there was less to mourn now than there was to celebrate.

*

Joanna sat where her mother had always sat, in the hard-backed chair beside the french windows. She tilted her head slightly to look at Sergeant Cooper. 'Does Dr Blakeney know you're telling me this?'

He shook his head. 'No. I rather hope you'll make the first move by offering to drop your challenge to the will if she agrees to honour your mother's intentions as set out in her letter to Ruth. A little oil on troubled waters, Mrs Lascelles, goes a very long way and it's in everyone's interests to put this sad affair behind you and go back to London where you belong.'

'In Dr Blakeney's certainly, not in mine.'

'I was thinking more of your daughter. She's very young still, and her grandmother's death has distressed her a great deal more than you realize. It would be' – he sought for a word – 'helpful if you pursued an amicable settlement rather than a continued and painful confrontation. Barristers have a nasty habit of unearthing details that are best left buried.'

She stood up. 'I really don't wish to discuss this any more, Sergeant. It's none of your business.' The pale eyes hardened unattractively. 'You've been seduced by the Blakeneys just as my mother was, and for that reason alone I will not negotiate amicably with them. I still find it incomprehensible that you haven't charged Jack Blakeney with assault, or, for that matter, Ruth with theft, and I intend to make sure my solicitor raises both those issues with your Chief Constable. It's quite clear to me that Dr Blakeney, ably abetted by my daughter, is using her husband and you to pressure me into leaving this house so that she can gain vacant possession of it. I will not give her the satisfaction. The longer I remain, the stronger my title to it.'

Cooper chuckled. 'Do you even have a solicitor, Mrs Lascelles? I hope you don't because you're wasting your money if that's the sort of advice he's giving you.' He pointed to the chair. 'Sit down,' he ordered her, 'and thank your daughter and the Blakeneys for the fact that I am not going to arrest you now for the illegal possession of heroin. I'd like to, make no mistake about that, but as I said before it's in everyone's interests, not least your own, if Dorset is shot of you. I should, by rights, pass on what I know to the Metropolitan Police but I won't. They'll find out anyway soon enough because, even with the capital sum Dr Blakeney pays you, you'll be quite incapable of managing. There'll be no more monthly cheques, Mrs Lascelles, because there's no old lady left to terrorize. What did you do to her to make her pay?'

She was staring out of the window but it was a long time before she answered. 'I didn't have to do anything, except be her daughter. She assumed I was like her, and that made her afraid of me.'

'I don't understand.'

She turned round to fix him with her strangely penetrating gaze. 'I watched her murder her father. She was terrified I was going to do the same to her.'

'Would you have done?'

She smiled suddenly and her beauty dazzled him. 'I'm like Hamlet, Sergeant, "but mad north-north west". You probably won't believe me but I was always more frightened that she would kill me. I've been sleeping quite well recently.'

'Will you go back to London?'

She shrugged. 'Of course. "When a man is tired of London, he is tired of life." Have you read Samuel Johnson, Sergeant? He was a great deal wittier than Shakespeare.'

'I will now, Mrs Lascelles.'

She turned back to the window and its wonderful view of the cedar of Lebanon that dominated the garden. 'I suppose if I fight Dr Blakeney you'll pass on what you know about me to the Metropolitan Police.'

'I'm afraid I will.'

She gave a low laugh. 'Mother was always very good at blackmail. It's a pity you never met her. Will the Blakeneys look after Ruth, Sergeant? I wouldn't want her to starve.'

Which was, thought Cooper, the closest she would ever come to expressing affection for her daughter. 'They certainly plan to keep her with them in the short term,' he told her.

('Ruth will need all our emotional support,' Sarah had said, 'and that includes yours, Cooper, if she's to get through the abortion and Dave Hughes's trial.' 'And if Hughes is acquitted?' Cooper asked. 'He won't be,' said Sarah firmly. 'Three more girls have agreed to testify against him. Women have plenty of courage, you know, when they're not pinned to the ground with knives held to their throats.')

'And in the long term?' Joanna asked him.

'Assuming the will isn't challenged, then Dr Blakeney will set up a trust fund for Ruth at the same time as she makes you a gift of the money your mother intended you to have.'

'Will she sell off the garden to do it?'

'I don't know. She told me this morning that Cedar House would make rather a fine nursing home.'

Joanna gripped her arms angrily. 'Mother must be turning in her grave to think the old ladies of Fontwell will be looked after at her expense. She couldn't stand any of them.'

Cooper smiled to himself. There really was a beautiful irony about it all, particularly as the first customer would probably be poor, bewildered Violet Orloff.

Jack watched Sarah out of the corner of his eye as he sat at his easel putting the finishing touches to the portrait of Joanna. She was staring aimlessly out of the window towards the wooded horizon, her forehead pressed against the cool glass. 'Penny for them,' he said at last.

'Sorry?' She turned to glance at him.

'What were you thinking about?'

'Oh, nothing, just – ' she shook her head – 'nothing.'

'Babies?' he suggested, without the usual trace of irony.

She moved into the centre of the room and stared at the painting of Mathilda. 'All right, yes, I was, but you needn't worry. It wasn't in hopeful anticipation. I was thinking that you've been right all along and that having babies is a mug's game. They bring you nothing but heartache and, frankly, I'd as soon play it safe and spare myself the anguish.'

'Pity,' he murmured, rinsing his brush in turpentine and wiping it on the kitchen roll, 'I was just getting acclimatized to the whole idea.'

She kept her voice deliberately light. 'I can take your jokes on most things, Jack, but not where babies are concerned. Sally Benedict destroyed any credibility you might have on the subject the day she destroyed your little mistake.'

He looked very thoughtful. 'As a matter of interest, am I being singled out because I'm a man or are you planning to lay that same guilt-trip on Ruth in years to come?'

'That's different.'

'Is it? Can't see it myself.'

'Ruth wasn't two-timing her husband,' she muttered through gritted teeth.

'Then we aren't talking about babies, Sarah, and whether or not I have the right to change my mind, we are talking about infidelity. Two different things entirely.'

'In your book, maybe. Not in mine. Committing yourself to a person is no different from committing yourself to a belief. Why, if you couldn't bear to impregnate your wife, were you so unconcerned about impregnating your mistress?' Two spots of colour flared high on her cheekbones, and she turned away abruptly. 'Let bygones be bygones. I don't want to talk about it any more.'

'Why not?' he said. 'I'm having a hell of a good time.' He linked his hands behind his head and grinned at her rigid back. 'You've put me through hell these last twelve months. You yank me out of London without a "by your leave" or a "do you mind?". Stick me in the middle of nowhere with a "take it or leave it, Jack, you're only my shit of a husband".' His eyes narrowed. 'I've put up with Cock Robin Hewitt strutting his stuff about my kitchen, leering at you and treating me like something the dog threw up. I've smiled while mental midgets pissed on my work, because I'm just the bum who likes nothing better than scrounging off his wife. And on top of all that I've had to listen to Keith Smollett lecturing me on your virtues. In all that time only one person, and this includes you, ever treated me as if I were human – and that was Mathilda. But for her, I'd have walked out in September and left you to stew in your own complacent juice.'

She kept her back towards him. 'Why didn't you?'

'Because, as she kept reminding me, I'm your husband,' he growled. 'Jesus, Sarah, if I didn't think what we had was worth something, why would I have married you in the first place? I didn't have to, for Christ's sake. No one held a gun to my head. I wanted to.'

'Then why—?' She didn't go on.

'Why did I get Sally pregnant? I didn't. I never even slept with the horrible little bitch. I painted her portrait because she thought I was going places after the Bond Street dealer clinched my one and only sale.' He gave a hollow laugh. 'She wanted to hitch her wagon to a rising star, the way she's hitched it to every other rising star she's ever met. Which is what I painted, of course – a lazy parasite with pretensions to greatness. She has hated me ever since. If you'd told me she was claiming me as the father of her unwanted baby I'd have set you straight, but you didn't trust me enough to tell me.' His voice hardened. 'You sure as hell trusted her, though, and you didn't even like the bloody woman.'

'She was very plausible.'

'OF COURSE SHE WAS PLAUSIBLE!' he roared. 'She's a *fucking* actress, and I use the word advisedly. When are you going to open your eyes, woman, and see people in the round, their dark sides, their bright sides, their strengths, their weaknesses? Dammit, you should have let your passions go, clawed my miserable eyes out, slashed my balls – *anything* – if you thought I'd two-timed you.' His voice softened. 'Don't you love me enough to hate me, Sarah?'

'You bastard, Blakeney,' she said, turning round and raking him from head to toe with glittering eyes. 'You will never know how unhappy I've been.'

'And you have the nerve to accuse me of being self-centred. What about my unhappiness?'

'Yours is easily cured,' she said.

'It damn well isn't.'

'It damn well is.'

'How?'

'A little massage to ease the stiffness and then a kiss to make it better.'

'Ah,' he said thoughtfully, 'well, it's certainly a start. But bear in mind the condition's chronic and needs repeated applications. I do not want a relapse.'

'It'll cost you, though.'

He eyed her through half-closed lids. 'I thought it sounded too good to be true.' He dug in his pocket. 'How much?'

She cuffed him lightly across the head. 'Information only. Why did Mathilda have a row with Jane Marriott on the morning she died? Why did Mathilda cry when you showed her your painting? And why did Mathilda leave me her money? I know they're all related, Jack, and I know Cooper knows the answer. I saw it in his eyes last night.'

'No massage if you don't get the answer, I suppose.'

'Not for you. I'll offer it to Cooper instead. One of you is bound to tell me in the end.'

'You'd kill the poor old chap. He goes into spasms if you touch his hand.' He drew her down on to his lap. 'It won't make it any easier if I tell you,' he warned. 'In fact it'll make it harder. I know you too well.' Whatever guilt she felt now, he thought, would be nothing compared with the agonies of wondering if she had unwittingly conned Mathilda into believing she was adopted. And what would it do to her relationship with Jane Marriott? Knowing Sarah, she would feel duty-bound to tell Jane the truth, and push the poor woman away with a surfeit of honesty. 'I made Mathilda a promise, Sarah. I really don't want to break it.'

'You broke it when you told Cooper,' she pointed out.

'I know, and I'm not happy about it, any more than I was happy about breaking my promise to Ruth.' He sighed. 'But I really did have no option. He and the Inspector were convinced the will was the motive for Mathilda's murder and I had to explain why she made it.'

Sarah stared at Mathilda's portrait. 'She made it because she was buying her rite of passage into immortality and she didn't trust Joanna or Ruth to deliver the goods for her. They would have squandered the money while she trusted me to build the "something worthwhile in her memory".' She sounded bitter, Jack thought. 'She knew me well enough to know I wouldn't spend a bequest on myself, particularly one to which I felt I had no right.'

'She wasn't that cynical, Sarah. She made no secret of her fondness for you.'

But Sarah was still absorbed in the portrait. 'You haven't explained,' she said suddenly, 'why you went to stay with Sally that weekend?' She turned to look at him. 'But that was a lie, wasn't it? You went somewhere else.' She put her small hands on his shoulders. 'Where, Jack?' She shook him when he didn't answer. 'It had something to do with Mathilda's weeping and, presumably, her will, too, though you didn't know it at the time.' He could almost hear her mind working. 'And whatever it was required your absence for that weekend without my knowing where you were going.' She searched his face. 'But for all she knew she would live for another twenty years, so why tell you something now that wouldn't have any real impact until after she was dead?'

'She didn't intend to tell me. I was a very reluctant recipient of her confession.' He sighed. Sooner or later, he realized, Sarah would find out that he had stayed with her father and why he had gone there. 'A year or so after Joanna was born, she had a second daughter by Paul Marriott, whom she put up for adoption. For all sorts of reasons she persuaded herself that you were her lost daughter, and she told me she'd changed her will in your favour.' He gave a wry smile. 'I was so shocked that I didn't know what to do. Say nothing and let you inherit under false pretences? Tell her the truth and shatter her illusions? I decided to put the decision on hold while I went to see if your father had something I could show her.' He shook his head ironically. 'But when I got back Mathilda was dead, the police were searching around for a murder motive, and I was the only person who knew Mathilda had left you a fortune. It was a nightmare. All I could see was that you and I would be arrested for conspiracy unless I kept my mouth shut. We couldn't prove I hadn't told you about the will, and you had no alibi.' He gave a low laugh. 'Then out of the blue you offered me my marching orders and I realized the best thing I could do was grab them with both hands and leave you thinking I was a miserable bastard. You were so hurt and angry that, for once in your life, you didn't try to hide your emotions, and Cooper received a hefty dose of transparent honesty. You showed him everything from shock about the will to complete bewilderment that I'd been able to paint Mathilda's portrait without your knowing.' He laughed again. 'You got us both off the hook without even realizing what you were doing.'

'Thanks very much,' she said tartly. 'And what would have happened if I'd been overjoyed to see the back of you?'

His face split into an evil grin. 'Well, just in case, I took out an insurance policy by moving in with Joanna. She's better-looking than you so you were bound to be jealous.'

'Bollocks.' But she didn't elaborate on whether it was the looks or the jealousy that was evoking her scorn. 'Did Mathilda tell Jane she'd had Paul's child? Was that what the row was about?'

He nodded. 'But she told her it was a boy.'

It was Sarah's turn to sigh. 'Then I doubt it's even true. She could have fantasized a baby just as easily as she fantasized her uncle's suicide' – she shrugged – 'or had an abortion or smothered the poor little thing at birth. I think it just suited her to resurrect the fantasy in order to create a thoroughly guilty and embarrassed legatee whose strings she could pull after she was dead.' She turned back to examine the portrait again. 'She used and abused us all, one way and another, and I'm not sure I want to be manipulated by her any more. What do I say to Jane and Paul if they ask me why she left me her money?'

'Nothing,' he said simply. 'Because it's not your secret, Sarah, it's mine. Duncan did her one good service by destroying her diaries. It leaves you free to build a memorial to her in any shape or form you like. In ten years, Fontwell will see her only as a generous benefactress because there'll be no evidence to prove otherwise.' He cupped her face in his hands. 'Don't abandon her now, sweetheart. Whatever her motives were and whatever she did, she entrusted you with her redemption.'

'She should have entrusted it to you, Jack. I think she probably loved you more than anyone in her whole life.' Dampness glistened along her lashes. 'Does she deserve to have people think well of her?'

He touched her tears with the tip of his finger. 'She deserves a little pity, Sarah. In the end that's all any of us deserve.'

This is the diary of Mathilda Beryl Cavendish. It is my story for people to read when I am dead. If anyone finds it they should take it to the police and make sure Father is hanged. He made me do something wicked today and when I said I was going to tell the vicar, he locked me in the cupboard with the scold's bridle on my head. I WAS BLEEDING. He cries a lot and says it is Mother's fault for dying. Well, I think it's Mother's fault, too.

It was my birthday yesterday. Father says I am old enough and that Mother would not mind. She knew about men's needs. I am not to tell ANYONE or he will use the bridle. OVER AND OVER AGAIN.

Mother should never have done such things, then Father would not do them to me. I am only ten years old.

I HATE HER. I HATE HER. I HATE HER . . .